Die I Will Not

the
Perpetual
Book Fund

A

Virginia F. Maner

Perpetual Book Fund
Book

WILLIAMSBURG REGIONAL LIBRARY
FOUNDATION

Books by S.K. Rizzolo

The John Chase Mysteries
The Rose in the Wheel
Blood for Blood
Die I Will Not

Die I Will Not

A John Chase Mystery

S.K. Rizzolo

Poisoned Pen Press

Poisoned Pen Press
6962 E. First Ave., Ste. 103
Scottsdale, AZ 85251
www.poisonedpenpress.com
info@poisonedpenpress.com

Printed in the United States of America

This book is dedicated to all my old friends and colleagues at the Buckley School. Dare to be true!

Acknowledgments

I would like to thank Barbara Peters and Rob Rosenwald for welcoming me back to Poisoned Pen Press after a hiatus of some years. I am thrilled to be publishing the third novel in the Penelope Wolfe/John Chase series due to their unfailing kindness and expert stewardship. Thanks also to Beth Deveny, PPP's supportive copy editor, and to fellow Poisoned Pen authors Mary Reed and Priscilla Royal, who have gone out of their way to offer valuable advice and friendship.

Thank you to John Langbein, Sterling Professor of Law and Legal History at Yale Law School and author of *The Origins of Adversary Criminal Trial*, for answering my question about the crown witness program during the Georgian era and to D.P. Lyle, M.D., for explaining stab wounds to the chest. And I must acknowledge historian Kathryn Kane—curator of *The Regency Redingote*, a website offering unbelievable riches for the Regency novelist—as well as my brother-in-law, Robert Rizzolo, an authority on Sicily and all things Italian. Any errors are mine, obviously.

My dear friends Susan Selvin, Andy Nelson, Nancy Booth, Kim Scolari, and Kathy Ouimette have my gratitude for being such wonderful company, as do Margaret and Peter Mason for their friendship and appreciation of my books.

Finally, I thank my suddenly grown-up daughter, Miranda, just because I'm so proud of her, and my ever-patient husband Michael, who rescued me from many a plotting pit of despair.

"Yet die I will not till my Collatine
Have heard the cause of my untimely death;
That he may vow, in that sad hour of mine,
Revenge on him that made me stop my breath."
                    —William Shakespeare, *The Rape of Lucrece*

What person, unacquainted with the true state of the case, would imagine, in reading these astounding eulogies, that this *Glory of the People* was the subject of millions of shrugs and reproaches!…That this *Conqueror of Hearts* was the disappointer of hopes! That this *Exciter of Desire…*—this *Adonis in Loveliness,* was a corpulent gentleman of fifty! In short, that this *delightful, blissful, wise, pleasurable, honorable, virtuous, true, and immortal* PRINCE, was a violator of his word, a libertine over head and ears in debt and disgrace, a despiser of domestic ties, the companion of gamblers and demireps, a man who has just closed half a century without one single claim on the gratitude of his country, or the respect of posterity!
                    —Leigh Hunt, *The Examiner*, March 22, 1812

PART ONE

The little Moth round candle turning,
Stops not till its wings are burning:
So woman, dazzled by man's wooing,
Rushes to her own undoing.
                    —Charlotte Dacre, "Simile"

Chapter I

March 1813

A woman crossed the street. Coach lamps winked at her out of darkness, dazzling her eyes. Her feet sloshed through mud and horse muck, soaking the bottom of her skirt. When she reached the other side, she threaded her way down the crowded footpath, forced to skirt a cluster of prostitutes. Next she encountered a crew of young men, out to enjoy themselves at the taverns or supper rooms nearby. One of them, a boy, called a jest to his friend, and she paused to gaze after him, thinking how lucky he was to walk in safety, to live without fear. He did not notice her. She bent her head, pressed on.

Reaching her destination, she flattened her body against the door of an adjoining shop-front to stand gazing up at the windows of the *London Daily Intelligencer*. Light blazed in the editor's room and in the printing offices above, where the pressmen and compositors would toil to produce the morning edition. As journalists came in and out of the building, speaking to one another in ordinary, cheerful voices, she withdrew to the shadows. She fixed her eyes on the window of Dryden Leach's private room. At this hour he would be working alone.

It was his settled habit to retire to his room with orders he was not to be disturbed so that he might finish his work. He would sit, a glass at his elbow, his Burke and his Shakespeare ready for apt quotation. He would think only of how to turn a profit, ingratiate himself, shout the desired opinion. He cared for nothing and no one. He was greedy, fawning, deceitful... cold. Once she had been fool enough to think he loved her, but in that she had been wrong. Always she had been the pawn of the men in her life. Hatred swelled in her heart.

She saw her chance when several parliamentary men piled out of coaches, returning with their reports of the night's session. When the porter came out to greet them, she slipped, like a restless spirit, behind him and into the hall, where voices reached her ears along with the creaking of floorboards. Swiftly, she mounted the stairs to the editorial offices on the first floor. Her hand went out to open the door to his chamber. Under her cloak, her other hand groped for the knife in an interior pocket, the solidness of its handle reassuring. Exultation overtook her; she threw open the door and went in.

The man at the desk looked up, annoyance settling over his handsome face. He was in his early fifties, dark-haired, with thin lips and eyes dulled by brandy. His gait a little unsteady, he came forward to meet her in the center of the carpet. Slowly, deliberately, she lifted her veil.

"Did you bring the memoirs?" he asked.

In her mood of dark liberation, it was surprisingly easy to achieve her purpose. She stepped closer and thrust the knife into his breast, pushing past his startled recoil, feeling it penetrate his coat, his shirt, the flesh underneath. She withdrew the knife to thrust a second time, more deeply. For a long moment, they stared at each other as wetness darkened his shirt.

"You fiend," he gasped. "How could you?"

"You had to be stopped."

Swaying, he fell to his knees on the carpet and bent over, coughing, his labored breathing the only sound in the room. She stepped away. At the desk, she reached out with shaking fingers to grasp some papers, her eyes frantically skimming a few sentences before she pushed the sheets into the pocket of her cloak. She could go now. But suddenly he reared to his feet and in two strides was at the desk. His hands came out to restrain her. Wrenching free, she ran out of the room and down the stairs.

But she heard his footsteps behind her and glanced over her shoulder to see him lurch into the wall and clutch the banister. Still, he managed to make his way to the bottom. The trembling in her hands made it difficult to get the front door open, but after an agonizing pause she had darted past the startled porter and into the street. Racing away, she looked back once as Leach emerged, the porter at his heels. No one stopped her, and she fled into the night. Only then did she remember to draw the veil over her face.

Penelope had not seen the barrister Edward Buckler since she was engaged as a lady's companion while living apart from her husband, Jeremy. When her daughter Sarah became dangerously ill, Penelope sent for Jeremy, but Sarah recovered, thank God. Almost a year ago Penelope had left the employ of Lady Ashe and returned to London, hoping to establish a new lease on her long-faltering marriage. It had seemed somehow unwise to resume her friendship with Buckler—she even avoided the lawyer Ezekiel Thorogood and his wife Hope, her dear friends, because they were first and foremost Buckler's friends.

And yet she often thought of her last strange meeting with Mr. Buckler, standing over the grave of an unbaptized child who had not been as fortunate as Sarah. They had staged a baptism ceremony so that this child's soul would not be lost, and, serving as co-sponsors, they placed their hands side-by-side atop the cloth bundle that held the remains and renounced all sin and corruption in the poor mite's name. Long after that day, Penelope's sense of loss remained, a nagging reminder of her own loneliness.

She felt this loneliness keenly when Jeremy sauntered in one morning to find her sitting over her breakfast. Chin covered in stubble, beautiful eyes bloodshot, coat crumpled beyond redemption, he still managed to look handsome and well satisfied. He poured a cup of coffee and threw himself in a chair. "You won't have heard the news. Rex said the matter is to be kept as quiet as possible. No notice to the papers and Bow Street not to be called in. He was terribly shaken when the message from the surgeon came." Jeremy had caught her interest, no doubt his intention, thus avoiding a shrewish reminder that he had broken yet another promise to return home early the prior night.

"What happened?"

"The damndest thing. Last night Rex's son-in-law, Dryden Leach, was viciously attacked in his own office at the *Daily Intelligencer*." He quirked an eyebrow. "Stabbed, my dear. Apparently, he ain't dead, though something close to it. Rex and Leach are not the best of friends, but I'm sure the family will rally round under the circumstances."

Penelope struggled to keep her expression neutral. Dryden Leach was the man writing the vitriolic replies to the Collatinus letters published in the *Free Albion*, a radical newssheet. Over the last fortnight she had followed the increasingly heated exchange. Finally yesterday she had decided to approach the newspapers but was not foolish enough to venture into Seven Dials, a dangerous rookery, to visit the office of the *Free Albion*. Instead she tried to see Mr. Leach, hoping he might know something of his adversary. To no avail. A polite but very firm assistant had refused her admittance.

Absently, she buttered another piece of bread, which she left untasted on her plate. "Who was the attacker?"

"No one knows. Leach is a rabid Tory who sees a traitor and an infidel in every quarter. There have been threats before, I'm told. Perhaps he went too far, made somebody too angry. He managed to give a description of the attacker: a tall man in a cloak and black crepe mask. Rex hurried off to inquire into the matter."

Alarmed, Penelope considered confiding in Jeremy, only to reject the idea, for he would only think her guilty of idle, womanish nonsense. She had intended to tell him the whole story once she had a chance to speak with Mr. Leach after which she wouldn't have minded a laugh at her expense if that meant she could dismiss her fears. But now her unease grew.

"I've been reading Mr. Leach's letters in the paper. He refused to back down for fear of the assassin's knife. It sounded like boastful posturing, but do you think Collatinus attacked him?"

"Very likely." Jeremy did not sound much interested. In one of his quick mood changes, a discontented look settled over his face as he sipped his coffee and stared out the window.

Penelope suppressed her irritation. "Haven't you been reading the exchange? Collatinus hints about hidden evil stretching back to the time of the treason trials, and Mr. Leach fires back with charges of villainy. I should think you would be interested given the amount of time you spend with his father-by-marriage."

"Jealous, my dear? Rex and the Countess were telling me about their acquaintance with your father. I hear he left London rather abruptly, though I fail to grasp why this ancient history should concern you."

"Has Mr. Rex mentioned Collatinus?"

Jeremy smiled. "We've had other topics to engage us. My career for one, which I should think you would be glad of. He has been immensely useful to me, so I wish I understood why you dislike him."

It was an old argument. Penelope had not been in favor of Jeremy befriending the well-known—some would say notorious—moneylender and gentleman upstart Horatio Rex. Born a Jew, he had divorced his first wife to marry an Anglo-Irish countess. A fiery pamphleteer and printer in his youth, he made his fortune as a money-broker but was taken to court numerous times for his predatory business dealings, spent several stints in the Fleet and King's Bench prisons, and twice fled the country to escape bankruptcy. These days Rex, who had anglicized his birth name of Hirsch Reyes, ran lending offices all over London, some more respectable than others, all catering to different segments of society. No, Penelope could not like this connection, though Mr. Rex had once been her father's friend. But as it was clear Jeremy did not share her views, she held her tongue. Instead, she would seek Mr. Buckler's counsel.

◇◇◇

Penelope went first to Ezekiel Thorogood's office in Lincoln's Inn Fields, catching him as he was about to step into a hackney. His weathered cheeks wrinkling in delight, he wrung her hand enthusiastically and said he was on his way to Westminster Hall to watch Buckler argue a crim. con. cause in the court of King's Bench.

"An attorney called Grouse has sued Buckler's client, a sugar broker, for engaging in criminal conversation with his wife. Grouse has demanded damages of ten thousand pounds." Shaking his large, gray head in disapproval, Thorogood explained that the plaintiff, no newcomer to the legal system, had already triumphed to the tune of a few hundred pounds in an earlier cause against his own coachman on the same charge of adultery with his wife.

Though the old lawyer kept his face somber, a gleam of humor lurked in his eyes. "Even though Grouse first challenged his coachman in court, he claims it was the sugar-broker Lionel Taggart who initially seduced his wife from the path of virtue. But I daresay Taggart makes the richer target." His humor faded. "Ruining the coachman was merely incidental."

Thorogood was utterly content with his wife Hope, a Quakeress who had braved her family's displeasure to marry him, yet he'd seen enough of the world to look upon the frailties of men and women with compassion. His sympathies were ever with the downtrodden, with those crushed under the weight of the powerful. As a result, he would feel little pity for one rich man striving to relieve another of his precious wealth. And this case marked a departure for Buckler, who was often dragged into Thorogood's more colorful—and less lucrative—projects to help the wretches accused of various crimes.

Curious, Penelope asked: "Has Mr. Buckler been employed in such a case before? I thought him mostly attached to criminal matters."

Thorogood grinned at her. "It's the first. Defending Taggart could be a big step for him. Some would say Buckler does well to wash off some of the Old Bailey dirt in a civil case. Accompany me, my dear, and give your opinion as to whether he has found a new career. Hope will not approve of my having exposed you to such scandalous proceedings, but, after all, there's a new pamphlet on the subject every other day. These cases are distressingly common among the fashionables." His eyes were kind, bearing no hint of insinuation. Still, Penelope knew he was well aware of the state of her own marriage.

Smiling back, she took his hand and allowed him to help her into the coach. In a courtly gesture, Thorogood used a corner of his cloak to dust off the seat, and they rumbled off in the rickety, smelly carriage that looked as if it might have been new some fifty years ago when George III came to the throne.

"You must tell me of your affairs. What have you been doing with yourself since your return to the metropolis? Hope will want to know all the details."

She shifted to face him. "My husband has taken lodgings with a gallery and painting room in Greek Street. We received an unexpected legacy from a cousin of mine, and this good fortune has enabled Jeremy to fulfill his ambition of setting up a studio."

"Excellent," he said too heartily. "Has the business prospered?"

"He has sold three portraits of a man, his wife, and his daughters. Now he has several other commissions to fulfill." If he could only be persuaded to complete them, she added silently, and to stop increasing the pile of bills on her desk. The three hundred guineas Jeremy had earned from these portraits had been swallowed up almost immediately.

Reading something of her chagrin, Thorogood arranged his bulk a little more comfortably and trained his benevolent gaze on her. "Tell me why you have come to see me, Mrs. Wolfe."

Chapter II

They arrived to find the court packed to bursting, the spectators having paid a fee for the privilege of hearing the secrets of the bedchamber aired in public. Recognizing Thorogood, the usher showed them to seats and accepted the proffered coin with a smile of thanks. When Penelope asked Thorogood to point out the plaintiff and defendant, he indicated curtains on opposite sides of the court where the two men could, separately, watch the case unfold in privacy. Mrs. Grouse, of course, was not a party to these proceedings. Once this case was resolved, her husband would likely seek a suit for separation in an ecclesiastical court, as well as a divorce in a private act of Parliament. And Mrs. Grouse would be utterly ruined.

Like everyone else in the spectators' gallery, Penelope observed the barristers—three for the plaintiff, two for the defendant—as they questioned the witnesses, their movements scripted, their voices perfectly modulated. As she settled in her place, a clergyman was deposing about the once-perfect state of harmony between the plaintiff and his wife. Pompously, he said, "They were indeed a happy couple before the serpent usurper invaded their paradise and set Mrs. Grouse on her ruinous course."

Burton Dallas, the other defense counsel, did his best in the cross-examination, but the witness had skin like leather. "Mr. Grouse is fond of congenial society?"

"As any gentleman is, yes. I have myself been the recipient of his hospitality on numerous occasions."

"Can you tell us anything of Mr. Grouse's other acquaintance? Friendships with women perhaps?"

The clergyman glared yet admitted, "He told me he was involved with another female whom he did not wish to marry, but I believe he broke off this connection upon his marriage."

"He cast off this woman?"

"No, he felt bound to make provision for her."

At this point Thorogood whispered loudly, earning a quelling glance from a nearby spectator, "Do you see, Mrs. Wolfe? Buckler and his learned friend attempt to establish that Grouse neglected his wife to pursue his own pleasures. It won't work, I'm afraid, though it may reduce the damages."

She nodded, feeling a little sick. What if Jeremy were to find himself in Mr. Taggart's position one day? Her husband often enjoyed flirting with the married women he entertained as clients, but what if he were to arouse the enmity of some wealthy man? The disgrace would be appalling. For a while she sat only half-listening to the testimony, breathing in the sweat and perfumes of the people in the gallery. She tried to examine her situation objectively as did the lawyers, arguing first her own case, then Jeremy's. She had married him much too young, partially in rebellion against her father's cold severity, partially in surrender to an overmastering infatuation. Jeremy had been weak to allow matters to go as far as they did, but she was the one who organized their plans. Truth be told, he saw her unhappiness at home and came gallantly to her rescue, even though he was not ready for marriage either. She could not condemn him now.

Buckler rose to cross-examine another witness, a housemaid called Naomi Clarkson, whose account of her mistress' activities had been particularly damaging. "You've testified that your mistress kept the drawing room blinds closed during Mr. Taggart's visits and this seeming need for privacy aroused your suspicions?"

"Yes, sir."

"And yet is it not the case that the sun shone strongly on this room and therefore the blinds were kept lowered for much of the day?"

She looked away. "That's as may be, but she always put the blinds down before he come."

"Did you ever notice the sofa cover disarranged?"

"No. But I saw the mistress with her hair on end and her dress tumbled when I brought more coals for the fire!"

As the afternoon wore on, Buckler and his colleague did what they could to defend their client, but the evidence against Taggart was strong. One servant after another gave damning evidence: the footman, the cook, the groom, even a child of fourteen who, when visiting Mrs. Grouse, had peeked through the study window and seen her locked in Taggart's embrace. One maidservant reported on Mrs. Grouse's habit of donning fresh undergarments whenever Taggart was expected.

Finally, a stir of renewed interest rippled through the court when Buckler rose to open for the defense. "Gentlemen of the jury, the learned counselors suggest that you are called on to guard the public morals of our country, which are endangered in this era of licentiousness and revolution. But I'm sure you are far too wise to stand in need of such instruction or to feel it your duty to preach lessons of morality.

"Mr. Taggart is deemed a calculating schemer, a seducer, and an adulterer. A man who sought to inflame the passions of an innocent wife and contaminate her heart. But adultery is unproved in this instance, and in my conscientious opinion this crime has not been committed." He paused to scan the panel.

"I do not mean to say that paying visits to a married woman in the absence of her husband is a proper thing or kissing her is not a censurable familiarity. However, a great deal more must be proved before anything like adultery can be established. I have never heard a charge of this nature made out on such slight grounds."

At Penelope's side, Thorogood gave a faint snort, which he turned into a cough. The spectators seemed to emit a collective breath of satisfaction that the defense finally had an opportunity to draw blood of its own. Journalists scribbled in their notebooks, and the judges in their enormous wigs frowned down upon the barristers.

Buckler went on to argue that the door of the room where Mrs. Grouse had received Mr. Taggart was never fastened and servants came in without notice, never discovering them in any indecent situation. His words dropping deliberately into the tense silence, he continued: "Can we infer adultery from Mrs. Grouse dressing herself with care when a visitor was expected? The witnesses are the plaintiff's own servants who owe their first loyalty to their master. One can only wonder why the prosecution has not put forth a stronger case."

Finally, Buckler allowed a note of derision to creep into his voice. "If I am to speak, however, of damages, I beg the jury to remember the provocation Mr. Taggart received and to consider what sort of woman this is for whom a husband has come a second time into a court of justice to demand reparation. The first verdict gave him a right to divorce this abandoned wife. A verdict now can offer nothing but pecuniary damages."

Penelope found herself leaning forward to catch every word of this speech, and yet it troubled her. The witnesses had testified that the plaintiff treated his wife with affection and she repaid him by carousing and cuckolding him. But how could the jurors know what happened between a man and his wife behind closed doors? How could these men know whether he treated her with cruelty, contempt, or indifference, or whether she was driven to act as she did? Then there was the role of Mr. Taggart. Perhaps Buckler was right to suggest Mrs. Grouse had enticed her lover, in which case the blame must rest more heavily on her shoulders. Still, Penelope pitied any woman condemned for her failure to uphold society's standard of purity when no such adherence was required of the male sex.

After the defense completed its case and one of the judges summed up, dwelling at length on Mr. Grouse's irreproachable character, the jury retired to consider its verdict. Thorogood took Penelope's arm to help her down from the gallery. Together they approached Buckler, who was talking animatedly to his colleague. Thorogood tapped him on the shoulder.

He turned toward them, recognition blooming in his eyes. For a moment, he looked happy to see her before wariness shuttered his expression. "Mrs. Wolfe! What brings you here?"

Penelope smiled. "I showed up unexpectedly to consult Mr. Thorogood."

"Then I am sorry to have delayed your business for so trumpery a matter as this." Glancing around to find himself the focus of several pairs of interested eyes, Buckler added, "Shall we leave the court and walk the hall? I must await the verdict."

"Not long, I suspect," said Thorogood, wringing his friend's hand vigorously, his genial countenance beaming all over with pleasure. "Ten thousand pounds? Your client may soon have a rather large hole in his pocket. Or if you're lucky, the jury has bought your insinuations as to the plaintiff's greed."

"We did our best." He lifted his hand to his head to pluck off his gray wig. Underneath he wore a tight silk cap, which he removed, allowing his reddish hair to spring free in all directions. Sensing his embarrassment, Penelope wondered whether it was the salacious nature of the case or the possibility of failure that discomposed him. Probably both.

They went down the stairs, joining the lawyers and laymen who strolled through the cavernous space under a vast hammer-beam roof. Buckler offered Penelope his arm. "How is Sarah?"

She laid her fingers on his sleeve, feeling a sense of rightness that banished, for the moment, the fears for her daughter's future keeping her awake at night. "She is well, thank you, sir."

"And your husband?"

When she did not at first respond, Thorogood said, "Wolfe has set up an artist's studio in Greek Street."

His gaze suddenly on her face, Buckler halted and drew her to one side. "You are looking rather tired, Mrs. Wolfe. Is anything the matter?"

Penelope forced a laugh. "That is hardly flattering, sir. But it's true I have not been easy of late." She paused, suddenly unsure of how to explain, not wanting to sound fanciful or, worse, involve Buckler yet again in her disreputable affairs.

She thought he looked alert…happier than when she had seen him in Dorset last spring. Healthy color tinged his cheeks, and he had a brightness about him, as if he'd been getting regular exercise or found a new interest. It seemed he was even securing employment these days.

With some reluctance, she went on: "A newspaper editor, a relative of my husband's friend, was stabbed last night in his office on the Strand. It is not known whether he will survive. This editor was engaged in a war of words with another man calling himself Collatinus."

Buckler reached up to remove an errant lock of hair that had fallen across his forehead, interest sparking in his eyes. "I've been following the exchange in the *Daily Intelligencer* and *The Free Albion*. The references are rather cryptic: an injured mother at the mercy of unscrupulous men, conspiracy, and foul murder. Collatinus—the repentant radical who claims he wants to atone for past folly but still manages to damn the aristocracy and anyone who benefits from the patronage of the great. Skating dangerously close to seditious libel with references to a 'bloated corruption' indulging in sordid intrigue. A not-so-subtle jab at the Regent, I should think. What have you to do with this commotion, Mrs. Wolfe?"

"My father used the name Collatinus as an alias before he went into exile." Penelope's father was Eustace Sandford, a renowned radical philosopher who had married a Sicilian woman and produced one daughter along with numerous works of political philosophy, which he sent from his island retreat to be published in his native country.

Buckler seemed to make light of her concern. "That need not worry you. Someone has merely adopted the alias. Some scribbler or other who wants to make a noise and hide behind a Roman patriot."

"You don't understand," she said, annoyed by the hint of condescension in his tone. "These letters betray details of a personal nature—details only my father or someone close to him would know."

"The murder? The writer hinted a murderer would be unmasked in a future letter. The language was remarkably obscure, and I took it for no more than contrived melodrama designed to sell a few extra papers. You think Mr. Sandford may be drawn into this affair?"

Thorogood broke in. "You are quick on the mark, my boy."

"He knew a woman who was slain." Penelope met Buckler's eyes, though speaking the words that cast the shadow of suspicion on her father made her sick at heart. She wanted Buckler to think well of her family—and of her.

"Who was she?"

"He never told me her name, but she may be the N.D. the letters allude to. My father said only that she died and he felt somehow responsible." Her throat tightened. She was remembering the night, her eighteenth birthday, when her normally repressed father, working his way through a bottle of brandy, had opened the floodgates. Slurring his words, he alternately raved and cried in anguish, but the next day it was as if the incident had never happened. A month later, she married Jeremy Wolfe, an artist who had braved wartime travel to tour British-protected Sicily.

Thorogood put a large, steadying hand on her shoulder. "I've seen the letters myself. Collatinus has expressed regret for betraying his own class."

"Your father said something similar?"

"Yes, Mr. Buckler. He told me he was born a gentleman but did not always act the part. And the woman died as a result. So, you see, these new letters fit."

Buckler regarded her soberly, and after a moment Penelope resumed her story. "We left my mother behind. I don't know why he brought me, but I suspect he thought he might not return to Sicily. We spent a short time in France before the Terror, then came here."

Thorogood shook his head ruefully. "You are both too young to recall the '94 trials in London. The government was terrified about the prospect of a bloodbath, the like of the one occurring in Paris. You can't imagine—habeas corpus suspended, spies and informers, the constant threat of arrest. An unwise remark overheard in a tavern, and a man might end in prison. Thank God for English juries. They found the men accused of high treason innocent. But unfortunately, the government just got Parliament to pass new laws and crush the radicals another way. Go on, Mrs. Wolfe. Explain the rest."

"My father escaped just ahead of his arrest. If he had stayed, he'd have taken his pick between being tried for a traitor or hanged for a murderer. I assumed he meant false evidence would have been trumped up against him." She was aware of the bitterness creeping into her voice, but before she could say more, a lawyer, hurrying by, interrupted her. "Make haste. The verdict is in," he called, his black robe flapping around spindly legs, the wig on his head slightly askew.

Buckler did not move. "You fear that Sandford is guilty of more than the folly of writing political letters? You fear he might be directly implicated in this woman's death? I am certain you are mistaken." His hand came out to grip hers.

"We will resume this conversation later," said Thorogood. "Buckler, I see Dallas beckoning."

They went up the stairs into the court, and Buckler took his place next to his colleague below the bench, where the scarlet-robed judges in their enormous wigs had resumed their position. The jury, upright and substantial men all, waited in the box. As it turned out, Thorogood had hit the nub of the matter: the jurors bought the defense's insinuations, after all. They had the power to find for the plaintiff but reduce the damages to reflect that Mrs. Grouse was not criminally connected to the defendant alone. And that is precisely what they did. Buckler and Mr. Dallas lost the case, damages awarded of one shilling.

Chapter III

After the trial Penelope dined with Thorogood and Buckler at a coffeehouse, where they resumed their interrupted conversation. Listening to the affectionate raillery of the two men raised her spirits, especially since they were generous in their offer of assistance. She told them of an assembly she had promised to attend with Jeremy that evening at the home of Mr. Horatio Rex and his wife, the dowager Countess of Cloondara. "Mr. Rex was the editor and printer of the journal that published the original Collatinus letters. I hope to question him, which may prove difficult in the crush."

"You can rub shoulders with the nobs, at any rate," said Thorogood. "For our part, we will ask around in the Temple and Lincoln's Inn to see what gossip we can glean from our finest legal minds. Buckler, now that your sugar-broker has been brought off finely, you will have plenty of time for such inquiries." Eyes twinkling, he added with spurious gravity, "Mrs. Wolfe, did I ever tell you about the time that Edward, coming home at twilight, spotted a large, white rectangle on his table, which he supposed, for a moment, to be a brief promising employment? His poor clerk had to tell him, 'Alas, it is only a napkin.'"

"Hardly original, old man," Buckler retorted. "I've heard that one before. You may add plagiarism to your other sins."

Smiling, Penelope turned the conversation and agreed to dine with her friends at the Thorogood home in Camden Town some three days hence, though she wondered whether she acted wisely to involve them. But the insuperable relief of turning to people she trusted quickly drowned any qualms.

After they made their farewells, Thorogood insisted on putting her into a hackney and paying the driver in advance. And as the coach wound its way through streets showing lights at the windows, the chill in the air intensified. She sat in the dim interior, huddling in her too-thin pelisse, thinking of her father, who often remarked that after years of residence in Sicily, the damp of an English winter would strike his bones like the coldness of the grave. His recent letters had been filled with exultant details about the new Sicilian constitution the British envoy had forced on King Ferdinand. As was typical with her father, he offered hardly any personal information.

What had he meant about being responsible for a woman's destruction? Had she been his lover? Did he abandon her and break her heart, or involve her in unsavory business? His radical activities had brought danger and suspicion from the authorities, and he had confessed to having failed this woman in some essential way. That was bad enough—if only Penelope could be sure he had done no worse.

When she descended from the coach in Greek Street, the front door of the town-house she shared with Jeremy was ajar, a pool of light spilling onto the street. She was about to hurry inside when she heard her daughter call, "Mama!"

She stopped short. "Sarah?"

Heart pounding, Penelope peered into heavy London smoke and fog that had settled under the dome of the sky, giving her the curious sensation of being inside an enormous, dark cave. Through tendrils of mist—shifting, swirling, settling again—she glimpsed a form bent over her daughter, who stood on the pavement some distance away. Penelope ran, snatching Sarah up, no doubt looking like a crazy woman as she ran frantic hands over her small body. Sarah's arms clung, she gripped her mother's waist, hard, with her sturdy legs, and Penelope looked up into the face of the man, who had straightened to his considerable height, arms folded across his chest.

He touched his low-crowned hat. Penelope could not see his eyes or the rest of his features clearly, though she noted he was decently dressed, clad in a heavy greatcoat and stout boots. From behind, a voice, on a rising note of panic, shouted Sarah's name. It was Maggie, the nursemaid. Relieved, Penelope answered, "I've found her, Maggie. Where is Mr. Wolfe?"

"In the painting room. Shall I fetch him, mum?"

"We'll be there directly."

Down the road in the direction of Soho Square, another hackney had stopped, and Penelope saw a passenger step out. She caught the sound of voices as the coachman on the box called a remark. Reassured by this evidence of ordinary life, she turned back to thank the man, but he spoke first.

"You must be more careful with the little 'un, ma'am. The city ain't safe for the pair of you."

Sarah tried to raise her head, but Penelope pushed her down and took a step back. "I beg your pardon?"

"Best go inside, ma'am." Before she could say anything more, the man touched his hand to his hat and walked away, melting into the fog.

Maggie met Penelope on the doorstep, carrying her son Jamie, a child less than two years old, in her arms. Her five-year-old son Frank hovered at her side with the hired housemaid and manservant waiting in the background, eager to take any gossip back to the servants' table.

"You'll be angry with me, mum," said Maggie contritely. "But indeed I thought she was safe with her dad. He took her while I was getting Baby settled. How she got out of doors is what I can't tell you. That door was locked."

Sarah adored her father, who liked to sweep in and bear her off to play, but his attention was apt to stray. While usually a biddable child, she had a streak of curiosity, occasionally causing her to act on impulse, especially when she thought no one was paying attention or when upset. Penelope remembered guiltily that she herself had been abstracted and short-tempered this morning when she sat down at her desk to try to determine if there were any bills she could conveniently settle. Examining the door now, Penelope saw what had happened. The child was just tall enough to reach the lower bolt.

She set Sarah down and knelt on the carpet to address her, holding her by the arms. "You must never wander into the street alone again. Do you understand me, Sarah?" She gave her daughter a slight shake. "It's not safe. You could be struck by a coach or worse. Mama doesn't know the person you were with—he could be a bad man."

Sarah fixed earnest eyes on her mother's face. "He's a moon-man, Mama. He comes out at night to watch the moon."

"Oh, Sarey. Why did you leave the house?"

Tears welled in her daughter's eyes, several fat drops trailing down her cheeks to drip off her chin. "I heard a carriage and thought it was you. So when you didn't come in, I went to look."

Penelope's heart twisted, and she pulled Sarah into a hug. "Don't cry, darling. Mama was gone quite a time. But listen to me. You are not to worry if I go out. You must know I will always come back to you." It was no wonder the child was afraid, she reflected. How much stability had she experienced? In her short life, they had moved from place to place, her father there one day, gone the next.

Jeremy's voice broke into her thoughts. "I see you're back, love." He stepped closer to kiss her cheek and throw an affectionate arm around his daughter. Attired in silk stockings, knee breeches, long-tailed coat, and pristine cravat, he looked every inch the gentleman. His artfully arranged locks framed a countenance alive with light and energy, his blue eyes sparkling at her, daring her to see the world as he did.

"Make haste to dress for dinner, Penelope. It will soon be time to leave for the rout." As she stared at Jeremy, speechless, he tweaked his daughter's nose. "Where did you get to, Sarey-bird? I thought we were playing a game."

Buckler and Thorogood had retired to Buckler's chambers in the Inner Temple to enjoy a punchbowl. With the delicacy of a connoisseur, Thorogood pared his lemons and poured the rinds and juice together over loaf-sugar. He bathed the whole in boiling water and mixed well with a long spoon. When he was satisfied, he added exact quantities of brandy and rum, stirring the whole.

Face screwed up in anticipation, Bob waited at Thorogood's shoulder. Buckler's clerk was a friendly young man with intelligent eyes, hollow cheeks, and a thin nose quivering as it inhaled the fumes. Fiercely loyal to his employer, Bob spent his days consulting dusty law books or attending to Buckler's rather meager correspondence. When there was no employment, he sat at his desk for hours at a time, scratching away with his pen on mysterious projects of his own. Once in a while, he made a half-hearted attempt to restore order to the piles of papers, dirty dishes, and clothing that bestrew the chambers. And when Buckler took to his bed in one of his periodic bouts of melancholia, it was Bob who made sure he drank his tea and ate his bite of buttered toast.

The fourth member of the group, a mongrel called Ruff, lay on the hearthrug in front of the fire, his head on Buckler's slippered foot and his nose stuck in the folds of his master's dressing gown. Ruff had been a rather dubious present from Penelope Wolfe when she rescued the dog after it was nearly run down in the street. Though Ruff could hardly be called an *expressive* animal, Buckler had learned to read the small signs indicative of alarm or content or disdain, as the case may be. When, as now, Ruff felt happy and peaceful, he sank his ugly face in his paws, folded his ears, and emitted faint wheezing sounds. Similarly contented, Thorogood smiled to himself, humming an old song.

"You look like a hag gloating over her cauldron."

"Quiet, Buckler."

Finally satisfied with his efforts, Thorogood removed his spectacles to wipe them free of vapor. He poured the mixture into three glasses and included a portion for Ruff, who roused himself enough to lap at the saucer. Thorogood then took his own glass and set it on the low table next to his usual armchair.

Packing and lighting his pipe, he was soon puffing away, smoke wreathing merrily around his head.

Only then did he open the conversation. "A near-run thing, Buckler. I was by no means certain you and Dallas would triumph today. *Quid enim sanctius, quid omni religione munitius, quam domus unusquisque civium?* What more sacred, what more strongly guarded by every holy feeling, than a man's own home? The jury might easily have decided to punish the adulterer."

"For Taggart's sake, I am relieved they did not." Buckler rattled the fire-tongs against the bars of the grate, making the flames leap higher. "And I'm glad to be quit of the business with some gold in my pocket."

"Left a bad taste in your mouth, eh?"

"Servants testifying to hearing nasty 'knocking noises' from adjoining rooms? I admit I find cases of this nature rather sordid."

"You cannot afford to be so nice, my friend."

"Too true." Buckler stared into the fire. "At this rate, I'll never get a chance to stand for Parliament. It's hard to know what's worse: defending adulterers or criminals. Always to suffer the fools who condemn me as an Old Bailey barrister willing to sell my voice to any purchaser. And to be told that at least three-fourths of my work is calculated to bring off the marauders who prey upon society."

"Console yourself that you are come up in the world to try a case at Westminster Hall," said Thorogood a little sternly, for this was an old argument between them. "After all, today you saved your client from a gentleman marauder." His tone too casual, he added, "Were you pleased to see Mrs. Wolfe?"

From his desk across the room, Bob's head popped up. "Mrs. Wolfe? Did you indeed see her today, sir? Is she well?"

Buckler chose to answer his clerk. "Not particularly. She seemed rather worn."

Relaxing in his chair, Thorogood sipped his punch with appreciation. "What did you think of her story? She is a sensible woman. I suspect she has good cause for her anxiety."

Bucker and Thorogood explained something of Penelope's situation to Bob, suggesting that the clerk might ask around about Collatinus among his own extensive acquaintance. Knowing Bob, who conversed freely with anyone he met, they thought he might happen upon a bit of gossip making its way through the taverns and coffeehouses.

"I should be delighted, sirs," said Bob, gratified.

Thorogood tapped his pipe against the table, relighting it with a spill he took from a vase on the mantelpiece and thrust in the fire. "What we need is someone who remembers Sandford."

"You mean an old rogue like you? I'm surprised you were able to keep out of Newgate without Mrs. Thorogood to curb your excesses."

The lawyer chuckled. "Oh, I was a pretty tame fellow then, Buckler. Later I discovered that respectability is vastly overrated."

"Speaking of respectability," said Buckler, "I'll have a word with Latham Quiller. There was a reference in the second Collatinus letter to "L. Q____er of the Temple. You know Quiller was once a member here before he became a serjeant? The letter mentioned something about a lawyer failing a lady in distress and savaging her reputation to boot."

At the mention of Quiller, whom he cordially disliked, Thorogood made a face, blowing out an indignant puff of smoke. "So shining a representative of the English bar would hardly do anything so shabby."

Bob rose to dig through a pile of newspapers discarded in one corner. "The letters are published in *The Free Albion*, did you say? Here's one." He scanned the columns. Lips thinning in disapproval, he quoted, "*To suffer the dignity of rank as a veil for depravity is to mock every sacred principle of our honor.*" He lowered the paper. "Ugh, why do you read such stuff, sir?"

"I don't know. It passes the time?" Buckler sent a whimsical glance across the room toward his ever-unreliable long-case clock. His relationship with time—in other words, his inability to master the productive use of it—was an old joke among them.

Bob ignored him. "Collatinus was a Roman, Mr. Thorogood? Why would Mrs. Wolfe's father choose this particular name?"

Thorogood leaned forward, a pedantic fervor kindling in his eyes. "Lucius Tarquinius Collatinus. Roman patriot who married Lucretia. When Collatinus was away, Sextus Tarquinius, the king's son, broke in one night to ravish her. He told her that if she didn't give herself to him, he would swear she'd committed adultery with a slave."

"What happened to her?" inquired the clerk in ready sympathy.

Buckler affected a groan. "Do not encourage him, Bob."

"Livy says she plunged a dagger into her heart to cleanse her shame, but that was not the end of it. While the king was away fighting a campaign, Collatinus and Brutus, the king's nephew, raised a mob and locked the gates of Rome against its rulers. They established a republic, and Brutus and Collatinus became joint consuls. A triumph for the people."

"You've forgotten the end of the tale," said Buckler. "Sandford's choice of name seems rather ill-omened when one remembers that Collatinus was soon ejected from his consulship. The people didn't care for the royal blood in his veins, and even Brutus didn't remain loyal to him. Collatinus became an exile, rather like Sandford, strangely enough."

Thorogood looked grim. "With an indignity suffered by a lady at the root of it all. What if this N.D. was wronged and Sandford sought to avenge her honor?"

"Possible, I suppose. In any case, if the author of these new letters realizes Mrs. Wolfe is Sandford's daughter, she may be at risk."

"What motive can Collatinus have?"

"It may be political, or he may intend blackmail." Buckler drained his glass and set it among the other dirty cups on the table. He felt a pleasant languor he hoped would take him into a restful sleep untroubled by dreams of Penelope Wolfe. "A touch too much rum this time, Thorogood."

"Nonsense. The punch was perfect."

As Thorogood prepared to depart, wrapping himself in his fur-lined cloak and muffler, Buckler said, his voice low, "I want to help her, Zeke. Mrs. Wolfe should not face this business on her own, and he is not the sort to care for anyone but himself."

Thorogood had no need to ask who "he" was. "We will do all in our power, of course. Buckler, be careful."

"Do you suppose N.D. was her father's mistress? It must make Mrs. Wolfe unhappy to suspect her father of infidelity, whatever else he got up to while he was in London."

"Yes, she is awkwardly placed, and I suspect history repeats itself in her own marriage." Thorogood plucked his white hat from the stand and faced his friend squarely. "But I was cautioning *you*, as you are well aware."

A frigid gust of wind hit Buckler as he turned away to open the door. "That bastard Wolfe does not appreciate his good fortune," he said.

Chapter IV

"A word with you," said Fred Gander. John Chase, sitting at his usual table in the Brown Bear tavern, did not immediately reply. Instead, he exchanged a derisive look with fellow Runner Dugger Farley, who stood nearby, casually holding the arm of their prisoner while he conversed with an acquaintance and quaffed ale with his other beefy hand. Farley loomed over the culprit, a man about forty years old, hunched over, defeated, with mud on his trousers and a deep rent in his shabby coat. Desperate eyes gleamed from his haggard face.

"As you see, I am occupied." Chase did not care for the journalist Gander, who made frequent sport of the Bow Street men in the press. In his last effort Gander had developed his witticisms around the theme of "bulldog" Runners drawing "badger" malefactors into the open and seizing them in an obstinate grip. The point being that there was nothing to choose between them in terms of "animal propensity": the one fiercely grasping his portion of the forty-pound reward for a capital conviction, the other clutching his illegal gains.

Chase turned his eyes toward the door. To Farley, he said, "The prosecutor should be here soon. Put the prig at a table and let's see if he can identify him."

"Why bother? We got what we need." Farley held up the packet of fine muslin handkerchiefs they had pulled from the thief's trousers after dragging him into a corner of the tavern to search him to the accompaniment of drunken shouts of encouragement from the tavern's customers.

"Just do it."

Obligingly, Farley took the prisoner to a table and sat him down, ignoring the protests of two men whose raucous drinking song had been interrupted.

Gander still hovered at Chase's side. "I will await the completion of your business." After pausing to exchange a few words with Farley, the journalist moved away to stand in front of the taproom fire. He ordered a pint from a barmaid.

Ignoring him, Chase nursed his own drink and tried to feel more interest in the proceedings. Of late he'd been troubled by a lingering sense of boredom and discontent. He stood guard for the Regent on state occasions, attended the occasional ball to lend protection to the nobles, raided disorderly houses, or chased down culprits from the never-exhausted fund of petty thieves who peopled the streets. He sometimes went out of town employed on private inquiries, which helped to break the monotony. But he knew it was not really dissatisfaction with his job bothering him. Rather, it was the growing realization his life was empty. Upon this thought, he touched his coat pocket where reposed a letter from Abigail, an American woman who had nursed him after the battle of Aboukir in '98 and borne him a son named Jonathan. She had not wanted to marry him; instead, she opted to return to Boston to raise their child in more affluence than Chase could offer.

Now she had sent word that Jonathan had joined the crew of a privateer as cabin boy to sail the seas in search of fat British birds to pluck—merchant ships carrying valuable cargos. For Chase, a former first lieutenant in His Majesty's navy who had become a cabin boy at the same age, this was unsettling news. Pride in his son was uppermost. Yet he worried for Jonathan's safety and wrestled with the knowledge that his own flesh and blood served the enemy. Since the Americans had almost no navy of their own, they relied on privateers to conduct the war, with unanticipated success. The many stings inflicted by these rampaging pirates could not sit well with an Englishman. So on this gloomy March night Chase was in no mood for sly, slinking Fred Gander.

The door opened, and the shopboy, radiating triumph, preceded his master into the taproom. He had served his employer well, first in trailing the thief to his hole in a ramshackle building, then in fetching the Runners to arrest him. He brought the linen-draper over to Chase's table.

"Here's Mr. Scoldwell, sir."

"You have recovered my property?" The linen-draper Scoldwell wore a neat, black suit and an unhappy expression, clearly knowing himself to be out of place in the taproom's low company. Old age had rounded his shoulders and carved lines of weariness around his mouth. He moved with hesitant steps, leaning for support on a cane decorated with a roaring lion's head.

Farley spread the wares on the table for him. "Yours?"

Scoldwell ran one finger down the material. "Yes, this is my property. Where is the thief?"

With a quelling glance at the ever-helpful boy who looked about eagerly, Chase said, "Have a look, sir, and see if you spot him."

The linen-draper's eyes traveled around the crowded taproom. Voices clamored, glasses jingled, and loud laughter rang out as he made his careful inspection. After a moment he lifted one bony finger. "There, sitting at that table."

"That's it then. I'm off to play nursemaid at the Theatre Royal," said Farley. He motioned to the landlord, who was watching with a complacent eye as the drama unfolded. The Runners were his regular customers. Though plans were afoot to expand Bow Street's premises across the way, the public office had long suffered from a lack of space. As a result, the Runners often used the tavern to conduct their business, stow stolen goods, and hold prisoners temporarily. This thief would remain in lockup at the Brown Bear until he could be brought before a magistrate.

After dismissing the prosecutor with instructions to appear in court the next day, and seeing the prisoner disposed in his cell, Chase and Farley were ready to depart.

Farley pointed across the room. "Gander's waving at you. You mean to speak to him?"

"Not if I can help it. I'm going home."

The journalist cut him off at the door. "A word with you, Mr. Chase? I wouldn't be so hasty. I might have something to say for your profit, a private matter."

"You mean a private matter between me, you, and your legion of readers."

"No, no. Let me buy you a drink, Chase. You'll want to hear the news of your friend Mrs. Wolfe."

Chase lifted the journalist by the shoulders and propped him against the wall. "Mrs. Wolfe had better not appear in one of your paragraphs, Gander. Do you understand me?"

Gander blinked back, alarm making his body go rigid and his booted feet twitch against the wainscoting. "No need to take me up like that, sir. I thought you'd want to know she might be in a bit of a fret. Friendly intentions, I assure you."

"You will explain yourself." Chase set Gander down, gently, and strode to his corner table without looking to see whether the journalist followed. A man who had appropriated Chase's seat took one look at him and scurried away.

Joining him, Gander made eye contact with the barmaid, held up two fingers, and contemplated Chase, his good humor restored. "Perhaps I can sweeten your temper, sir. What would you say to a job? For the usual fee, of course."

Chase just looked at him and waited. After reflectively smoothing his collar and taking several long pulls from the tankard the barmaid set in front of him, Gander said, "I want you to look into a bit of havey-cavey business I chanced upon just before the curtain descended on an interesting scene. I'm sure you've noted, and given due honor, to my humble contributions in the *London Daily Intelligencer*? Last night I stopped to have a word with an editor fellow there by the name of Leach, but he was suddenly taken ill. Bundled off home, no questions asked. Deuced odd, all the way around."

"Why odd?"

"He'd run out of the building before he swooned. I arrived to see our porter practically carrying the poor fellow to a hack, and there was Leach waving his arms to keep everyone at bay. I caught a glimpse of him, and he looked like death."

"So the man was sick. Maybe he didn't want people gaping at him. What's your theory, Gander? I take it you suspect some sort of foul play, but what reason could there be to conceal it?"

"That's what I don't know. I thought you'd poke around, maybe ask a few questions. The place to begin is with the porter. I had a word with him, but he's not opening his budget to me. I'm too well known to him, see, and he won't risk losing his place. You try him, Chase. He'll blow the gab with you if you treat him handsome."

"What's your interest in Leach?"

Gander grinned. "The story, what else? Deuced smoky that the editor of a major daily newspaper disappears with no real explanation and no announcement as to when he might be back. Leach is well paid for his loyal support, which, I can tell you, is needed now that Prinny has turned his back on his Whig friends. I've seen the Prince's man around lately—there's bound to be something in the wind." He added judiciously, perhaps to show he intended plain dealing, "I don't mind telling you I've another interest in this business. Have you been following the noise in the papers about the Princess of Wales?"

"Who can escape it?"

As all the world knew, the Prince Regent's long-estranged wife, Caroline, had sent him a letter protesting her separation from her seventeen-year-old daughter Charlotte, heiress to the throne, even though Caroline had been acquitted of adultery in an earlier investigation. When the Regent twice declined to read this missive, Caroline submitted it a third time, only to be told he'd been informed of its contents and did not choose to respond. Then the letter made its way to the papers, sparking a national uproar, a debate in the House of Commons, and a meeting of the Privy Council, which ruled that the Regent's restrictions on his detested wife's contact with Charlotte must be upheld. Now the clamor had increased in volume as many championed the injured mother's claim that she was the victim of "suborned traducers"—those paid to commit perjury, according to the explosive phrase used in her letter.

Gander leaned closer. "You've heard of *The Book*, Perceval's report of the inquiry into Her Highness' conduct back in '06? The 'Delicate Investigation' aiming to pin a by-blow on her to get the Prince of Wales his divorce? Well, the boy living with her truly was an adopted son, not a cuckoo in the royal nest. Perceval destroyed most of the copies of his defense of the Princess in a big bonfire when he got himself in office, but a few escaped the flames. The Prince tried to buy them up, but it seems he missed some. It may be I have one in my possession." His eyebrows did a little wiggle that made Chase want to smack him.

"You bought one, eh? I suppose you seek a return on your investment. Publish it then. The time is ripe."

"I tried once before, but an injunction from the Lord Chancellor soon put paid to that. Never fear, I won't let anyone steal a march on me, especially since the Regent himself is said to have leaked Lady Douglas' testimony to the papers. She's the shrew who falsely accused the Princess, you know. Maybe the radicals will get Lady D. for perjury in the end."

"What's this to do with Leach?"

Gander looked smug. "That's what I mean to know. A big defender of the Regent is Mr. Leach, and he's been striving mightily to refute some base insinuations leveled against His Royal Highness in letters written by a radical hack named Collatinus. Leach uses his replies to Collatinus to attack Caroline's fitness as a mother and general unsuitability as a wife. He even implies Collatinus is one of her supporters. I want to know the real story, Chase, to spice up my pamphlet."

"What exactly does Leach say in these letters?"

"Oh, the usual rant. He calls Collatinus a coward who fled in disgrace in '94 when the authorities were forced to take strong measures. Says he hopes they'll crush the malefactors now in wartime. Trots out the sacred honor of the royal family and His

Highness' rights as a father." Gander pursed his lips to convey his dismay at the depravity of the modern era. He allowed Chase a moment to absorb his words, then added, "Leach was about to reveal the identity of Collatinus, though I suppose this treat is no longer in store for us."

"How does Mrs. Wolfe figure here?"

"That's for you to find out, isn't it? I'll tell you two things, though. Her husband is an intimate of a man called Horatio Rex, father-in-law to the journalist. And, strangely enough, Mrs. Wolfe paid a visit to Leach on the very day he took ill. What do you suppose she wanted?"

Chase kept his face blank, but inside his thoughts churned. He had heard of this Horatio Rex. Some years back, Rex had been questioned at Bow Street on charges of assaulting two prostitutes. Though the two victims had quickly recanted their testimony, Rex was later convicted at trial. Had these women attempted to extort money with a false accusation, or had he paid them off to silence them? Whatever the truth, and despite his hard-won social position, Horatio Rex had a murky reputation. What was Mrs. Wolfe embroiled in this time? Chase knew her for a woman honorable to a fault but prone to heedless impulse. "I'll look into the matter," he said.

Reaching into his waistcoat pocket, Gander pulled out his watch. After consulting it, he grinned. "I thought you might agree. Then you're sure to enjoy the show at Mr. Rex's rout-party this evening. Just say you've come to guard the family jewels."

Horatio Rex and the Dowager Countess of Cloondara resided in Fitzroy Square, a newer terrace of houses faced with Portland stone just south of the New Road and north of Oxford Street. The square itself had been built only on the east and south sides, for the work had been halted upon the breakout of the war when trade stagnated. It had an air of aspiring to big things in a location not quite promising enough to deliver them. Two or three hundred people were there to guzzle Mr. Rex's excellent champagne and revel in the overpowering grandeur of his drawing rooms. At the head of the stone staircase, Mr. Rex, a slim man of sixty dressed with restrained elegance, waited to greet his guests, the Countess at his side. In recent months, Mr. Rex had been eager to offer Penelope and Jeremy his friendship, but Penelope, not liking the banker's circle of dissolute gentlemen and worried that Rex encouraged her husband in idleness, had done her best to stay aloof. However, Jeremy nourished hopes of preferment; it had even been hinted he might be introduced to the Prince Regent, a noted connoisseur of the arts.

The Countess of Cloondara, some years her husband's elder, held herself like a much younger woman, though wrinkles were scored over the remains of a striking beauty to form a cracked mask. Jeremy received a smile as he lifted her hand, spotted and twisted with age, to his lips. To Penelope, the Countess murmured a polite greeting. Gazing into her still vivid eyes, Penelope was taken aback to discern a flicker of dislike, though for what reason she could not fathom. Her father had mentioned that the Countess had been kind to her when she was a child.

Penelope turned away to allow the next guest to approach, accompanying Jeremy through the glittering throng of ladies and gentlemen, laughing and chatting under chandeliers that blazed with light. Whatever her host's personal history, he had done well for himself, she reflected. Softly, she asked Jeremy how Mr. Rex had come to wed an Irish Protestant peeress in the Anglican Church, but he merely laughed. "You mean, if they really *are* married. They've been a devoted couple for over thirty years, so I don't suppose it much matters anymore."

While Penelope made inconsequent conversation, she felt a growing impatience. She must use this opportunity to discover if Mr. Rex would tell her something of N.D. and Collatinus. Her father's old friend was the obvious person to ask; he must know a great deal about the letters he himself had published. In fact, it was possible Rex himself had been the one to resurrect Collatinus. He seemed an obvious suspect, but, then again, so was Penelope herself, particularly if someone knew her father had penned the originals. She was a radical's daughter, after all.

Dutifully, Jeremy remained at her side, bringing her a glass of champagne and introducing her to a government minister named George Kester and a married couple, Mr. and Mrs. Ralph Hewitt. She had heard these names before, for Jeremy had been enthusiastic in his praise of his new acquaintances' stature in society. Penelope was less impressed. An aging beau in a too-tight coat, Kester was clearly bored with the company. Similarly, Hewitt, a balding, good-humored man, smiled and nodded at acquaintances in the crowd as he listened to his wife's prattle with only half an ear. For her part, Mrs. Hewitt couldn't take her eyes off Jeremy.

"We've just heard the most shocking rumor, Mr. Wolfe. Mr. Rex's son-in-law Dryden Leach slain in his own office. I vow it terrifies me to think of it. Mr. Rex won't confirm the rumors, but I had it from the Countess—"

"We don't yet know the truth of the matter," said Hewitt.

George Kester shook his head. "A strange business. If something did happen, it wasn't reported in this morning's paper. And what of this masked man?" Leaning toward Hewitt, he lowered his tone. "Is the masked man Collatinus, do you think? These letters have caused concern in some quarters."

Ralph Hewitt gave a crack of laughter. "You mean, with half the men in London terrified of finding themselves the subject of a paragraph in the newspaper? You include yourself, I take it?"

Smiling blandly, Kester steered the conversation into a new channel. Penelope raised her brows at Jeremy, hoping he would encourage further discussion, but he ignored the message. After a while, Penelope tried again. "Are you acquainted with Mr. Leach?" she asked Hewitt.

"We all are. I believe your father is also an old friend of the family? You are the daughter of Eustace Sandford, Mrs. Wolfe? I met him once. He is quite celebrated in his way, though I don't claim to have read any of his books."

She grew uncomfortable under his ironic assessment. "My father has not returned to his native country in nearly twenty years, sir. Though I visited England with him when I was a small child, I was raised abroad."

This drew Kester's wandering attention. His eye lingered over her face and moved lower. "You must have been a mere babe. I must say you have matured delightfully, ma'am." He exchanged a smirk with Hewitt that made her suddenly angry.

"She has indeed," said Hewitt. "Where have you been hiding her, Wolfe?"

"Oh, I'm afraid my wife doesn't approve of the fashionable scene."

Penelope stiffened. "You make me sound a Puritan." She paused. "Has Mr. Leach been successful in the newspaper business, Mr. Hewitt?"

"There were lean times at the start, I believe, but he made a name for himself at the *Daily Intelligencer*. It didn't hurt to have Rex's blunt behind him. Mary Leach was well dowered, and that's how Leach found the capital to become editor-proprietor of a newspaper. Of course, Rex had no notion he was hatching a Tory."

"Oh, poor Mrs. Leach," said Mrs. Hewitt, wringing her plump hands. "She must be beside herself with worry."

Her husband patted her arm. "You may visit her one day soon, my dear."

With dismay, Penelope saw Jeremy's eyes straying in the direction of the card room, and he smiled, murmuring, "Will you excuse us, ladies? Kester, Hewitt—shall we go have a word with Poole?"

Disappointed, Mrs. Hewitt smoothed one hand over her ostentatiously ugly gown and gazed up at Jeremy. "You may depend on me to keep your wife company." She gave an irritating titter. "I'll call on you to discuss having my portrait painted, sir. Mr. Hewitt was just saying he should like to find someone to execute the commission."

Jeremy bowed. "I would be honored, madam." With a wry glance at Penelope telling her he would rather paint a turnip than Mrs. Hewitt (but that he would, of course, accept the commission for her sake), he moved away gracefully with his friends.

Having resigned herself to hearing particulars of this woman's wardrobe and servants and carriage, Penelope was not displeased when their host approached. He greeted Mrs. Hewitt, then lifted Penelope's gloved hand to his lips, his hair glinting silver in the candlelight.

Smoothly, he detached her from her companion with the excuse that he must further his acquaintance with the daughter of so old a friend. As he led her to a sofa against the wall, he said, "You are in fine looks this evening, ma'am." With obvious approval, he examined her amber crepe dress over white sarsnet, trimmed with white beads. Jeremy had helped to choose the gown from a fashionable modiste, even as Penelope had protested its expense, but she was glad of it now since its rustle and gleam bolstered her confidence. At her throat she wore her mother's pearls, one of the few pieces of jewelry she possessed, and when Mr. Rex complimented her upon them, she explained their origin.

He smiled at her. "I regret I never had an opportunity to meet your mother, though your father often spoke of her to me. I understand she died when you were young?"

"Of influenza, sir, when I was ten years old. My father always thought an English doctor might have saved her, but she was never strong."

"Tragic but all too common." A look of melancholy settled over his face, and after a moment he added, "I remember you as a little girl, Mrs. Wolfe. You were a bright little thing but rather sad. I'm sure you must have been missing your mother."

Memory stirred. She sat in a coach while her father climbed down to speak to another man in hushed, urgent tones. It was very early in the morning; she was cold and frightened. Where were they going? Was this the day they fled England? She did not recall, but the man her father had been talking to was Horatio Rex. Despite the quiet voices, they were furious, so furious that she had shrunk into a corner of the coach, whispering to the doll in her lap and trying to pretend they weren't there....

"Yes, I was about five, a little older than my daughter Sarah is now."

"Perhaps it is best your mother did not accompany your father to England. Those were not happy times for our country, and matters are not much better today. However, we've got Boney on the run at long last."

"My father rarely speaks of those days."

"Wise of him. We'll let the ghosts of the past rest, my dear. You are enjoying London?"

"Very much. Jeremy has been grateful for your patronage, sir." She paused. "Forgive me, but he said you have experienced an unhappy event in your own family?"

Rex slanted a glance at her that was neither surprise nor resentment at the pointed question but instead a kind of watchfulness. "Your refer to my son-in-law. I was terribly shocked when the news first arrived, or I would not have spoken of the matter to Jeremy. I know I can rely upon your discretion."

Penelope was taken aback. "I heard Mr. Leach was gravely injured. Will he recover?"

"Little chance of that, I'm afraid. His death is hourly expected. You must be surprised to find us entertaining guests under the circumstances, but I do not choose to trumpet our affairs to the multitude. Besides, these little entertainments are expected of me." His cynical gaze took in the long windows hung with gold-embroidered damask, the matching gold brocade furnishings, and the array of richly dressed guests who looked as if they hadn't a care in the world.

"Is it known who did such a horrible thing?"

"Leach is not an easy man to like—he has made many enemies in his career. Of course, the Countess and I are distressed for my poor Mary." He gave another smile she found difficult to interpret. "You remind me of Mary. She is years older than you are, of course, but there's the same…vulnerability. And something of the same ambition? Before her marriage, she published a volume of poetry and several Gothic romances, though she has since turned her talents to the composition of paragraphs for her husband's newspaper." At this reference to Leach's Tory agenda, he did not bother to hide his contempt. After a pause he said, "Jeremy tells me you are also a writer?"

Why did every word out of this man's mouth seem to carry a double meaning? She replied lightly, "I've had occasional work, Mr. Rex. Perhaps one day when my life is more settled I will try to achieve more in that line. You must be very proud of your daughter's accomplishments."

He sighed, melancholy descending again. "We've not been on easy terms. She blames me, with good reason, for abandoning her mother when she was a mere child, but I hate to think I drove her into the arms of a man like Leach. She must have thought he offered a kind of safety, a haven from the dangers of holding views at odds with society." Stretching his arm along the back of the sofa, he assumed a careless pose. "At all events, I am the more ready to come to her assistance in this emergency. I shall help Mary manage the parish authorities and the funeral arrangements when the time comes. She's had a sad time of it in the past year. She lost her eldest son to a sudden fever and now this business with her husband. We thought it safer, until we know more, to put it out that Leach is ill."

"How truly dreadful. Will you employ a Bow Street Runner to investigate the crime?"

His lip curled. "I have no love for Bow Street."

"May I ask why, sir?"

"The Bow Street banditti once bribed two women to say I had assaulted them. While I stood in the very court, my hat was stolen, my pockets rifled. The magistrate only laughed and refused to prosecute my accusers for perjury. No, I have no use for Bow Street. Magistrates, police, lawyers, the justices in Westminster Hall, the journalists who ruin a man's reputation for gain…They are all the same. Villains who seek, in one way or another, to gratify a cankered heart."

"Is the attack on Mr. Leach connected to the recent letters in the papers? If we could only understand—"

She broke off, nonplussed, to find him smiling again—it seemed she amused him. Horatio Rex was a man who looked for hidden motives in everyone he met. In his battle against a prejudiced English society that viewed him as an outsider and an interloper, even as it fawned over him for his power and wealth, he was justified, she thought. But she had the strangest feeling they played a game only he understood.

"I cannot tell you what role the Collatinus letters played in Leach's fate, Mrs. Wolfe. A dangerous business from the start. Profit is one thing, but one has to know when retreat is in order. A lesson I have learned the hard way."

"How could there be profit, sir? I thought the intent political."

"Political, no doubt, but other motives may come into play. Blackmail, for instance. Hush money. If this Collatinus had information someone would prefer be kept secret, writing to the newspapers might seem rather clever. Write one or two letters, then make it known in the proper quarter that a certain sum will ward off further revelations."

"But why attack Mr. Leach?"

"He made himself quite insulting to Collatinus, and I suspect he was about to unmask him. Did he not promise such a revelation? He was stopped before his final reply could be published."

Hearing again a note of warning in his tone, she was at a loss. Then she gathered her courage. "Collatinus mentions a woman referred to as N.D. I wonder if you or my father once knew someone with those initials?"

Rex reached over to take her chin in his hands, turning her toward him, one white finger stroking her cheek. "Oh, my dear. What am I to say to *you* on that subject? She was a beautiful woman, that's all." He released her, saying harshly, "Leave it alone. You don't know the harm you might do. Your father would not thank you for bringing ruin upon your family."

"I am sure my father is innocent of any real wrongdoing."

He let his hand drop from her cheek. "The evidence against him was persuasive, my dear."

Before Penelope could respond, a movement drew his attention. He frowned. Rising to his feet, he excused himself to hurry toward a late arrival. Mr. Rex stepped around the people who stood in his path with only a brief word of apology and bore down on the newcomer.

This was a man over forty who carried an ebony baton in one hand, the symbol of his authority to search and seize malefactors. Hair tied in an untidy graying queue, he wore a truculent expression and boots too scuffed for Mr. Rex's gleaming floorboards. He advanced among the guests, his keen-eyed gaze scanning the drawing room, seeking someone. His eyes fastened on Penelope—and held. It was John Chase.

Chase started to move in her direction, but Mr. Rex grasped his arm. "You trespass in a private dwelling, sir."

The Countess hurried forward to join her husband, and several broad-shouldered footmen now flanked their master. As the footmen began to maneuver Chase back toward the door, a buzz of gossip broke out among the observers. Seeing him wince in pain, Penelope realized they had jarred the old knee injury he suffered while fighting for his country. Indignant, she swept across the room to confront her host, ignoring the Countess' basilisk stare.

"This man is a friend of mine, sir. He came to speak to me."

Astonishment widened Rex's eyes, but he resumed his polished mask. "You call a Bow Street Runner friend, Mrs. Wolfe?" He motioned to the footmen, and they let Chase's arms drop.

"I do." Penelope held out her hand, which disappeared into the Runner's grasp. "I am pleased to see you again, Mr. Chase."

Chapter V

John Chase awakened in good spirits despite a noisy neighbor having disturbed him several times in the night. His landlady, Mrs. Beeks, had recently rented the room behind his to a seamstress named Sybil Fakenham, and Chase would often hear her muttering to herself or slamming her drawers shut. Once or twice he had glimpsed her on the stairs: a gaunt young woman with wispy, brown hair, a sullen mouth, and glassy eyes that made her seem not quite present in the world. When he'd asked Mrs. Beeks about her, she folded her lips in disapproval. "She bothers you, Mr. Chase, you have only to say the word. I'm that close to showing her the door. Try to offer a little Christian charity, and there's the thanks I get."

"Never fear. I'll say the word if necessary. Why is she in need of charity?" After some years as Mrs. Beeks' only lodger, he was jealous of his hard-won peace and privacy—such as it was for the resident of a district filled with gin shops, coffee-rooms, and brothels that never slept. But in reply, Mrs. Beeks had only shaken her head and lumbered off to her kitchen in the nether regions.

Again today after breakfast, Chase encountered the young woman in the entrance hall. Dressed in the same faded gown and bonnet she'd worn the last time he saw her, she carried a large box and was on the point of going out.

Chase moved to open the front door for her. "Good morning, Miss Fakenham."

His reward was a freezing glare accompanied by a disdainful elevation of her chin. Without returning his greeting, she swept out the door and walked away without a backward glance.

Leo Beeks, observing the exchange, spoke from behind him. "Your courtesy is wasted on her, sir. She doesn't like anyone." He sounded aggrieved, and Chase, amused, thought the seamstress must have rebuffed his puppy overtures of friendship.

"Courtesy hurts no one, Leo."

The boy gazed up at him out of fearless, deceptively angelic blue eyes that missed nothing. "Yes, sir," he said a little scornfully. Then, moving on to more important matters, he added, "Any word from Jonathan?"

Inwardly, Chase groaned. He had made the mistake of telling Leo about his son in America and as a result had to endure persistent questioning about his correspondence. Mrs. Beeks would not thank him if he told her son about Jonathan having joined a privateer, for such news would only fire the boy with renewed determination to seek his own fortune at sea. But his landlady had other ambitions in view for both her sons: William with the scholarly bent to become a secretary or a tutor, Leo to be safely apprenticed in some worthy trade as a printer or an apothecary's assistant. At least Leo had stopped talking about becoming a Runner, to Chase's great relief.

"No word since the last time you inquired." Chase nodded in dismissal.

Retrieving his hat and coat, he walked from his lodgings in King Street through Covent Garden Market to the public office. Though the air remained chill, a stiff breeze had blown away the clouds. He felt the occasional twinge in his bad knee, but he was reasonably whole and rested. With the ease of long practice, he weaved through the market, avoiding the refuse, animal droppings, cabbage leaves, and general muck that littered the pavement, barely registering the raucous cries of the aproned stall-keepers as they strove to attract customers.

After fetching his prisoner from the basement cell at the Brown Bear, Chase marched him across the street to join the assorted thieves and vagrants waiting a turn for their committal hearing. In the airless, grimy courtroom, Chase and Farley lounged at a table in the well below the magistrate's bench along with the clerks and shorthand reporters. On the opposite wall was the elevated dock where each prisoner would face the magistrate. Adkins and a new Runner called Victor Kirby, who had recently been promoted from conductor of the patrol, guarded the prisoners.

Farley spoke out of the corner of his mouth. "Word is Kirby's been summoned to Great Marlborough Street." This was the location of one of the other public offices.

"For what purpose?"

"Magistrate there wants to pull him into a delicate inquiry. Instructions from on high. They say it's something to do with the Princess of Wales. I reckon they're after more dirt, if they can find it."

Chase's professional pride stirred. "Why Kirby? He was a good patrolman, but he's too green a principal officer as yet."

"Maybe that's the point," said Farley shrewdly. "No time to have formed his loyalties among us. He'll keep it quieter."

That made sense, Chase reflected. He thought of Gander and his pamphlet designed to capitalize on the Princess' growing popularity. It seemed Carlton House had formed new plans to discredit her, no doubt with her vengeful husband lurking in the background, instructing his minions to send anonymous paragraphs to the papers. But Chase had little pity to spare for the Princess since, like everyone else, he had heard the persistent rumors about her many scandalous liaisons. Everyone knew that the commissioners of the Delicate Investigation, while acquitting her of outright infidelity, had nonetheless admonished her to conduct herself more circumspectly in future.

The case of the linen-draper Scoldwell and the shoplifter was soon over. Scoldwell and his boy were called to give their evidence, and, to no one's surprise, the shoplifter was remanded for trial and sent to Newgate. As they left the office, Farley asked,

"What did Gander want last night?" His round, red face wore a look of curiosity.

"A small matter he wants me to look into." Chase liked Dugger Farley; however, he was never sure of the man's allegiances. Thus, he tended to keep his own counsel with Farley and everyone at Bow Street. Chase might have confided in Mr. Graham, the magistrate who had helped him obtain his position, but Graham was in failing health, and Chief Magistrate James Read was far less approachable.

Farley grinned at him. "Make Gander pay for your trouble, John. Your chance to get a bit of your own back at the gentlemen of the press."

Bidding good-bye to his colleague, Chase was free to turn his attention to Penelope Wolfe. Their brief encounter the prior evening was responsible for the lightening of his mood. *This man is my friend,* she had said as she held out her hand, ignoring the cold stares her unconventional behavior provoked. He had not been encouraged to loiter in Rex's reception rooms after she came to his defense, but he and Mrs. Wolfe had stepped aside for a moment to fix their meeting. Even in the costly gown, far grander than anything he'd ever seen her wear, she did not shun him but greeted him like an old and valued friend. He hoped the gown indicated that Mrs. Wolfe had found her way to prosperity—the last time he'd seen her she was employed as a lady's companion and a very unsuitable one at that. He had no knowledge of her present circumstances beyond the address on Greek Street, which she hurriedly recited for him before Rex's footmen escorted him out.

Today he intended to ask about her visit to the *Daily Intelligencer* and get her impressions of Leach and his father-in-law Mr. Horatio Rex. He stood for a moment examining the typical London row house with basement, three stories, and garret. Knocking at the door, he waited until a neatly dressed, impassive maid opened the door. "The mistress told me you would call, sir. She is with the master in the painting room," she said when he gave his name.

He followed the maid up the stairs and down the passage to a room at the rear where, announcing him, she moved aside for him to enter. He stepped over the threshold to find Jeremy Wolfe pacing, brush in hand, while Penelope reclined on a divan at the opposite end of the room. Her dark hair draped across one half-exposed shoulder, she wore a white linen tunic, tied at the waist, and sandals on her slender feet. The brilliance of her tunic gleamed against the heavy folds of scarlet drapery on which she lay, this drapery sweeping up from the divan to form a sort of canopy over her head. A jeweled butterfly dangled from a golden cord at her waist, and in her palm rested a small padlock in the shape of a heart. But, as Chase approached, he saw that her arms and shoulders were prickled in gooseflesh, for the room was cold, and a meager fire on the hearth offered little in the way of warmth. Still, she seemed to come from another world, one brighter and more beautiful.

Penelope pushed back her hair and jumped to her feet, a blush covering her cheeks. "Mr. Chase! I beg your pardon. Jeremy has kept me beyond my time."

"No hurry, Mrs. Wolfe. I await your convenience."

Chase had noticed the artist's flash of irritation at the interruption, but Wolfe came forward with a pleasant enough smile. "John Chase? I missed your entrance last night at Rex's party. I am pleased to make your acquaintance, sir. My wife has told me of the assistance you've given her in the past. Allow me to express my gratitude."

So this was the elusive Jeremy Wolfe. Despite everything Chase had heard of him during the Constance Tyrone inquiry when he first met Penelope, this was the first time he had actually met her husband: a man at least fifteen years Chase's junior with a face that, by all rights, should be stamped on a Greek coin. The artist displayed a practiced charm and a willful spirit revealing itself in restless movement. In all of Chase's dealings with Penelope Wolfe, he had often imagined her perennially absent, ever-troublesome husband. He now found that his imaginings had not been far off the mark.

Chase bowed. "Thank you, sir." His gaze took in the easels; the stretching frames; the color palette on a stand; the low dresser bursting with clothing and costuming accessories; the canvases stacked against the walls, four and five deep; and the wooden lay-man next to the window. Most of the canvases seemed to show only heads in various stages of composition. He turned to Penelope. "I have interrupted your sitting."

She had recovered her complexion. "We are finished, Mr. Chase. If you'll excuse me, I'll go change. I'll have Lydia bring tea to my sitting room if you would join me there in quarter-of-an-hour?" She didn't wait for his response but let the heart-shaped padlock drop from her fingers onto a low table before quitting the room. He picked it up to examine it, a piece of inexpensive brass wrought in cunning design with a tiny key attached.

Pacing again, Wolfe studied his painting for a moment before drifting away to examine it again from a different perspective. He had forgotten Chase's presence.

"The butterfly and the heart padlock. What do they signify?"

Wolfe looked surprised. "Penelope poses for me in the guise of Psyche—the soul. The butterfly, her symbol, indicates transformative powers. Psyche also suggests fidelity because she remained true to her Eros in all her trials. The padlock suggests a similar meaning. You have the key to my heart, and only you can unlock it. That sort of thing is popular, especially among the ladies." He smiled engagingly at Chase. "I mean to make my fortune with this portrait, sir. My wife says I must consider our short-term advantage and fulfill commissions that do not appeal to my imagination." He gestured vaguely in the direction of the half-finished canvases. "I prefer to take the longer view. If I can cause a stir among the critics with one important painting, my career will be made."

Ah, now that sounds promising, Chase thought wryly. But Jeremy Wolfe seemed to believe in his own prophecy. Too bad he had not observed the expression on his wife's face as she put aside the cheap trinket.

◇◇◇

Hair confined by a simple knot and garbed in a sensible gown, Penelope awaited him in her sitting room on the ground floor. Chase looked around with interest. This was clearly her domain. A writing table, covered in messy piles of paper, stood near the window. A comfortable wing chair reposed by the hearth, where a hearty coal fire warmed this much smaller room. On a low table drawn up next to her chair were an open book and a folded newspaper; under this table a doll lay on its back, staring vacantly at the ceiling, presumably abandoned by Sarah. Chase sat on the sofa Penelope indicated.

She handed him a cup of tea. "Did you come to Fitzroy Square to find me last night?"

"Partially. I must admit I wanted to see the kind of establishment kept up by Horatio Rex, and I sought more information about his son-in-law."

Penelope's face went still. "Mr. Dryden Leach? Why should he interest you?"

Chase watched her with a mixture of sympathy and exasperation. Her tone was too elaborately casual, her countenance too neutral, as she perched upright in her chair and took a sip of her tea: all in all, a poor pretense at unconcern. He remembered that Penelope Wolfe had always worn her feelings close to the surface and was apt to blurt her thoughts. He remembered too that he both liked her honesty and found it irksome when she sometimes seemed oblivious of the dangers inherent in an open temper. But now she thought to fence with him.

"I came to ask you the same thing," he answered.

She laughed, pleased to have her guess confirmed. "I was sure of it. Why else should you invade a banker's fashionable party when your services had not been requested? There had to be some devilry at work." The smile quickly faded. "So you've heard about the attack on Mr. Leach? I'm glad you are engaged in the affair, Mr. Chase. I've been to see Mr. Buckler and Mr. Thorogood, but you will have far greater resources at your command."

"Attack? Gander told me Leach was suddenly taken ill. What do you know of the matter?"

"Wasn't Mr. Gander the scribbler who made himself obnoxious during the Tyrone affair when you and I first met? I don't think much of your friends, sir."

"Not my friend but my employer, as it turns out." Chase told her something of Gander's ambition to publish a pamphlet defense of Princess Caroline with extracts from the investigation into her conduct, adding mention of Gander's interest in the Collatinus letters. As he described the letters, Penelope's expression shuttered, and she smoothed her dress with one hand, her fingers toying absently with a bit of braid on her sleeve.

"You haven't answered my question," Chase said when he was finished.

Abruptly, her eyes met his. "I'm not sure I should tell you, Mr. Chase—not when your first loyalty must be to Mr. Gander. There is someone involved besides me, you see. Someone I must protect."

"You called me friend last night," he reminded her. So she had chosen to judge him based on the reputation of the Runners as grasping thief-takers for hire, and the knowledge stung. "I owe no loyalty to Gander beyond giving him my professional services. I am under no obligation to tell him what I know and certainly under no obligation to share my personal business. 'Twould be easy enough to return his retainer and be done with him altogether."

"I won't ask you to do that."

She had made up her mind to keep her knowledge from him, and, in typical Penelope fashion, told him so instead of dissembling. A bitterness that utterly destroyed the more charitable mood he had awakened with this morning grew in him. He put down his cup and rose.

"Mr. Chase!"

As his surge of anger subsided, he saw she now looked thoughtful, as her mind seemed to take up possibilities and evaluate them, one-by-one. After a minute of consideration, she came to a decision. She reached for the newspaper on the table and folded back a page; then she put the paper in his hand. "I do trust you. I need to know the identity of this Collatinus. Will you help me?"

He listened carefully to her story and read the letter. "How many of these have been published?"

"This is the third."

"Interesting. Collatinus promises to reveal the identity of N.D.'s killer but first tantalizes his readers with hints about her death and the people she knew."

"Yes, along with charges of corruption in high places."

"But who is N.D.? It shouldn't be too difficult to discover her identity if she was murdered." He looked down at the page and tapped it with one finger. "Collatinus quotes her here: '*Lord _____ pinned his gaze on me as I sat in my opera box. He too became my devoted slave.*' No initials this time, I see, though Collatinus notes that the besotted lover was a gentleman of rank. I'll tell you one thing about her, Mrs. Wolfe. She was a courtesan. She displayed herself in an opera box to attract her protectors."

Penelope smiled at him. "I had thought of that myself. The letter goes on to describe N.D.'s other admirers. I don't recognize anyone, do you?"

"No, but others might. Even twenty years later."

"I met a man called George Kester at Mr. Rex's party. He asked his friend Mr. Hewitt for information. Mr. Kester seemed concerned about what these letters might contain."

"Any idea why?"

"None at all. Mr. Hewitt made a joke I don't think was appreciated, but they both seemed interested in Collatinus."

Chase returned his attention to the newspaper in his hand. "What of this allusion to a 'contemptible hireling scribe' who would sooner serve the great than stand up for truth and justice? The reference sounds a bit more contemporary. From what Gander told me, I assume Collatinus refers to Dryden Leach. You say it was Leach's father-in-law who told your husband about the masked man? Were Wolfe and Rex together the entire evening?"

She shook her head. "Jeremy encountered Mr. Rex at a gambling hell quite late, and Mr. Rex invited him to come home with him for a drink. The message about Mr. Leach arrived while Jeremy was there."

"So Rex has no alibi for the attack," murmured Chase.

Chapter VI

Chase and Penelope emerged from the house on Greek Street to find an empty hackney coach that chanced to be passing. When the jarvey observed them hesitating on the flagway, he pulled up his horses to wait. Chase glanced at the coach number and gave the driver the measuring look habitual with him. As Chase let down the steps to help Penelope get in, he noticed that this vehicle seemed in better repair than was typical with hacks, and its horses were not the ill-bred, broken-down brutes one usually encountered. Inside, the upholstery was clean, the side-glasses free of London soot, the glass intact.

As they drove to the office of the *Daily Intelligencer*, Chase was busy with his own thoughts. Shaking his head at his own folly, he wondered why he had agreed to allow Penelope to accompany him. "A lady does not show herself in a newspaper office," he'd told her.

"I went before," she had replied unanswerably. "And fully intend to go again."

Because Chase thought her presence might serve as a useful blind to his own activities, he'd acquiesced, and, besides, he was strangely loath to disturb their newly reestablished harmony. Now, as the coach inched toward the Strand in heavy traffic, he said, "Gander told me to inquire for him. He's taken an office there for the time being. If he can manage it, he'll take us up to Leach's room and let me have a look around. But there's to be no bustle about it. Anyone challenges us, Gander will claim we bluffed our way in with a tale about having a story to sell."

"I could say I'm a lady's maid who's been dismissed and wants to sell her mistress' secrets for revenge. I always wondered how the newspapers obtain fresh material for their paragraphs. Their sources must be either servants or perhaps the ladies' rivals." She said this demurely from under her plain straw bonnet.

Chase raised his eyes to the ceiling of the coach. "You don't look the part of lady's maid, Mrs. Wolfe, not nearly lofty enough. They are more likely to think you a schoolgirl escaped from her governess. We must be careful. A Bow Street Runner will not be welcome since Leach's attack remains largely a secret."

But why? he asked himself. The Tory press would have seized upon the story of a masked man wielding a knife. It made Leach's point about the danger of radical elements in society more eloquently than any words the man could pen. If the tale were true, it seemed incredible that the editor of a major London newspaper had suffered a brutal assault in his office with no one the wiser. Witnesses must have seen this masked man, yet somehow their tongues had been stopped. Chase also considered what Penelope had told him of Eustace Sandford. Clearly, Sandford had involved himself in some sort of low treachery. It was possible he had betrayed a young woman to her death and someone seeking hush-money was still interested in this crime—or this person might wish to resurrect old secrets for reasons of his own. But how could Sandford, far away in Sicily, still be involved?

When they entered the lobby of *The Daily Intelligencer*, they found themselves in a hall, with several doors bearing plaques that announced the letter and inquiry department as well as the advertising office. A staircase rose to the floors above, and Chase glimpsed a second staircase at the rear. A man sitting in a hard chair glanced up as the bell jingled. Laying aside the sporting magazine he'd been reading, he unfolded awkwardly from his chair. "Help you, sir and madam?" With his shiny, shabby coat, long face, and eager eyes, he looked hungry, thought Chase, like a dog too long abandoned by its master.

"John Chase to see Mr. Dryden Leach, if you please." On an impulse, Chase had decided to ask for the editor to see how the porter would respond.

"Mr. Leach is not available at present."

"You recall this lady who was here two days ago? Mr. Leach was not at liberty then either. Do you expect him soon?"

"Can't say, sir."

"Not ill, is he?"

The man seized upon this. "He *is* ill, and I dunno when he'll be back."

"A pity. I gather the illness was sudden?"

"It was." The porter wet his lips and stared at his boots.

Penelope spoke. "Was Mr. Leach fortunate enough to take ill at home where his wife may care for him?"

A furtive expression flickered. "Can't say, madam."

Slowly, Chase retrieved his purse. Opening it, he pulled out a coin and dropped the money in the man's waiting hand. "For your trouble. Were you here when Mr. Leach took ill?"

The porter took the money, secreting it somewhere on his person so quickly that Chase did not see the pocket into which it disappeared. The man gave several rapid glances up and down the corridor. "Maybe I was; maybe I wasn't. Not for me to speak further. Now, sir, is there something I can do for you?"

Chase's instincts told him Gander had been right. This man would be willing to sell his knowledge at the right price. "What's your name, porter? Maybe there's a tavern close by, a favorite of yours?"

"Could be." A gleam of interest enlivened his stolid stupidity. "The name's Peter Malone, sir."

"You live nearby, Malone?"

"Place called Feathers Court, sir. There's a pub there too. You know it?"

"I can find it, Malone." Chase exchanged a long look with him. Then he said in an authoritative tone that brooked no argument, "If you can't fetch Mr. Leach for me, I'll speak to Mr. Gander. Is he in?"

Nodding, the man took himself up the stairs, and they heard him knocking at a door on the next floor. Chase said to Penelope, "If the attacker came through the front entrance, the porter would have seen him enter and depart."

"Do you think he knows something?"

"Maybe."

Soon Gander himself appeared, Peter Malone at his heels. When the journalist saw Penelope, his ferret face brightened, and he gave her a wide grin. "Mrs. Wolfe? Well now, come this way, the pair of you. I see it's up to me to introduce you to my domain." For Malone's benefit, he added, "We'll just step upstairs and discuss the morsel of news you've promised me, shall we?"

They followed Gander up the staircase. "You've come at a good time," he said to Chase quietly. "In an hour or so, the beast will stir from its slumbers. Some of the men are still home sleeping off last night's labors."

"How have you been producing the paper without Leach?"

"The sub-editor Mr. Blagley has stepped into his shoes. He even had to write the leading article at the last minute the other night, as Leach's could not be found. I take it you went to Rex's party. What news?"

"Nothing yet. Where is Leach's appointment book?"

"Blagley took it, but I've already checked it: nothing out of the ordinary there. When can I expect a report?"

"Be patient. Let me speak to Blagley."

"Best not. I got something for you, Chase. You recall that Leach had bragged about getting ready to unmask Collatinus? According to Blagley, it wasn't just talk. Leach had stumbled on a big story. He told Blagley there might be trouble for the paper if he published, but he was determined. See if you can get a word with his wife. She might know something. She used to write the odd paragraph or poem for the paper. He might have confided in her."

Gander led them into a spacious chamber that overlooked the bustling thoroughfare outside. Sunlight poured through large windows to pool on the carpet, illuminating the rosewood desk, leather chairs, and tall bookshelves lined with expensive volumes. The journalist nodded to Chase. "Leave you to it, shall I? I'll stand guard, but you'll need to be quick." He went out, closing the door behind him.

Penelope looked around with interest. She pointed at Leach's imposing, high-backed chair. "Mr. Leach would see anyone who entered. If a masked man broke in, why didn't he give the alarm?"

Chase approached the desk. "The assailant rushed in on him too quickly, or possibly Leach recognized him and felt no fear. Or maybe he called out and nobody heard."

Donning his spectacles, he began opening drawers and sifting through papers. The neat stacks of correspondence revealed Leach as a convivial man who, in his capacity as editor, had received many invitations. Some were addressed to him and his wife at their home in the Adelphi Terrace, some to him at his Strand office. Chase perused a chatty note from one of Leach's acquaintances as well as a handbill for a debating society at a coffeehouse. He next unearthed a steep bill from Leach's tailor, an effusive report in someone else's hand describing the guests at a Venetian breakfast, and a gilt-edged card bidding the editor to attend a dinner in St. James's Square. Leach's connections to the current administration were numerous, and he was likely paid for his loyalty in social advantages as well as bribes to swell the newspaper's profits.

The only discordant note in the picture of Leach as gentleman and *bon vivant* was a hysterical plea from a woman called Mrs. Montclair begging him not to publish a paragraph in his newspaper, and across the bottom of this letter he had scrawled the single word "PAID." Chase knew it was common practice for newspapers to earn revenue through publishing puffs, essentially purchased public praise allowing politicians and other notables to receive favorable press, but the process worked the other way too. Newspapers often extorted suppression fees to halt the publication of private, embarrassing "anecdotes" or to contradict one already printed.

He lifted his eyes from the stack. "Any number of people had a motive to attack Leach. In addition to his political pandering, he traded in secrets and information. I doubt he had any scruples about ruining anyone." He set Mrs. Montclair's letter aside and slid open another drawer.

"You see nothing about Collatinus?"

"Nothing. Did you say Leach wrote of having received threats? You would think he'd be ready to defend himself."

Penelope had been walking slowly around the room, arms behind her back. She now paused in the center of the Axminster carpet and bent lower for a closer inspection. "I've found something." He closed the drawer he'd been examining. Joining her, he got down on his haunches to examine the medallion.

"Good eye, Mrs. Wolfe."

Lightly, she ran a hand over the pile, then rubbed her fingers and thumb together. "I suppose I'm used to checking for paint spatters on the floorboards that the maid has missed. This carpet has had time to dry. It won't be easy to remove the marks."

Together they contemplated the floral design, and Chase drew in a breath of satisfaction, for he had begun to think they might be chasing a fantasy. Like the rest of Leach's chamber, the carpet struck a note of restrained elegance and good taste. But mixed in with the greens and pinks of the bouquet were several reddish-brown smears that might have gone unnoticed, blending as they did with the lighter rose tints.

"That looks like blood, Mr. Chase. The stabbing occurred just here. Mr. Leach must have risen to meet the assailant. If he knew the man, he might not have observed the knife in his hand in time to ward him off."

"Not a great deal of blood, if blood it is. But you may be right."

"I'm sure I am. He stood here a moment"—her eyes went distant as she envisaged the scene—"and then retreated to his desk. Was he defending the article he was writing or looking for a weapon?"

She took a few steps backwards, but, turning her head, caught sight of something resting in one corner of the desk's gleaming expanse. She pulled out a book lying in the middle of a stack of other volumes. It was a finely bound copy of a work entitled *Thoughts on English Liberties in the Present Day*—by Eustace Sandford.

Chase removed the volume from her hands. Leach had marked a page in the text with a small slip of paper. Opening the book carefully so as not to dislodge the marker, he read the page. It meant nothing in particular to him; the passage seemed to be about the lengths to which any freeborn Englishman should go to preserve his political liberties. He examined the marker, which was blank, and set the volume aside.

"Leach's reference material for his missing article?" he said musingly, then looked sharply at Penelope. "Don't jump to conclusions, Mrs. Wolfe. Wait until we know more."

John Chase would readily admit to being a suspicious man. In his work as a Runner, he had learned to trace the lines revealing a design, the hidden motivation behind a particular crime. He knew this watchfulness set him apart from his fellow man, for most people seemed to live comfortably enough on the surface of things. But he could not. So when, for the second time that day, he was presented with a strangely convenient hackney coach, drawn by an unusually sound and spirited team, he took Penelope's arm and drew her away. "There's a coach-stand around the corner. We'll go there."

"This one displeases you for some reason?"

He didn't answer since he was too busy memorizing the number on the coach's plate and stealing a glance at the driver, who looked harmless enough: a typical London jarvey, wearing a many-caped benjamin and a wide-brimmed hat. When the driver saw he had lost his fare, he merely picked up the ribbons and set his horses in motion as soon as a break in the traffic allowed.

As they moved down the pavement, Chase's senses were alive to every detail of the familiar scene: shoppers flowing in and out of the cutlers, wax-chandlers, hatters, bookstalls, mapmakers, tobacconists, and tailors that lined the street. A man wearing a

signboard that advertised a lotion for loose teeth stumped by, and
a street hawker selling oysters struggled to be heard over the din.
But, after a minute or two, Chase noted that they had picked
up another interested party. This was a man in a brown felt hat,
who had been standing outside the newspaper office when they
emerged. The fellow had carefully kept his face turned in the
other direction, apparently absorbed in reading a bill pasted to
the wall, but Chase had felt the watchful attention on his back
during their brief flirtation with the hackney. Observing that
the man in the brown felt hat slouched down the street in their
wake, he cursed under his breath.

To test his theory, he led Penelope out of the stream of pedestrians over to the window of a pastry cook. When she opened her
mouth to question him, he gripped her arm in warning, feeling
her give a little start of surprise, but she followed him obedi-
ently enough, even showing the good sense not to glance over
her shoulder. Behind them, the man in the brown felt paused
to examine another shop window.

While Chase pretended to ogle the tarts, pies, and jellies on
the other side of the glass, he fumbled at his purse to make sure
he had his money ready. "There's a man following us. We'll move
again in a moment and nip round the corner to the stand."

Her nod was a barely perceptible inclination of her head,
the stiffness in her posture betraying apprehension. Giving
her arm a reassuring squeeze, he guided her back into the line
of pedestrians, and they set a rapid pace, weaving in and out
of the passersby, several of whom erupted in protests at their
rudeness. As Chase and Penelope made an abrupt right turn,
the coach-stand came into view. Three hackney coaches were
drawn up awaiting custom, and the waterman sat on a barrel
at the curbstone next to the pump used to supply the horses.
Confound it, thought Chase, there would have to be more than
one coach available.

The waterman leaped to his feet. "Where to, sir?" He
motioned to the conveyance at the head of the line. The box
was empty, the jarvey having gone inside the pub to grab a pint

while he waited. The driver of the second coach in line looked up indifferently and went on polishing a panel of his vehicle with a filthy cloth.

"Greek Street." Chase slipped a large tip in the waterman's hand and leaned closer to whisper in his ear, simultaneously showing his Bow Street baton. The waterman brightened. "Yes, sir! Never fear. I'll attend to it." Turning his head, he bellowed for the driver of the first coach, who stepped out of the taproom and mounted the box. The waterman opened the door of the coach and touched his hat politely to Penelope; the driver set his horses in motion, and they rattled off.

When they had gone a short distance, Penelope said, "What did you tell him?"

The side-glass was too small for Chase to get his entire head out, but he caught a glimpse of the man in the brown felt hat jumping into the second coach. The driver seemed to be finding it difficult to get his restive horses under control. As loud execrations followed them down the street, audible even over the cacophony of carriage wheels and voices, he leaned back, satisfied. "The jarvey will take our friend on a pleasant detour."

Penelope's eyes gleamed with admiration. "An immensely clever trick, Mr. Chase. But who on earth was the man, and why should he follow us?"

He waved away her praise, absorbed in an attempt to assemble the facts as he knew them. They were meager at best: letters with cryptic references to some nameless woman dead nearly twenty years; attempted murder that had been concealed; and pursuers following either him, Penelope, or the both of them. Perhaps his attendance at Rex's rout-party had sparked the interest of these pursuers, or the interest stemmed from her relationship to Eustace Sandford, the former Collatinus. His worry increased. "This business has a nasty smell, Mrs. Wolfe. Until we get to the bottom of it, you must watch yourself."

"I don't understand. Are we being shadowed because of the Collatinus letters?"

"I had entertained the possibility."

"There was something in the way Mr. Rex spoke to me last night," she said unhappily. "It occurred to me that he might believe me capable of writing these letters."

"The idea may have occurred to any number of people, assuming they know who your father is."

A new, even more disturbing thought seemed to present itself, for she went pale, twisting her hands in her lap. "Could it be—"

Chase found he very much disliked that particular expression on Penelope Wolfe's face. "What is it?"

"Last night I saw a man. Sarah had run outside. I found her there when I arrived home. This man was standing over her, as if he happened to be passing by and chanced upon her. The whole thing seemed strange somehow."

"Why didn't you tell me this before? Did he frighten or hurt her?"

"No, she was perfectly fine. I picked her up and brought her inside. I thought little of it. I suppose I had other things to think about last night. But now—"

He listened while she stumbled through a description of the incident. When she had finished, he said, aware of sounding terse and unfeeling, "Keep the child close. Warn your servants to be on guard for anything out of the common, and tell your husband about the lurkers and your connection to the Collatinus matter. He will take steps to ensure your safety."

She looked stricken. "Yes, I should have told him before. And you, Mr. Chase? How do you intend to get more information about Dryden Leach? His assailant may be Collatinus or lead us to him."

"I've sent a message to Noah Packet."

"You mean the little man you introduced me to in the street when I attended the St. Catherine procession. The thief?"

"Aye, but a useful one." He smiled at her disapproval.

"What will you do?"

The answer seemed obvious: he would trace a few lines and hope to reveal the design. "I shall find the masked man."

"I own I find it all rather perplexing. The blood on the carpet suggests Mr. Leach was attacked, and Mr. Rex admitted as much to me. He claimed there were reasons why the attack must remain a secret for the present. That would explain Leach's supposed illness and the two conflicting versions of events. But the whole thing seems unlikely, almost a Gothic tale. Why are there no witnesses? Why did no one report the crime to the authorities?"

"Unlikely, I agree. You are certain the source of the story was Mrs. Leach herself?"

"Mr. Rex received a note from the surgeon called to the wounded man, but surely it must have been Mrs. Leach who summoned this surgeon? Her husband would have told her about the masked man."

"Don't worry. I'll ask her." Anticipating the next words out of her mouth, Chase added, "That is, after I've escorted you safely home."

Chapter VII

Not far from the office of the *London Daily Intelligencer* sprawled
the Adelphi, a stately terrace that seemed one vast structure
with its uniform brickwork and pilasters decorated in ancient
motifs. At the Leach residence in the center of the terrace, the
knocker was muffled, and when Chase knocked, a footman in
livery answered, informing him the mistress was not at home
to visitors. The footman appeared to feel that a plainly dressed,
middle-aged man of uncertain origin ought to have gone to the
servants' entrance, and he made to close the door in Chase's face.
To stop him, Chase gave his name quickly. "If your mistress is
not available, be so good as to fetch her maid to me. My business cannot wait."

A shade of uncertainty crossed the young man's face. He
took a step back, allowing the door to crack wider. Chase did
not hesitate but pushed past him to find himself in a groin-
vaulted entrance passage dominated by a staircase of stone and
iron. The first thing that struck him was the deathly quiet in
the house, as if life itself scarcely thrived here. The hall, hung
with ugly portraits and perfectly spaced gilt-framed mirrors,
was clean and cold, offering no hint of the owner's personality.
Somewhere above, Dryden Leach would be breathing his last,
though a pall of mourning had already descended. Through an
open door leading off the entry, Chase glimpsed a spacious, richly
appointed library with large windows and decorative columns.

The footman left him standing there, and some minutes passed before a woman came down the stairs and moved toward him, her feet making no sound on the marble floor. She was a thin, drab, bespectacled person, sporting the single adornment of a shiny silver crucifix around her neck. She had brown hair confined in a tight bun and prim, colorless lips that did not smile.

"Good day. I am the children's governess, Miss Elliot. Albert said you have an important message for the family, Mr. Chase, and I thought someone should come down to receive it. Would you wish to write a note?"

"I much prefer to talk to you." When she glanced around in dismay, as if wondering where to conduct this unauthorized conversation, Chase added, "Do not trouble yourself. We can speak here, Miss Elliot. I will take but a few minutes of your time."

"I'm not sure how I can be helpful. Are you a friend of the family, sir?"

"In a manner of speaking." He was not surprised by her puzzlement as he hadn't told the footman he was a Bow Street officer. He went on quickly before she could ask him to explain his presence. "I understand your employer is gravely ill. How is he today?"

"I wouldn't know. I have been with the children all day."

"Has the doctor seen him?"

"I believe he came this morning, but we have not been told—"

"Can you tell me the surgeon's name, Miss Elliot? I might have a word with him to see whether anything further can be done for his patient."

She hesitated, then said, "A Mr. Thomas Fladgate."

"What of your mistress? She must have assistance in the sickroom, surely? A nurse?"

Miss Elliot's voice rose in distress. "She allows no one to share the burden with her. I've scarcely seen her since Mr. Leach was brought home in the hackney."

"It seems a great a responsibility. I suppose the footmen carried your master upstairs?"

"Yes, sir, he was in a dead faint."

"Who paid the driver?"

"The butler, Mr. Isherwood."

"Has anyone spoken to Mr. Leach?"

"Just the surgeon and Mrs. Leach. I understand the patient has been prescribed laudanum to ensure his rest. I…I didn't know what to say to the children—" She looked at him with huge eyes framed by tiny, gold-rimmed spectacles. "I must return to my duties, Mr. Chase. Is there a message?"

A new voice spoke. "That will not be necessary."

Startled, Chase looked up to see a tall, black-draped woman standing at the bottom of the staircase. She had descended so quietly that neither he nor the governess had caught her approach. One hand resting on the banister, she stood for a moment watching them before she glided forward. "Thank you for your assistance, Miss Elliot, but I will attend to our visitor."

The governess bid Chase a hasty good-bye and scurried up the stairs, but his attention was focused on the woman who now confronted him—Mary Rex Leach. Under her cap, her face was composed, though lines of immense fatigue were evident, and her skin seemed too tightly drawn over her cheekbones. Blue eyes, sunken in their sockets, assessed him without ostensible interest. As Chase took in all her unrelieved, lusterless black, he remembered what Penelope had told him about Mrs. Leach having lost a child before this imminent bereavement.

"I am Mary Leach. You wished to speak to me? Let us step into the library, sir."

He bowed and held the door for her to enter the room. Once inside, she gestured toward a chair and perched, her back straight, on a small sofa. Then she turned her eyes on him, clearly implying he must account for his presence—or get out.

"I beg your pardon for calling at such a time, ma'am."

"You have a message for my husband?"

"For you, in fact. My friend Mrs. Wolfe is anxious to be of service to you. She has heard from Mr. Horatio Rex about the assault on your husband."

"You know Mrs. Wolfe? My father has told me of his acquaintance with her husband, but I've not seen Penelope since she was a child of five years old. Yes, I must speak to her one day soon about a personal matter relating to her family." As she uttered this statement, she punctuated it by clasping and unclasping her hands so that the skin at her knuckles whitened. After a moment, as if becoming aware of this convulsive motion, she laid them flat on her lap and sat up straighter.

"Your husband, ma'am?" Would you describe what happened to him and his current state of health?"

"He is very weak. I'm afraid I cannot tell you much more at present. I must return to the sickroom." She rose to her feet, and he was forced to do likewise.

"Has Mr. Leach identified the masked assailant? You must be eager to see him apprehended and strung up as he deserves."

"Oh, do not fear, sir. He will get what he deserves."

Chase stared at her, nonplussed. In the twist of her lips and the flash of her eyes, he had glimpsed a marked resemblance to her father, a bitter humor that was more despair than anything else. "Your husband had been waging a public battle with a Jacobin called Collatinus. Was Collatinus the masked man, Mrs. Leach?"

"The masked man? You've got it wrong. You really must excuse me, Mr. Chase." Mary Leach was already starting to turn away.

"Tell me how I am wrong, ma'am."

"Dryden Leach had an enemy." She shook her head helplessly. "I can say nothing more."

This was surely an odd way to refer to one's husband lying at death's door; there was no emotion in the soft, precise voice, as if she gazed into a void only she saw and couldn't hope to describe. "Wait," he said, his urgency growing. "May I carry a message to Mrs. Wolfe for you?"

Mary Leach was at the door, but at this she turned back to address him once more. "Tell her to be careful."

In later years, Chase would recall her face as she spoke these words, and he would wish he had induced her to trust him.

He strolled toward Feathers Court at the southern end of Drury Lane. While he waited for Peter Malone, he intended to confer with Packet to see if the thief had turned up any information about Dryden Leach. But this was hardly a salubrious district to conduct one's business, and Chase kept a firm grip on his purse and watch, as he picked his way through a crowd of ragged men, women, and children. They were tenants of the foul courts opening from Drury Lane, many of them drunk, ill with consumption, or hungry—all of them cursed with poverty. Straight ahead, the spire of St. Mary le Strand, where most of them had probably been baptized, poked a finger into the darkening sky. And when they died, their bodies would mingle with a crowd of another sort in the tiny, overburdened burial ground nearby.

As Chase approached the archway that led to the court, his eyes fell on a woman lingering at the entrance: a plump whore in a low-cut gown and a frayed shawl fastened at her breast by an ornamental pin in the shape of a rose. At her feet sat a straw basket in which lay an infant who seemed to be asleep. As Chase watched, the woman extended one foot, clad in a torn and dirty slipper, and nudged the basket gently, her expression softening. But once she noticed his scrutiny, a hard mask descended. She lowered the glass of gin in her hand to leer at him. "Want company?"

"Not at present."

"Later?"

"You know a man called Peter Malone? Likes to come here of an evening, lives hereabouts?"

She thought a moment, then jerked a thumb over her shoulder. "Not to speak to. Lives in that court there with his wife and kiddies. He ain't been around yet if he's the one you want."

Chase extracted a coin from his purse. "Here's a sixpence for you with a chance for another later. You keep your eyes open, eh? You see anyone following Malone, anything looks different, you come tell me in the Blue Anchor."

She stooped to slip the coin under the baby's blanket, carefully balancing her glass so that its contents wouldn't spill. Roused from its slumber, the baby gave a whimper, too faint to be called a cry. When the money was safely stowed, the woman said wearily, "Not much happens here unless you want I should tell you when some poor sot starts banging on his wife and she sets up a screech."

"Strangers, anyone showing unusual interest, anything that seems amiss. Can you do it?"

At her nod, Chase was about to walk away, but he paused. "This your usual patch, miss, or maybe you walk the Strand of a night? A man was attacked at the newspaper office round the corner. You hear anything about him?"

"Can't say I did."

"Two nights ago. Nothing out of the common?"

"It was a slow night. Took myself off to bed early."

"Listen, if you hear anything, will you bring word to John Chase at Bow Street? I'll pay for the information."

She nodded again, and he went under the arch and into the court. It was a confined space hemmed in by high buildings where families inhabited one room each. The hideous odor of the cesspool assailed his nostrils, and he had to dodge some low-hanging laundry strung across the yard. Chase had seen many courts like this, and they were always the same: stench, squalor, criminality, despair. And yet there was always the local public house. Ignoring the tenants peeking furtively from their open doors, Chase entered the taproom of the pub. Redolent with ale, sweat, and smoke, the large room offered a cheerful contrast to the fetid court outside. A fire blazed in the hearth, and barmaids circulated, hoisting heavy trays in muscular arms. Other smells of uncertain origin greeted Chase, but, on the whole, the place was reasonably clean and inviting, its tables filled, its patrons eager to lay aside their worries for a short while and, at this early hour, not yet drunk into insensibility. An arm waved at Chase from a table against the wall near the bar, a position, he was not surprised to see, commanding a view of the entire room. The arm was attached to the diminutive form of Noah Packet.

Pulling out a chair, Chase joined him. It took him an instant to determine why the thief looked so unfamiliar; then he said, "New coat, Packet?"

Packet preened—there was no other word for it. "Like it?"

Chase did a thorough examination. Too large for Packet's slight shoulders, the coat was a handsome specimen nonetheless. Bright blue, double-breasted with large shiny buttons, it was made of quality warm, thick wool. This was certainly a change from the old black suit he had worn for years, but Chase told him he thought it a little conspicuous for one in Packet's profession.

"You may be right. Guess I couldn't resist."

"How'd you manage to lift something like that?"

"Naw, I bought it. Came into some blunt unexpectedly." His eyes skittered away.

Chase sighed. "Now what? You meant to play least in sight for the foreseeable future after the trouble you had last year." When Packet had accidentally chosen an underworld crime king as a mark, he'd been forced to participate in a burglary, an offense more serious than his usual petty thievery. Catching him with the gains, Chase had been given an opportunity to peach and collect the reward, but he had not taken this opportunity. For one thing, the thief had repeatedly proved his worth in ferreting out bits of gossip from servants and tavern wenches. For another thing, Chase liked him too much to see him rot in prison.

Packet's eyes returned to rest briefly on him. "Ain't like that. I did a turn for a gentry-cove in the shipping line. Legitimate like. Never thought I'd go on the square, did ye?"

"Maybe we should pin a medal on you."

Packet burst out with the hoarse sound that served as his chuckle. "Stubble it, Chase. You think I might have something for *you*, too?"

"I was hoping so. Cut line before the porter fellow arrives. Maybe you can watch him while I'm talking to him, see if you think he tells me true."

"To be sure," he said modestly. While Chase was pretty good at observing people, the thief was even better. Packet took out a pocket-handkerchief and began to polish one of his shiny brass buttons that had been spattered with a drop of porter. It was his peculiarity that he never looked a man directly in the face when about to divulge information. "Seems Malone may have come into a bit too," he said, inspecting his cuffs. "He was here last night and heard to say he'd be taking his wife and childer to new lodgings."

"A secret to sell? I thought as much."

Packet shrugged. "I'll tell you something." His muddy brown eyes traveled past a plaque announcing the age of the pub to drift indifferently over a buxom tavern maid, who had bent to serve a customer at the next table.

"Yes?"

"I had a word with your Mr. Leach's scullery maid—taking little thing, she is. She says as how her mistress seems mighty interested in keeping this affair dark. Mrs. Leach won't even admit her own father to her husband's room. This Mr. Rex went to the Adelphi on the night his son-by-marriage got used up but was sent off with a flea in his ear."

"It's common knowledge there's bad blood between Leach and Rex."

"Things ain't none too rosy with Mr. and Mrs. Leach neither. The girl told me there's been talk. Leach let it be known below-stairs that he wants his servants to keep an eye on her comings and goings and visitors."

"An affair?"

"Could be. Maybe she found a young spark to keep her company."

"See if you can find out more, Packet. Jeremy Wolfe says Rex received a message from the surgeon treating Leach, and that's how Rex found out about the attack. The surgeon apparently didn't think a woman could handle the crisis."

"Wolfe? The artist cove as is wed to your friend Mrs. Wolfe? I got a weakness for a young gentry-mort like her. Very pleasant was Mrs. Wolfe when I had the privilege of making her acquaintance."

"She doesn't return the sentiment. At all events, she's in some difficulties." Chase told him about Penelope's encounter with the stranger in the street and about the men tracking them earlier that day. Whatever this was, it clearly constituted an organized effort by someone with the means to pay for spies and coach drivers; Horatio Rex certainly had these means, Chase reflected. Did Mary Leach refuse to admit her father to the sickroom because she suspected him of being behind the attack? If Rex were Collatinus, that might make sense.

Packet listened with interest. "Never fear. I'll nose around some more."

"See what you can discover about Leach's attacker. I've just come from the Adelphi Terrace, where he is about to meet Old Mr. Grim. His loving wife cares for him."

"Oh?"

"She doesn't leave his side."

"You think maybe she's covering for someone? Maybe she don't relish the scandal?"

"This is her husband, Packet. Wouldn't you think she'd want his killer caught?"

"Who do you reckon this masked man was? Collatinus?"

"I've no notion, but Mrs. Leach informs me I've got hold of the wrong handle somehow."

"Aiming to throw dust in your eyes," suggested Packet.

"You may be right." Chase removed his watch from his waistcoat pocket to check the time. "Let's hope that porter will be along soon."

When Malone arrived ten minutes later, he hesitated as his eyes adjusted to the light, then began to scan the tables. He caught sight of Chase, froze, turned his back, and slipped back out the door, banging it behind him.

"What the devil?" Chase was already on his feet. "Wait here," he said to Packet, but the thief remained close on his heels.

As they ran through the court and onto Drury Lane, the prostitute still loitered in the archway. "Your man is getting away. Be quick! There he goes," she gasped, excitement making her look younger. She pointed down the street at a fleeing figure.

"I can see that," Chase barked at her.

He set off after the porter, but his bad knee, which had stiffened as he sat over his ale, gave out, and he nearly lost his footing, his spectacles bouncing to the bottom of his nose. Ahead of him, Malone rounded a corner, disappearing from view. He cursed.

But Packet, who had sprinted after Malone, called over his shoulder, "My chance to return a favor." His hoarse chuckle floated back. "I'll see you later at the Brown Bear."

Chase turned away. Retrieving a coin from his purse, he walked slowly back toward Feathers Court to approach the woman with the baby in her arms. Awake now, the infant rooted at her neck, and the whore looked at him with a glint of mockery in her too-old eyes. Chase sighed.

"Your sixpence, miss." He put the coin in her hand.

Chapter VIII

Penelope and Maggie spent the evening in front of the fire. Though a basket of plain mending lay at Maggie's feet, she liked to take an hour in the evening to do some fancy work, a skill she'd been taught by the patroness of the rather unusual charitable organization where she and Penelope had first met. Tonight Maggie was busy adding a floral and leaf design to the hem and neckline of one of Penelope's muslin gowns.

Maggie listened as Penelope described the Collatinus letters, N.D.'s mysterious death, and the recent attack on Dryden Leach, but she refused to credit that Eustace Sandford, a man she'd never met, could have done anything seriously amiss. "He's your dad, isn't he? You'd know if he had something wrong in his nature." Unerringly, she had hit upon the reassurance that would be most welcome, and Penelope was grateful.

On the whole, Maggie seemed to welcome these developments as a way to enliven the dull domestic round. Her face bright with interest, she said she wasn't one to wish ill on anyone, but she thought Dryden Leach sounded like a coxcomb who had likely asked for his scurvy treatment, what with writing nasty articles and getting himself involved in low shams. And she thought Penelope worried too much about what she called a bit of fiddle-faddle in the papers that may or may not be based in sober truth. Still, Maggie promised to redouble her vigilance over Sarah and the other children.

The lamplight played over her freckled countenance, striking fire on her red head, as she added her bit to the conversation. "Today I went to the baker's shop to buy some of them buns the children like for their tea, you know, mum. When I went in, the lady as owns the shop was not so friendly as usual—" Color stained her cheeks.

"You thought it was because we had not paid the bill."

"That's just it, mum. Mrs. Vane said to ask when it might be convenient for you to make all tidy. I said I would, frowning her down like, but then she said as how a man come around asking about you and the master. Wanting to know how long you've lived in the neighborhood, do you settle your accounts, do the neighbors think well of you, that sort of thing. She said it like I should know what it meant, and maybe like I was trying to hide our wickedness. She wrinkled up her mouth like she was aiming to spew her guts."

Her mimicry of Mrs. Vane was so uncannily like the original that Penelope had to laugh, and yet there was little enough to laugh about in this additional sign of a formless menace lurking in the background of her life.

Grinning in response, Maggie picked up her needle and resumed her story. "I told Mrs. Vane that Mr. Jeremy is to paint the portrait of a Duke. I said His Grace's people are inquiring into our way of life to make sure we're respectable."

"Did she believe you?"

"Oh indeed, mum. I'm sure she did, for I pretended I couldn't tell her the Duke's name, as he was too high in the instep to have his private affairs spoken of. I told her all about how he is to be married to a great heiress and wants a portrait in honor of the occasion. I said if he likes Mr. Jeremy's work, he'd likely commission another of the bride. She swallowed it!"

Penelope went to the mantelpiece and shook out some coins from a box she kept there. "Will you take this money to Mrs. Vane in the morning?"

"Don't be giving that sourpuss all our rhino, mum," Maggie

warned, though she took the coins and stored them in a little bag hanging at her waist.

"Did Mrs. Vane say anything more about this man? Young or old? Well dressed and polite or rough and low?"

"Well-spoken, about thirty or thereabouts, plainly but decently dressed."

"Be on your guard for anything out of the ordinary, Maggie."

The two women lapsed into silence. Penelope was thinking about how much she had come to value Maggie's companionship. An Irishwoman whose husband only showed his face when he wanted to appropriate her hard-earned funds, Maggie fended for herself with her two young children. She often fervently expressed her gratitude for her position as Sarah's nursemaid, but, in truth, the obligation was mostly on Penelope's side. Being in Maggie's company was often a relief, for it was never necessary to pretend with her. She understood what it meant to live with uncertainty, and treated the children and her mistress with humor and kindness. Penelope admired her ability to take the world as she found it.

Trying to gather her scattered thoughts, Penelope took up her pen. She had been rereading some of her father's works and taking notes with the idea of perhaps writing his biography, though she was finding it enormously difficult to concentrate. When she realized she had read the same passage for the third time, she allowed her mind to return to Mary Leach. Penelope was curious about this woman who had cut herself off from her family and her career as an author to live a more conventional married life. At least her husband had encouraged her to use her literary talents in some form, albeit in the Tory cause. What would happen to Mary? Would she experience her husband's death as a release, a liberation? Mr. Rex had suggested that Mary sought a refuge in wedding her unlikable husband, but this attempt was unlikely to have been successful. To marry for the wrong reasons rarely was, Penelope thought wryly, but then again to marry for love was apt to be just as risky.

She wondered what her own life would have been like had she herself chosen otherwise, and, unbidden, the image of Edward Buckler rose before her. It had been a relief to see him so full of energy and purpose, for she had sometimes pictured him spending his days in his chambers among his books and papers with little to do but indulge in gloomy thoughts. He was a man who needed to put himself in the current of life. What he really needed was a wife, she decided with a sternly repressed pang.

Maggie, beginning to nod over her embroidery, gave a wide yawn and folded up the dress. "I'm off to bed, mum. Waxing moon tonight—grand it is. I saw it from the nursery window when I put the children to bed." She crossed herself unselfconsciously. "*God and the holy Virgin be about me. I see the moon, and the moon sees me.* Reminds me of my mam. Best not take chances, she used to say." Despite her robust commonsense, Maggie had a superstitious streak that revealed itself at odd moments, a trait Penelope shared, her own childhood having been filled with Sicilian lore whispered to her by an old nurse.

Later, having retired to her bedroom, Penelope listened to faint creaks as the house settled around her, quiet and peaceful. A candle burned on the table, and the room was mostly in shadow. The maid and the manservant had retired to their rest in the attics above, the cook was asleep in her basement apartment, and Jeremy had not yet returned from an engagement. She felt restless, the novel on her bedside table failing to hold her attention. Finally, she tossed aside the bedcovers to approach the window. Taking care not to be visible from the street, she gazed out through a crack in the blind for some minutes, unmoving, her heart troubled. At this hour the street was deserted but for the occasional coach passing by, and she watched the neighbors' lights blinking out, one by one. For once, the air was clear enough that she could admire the gibbous moon floating among a few visible stars. In this hour of mystery, the chimney pots reminded her of the turrets of a castle in some remote country, and she began, idly, to spin a foolish tale of forbidden love and ancient curses. Then the cry of the night watchman broke the stillness. Penelope let the blind drop and went to bed alone.

Noah Packet crept into the Brown Bear as Chase sat over a glass of hot gin and a half-eaten lamb chop. "Hungry?" Chase asked.

"Won't say no to a morsel."

"You've earned it." Chase nodded at the barmaid and sat back to regard Packet. His hat was missing. He was liberally bedaubed in mud from his tousled hair to his cracked, old boots, a smear decorating each cheek. One side of his face was bruised and bleeding, one of his eyes swollen shut. Moreover, the glory of his new blue coat was quite dimmed: it too was covered in filth, and he had lost one of his shiny buttons. Exhausted, he slumped in his chair, avoiding Chase's gaze and wrinkling up his nose at the musty smell that rose from his clothing as it began to dry in the tavern's warmth. He looked like a gnome that had crawled out of the earth.

"What happened, Noah?"

"I followed the fellow, but he smoked me."

When the tavern maid slapped a plate and glass in front of Packet, he paused a moment to wrap his hands around his gin and take a long swallow, his throat working convulsively. When he spoke again, his voice had dropped to a whisper. Chase had to strain to hear over the cacophony of boisterous conversations and tankards thumping the wooden tables.

Packet had chased Malone down Drury Lane, passing the Cock and Pie public house and turning left onto Wych Street to head toward Lyons Inn, a disreputable Inn of Chancery inhabited only by the lowest of lawyers. People lounged listlessly against the ramshackle houses, the women on the doorsteps quarrelling and laughing among their confederates, barefoot children tumbling everywhere. Foul gutters ran down the center of the street, and over the whole hung a miasmic vapor that choked the lungs and made Packet, Londoner born and bred, long for some fresher air. Malone circled round the back of the Inn and, crossing Holywell Street, ducked down an alleyway called Half-Moon passage linking to the Strand. Gamely, Packet followed.

"He were waiting for me as I come round the corner." Packet sawed away at his chop, popping a piece into his mouth, his slender fingers trembling. His eyes lifted from his plate to skim over Chase's face and flitted away.

Taking a few uncertain steps forward, Packet had been peering into the murk to see if he could spot his quarry when a bony arm reached out to seize him. This arm raised him up, and he found himself confronting a pair of blazing eyes.

"What do you want, little man?" Malone shook him, like a terrier with a rat in its mouth.

Packet hung his head, trying to look pathetic, and, after a moment, Malone stopped shaking him but kept a firm grip on the lapel of his coat with one hand. The other hand drew back. "What've you got to say for yourself?"

"Begging your pardon. Thought you was someone I knew."

"You lie. Tell me, or you'll be sorry. That John Chase you were with—he's a Runner?"

"He just wants your information, Malone. Profit for you in it."

"I ain't a fool. I know when doings are too big for me. Let them nobs run their rigs, for all I care. You tell the Runner to stay away from me. Maybe you need a little encouragement to deliver my message?"

Packet could only shake his head as a fist took him in the face. Rustles in the darkness told him they had an audience, but the watchers stayed well back. He did not cry out. He wanted to save his strength to run if an opportunity came. But before he could make an effort to extricate himself, Malone dropped him in the muck of the street. Taking to his heels again, the porter was soon lost in the crowd. Slowly, Packet picked himself up. By the time he staggered out onto Holywell Street again, Malone was long gone, and Packet was left to stare up into the stern countenance of a half-moon shop sign sailing placidly above his head.

Now, Packet shivered, glaring at Chase. "I should never have hoofed it after that fellow. It's you as I blame. Had your voice in my head, saying like always, 'I got to know.' I told you before—you a plague of God, you is."

"You said it yourself, Packet. You owed me. How'd Malone find out I'm a Runner, do you suppose?"

"Queers me. He had the smell o' fear on him, and that made him mean."

"He was eager enough to sell his information until someone scared him off after I spoke to him at the *Daily Intelligencer*. You think we got some big men behind this little drama?"

Packet pushed his plate away. "The next time I decide to do you a favor, you have my permission to darken my daylights yourself. You leave this one alone."

Chapter IX

Chase would do no such thing. The next morning saw him up betimes and well rested, his neighbor having kept quiet for a change. After breakfast, he walked up St. Martin's Lane to the rookery around Seven Dials, where seven streets came together in a poor, criminal district even a prigman like Packet might hesitate to enter. Chase wanted to locate Samuel Gibbs, editor and printer of the *Free Albion*, but this was easier said than done. Fly-by-night printers tended to pack up and move their premises whenever they feared the weight of authority might descend on them with an indictment for seditious libel.

He finally found the office on Monmouth Street, but the shutters were fastened, no one answering his knock. And when he attempted to interview a neighboring dealer of pigeons, fowl, and other more exotic birds, the man could—or would—tell him nothing. After trying the rag-and-bone man and the dealer in old iron with similar results, Chase walked the streets. He kept his hand on the pistol in his pocket and his Bow Street baton conspicuously displayed as he asked questions of the men leaning against doorposts and the women sitting on steps. There was little to see but gutters choked with refuse and rows of shabby buildings with endless lines of broken or patched windows. He decided to take himself back to civilization.

Then he was off to the hackney-coach registry office in Essex Street to see about tracing the suspicious coaches. Again showing his Bow Street ensign, Chase gave the clerk the plate numbers and was soon in possession of the drivers' names, as well as the names of the yards where they stabled their horses. On the other hand, without a plate number, he was unlikely to trace the hackney coach that had transported Dryden Leach back to the Adelphi. He would have to hope Packet discovered something by inquiring at the coach stands in the vicinity of the Strand, and Chase had also asked him to check the coaching inns in case Peter Malone had been spotted leaving town.

At the first coach-yard, Chase found the driver himself, sitting over a tankard of ale in the taproom. Scanning his features, he did not believe this to be the same jarvey from Greek Street, a conclusion confirmed when the man took him outside to display his coach: a battered specimen with a faded coat of arms and a broken door fastened by a peg. It was not the same coach he and Penelope had ridden in the day before. After silencing the man's curiosity with a generous tip, Chase went on to the second yard but was informed that this particular coach had been out of service for a week due to the driver's illness. When Chase asked if the vehicle happened to be a particularly handsome equipage, the landlord laughed. "If you're fond of mud, broken springs, and doddering horses, sir." So there it was. The number plates had been falsified.

Last night, Chase had asked the harlot with the baby to show him the porter's lodging in Feathers Court, but a suspicious neighbor told him Mrs. Malone and the children had stepped out. Upon his return today, he was not terribly surprised to learn that the family's belongings had been removed. They were gone; no one in the court would admit to knowing where. And Chase's mind moved again to Mary Leach and her desperate vigil over her dying husband. What had really happened at the newspaper office?

As he left Feathers Court, he barely noticed the dreary drizzle of rain soaking his hat and coat, for he had much to digest. Suddenly he recalled Farley's tattle about the Runner Victor Kirby and his involvement in a secret investigation of Princess Caroline, and he remembered that the wounded journalist Dryden Leach was a sycophant, a word-man for hire, who polished the reputation of his royal master with fawning paragraphs in his newspaper. Surely, the Home Office men had no reason to attack Leach, though they might have an interest in knowing who did. Possibly, Peter Malone had seen the masked man, and the government either wanted to obtain this information, or prevent Malone from revealing it to anyone else. Yes, that could be true, Chase thought, particularly if the watchers were not in the pay of Horatio Rex, after all. Chase would have a word with Kirby.

But what in heaven's name could an inquiry into Princess Caroline have to do with Penelope Wolfe? Was it possible the Home Office was watching Penelope's movements because she was suspected of being connected to Collatinus, who was a threat to the Regent? Though Chase had kept a sharp eye out today, he had not observed anyone following him. Which told him yesterday's watchers had been more interested in Penelope than in him. Nothing added up, and instinct told Chase that the stubborn darkness of this inquiry would not readily yield to enlightenment.

For much of the afternoon he toasted his boots in front of a small fire at Bow Street, waiting to see if Victor Kirby would appear, and was rewarded for his patience when the Runner strolled in about five o'clock. A man of medium height with ropy arm muscles and pleasant, nondescript features, Kirby walked to the table, picking up a copy of the *Hue and Cry*. He greeted Chase respectfully and began to flip the pages.

Chase rose to join him. "I hear you've been working out of Great Marlborough Street these days."

Kirby kept his attention on the gazette as if absorbed in its descriptions of stolen property and felonies committed. "I'm sure you'll pardon me, Chase, but I'm not at liberty to discuss the matter. Magistrate's orders."

"Look, I know there's a to-do with letters written by a radical hack called Collatinus, so don't pitch the gammon with me."

"It's not that I don't want to tell you," said Kirby awkwardly, "but my career won't be worth a jot if I blab. Maybe after it's all over—"

Chase studied him. "Let's try this. I speak; you listen. Just say me yea or nay." He paused, keeping his eyes fixed on the other man's face. "Well then, you have been told to examine the private affairs of the Princess of Wales to prepare the way for the Regent's divorce. Maybe like the last investigation? Interviewing her servants, noting her movements, maybe even inspecting her linen and reading her love letters?"

The younger man's expression remained stony, but a little color crept up his cheeks. Chase smiled, allowing the silence to stretch before he said, "I wonder, Kirby, whether you've seen the Collatinus letters? They allude to the Regent in no respectful terms. Have you and your new colleagues been charged with the task of finding this scribbler and stopping his mouth?"

At this Kirby looked angry. "I have no idea what you're talking about, and, even if I did, I can't tell you, as I've made plain." He tossed the gazette back on the table. "I'll take myself off now. Business to attend to."

Chase stepped in his path. "One moment, Kirby. Skinny man in a brown coat, name of Peter Malone. He's the porter at the *Daily Intelligencer*. You know him?"

There was no reaction except that Kirby's defiance seemed to harden. Then the door opened, and one of the clerks thrust in his head. "John Chase? Mr. Read needs to see you right away." Kirby shoved past the clerk and went out.

Chief Magistrate James Read had pulled a lamp close to him on the desk in order to work in the gathering gloom. Light flickered over his austere features, illuminating the fleshy pouches under each eye and the wrinkles on his heavily lined forehead. He drew himself upright, readying himself for yet another unpleasant task in an already long day, and indicated a chair in front of the desk. Taking a seat, Chase waited for the magistrate to speak.

"You've been poking your nose where it has no business to be. Oblige me by steering clear of this Collatinus affair."

"Who gave you the word, sir?"

"None of your business, Chase. Let's just say I heard it from those you would do well not to cross and leave it at that. What's your interest in the matter?"

This was not an easy question to answer. If he said he was trying to find the author of the letters, Read would wonder what possible reason he could have. If he said he was trying to find a masked assailant—whose supposed victim had never even reported the crime—Read was likely to question his sanity. Chase answered carefully, "A friend of mine, a lady, is in trouble and has asked for my help."

"What trouble?"

"I won't betray the lady's confidence at present, except to say that the inquiry relates to a journalist, stabbed while sitting alone in his office. The man is not long for this world, and yet no notice has been taken by anyone. In fact, everyone seems deuced eager to pretend the attack never happened! I didn't think you'd wish me to ignore foul murder, sir."

"That would depend, Chase. I gather some unpleasantness is afoot, but I've been told the Home Office has the matter well in hand and affairs of state are at stake. No call for your interference. Who is guilty of the crime, do you think?"

"A masked man, supposedly, but I find I credit his existence less and less."

Read's look seemed a curious mixture of amusement and disapproval. "You say you aim to help a lady?"

"Yes, sir."

"This wouldn't be she, by chance, whom you met at Mr. Horatio Rex's rout?" He gave a sour smile at Chase's start of surprise. "I suppose you think I do nothing but nurse thieves and molls in court and bury my head in papers the rest of the time, but I do like to know a thing or two about the men on my staff." Reaching over to one of his neat stacks of correspondence, he extracted a single sheet. "Let me see, I think I have the letter here. *Rascal. Interloper. Rudesby.* Would that be you, Chase?"

"Rex sent a letter of complaint. I should have known he would."

"Yes, you should." The smile was gone from Read's eyes. "Some of the fashionables may like to have a Runner attending their fancy parties, but in future you will wait to be invited. You were trespassing, as Mr. Rex charges with perfect justice."

"I beg your pardon, sir." Chase didn't bother to imbue his speech with false contrition as he believed Read would not care overmuch to indulge the complaints of a moneylender, however plump in the pocket the "gentleman" might be.

The Chief Magistrate brushed aside this apology with a wave of his hand. "I don't doubt you've been after Victor Kirby too. You leave him alone, Chase. Indeed, this must all stop immediately, and you'll return to your other duties. I would assume you have some? Otherwise, I may start to think Bow Street has outlived its usefulness."

Chase grinned. "I can find a trick or two to keep me busy, sir. But is there nothing you can tell me about the Home Office's interest in this case? A valuable witness to the attack on the journalist has disappeared."

"Not a thing. The matter is out of my hands. They haven't told me much, though I know enough to be glad I'm well out of it. It seems Conant over at Great Marlborough Street has taken the lead." He paused, then added reflectively, "Ambitious man is Conant. He'll be nipping at my heels."

"I trust not, Mr. Read." This time Chase was sincere. While he knew next to nothing about Read's life outside the office, Chase had always been impressed by the Chief Magistrate's refusal of the knighthood that traditionally accompanied the magistracy of Bow Street. It seemed Read cared more for the substance of his job than for worldly advancement.

Read stretched his shoulders, glancing down at his papers. "We're finished here. Do I have your assurance you'll let the matter drop?"

They looked at one another, and the only sounds in the room were the carriage wheels and street cries from outside. Chase finally said, "No, sir. You don't."

Thunder descended on the magistrate's brow. "You are insubordinate. Cross me in this, and I can't be answerable for the consequences. You won't like to lose your situation."

Chase did not answer.

"Blast it. I don't have time for this. Do as I say, or you'll be sorry. Tell your lady-friend, with my apologies, to find someone else to fight her battles." Turning away, Read picked up his pen, and Chase left the room.

He walked home in the twilight under roiling clouds that weighed upon the city. There was no question in his mind about whether he would continue his investigation, but he supposed he would have to be more circumspect in the future. He must proceed in a more private capacity without resorting to the convenient authority of Bow Street.

As Chase picked his way through the crowd of pickpockets, low women, and pleasure-seeking gentlemen in the market square, Packet suddenly materialized at his elbow, motioning him into a shop doorway. Chase was not surprised to see him since his line of business often brought him to the square, which provided enormous scope for his talents. Tonight the thief wore his rusty, old coat again. His eye was still black and blue, but the swelling on his face had subsided.

"Got news," he hissed.

"Let's hear it," said Chase. "But be quick. It's about to rain."

With a quick look up at the threatening sky and another look around to make sure no one overheard, Packet murmured to Chase's cravat, "I asked about Leach's surgeon, fellow called Fladgate. Nothing. He were well greased in the fist to keep quiet, I warrant. But I got a chambermaid as says she found her mistress' muddy boots and soiled skirt on the morning after Leach was hushed. Seems Mrs. Leach went out in the night, and there ain't no one to say just where she went."

"Did you inquire among the molls on the Strand? Anyone see Mrs. Leach?"

"Not for certain, except for one interesting thing. One of them gals says as how she saw a veiled woman a-running down the street, like the hounds of hell were after her. Might a been Mrs. Leach, might not, but strange all the same, eh? You reckon she were hand in glove with the masked man?"

"No, I think she made him up." Chase dropped several coins in Packet's hand and walked away.

At home he found an unexpected invitation from the lawyer Ezekiel Thorogood to dine the next day as well as a coyly urgent note from the journalist Fred Gander, seeking fresh intelligence on the inquiry. Chase would have to get rid of Gander somehow. As he ate his dinner with Mrs. Beeks and the boys, Chase kept his attention on his plate, dimly aware that he hurt Leo's feelings with his monosyllabic replies to a stream of eager questions. Leo's brother, William, a much more self-contained and reserved child, thankfully paid Chase no mind.

Listening to the rain drumming on the windows as he pondered Packet's information, Chase turned over a startling possibility in his mind. If he was right about the masked man being invented, could there instead have been a masked *woman*? He thought he now knew who had attacked Dryden Leach, but what he didn't understand was *why*—or for that matter why Mrs. Leach hadn't simply finished off her victim since she had him completely in her power. As for motive, he might have presumed she had a private reason for attacking her husband had she not removed Leach's reply to Collatinus, which the journalist planned to publish the next day. Chase thought the answer must lie in the past with the events surrounding the original letters and the relationship between Horatio Rex and Eustace Sandford. But what was he to do with this knowledge? For one thing, he had no proof, and for another, the Chief Magistrate had told him in no uncertain terms to stay out of the matter. And Chase could hardly accuse a wealthy and well-connected lady of murder without more positive evidence.

Chapter X

For centuries, the effigies of knights at rest in the Temple Church had spoken of ancient times and lost glory. These armed knights had not been Templars, the once-powerful order of warrior-monks who had built the round church, but were instead noblemen who had chosen to be buried here, probably in exchange for a fat donation. In sadly dilapidated condition these days, the marble forms reposed, some with legs crossed to signify a crusader's vow. This spot often drew Edward Buckler since he liked to breathe the air of the past and escape, for a time, the relentless pace of modern life. Here in the church in the middle of the day, he found Latham Quiller, serjeant-at-law, leaning over the iron railings to gaze upon the effigies.

As Buckler approached, Quiller loosed his grip on the iron and straightened up. After a brief exchange of greetings, the serjeant said, "You've made an enemy of Richard Grouse. I shouldn't be at all surprised if he made himself unpleasant." Quiller referred to the plaintiff whom Buckler and Dallas had humiliated in the crim. con. case when the jury had awarded Grouse the ludicrous damages of one shilling for his wife's adultery. It was Buckler's luck that the man was also a solicitor with the power to hurt him professionally.

"Grouse is above my touch in any case. I doubt he would ever offer me a brief."

"Likely not. But you should be on your guard lest he turn other solicitors against you."

It was the custom of the English Bar that no barrister obtained his own employment but required an attorney or solicitor to serve as a bridge between him and a client. In truth, many a barrister's career had foundered through an inability to cultivate profitable relationships with the lower branch of the profession. So Quiller's advice was sound, though he spoke as if Buckler's fate could mean nothing to him personally. Buckler had often wondered what Quiller thought of the decline of his own order—the serjeants had once been at the very top of the legal heap, but their privileges and rights of precedence had long been under siege from an encroaching army of King's Counsel. These days the order seemed largely populated by second-rate lawyers, excepting Quiller and a few other talented, ambitious men. In his mind Buckler heard his Thorogood's voice intoning *Sic transit gloria mundi*. Thus passes the glory of the world. Impatiently, he shook off this ill-timed fit of whimsy.

"Your clerk told me I might find you here."

"An hour of recreation before I must return to my business."

"My apologies for the interruption, sir. I have a few questions I'd like to ask you."

"About a brief?"

"Unfortunately not," Buckler said wryly. "Some business I am looking into for a friend. Can you spare a few minutes?" He kept his tone deferential.

Quiller gave him a sharp glance followed by a wary nod, perhaps because he was all too familiar with impecunious young barristers soliciting his patronage. Before his elevation to the Order of the Coif and removal to Serjeants' Inn on Chancery Lane, he had been a member of the Inner Temple. It seemed he still enjoyed a return to his old grounds and, if Buckler was lucky, a lingering wish to aid his former brethren. But Buckler noted that Quiller pointedly did not invite him to sit down in one of the pews.

"Glad to help," the serjeant finally responded without any noticeable enthusiasm.

"Have you seen the Collatinus letters?"

Distaste hardened his expression. "I've read them, yes."

"I wanted to ask you about a paragraph that seems to refer to you—one of those nasty hints with no basis in anything but malice, I'm sure. I am interested in the writer of these letters."

"Whoever he is, he's a wretch. I take no notice of such rubbish."

"Can you tell me anything of the lady whom Collatinus seems eager to defend?"

There was another pause; then Quiller said, "I suppose you mean Nell Durant."

"Was that her name? Who was she, sir?"

A strange look crossed the other man's face, but it was gone so quickly Buckler might almost have imagined it. He had read scorn and dismay and some other unidentifiable emotion.

"A courtesan. The mistress of any number of powerful, influential men. A whore, dead these twenty years."

"Did you know her?"

Quiller's hand reached out to grasp the iron railing again, and he slumped slightly in renewed contemplation of the effigies. "I met her years ago on two occasions soon before her death. She came to me for legal advice, even though I told her she should consult a solicitor. And you see what comes of contact with such a woman. I should have tossed her out on her ear as indeed I did—the second time."

"What sort of advice, sir, if you don't mind my asking?"

"I see no reason to respect her confidence now. She was being sued for debt and wanted to be freed of her creditors by asserting the status of a married woman. But the proof of her so-called marriage to a Joseph Durant wouldn't have stood up in court, as I informed her. I certainly never savaged her reputation as the paragraph in the newspaper charges."

"I take it this Durant was nowhere to be found?"

Quiller nodded. "Mrs. Durant claimed he was in France. I doubt there was such a person."

"And the second consultation?"

"The least said on that subject the better, Buckler. The lady tried to embroil me in her low intrigues. Nothing less than an attempt to bring disgrace on royalty itself."

"Disgrace?"

"She'd briefly taken the Regent's fancy, but she turned nasty when he refused her a settlement."

Buckler opened his mouth to press further and shut it again, for Quiller's stiff posture warned that he did not take kindly to intrusive questions. It would be better to circle around the matter delicately. "Do you know a journalist called Dryden Leach?"

The serjeant looked surprised. "I've read his answers to Collatinus in the *Daily Intelligencer*. Leach is a good man to take up the charge against the blackguard."

"Perhaps you know Nell Durant was connected to another Collatinus back in the '90s?"

"Yes, there was a bit of a bustle, as I recall. But I shouldn't think the same scribbler has written these new articles after all this time. Unfortunately, it has proven impossible to root out the radicals completely for all that the government has scored some successes. The weeds spring back, however. My friend Reeves, who led the Crown and Anchor Association, did his best to counteract the evil."

"I thought the Crown and Anchor tavern was, and still is, a site for radical gatherings, sir?"

"Very true, but Reeves tried to change all that by using the place for our loyalist meetings and even adopting the tavern's name for our society. While it lasted, we did our bit to foil the designs of the levellers. We wrote anti-Jacobin pamphlets, acted on anonymous information. And tried to dislodge the radicals at the Crown and Anchor."

This was the first time in their acquaintance that Buckler had observed enthusiasm in Quiller, so he asked his next question quickly. "Did you happen to compile information about well-known Jacobins? For instance, there was a man called Horatio Rex, editor of the paper that published the Collatinus letters."

Quiller shot him a look of proud derision. "'Jew' Rex? That infamous scoundrel is still very much in the public eye. He gives a lot of vulgar parties and gets his name in the gossip columns. But you're right. At the time he was a traitor as well as a sharper and a usurer. I recall *him*, all right. Reeves used to receive dozens of letters from informers wanting to help us stamp out the corruption, and I can tell you this Rex figured in a good portion of them."

"Can you recall the details?"

"There *was* a rumor we discussed at one of our meetings. A member of the association heard of Rex having an instrument among the gentry. It turns out this Collatinus was a 'gentleman' wicked and greedy enough to betray his own kind. He sold information to Rex. Cuckoldry, gaming debts, whoring—the secret histories of people of fashion. Of course, a scandalous paragraph would only serve to color the radicals' portrait of the aristocracy as monsters of rapacity, or the paragraph could be held back, for a price."

"But not the tattle about the Regent?"

"Too important to the villains. They chose to spend it as political capital. Collatinus made His Royal Highness look a fool and a profligate in order to promote his revolutionary cause. Quite damaging, I don't mind telling you."

Buckler would have to tell Penelope about this conversation, and imagining her distress, he dreaded the prospect. He could not know for sure that this "gentleman" was Eustace Sandford, but it would be foolish to deny the probability since Sandford had confessed to being the original Collatinus. "Was this gentleman named?" he asked almost unwillingly.

"I'm afraid not. But I can't think how a man of breeding went so wrong. As for Rex, he proved a turncoat in the end, unfaithful even to his own kind. He gave money toward the defense of the traitors, but all the time he was working in secret for the Home Office in order to entrap his cohorts and save his skin. Later he announced his opposition to the French and published a defense of the English constitution." Quiller lifted his brows. "No doubt it's a good thing for England when our enemies fall out, yet the flesh creeps at the thought of such an ally."

His vehemence took Buckler aback since he'd always thought Quiller a rather cold man, all polished surface and eloquent learning, a highly able advocate but not one inclined to moral indignation. Buckler drew breath to ask his final question since he sensed the other lawyer's eagerness to depart. "Tell me what happened to Nell Durant."

"She was mentioned at a subsequent meeting after Rex had renounced the republicans and the Collatinus letters had stopped. One of our members had heard an ugly tale that she'd fallen in with the radicals and allowed herself to become their tool." His mouth tightened in fastidious disgust, but he went on dispassionately enough. "Rumor was they killed her when she got frightened and tried to extricate herself."

"Killed how?"

"One of them broke into her house, raped her in her bed, and stuck a knife in her. A terrible ending for any young female, whether or not she brought it on herself."

Buckler thanked him, struggling to keep his dismay from showing, but the serjeant, gazing again at the effigies, did not appear to have observed his reaction.

After a moment, Quiller pointed at a stone knight about seven feet in length. "Do you see how his feet are trampling those two heads with wooly hair? They look rather like lawyers in their wigs, I've often thought. A warning to us men of law that our time must pass, eh Buckler?"

He had intended to request a private interview with Penelope to tell her about his conversation with Quiller, but when they met at the Thorogood home for dinner, she said, "No, Mr. Buckler. Whatever it is, I prefer you speak out before us all. There can be no secrets among us. Besides, Mr. Chase will be joining us. He will want to hear your information."

He bowed his acquiescence, and they went up the stairs to join the others in the Thorogoods' cheerfully informal drawing room. Pleased on his own account that John Chase would be in attendance, Buckler was also glad for Penelope's sake since she would need the Runner's professional expertise. Chase interested him: a man of action whose actions were fuelled by the power of contemplation and logic. Buckler, who often had difficulty in translating thought into action, particularly admired this trait.

When the maidservant showed in the Runner a few minutes later, Hope Thorogood, a plump, fair-haired woman, went forward to greet him with a glowing smile. Just being in Hope's presence humbled Buckler, for she was someone who understood how to appreciate life. Flattery, prevarication, bigotry, venality, snobbery, cruelty—Hope saw these things clearly in the world around her, but she did not allow such ugliness to weaken her essential humanity. Buckler quite frankly loved her and by no means only for her husband's sake.

He went forward to add his greetings to hers. "Mr. Chase. I have been hoping to see you again. How do you do?"

Chase appeared rather surprised by the warmth of this greeting. "You look well, Buckler. I take it the law agrees with you?"

"Like indigestion," boomed Thorogood. He advanced on his guest, saying: "Bring him in; bring him in. Here's a place for you, Mr. Chase." He swept down upon an armchair by the fire to remove a toy and stood back, beaming.

Buckler went to sit in the matching armchair, striking up an innocuous conversation with Chase about the news from Bow Street and the early spring weather, but all the time, he was watching Penelope, who knelt on the hearthrug, playing at spillikins with the children, crowing over her successes and pretending to pout when she failed to hook one of the ivory sticks with sufficient care. His gaze lingered over her wine-dark silk gown, shining hair, and brown eyes bright with laughter.

"You're so silly, Mama," said Sarah each time Penelope made a mistake, and David, Hope's son from her former marriage, heaved a sigh and leaned over to demonstrate the correct move with an air of masculine superiority.

Chase turned to Buckler, keeping his voice low. "Wolfe won't be here tonight?"

"Prior engagement."

They exchanged a glance; then Chase observed, "Mrs. Wolfe will need her friends before this matter is resolved, I do believe."

"You're right. She has written a letter to her father to ask him about the murdered woman and has explained the whole affair to her husband. But no more now, Chase. We are to put our heads together after dinner."

They went down to the dining room, Chase escorting Mrs. Thorogood and Thorogood leading Penelope, with Buckler and the children trailing behind. On this occasion, Thorogood's grown children and their families were not in attendance, but Hope's daughters, Faith and Charity, dined with the guests, as did David, Sarah, and Thorogood's daughter Sophia, who was quite the young lady nowadays. This was unusual, but then the Thorogoods had never much concerned themselves with the conventions. To them, their children were as much a part of the family as anyone else. The table was merry, the conversation general, while Thorogood presided grandly over the carving of the meat and Hope saw unobtrusively to the comfort of her guests.

When, at length, the nuts, fruits, and sweetmeats had been served, Thorogood, never so happy as when playing host, rose to give a toast. "I welcome you all to my board on an occasion made auspicious by the presence of our esteemed guest. I propose the health of Mr. John Chase, Principal Officer at Bow Street. A man who brings great wit and a stout heart to his work. Let the villains quake in their boots and the honest folk rest more soundly in their beds because of his efforts on our behalf. To your health, Mr. Chase!"

All except Chase rose, lifting their glasses to the Runner, who sat in the place of honor to his hostess' right. As Buckler raised his own wineglass and chinked it against Sarah's empty one to her immense delight, he saw that Chase's face wore an arrested look, as if some new vista had opened before him. When Thorogood had finished, he got on his legs to reply, speaking with some awkwardness but obvious sincerity. "I am very much obliged to you, Mr. and Mrs. Thorogood, for the honor you have done me and for your gracious hospitality. May you enjoy your present happiness for many years to come." Chase gave a little bow and resumed his seat to general applause and a few "hear, hears" from the children.

Buckler was glad to have enjoyed this time of lighthearted fellowship because the tone of the evening turned somber once the party returned to the drawing room. The children went off to bed, and Sophia took Sarah upstairs to listen to a story, leaving the adults to discuss the Collatinus matter. At dinner, Penelope had smiled and conversed freely, but Buckler, studying her surreptitiously, perceived that her thoughts were often far away. Now as she handed a cup of tea to Chase and moved away, her carriage erect, the Runner's eyes followed her. This would not be easy for her, and Buckler thought Chase understood her feelings as well as he himself did. She had withdrawn behind a wall designed to keep even her close friends at a distance.

Thorogood seemed too restless to sit and drink his tea. He planted himself in front of the fire, standing with arms clasped behind his back. His characteristic good humor had dimmed, and Buckler could read his regret that the pleasantness of the evening had come to an end. When everyone else was settled on the sofas and chairs, Thorogood glowered in Buckler's direction, his eyebrows meeting in a bushy line across his forehead. "Well, Edward, would you care to begin?"

Chapter XI

As he described his interview with Quiller, Buckler felt he spoke to Penelope alone, though he took care not to insult her by softening the tale of treachery, blackmail, and murder. When he was finished, Thorogood said to her, his tone gentle, "I'm sure you won't wish to judge your father when he is not here to speak for himself. Wait for his reply to your letter, my dear." At Penelope's nod, Hope, sitting next to her on the sofa, pressed her hand.

Thorogood looked around the group. "I recall the murder of this courtesan. The papers were full of the story for a few days—and then nothing. It was assumed the culprit had fled the country. I didn't take much interest at the time."

"*An injured mother*," quoted Buckler. "Something Quiller said has made me think—could Nell Durant have borne the Prince's child?"

A startled silence greeted this question.

Chase sat with one of Hope's delicate teacups balanced gingerly in his large hands. "A political disaster in the making, Buckler. A royal inamorata turned radical and blackmailer? God knows what sensitive information she had."

Thorogood stroked his chin thoughtfully. "What can you tell us, Mr. Chase? I assure you that anything we discuss stays in this room."

"I fully intend to be open with you, sir. From now on, I will proceed in a private capacity on Mrs. Wolfe's behalf."

Penelope said, "I am grateful to you, but you must have other business."

Their eyes met, hers questioning, his grave. "None that concerns me at present, Mrs. Wolfe." Chase went on to describe his visit to Dryden Leach's office, his interview with Mary Leach, the disappearance of the porter Peter Malone, and his speculation about the connection between the Collatinus letters and the Princess Caroline inquiry.

"Poor woman," said Hope. "She has been much tried by her husband. I understand why she fights to uphold her honor."

"Yes, Mrs. Thorogood," Chase agreed politely. "Collatinus is a threat to the Prince Regent's reputation and therefore a weapon he would not choose to see placed in his enemies' hands. It may be the Home Office has its own agents and informers at work to discover the author of these letters. Which would explain the interest in Mrs. Wolfe if it is known in official circles that her father wrote the originals."

Hope smiled at Penelope in reassurance. "If these men are employed by the government, they pose no physical threat to you or your family. Once they see you are innocent of any conspiracy, they will go away."

Penelope's answering smile went a little awry. "I suppose Mr. Chase's theory may also explain why questions about my family have been asked of the local shopkeepers." As she related the story about Maggie and the unpaid baker's bill, Buckler entertained himself with a pleasing vision of a dark alley and Jeremy Wolfe's face at the mercy of his fists. He kept his glance lowered so that no one would observe his emotion.

Chase said, "The government may want to know what happened to Dryden Leach as much as we do. I went back to the Adelphi Terrace this morning and caught the surgeon, a man called Thomas Fladgate, as he departed."

"Has Mr. Leach's health improved?" inquired Thorogood.

"An inflammation of the lungs has taken hold. Leach isn't long for this world, I'm afraid. His wife is nursing him."

"Mary?" broke in Penelope, and they all looked at her in some surprise. Chase leaned back in his chair, observing her, his gaze intent on her face.

"Penelope? Why do you sound so strange?"

She did not immediately respond to Hope, though she laid a hand on her friend's arm. "What else did the surgeon say, Mr. Chase?"

"That he had rarely seen such devotion in a wife. She allows no one to do for her husband what she can do with her own hands and stays with him throughout the day and night. I asked Fladgate outright about the masked man who attacked his patient and the wounds received."

Thorogood frowned in concentration. "The crux of the issue."

Penelope rose to her feet and began to pace the room. She looked at Buckler then at Chase, and she appealed to both for understanding. "I've been thinking of Mary Leach."

"Tell us, Mrs. Wolfe," said Chase, and Buckler thought he tried to steady her with this matter-of-fact response.

"This extreme devotion rings false. Mr. Rex implied that her marriage isn't very happy. Also, he told me she once had literary ambitions and now has an occasional pseudonym of her own, which she uses to contribute poems and squibs to her husband's paper. But what if she grew tired of serving his agenda—tired of serving *him*?"

Everyone stared at her, but Buckler had the distinct impression Chase had known what she was going to say.

"What the deuce!" expostulated Thorogood. "Do you mean to suggest the lady herself has some knowledge of the crime?"

"You are astute, Mrs. Wolfe." Chase gave them Noah Packet's information about Mary Leach having been abroad on the night of the attack and repeated her cryptic remark about Leach having had an enemy. He paused, waiting for Penelope to come to her own conclusions.

"What if Mary meant *she* was Leach's enemy? What if there was no masked man? What if she had to come up with a story to explain the attack at a moment's notice? She might have been in league with Collatinus or even written the letters herself. Perhaps she had reasons of her own to prevent her husband's revelations in the paper. Or she hated him and sought revenge for some injury. I can't think how else to explain her behavior."

Chase nodded, as if pleased by a pupil's correct response to a lesson. "I believe you're right, Mrs. Wolfe. Leach neither defended himself nor gave the alarm, possibly because he wished to hush the scandal and avoid implicating his own wife. Mrs. Leach has likely bribed the surgeon to keep his mouth shut."

Hope looked appalled. "She wouldn't get away with murder."

"Petty treason, actually," Buckler corrected her. "It is considered even worse than murder. Not so long ago a woman convicted of killing her husband was burned at the stake, though the executioner would strangle her first. At least we no longer indulge this particular barbarity. Now she would merely be hanged."

A ripple of discomfort passed through the room, as they absorbed that they might hold the power of life or death over a woman most of them didn't know. With a kind of detached interest, Buckler debated whether he could bring himself to resign a lady to the tender mercies of the English justice system, however much he deplored her deed. He would want to learn a great deal more about Mary Leach and her motives first, but he could not shield a murderess. He turned to Penelope. "You were once acquainted with Mrs. Leach?"

"Yes, though I don't recall those days very well. My father took me to visit her and her stepmother, the Countess of Cloondara, a few times. She was called Mariam then, the name given her by her mother. She was extremely pretty but quiet and rather meek. I don't think she much liked her stepmother."

"Could a woman do such a thing?" said Hope in wonderment. "And to nurse him afterwards…" Shuddering, she glanced up at her husband's robust form, probably recalling her own loving care when he had caught a dangerous cold the prior year.

Chase answered her. "Mrs. Leach may seek to hide her crime. She can always claim her husband told her to keep silent for his safety. She and the surgeon are the only ones with access to the sickroom, and it wouldn't be difficult to keep Leach quiet with regular doses of laudanum. When he dies, presumably the surgeon is prepared to swear to a false cause of death. A little bribery to the parish officials to head off a coroner's inquest, a quick burial, and the thing is done. And perhaps the Home Office would not be averse to this tidy solution so long as the Regent's name can be kept out of the business."

"How could she?" Penelope walked to the window and stood for a moment with her back to them. "She has children. If she is executed, their lives will be forever ruined. She would destroy herself utterly."

"If Rex revived Collatinus and Leach was bent on unmasking him in the papers, Mrs. Leach might have killed her husband to protect her father."

Penelope faced Chase. "What of *my* father? We mustn't forget Nell Durant. I must learn who was responsible for her death. I am determined the truth must come out at last."

Buckler could not help himself. He went to stand at Penelope's side, though he did not touch her. "We are agreed then. But there's something else we must consider. If Nell Durant had a child, where is that child now?"

◇◇◇

During the bustle of departure, there was just time for Buckler to exchange a few words with Penelope. Thorogood was busy making the arrangements to send her home in a hackney he had summoned, Chase had already taken his leave, and Hope was upstairs checking on the children. Buckler and Penelope stood together in the hall.

She laid a hand on his arm. "I must act for myself, you know. This case is…sordid and possibly dangerous. You must allow me to decide. You must indeed. I would not wish for harm to come to any of you."

"We don't think of that when you are in need." Lines from Shakespeare came to Buckler as he stood looking down at the top of her bent head. *The very instant that I saw you, did / My heart fly to your service; there resides, / To make me slave to it…*

And he realized it was true. Thorogood had brought Penelope to him for a legal consultation after her feckless husband had got himself briefly confined in Newgate on suspicion of murder. Since then Buckler had wanted nothing more than to protect her, though only recently had he begun to understand the depth of his feelings for Penelope Wolfe—another man's wife. What he wasn't at all sure of was whether she had ever thought of him in this light, not that it mattered since she wasn't free and he could never tell her of his love.

She lifted her eyes to his. "You must, at all costs, avoid a scandal, Edward. You have a career to make, and Mr. Chase has his employment at Bow Street. But I thank you for your loyalty most sincerely."

"You know I would do anything to serve you, as I told you once before."

"I remember. It was the day we walked together in the Temple Garden. You said I was too alone."

Buckler took her hand and raised it to his lips, retaining it for a moment, but he had to let go when Thorogood's voice was heard calling them. He attempted to banish his regret with a smile, which she returned rather tremulously. Then she turned away as Thorogood bustled in.

"Go and carry Sarah down to the coach, Buckler. And, for heaven's sake, take care not to wake her."

Chase sat in his armchair by the fire, a glass of brandy on the table at his side. After a while, out of long habit, he fetched his prized miniature of Abigail and baby Jonathan, holding it in his hands and studying it in the glow of firelight as he let his thoughts drift. Abigail's last letter had informed him that she had commissioned a new miniature of Jonathan so that he could see how his son had grown toward manhood. A peace offering of sorts, he thought, since she must have assumed he would be disturbed by the news of Jonathan having gone to sea. The rain and wind lashed at the windows, and it was pleasant to sit in the warmth, thinking about his son and imagining his adventures, thinking too about Penelope and the dilemma she faced as she peeled away the layers, stripping bare her father's past. She had probably been a dutiful daughter before her marriage to Jeremy Wolfe. Eustace Sandford had raised her after her mother's death, and it must have been he who taught Penelope to think for herself. How certain and firm she had been in saying the truth must be primary with her, but how would it be with her if this truth branded her father a killer?

From time to time, Chase heard the tenant in the next room, moving about and muttering as she paced the floor. He ignored the noises, hoping they would soon stop. But later as he lay in bed, sleepless, the din next door increased. Miss Fakenham began with slamming her drawers and proceeded to stamping her feet, crying, and talking to herself in a voice that rose to shrillness and fell to softer moans. Finally, he threw back the bedcovers and used his walking stick to pound the wall. When a welcome silence greeted his ears, he soon drifted off to sleep. But then, as if a caged beast had grown restless in its cell, the noises began again, louder.

Cursing, Chase rose and donned his dressing gown. Angrily thrusting his feet into slippers, he went out in the corridor. He put his ear against the woman's door to see if the noise had abated, hearing several loud thumps followed by a sobbing breath. He tapped on the door.

"Yes?" came the faint reply.

"Keep the noise down, miss. You will rouse the house." What he really meant, of course, was that she was bothering *him*, for he assumed Mrs. Beeks and the boys would be sleeping soundly on the floor above.

There was no answer, so Chase, irritated beyond all measure, opened the door and put in his head. Miss Fakenham sat in the middle of the floor, her disheveled hair framing a pale, wild face wet with tears. A blanket was draped over her thin shoulders, and a purple gown spilled across her lap. She was shivering violently.

"How dare you enter my room!" She was shaking so hard that she got out the words only with difficulty. Chase's gaze swept around. It was a bare place. He had been in this chamber once or twice, but Mrs. Beeks had removed her bits and pieces to leave space for the tenant's belongings; only the young woman didn't have many to speak of. The room contained a narrow bed, a washstand, and a few other pieces of shabby furniture, including a scratched up old chest of drawers on top of which were a silver-backed brush and an old, clouded looking-glass. The grate was cold and empty.

Chase opened his mouth to deliver a blistering scold—but stopped himself. "What is the matter?" he said instead.

She gazed at him, eyes huge and tear-drenched, and spoke with as much dignity as she could muster. "I beg your pardon, sir." Lifting the gown in her arms, she scrambled to her feet and laid it over the back of the chair. "I've spotted the silk," she said dully. "Don't worry. I'll not disturb you again."

"See that you don't." Her tears made Chase uncomfortable, so he withdrew hastily to his room. In bed, he lay staring at the ceiling. She had been as good as her word. Silence had descended over the house. But, after a minute or two, Chase got up again, cursing. Moving to his small sideboard, he put his tinderbox in his pocket, poured some brandy in a glass, and lifted the coal bin in his other hand.

Returning to Miss Fakenham's room, he set down the bin and knocked briefly before entering. This time she stood by the window staring out at the rain, her head bent, her shoulders shaking. Chase did not speak. Approaching her, he lifted her hand to fold her fingers around the glass of brandy. Then he stepped to the grate and soon had a fire blazing away.

"Sit down," he told her roughly. He removed the gown from the chair, tossing it on her bed, then pulled the chair closer to the fire. Without looking at him, she obeyed. After a few minutes her sobs subsided; her tremors stilled. But as her physical comfort increased, her embarrassment grew, a fiery blush mounting in her cheeks.

Chase, standing over her as she sipped the brandy, repeated his earlier question. "What is the matter with you?"

"My hands shake with the cold, and I make mistakes in my work. I try to move around to get my blood up, but that doesn't help much. Sometimes I talk aloud in order to keep myself from falling asleep. I *must* finish this gown by tomorrow morning, or I will lose my employment."

Chase felt curiosity stir. Now that she wasn't crying or biting his head off, Miss Fakenham's voice was low and pleasant, her accent refined, and he found himself wanting to know what had brought an educated young woman to this shabby, little room where she must labor for every penny if she hoped to keep food in her belly and shelter over her head. But all he said was: "Finish your work if you must. I've built the fire to last. Goodnight, miss."

She raised startled eyes to his face. "You've been very kind, sir." She spoke as if kindness was an extreme rarity in her experience.

Chase murmured something noncommittal and got himself out of the room. When he had returned to his bed and was finally slipping into welcome oblivion, her words came back to him. *Kind?* She had called him so, but he was not accustomed to seeing himself thus. He was getting decidedly soft in his old age.

Chapter XII

A thunderous knocking roused Penelope from a deep slumber. At her side Jeremy cursed. He sat up in bed, threw back the covers, and jumped out, wincing as his bare feet encountered frigid floorboards. "Stay here. I'll see who it is."

She heard rapid footsteps as one of the servants joined him, their voices fading as they descended to the lower part of the house. Penelope got up. After putting on her own dressing gown, she glided down the corridor to the nursery but found her daughter curled up, peacefully asleep. She eased the door shut and followed her husband down to the hall where Jeremy stood talking to Horatio Rex. Rex's tall form was enveloped in an evening cloak, beads of moisture sparkling in his gray-black hair. His cool composure appeared to have deserted him; he looked haggard. When he saw her, he cried, "Mrs. Wolfe! I must speak to you."

Jeremy stood in hostile stance, arms folded, eyes narrowed. "Do you know what time it is? What business can you have with my wife at this hour?"

Rex ignored him. He came forward to meet Penelope, taking her hand in his gloved one. "Dismiss your servants, Mrs. Wolfe."

Glancing up, she saw they had several interested auditors. Cook had not awakened apparently, but the other servants clustered on the landing, Maggie's red head among them. "Nothing to worry about," Penelope called to them. "Go back to bed, please." She led Rex down the passage to her sitting room. After fumbling for the tinderbox she kept on a shelf by the door, she soon had a candle lit. They faced each other.

"What is it, Mr. Rex?"

"Leach is dead. I meant to wait till morning, but I couldn't bear the thought of Mary being alone tonight. She wishes to speak to you."

"What can Mrs. Leach want with my wife?" said Jeremy.

"I hardly know how to answer you, Wolfe." He stretched out a hand to Penelope in supplication. "She is alone. Will you deny her in her need, ma'am?"

"No, of course I won't."

"You'll go nowhere in the middle of the night. Whatever this is, I don't want you involved."

Penelope was utterly taken aback, unable to recall the last time her husband had attempted to exert any authority over her. She touched his sleeve. "I *must* go, Jeremy. If Mrs. Leach needs comfort, I would not wish to desert her."

Rex nodded. "That's just it. She has no one—no other lady in the house, I mean—just her maid and a mouse of a governess who can be of no use at all. Her husband is dead, and my Mary is sorely troubled in her mind. Your husband may accompany you if he does not wish to entrust your safety to me."

"I will come," Penelope said. "Do let us both get dressed, Jeremy, so that we may accompany Mr. Rex."

Jeremy continued to argue as they went back up the stairs to their bedchamber. "I cannot like this. The woman has entangled herself in some nastiness that has nothing to do with us! Better to stay away, especially after what you told me about your father and the Collatinus letters. Why should we put ourselves at risk for a stranger?"

"She is not a stranger, and Mr. Rex is your friend. He has been your patron in helping you obtain clients and your host too many times to count. We must go; you know we must." As Penelope spoke, she was dressing herself in a warm merino gown and hastily bundling her hair into a knot. She rummaged through her dressing table to find a bottle of smelling salts and a clean handkerchief, stowing them in her reticule.

"I cannot like it," Jeremy repeated. "What business has the fellow to involve my wife in his private affairs? Have I been wrong, after all, to cultivate him?"

"But you did cultivate him. We must go, so let's not discuss the matter anymore."

"Oh very well, but I won't leave you. The woman has clearly come unhinged."

She did not answer him. How was she to explain? She chose not to believe Mary was dangerous, but Chase and Buckler would be horrified that she had agreed to Mr. Rex's request, even with Jeremy along for protection. But the truth about Collatinus might be revealed at long last. Besides, if she was right in her suspicions, Mary's agony of mind must be profound. She was a human creature in pain. Penelope could not turn away.

They were silent in the carriage, Rex absorbed in his thoughts, Jeremy sitting in the opposite corner, eyes shut, leaning his head against the cushion. But Rex seemed oddly nervous. Sweat beaded on his forehead. He kept glancing out the side-glass, and once, when they came to a stop, he opened it to gaze into the night.

"What is it?"

"We are being followed, Mrs. Wolfe. I saw that coach in Greek Street, and it is still with us."

"What!" burst out Jeremy, his eyes flying open.

"Don't worry. The men won't bother us. They are only watching to see what we do. They seem to have been told to keep their distance."

"That's comforting. Who are they?"

"I don't know, Wolfe," Rex said heavily. "Home Office agents, I suspect. I've seen them lurking outside my house, and I suppose this means they are interested in your wife too. Something to do with those letters."

"You and your daughter have drawn her into mischief. For God's sake, she was a little child when you and Sandford were up to your tricks. What can any of this have to do with her?"

Penelope grabbed Jeremy's hand and squeezed. "Leave it. We must first speak to Mary."

Their journey through the empty streets was rapid, and soon they had arrived in the Adelphi Terrace. As they stepped out, Penelope risked a quick look behind her. Rex was right. A carriage had pulled up down the street, its lamps glimmering faintly in the darkness, though no one emerged from its interior. They went quickly into the house, and Leach's butler met them in the hall.

"How is everything, Isherwood?"

"All quiet, Mr. Rex. The mistress is upstairs with Mr. Leach." The butler turned respectfully to Penelope and Jeremy. "Good evening, sir and madam."

"Come with me," said Rex, brushing aside the butler's attempt to relieve them of their outer garments. They went rapidly up the stairs to one of the principal bedchambers, and Rex knocked at a door. "Mary, I've brought Mrs. Wolfe to see you."

When there was no reply, Rex knocked again, louder. "Mary? Open the door at once, I say. No time to waste. We must discuss the arrangements for your husband."

Suddenly, a woman leaned over the banister from the landing above and then slipped down the steps to join them. A small, frail creature with a pinched face, she was clothed in a voluminous dressing gown, her hair drawn back from her face in a straggling plait that dangled over one shoulder. The governess, Penelope supposed. The woman said timidly, "You will wake the children, sir. They'll be frightened."

Rex did not appear to have heard her. "We must get inside. I am afraid. I am afraid of what Mary has done." He confronted the butler, who had joined them in the corridor. "The key, Isherwood?"

"Mrs. Leach has the only key. We had orders Mr. Leach was not to be disturbed on any account."

"We must get in. Fetch an ax at once."

The butler went rigid. "An ax?"

"Yes, you fool. Send one of the servants to the garden shed. Hurry!"

Penelope addressed the governess. "Go to the children and stay there with them. They mustn't be alone if they awaken." The woman's eyes widened, and she withdrew, stumbling over her feet in her haste.

Rex went on calling Mary's name and pounding on the door. When the butler and two half-dressed footmen returned with the ax, Rex hefted it. "Stand back," he commanded in a grim, determined voice.

With a grinding noise, the blade crashed into the wood around the lock, sending splinters flying. Wresting the ax free, Rex raised it again, but after the second strike, Jeremy took it from the older man, who was breathing heavily. Jeremy leveled a few more blows, the door shivering in its frame; finally, he was able to wedge the blade and part of the handle between the jamb and the door. As the footmen used their shoulders to increase the pressure, he pulled back with all his strength. There was a loud crack. The door burst open, hanging drunkenly on its hinges. Jeremy swiped a hand across his brow. "Wait here, Penelope."

After a moment she heard Rex say blankly, "Mary isn't here. Where could she be?"

Penelope entered, careful not to catch her dress on the splinters from the doorframe. She found herself in a well-appointed bedchamber warmed by the remains of a fire in the grate and lit by a candelabrum with several guttering candles that left much of the room in shadow. Her eyes took in mahogany furnishings, a white marble mantelpiece, and fringed curtains of green damask at the windows. Her gaze then fell on a table, which held various accouterments of the sickroom: a basin, rolls of bandages and lint, medicine bottles, a dosage spoon, and a pastille burner to freshen the air. So ordinary, she marveled.

Rex swung back to the butler. "Have the house searched at once."

As Isherwood hurried off to do his bidding, Penelope stepped closer to the large bed and looked down into the dead man's face. Dryden Leach lay under a green silk coverlet tucked neatly around his chin, its vivid color in stark contrast to the waxy eyelids that had closed out life forever.

When it became clear Mrs. Leach was not in the house, Penelope urged Rex to send a message to John Chase, but he refused angrily. Having assembled the servants in the hall, he rapped out a series of questions as they gaped at him. When had they last spoken to the mistress? Had anyone observed her departure? Was it possible they had all been *asleep* in her hour of need?

Isherwood winced visibly. "You gave us strict instructions to stay away, sir. Dora carried up some beef tea about six o'clock, but it wasn't wanted. Later Henry spoke to the mistress. That was about eleven o'clock after you'd been gone for some time. The master was then breathing his last."

The housekeeper stepped forward. "You can be sure I will question everyone, sir. Could Mrs. Leach have stepped out to fetch the surgeon or seek some religious consolation?"

"At this hour?"

Penelope broke in. "Did Mrs. Leach allow the children to bid good-bye to their father?"

The housekeeper evaded her gaze. "No, madam. But Miss Elliot explained what was happening to them. They were terribly upset, as you can imagine."

Both the housekeeper and the butler looked shaken too. The last few days—with the household thrust out of its normal routines and filled with such fear and suspicion—must have been enormously trying. They would have wanted to uphold their authority and the credit of their employers, yet it would have been obvious that something even graver than their master's illness was afoot. They must have been puzzled by Mrs. Leach's unaccountable behavior: her determined isolation, her refusal to accept any assistance, her secrecy.

Rex turned to address his daughter's personal maid, a young woman in an elegant dressing gown, probably a cast-off from her mistress. "When was the last time you saw my daughter?"

"I've hardly set eyes on her since Mr. Leach was brought home," she replied in a colorless voice. "My services have not been required in this emergency."

"Have you determined whether any of her garments are missing?"

"Her mourning cloak and bonnet, sir. A pair of boots along with the gown she was wearing."

Henry, one of the footmen, said, "I went up to bring more coals and trim the lamps in the other rooms, Mr. Rex. The mistress opened the door to speak to me, and I heard the master's gasping breaths. It sounded quite like he was choking or drowning. It was horrible." Embarrassed by his distress, he stared at his shoes.

Rex's glare raked down the line of faces watching him with varying displays of sleepiness, defiance, fear, and avid interest. "Someone must have seen her. Could you have allowed your mistress to go out alone without a word from any of you?"

Albert, the other footman, spoke up. "Mr. Isherwood had asked me to sit in the hall, sir, in case I was needed. Mrs. Leach did not leave the house by the front door."

"How then?"

The butler said, "Out the kitchen perhaps, Mr. Rex. I found the door unlocked some time after midnight. Ordinarily, I would have made my rounds to secure the house earlier, but we've been in turmoil today. I fastened the bolts and thought no more of it. Mrs. Leach must have gone that way. Perhaps she intended to meet a friend? I own it seems strange she would wish to see anyone under the circumstances, but—"

Jeremy took a step toward the door. "No doubt she will soon return. Rex, I'll bring my wife back tomorrow when Mrs. Leach is ready to receive her."

"No, no. I don't believe it. Something is wrong. She would not go out for more than a few minutes without a word to anyone. What reason could she have?"

"She received a letter," faltered Albert.

"What's this, Albert?"

"The carrier rang the bell to give me a letter for the mistress late this afternoon, Mr. Isherwood."

Rex's cheeks flushed with rage, and he moved closer to the footman, his fists clenched. "You didn't tell anyone until now? You didn't think it might be important?"

"She asked me not to, sir," Albert said simply.

"Did you note the receiving house stamp?" asked Penelope.

"The letter came through the Westminster Office but where before that I can't say. Twopenny post, madam. London origin."

Rex looked around wildly. "We are wasting time. We must search for her. Will you accompany me, Wolfe?"

"Of course, if you really think there's a problem. But in all likelihood, she's just gone out for some reason." Observing his friend's distress, Jeremy seemed to soften. "Let's go then. Never fear, Rex. We'll soon settle this business."

Taking torches and lanterns, Rex, Jeremy, and the footmen split up to search the neighboring streets—to no avail. When they returned an hour later, they brought the local watchman, who had come upon one of the searchers while making his rounds.

Penelope met them at the front door. "You must send for Mr. Chase, sir."

Jeremy went to stand with his wife. "She's right, Rex. I doubt Mrs. Leach has gone far, but Bow Street will know what to do."

"Best do as the gentleman says, sir," urged the watchman, a bedraggled figure in a shabby, old-fashioned coat. He gestured with his truncheon as he spoke.

Rex's indecision was clear. At length, he said, "I know he's a friend of yours, Mrs. Wolfe, and I'm sure you plan to tell him of this night's business. I'd be amazed if the fellow is to be trusted, but I'll let him help us locate Mary—though I tell you to your head that I'll not stand for any interference in my family's affairs."

Before he could change his mind, Penelope scribbled a message and gave instructions to a footman to carry it to Chase's lodgings in King Street. While they waited, Rex and Jeremy walked off together toward the Strand. After waiting in the entryway for a quarter-hour, Penelope suddenly said to the hovering butler, "Please conduct me to Mrs. Leach's apartments. She may have left some clue as to her intentions."

Though Isherwood seemed surprised at this request, he bowed. "Yes, madam. Please come this way."

They ascended the staircase to the second floor, and Isherwood opened the door to the room next to Leach's, pausing to light a branch of candles for her. When it seemed he meant to remain, Penelope dismissed him. "Thank you. I expect you want to be downstairs in case Mr. Rex returns. I'll soon rejoin you."

After Isherwood was gone, she made a slow circuit, briefly examining a wardrobe hung with stylish gowns, then stepping in the adjoining dressing room to lean over a table with jars and perfume bottles scattered across its surface. In the bedroom a wing chair was drawn close to the fire near a small satinwood table upon which rested several books. The neatly made bed with blue damask hangings offered no clue as to when Mary had last taken her rest, and there was a fine film of dust on the furnishings, the housemaids apparently having slacked in their work during their master's illness.

About to approach a small drop-leaf writing-table, she hesitated. What if Mary should return to find a near stranger rifling her private papers? Penelope knew that vulgar curiosity was part of her motivation for being here, but she felt a growing urgency. What if Mary had done something desperate? Was that why Rex's manner had seemed so strange because he too feared something of this nature? She still did not trust Horatio Rex, though he seemed genuinely worried about his daughter.

Penelope went to the desk. It had two small drawers with a built-in workbasket underneath. This contained delicate stitchery tools, tambour frame, and embroidery threads along with a pen-knife, quills, and sticks of sealing wax. After a cursory examination of these items, she turned her attention to the drawers, first opening the top one, which contained only a writing board and some blotting paper. The other drawer was empty. While there was no sign of the letter Mary had received tonight, Penelope supposed she might have put it in her pocket or destroyed it. But what had happened to the rest of her correspondence? Mary had swept her desk clean of every scrap of paper except for her pocket memorandum book.

She had divided the pocketbook into the categories "Letters upon Business," "Daily Occurrences," and "Memorandums and Accounts." In this small volume, she had recorded housekeeping details and the particulars of servants' contracts, as well as information about domestic purchases and taxes. Penelope was about to set the book aside when she discovered a short note written in the flyleaf. Dated this very day, it said in a ladylike, flowing script: *If I cannot return, summon my husband's cousin Elizabeth Moore. She is a kind soul and will not judge my darlings by the sinful wretches who are their parents. I beg her to persuade the children that they would be better and happier in new lives.* Sick at heart, Penelope read this note several times as dark trepidation stirred anew. If she could hope that Mary had gone on an errand and would soon return, she would feel less oppressed. As it was, it was too easy to imagine Mary Leach making a hole in the river, a creature driven to seek her end. Perhaps she had been unable to live with the guilt of her husband's death, or had thought she would inevitably be exposed for her crime.

Penelope returned to her task. After a few minutes of unproductive search for any hidden drawers, she gave up to approach the chest, a mahogany piece with lion's paw feet. Isherwood would be wondering what was keeping her. She sorted quickly through a pile of stockings, shifts, stays, and gloves, finding nothing of interest here either. But as she rummaged through the bottom drawer, she unearthed a small leather purse with a fold-over, silver-edged lid fastened by a clasp. Slowly, she lifted the clasp. Nestled in the white silk lining were a silver fork and a silver-bladed fruit knife, both with tortoiseshell hafts decorated with small, curving gold plates. Below these plates, the hafts were engraved with a triple plume emerging from a crown, which was inscribed *Ich Dien. 'I serve.'* This was the heraldic badge of the Prince of Wales, she remembered. The set was a lovely keepsake, the sort of pretty trifle a lady might receive as a gift from an admirer—a royal one in this case.

She was replacing the fruit knife in its sleeve when she noticed a larger silk compartment holding a third item, and her fingers closed over the object to pull it free. In her hand she held a larger, sturdy pocketknife with a matching handle decorated with the same triple-plume device as the other pieces. Penelope extended the blade; it was about four inches long and fashioned of steel, not the precious metal of the other knife that could only be intended for cutting soft fruits. This one looked well able to do some damage, she thought, as she examined it more closely. On this piece, the small inlaid gold plate on the knife's haft was engraved with the initials "N.D." Nell Durant. The set must have been a present from the Prince Regent to Nell, but why did Mary have it?

She was still inspecting the knife in her hand when the door opened, and John Chase entered the room. "Mrs. Wolfe!" He hurried toward her and took the knife, laying it atop the chest of drawers. She looked up into his tired face. Stubble bristled on his chin, and strands of graying hair had escaped from his queue to lie across his weathered cheek. She felt immense relief at the sight of him, for she knew him well enough to recognize the concern under his curtness.

"Where is Wolfe? I had understood he accompanied you to this place."

"He went with Mr. Rex to seek Mary. Mr. Chase, I've found—"

"Wait a moment." Chase addressed the butler, who stood watching them. "Leave us now. I will organize the search presently."

Isherwood withdrew, his disapproval clear, and Chase went to close the door. "Tell me now from the beginning."

When he had listened to her story and read the note in the memorandum book, he removed the fruit knife and fork from the case in order to run his fingers along the interior of the lining.

"Could Mary have used this pocketknife to attack her husband?" asked Penelope.

He picked up the larger knife, weighing it in his hand. "Without a doubt, but we cannot know for certain. See here. A few spots of blood have stained the lining. It seems Mrs. Leach didn't get the knife quite clean before she restored it to its place." Chase held up the purse to show her, and Penelope shivered, thinking of Mary returning home with a bloodstained knife in her pocket. And to have her husband—her victim—placed in her tender care!

"We must find her, Mr. Chase. Her guilt and her grief may have driven her to take her own life."

"I've questioned the servants about the letter delivered to Mrs. Leach, and you'd think they would have observed something to the purpose. But they can tell me very little. Perhaps she ran away to avoid any questions about her husband's death."

"We were followed here tonight, so I doubt the watchers could have observed anything of Mary's movements. Unless you think there were others?"

"The local watch might know, but I doubt it. Mrs. Leach is the wife of a loyal ministry supporter. Why should anyone suspect her? Regardless, we can but look for her and put out inquiries in the morning. Since Rex and the footmen have failed to turn up anything in the surrounding area, the watchman has suggested we search the Dark Arches."

"Dark Arches?"

"A maze of underground passages supporting these buildings. They lead to a wharf by the river where the products that are stored there can be shipped. Beggars and homeless children use these subterranean streets as a dossing ground. Thieves take refuge there too. Bow Street has long wanted to have the area cleared. "

"The river?" She heard the tremor in her voice but was unable to control it, and she couldn't seem to stop echoing Chase. "You must go at once."

"First, one thing must be settled at long last. Stay here."

He went swiftly out of the room, and Penelope heard him stepping over the shattered door to enter Dryden Leach's chamber. Exhausted, she sat in the wing chair by the cold hearth, leaning her head back. An interval elapsed before his return.

Penelope opened her eyes to find Chase watching her. "Mr. Leach?"

He reached down to help her to her feet. "The corpse has two wounds to the chest. One was the mortal blow, the other less serious. As to cause of death, it was exactly as we thought, Mrs. Wolfe. He was murdered."

Chapter XIII

Daybreak would not arrive for some hours yet. The searchers, including servants from neighboring households, fanned out from the Adelphi Terrace with Chase leading several of the men down Durham Street toward the entrance to the Arches. Going under a heavy stone arch and continuing down a road that descended toward the river, they soon found themselves in a gloomy warren of passages.

After a brief consultation, the men separated, but at Chase's heels came the watchman emitting a stream of bright chatter. "You from Bow Street, sir? I am honored to make your acquaintance," cried the watchman, whose name, he proudly announced, was Abraham Deeds. "I warrant your work takes you high and low, dear sir. Human nature in all its glory—big as life! As soon as I heard the lady was not to be found, I said you ought to be called in. Indeed I did. We'll find her now, sharp-like. All will be well, you mark my words."

"Hold your tongue." Swinging his lantern into one of the recesses, Chase illumined the frightened face of a girl huddled with her back against the blackened brick vaulting. Wrapped in newspapers against the cold, she had been asleep, for she jerked when he shined light over her form. "Wha—, what do you want?" she stammered, and, bending over her, Chase smelled the spirits on her breath. This was a very young girl, perhaps fifteen or so, and her face glowed white and sickly.

"You seen a lady tonight?"

She gaped at him. "Lady?"

Chase repeated the description Rex had given him. "A lady, someone who doesn't belong here. Dressed finely in a black cloak and bonnet. Dark brown hair and blue eyes."

The girl's gaze slipped past him. "I ain't seen no one."

He left her to regain her slumber and went on through the darkness, the watchman still dogging his heels.

"Do you make your rounds down here, Deeds?"

"I do, sir. But it's taking my life in my hands to put my head down some of these passages. I takes a peek, though, so as to say I did my duty. I don't linger here, no, I don't."

"You've seen nothing out of the ordinary tonight?"

"No, I haven't. Only one of me, you know. I can't be everywhere at once."

A mild defensiveness had crept into the watchman's tone, but he went on, irrepressibly cheerful. "I expect the lady will have returned home. Perhaps we ought to go see for ourselves."

"You go, Deeds."

"No, sir, I'll stick with you if you've a mind to keep looking." Chase heard a yelp as Deeds kicked a stray cur out of his way.

From somewhere nearby, the voices of the other searchers called Mary Leach's name, and other men would be traversing the open-air streets above. But she had been gone for over three hours and might be miles away. It was possible she had decided to flee, believing her role in her husband's death could not remain hidden, but Chase didn't think so. She would have left word and would have packed at least a small valise. Besides, he felt an all-too-familiar, uncomfortable sensation of dread that he tried to ignore, concentrating instead on the business at hand. Soon they came upon another flight of stairs and descended to yet another level where stone vaults towered above them in tiers.

Here he found the wine cellars, tucked under a series of low archways and all heavily padlocked against the depredations of thieves. As he went, Chase shined his lantern on the locks, though nothing seemed to have been disturbed. But after the passage suddenly turned in a new direction, Chase and Deeds nearly stumbled over a huddle of boys sleeping on a straw bed in one of the niches.

"Hey you," shouted Deeds, brandishing his club and prodding one of them with his boot in much same way he had kicked the dog. "You've no business there. Get up; get up, I say!"

The boys stumbled to their feet, and the tallest one, the leader, addressed them. "We ain't doing no harm, just sleeping. What's it to you?"

"Damned street scum," said Deeds fiercely. "You seen a lady around here? Not that you'd know one if you saw her, you filthy gutter rats!" Then he addressed Chase with his usual fawning good cheer, "This lot won't be any help to us, you can bet your last groat on that, sir. Let me drive 'em out."

"Wait." Chase looked at the taller boy. "How long have you been here?"

"Dunno. A while."

"You see anyone else?"

"A few whores and some little 'uns. The usual."

Without taking his eyes from the boy's face, Chase reached in his pocket for a coin. He held it up, and it caught the light of his lantern.

"He'll just lie to you, sir," warned Deeds. "He don't have a truthful bone in his body. I seen that one around, all right. Every night I pokes him with my stick and sends him about his business."

"Be quiet." Chase addressed the boy: "What's your name?"

"Simon, sir."

"I'll ask you again, Simon. Did you see anything out of the usual tonight? Anything at all you can tell me?"

"I was heading over to the Fox-under-the-Hill for some grub. The pub down by the river, sir." He gestured vaguely. "I saw a man. It were dark, so I didn't see him plain. He went down the tunnel and out to the street."

"You didn't follow him?"

"No, sir. He'd a thought I was out to draw 'im—pick his pockets—and I wasn't having any trouble. I just wanted my grub.

I had a penny earned on the square, and I knows the landlord would give me a pie or summat. Besides, there was that about 'im as told me to stay clear in case he were up to no good."

"What time was this?"

Simon shrugged. "After midnight, I reckon."

"You never saw him again?"

"No, sir."

"Would you recognize him?"

"Don't expect I would. I didn't see his face."

"Big man? Tall man? Can you tell me anything else about him?"

"Not so big you'd notice. Not so small neither. He'd his scarf pulled up over his nose. He walked bravely like a gentleman what owned the night."

Chase put the coin in Simon's palm. "Come, you show me exactly where you saw him, and I'll give you another one."

With alacrity, he set off down the passage, the other boys flanking him like an honor guard. Chase had offered his lantern, but Simon moved assuredly through the darkness, making several turns and descending and ascending several flights of stairs with scarcely a check. Listening to Deeds mutter at his back as he struggled to keep up, Chase realized he would not be in much better shape come morning, for his knee was bound to be stiff and painful after this adventure. On they went as they moved deeper into the massive, stone, fortress-like structure, and the air became close, turning rank as if to repel their intrusion. Then a new smell hit Chase's nostrils.

Simon halted. "He came from there, sir."

Chase looked around. They stood at the intersection of several streets wide enough for the drays and carts that would wind through here in the daytime, carrying goods to the river. Simon's raised arm pointed toward the opening for a smaller passage. Chase gave him his payment, dismissed the boys, and set off in the direction indicated.

"There ain't nothing hereabouts but horses and cows." Deeds had lumbered up, breathing heavily. "Cripes, what a stench."

Ignoring him, Chase began to inspect the doors of the cow-sheds. Like the wine cellars, they were secured for the night, but the wooden doors were battered and rickety, and the locks looked flimsy. He went on in this way for a quarter-hour or more and was beginning to think he was wasting his time when he came upon a stable with the door slightly ajar. Chase pushed open the door and entered.

He heard the snuffling sounds of cow breath along with an occasional soft lowing and a rustling in the straw. Chase picked out a line of stalls behind which he dimly perceived the dark, heavy shapes of the beasts. Several milking stools were stacked in one corner next to bins of feed and several shovels. A trough stood in the middle of a wooden floor. As Deeds started to blunder in behind him, Chase held up a hand to stop him, for he could see markings that looked like footprints in the dust at his feet. This meant nothing, of course. The cows would have attendants responsible for milking and feeding them, and Chase doubted that cleanliness was much of a virtue down here.

But then his beam fell on an overturned wooden crate, and he picked his way across the stable to bend over it. Someone had left a candle stub in a rough iron holder atop this crate. Kneeling down, Chase prodded the blobs of wax dripped around the candle: they were dry and hard. He reached lower to grope around on the dirty floorboards and grimaced in distaste as he encountered spider webs.

"What is it?" Deeds took a step into the cowshed.

"Stay back, you imbecile," Chase snapped. There was a strange prickling at the back of his skull, and the watchman's presence was a distraction not to be borne. He felt…something, and he needed perfect silence and concentration in order to identify the source of the feeling. His eyes went back to the water trough. What was it doing there? It had been placed deliberately in the center of the room to serve some purpose, like a prop on a stage that needed to be seen clearly by the spectators. And indeed when he moved closer, careful to step lightly with his feet, he saw drag marks in the dust. He stooped to feel with his hands around the base of the trough, and after a moment his fingers pinched up a tiny metal object. It was sharp, pointed at the end, less than an inch long—a pin. He found another and still another until he had a row of pins in his hand. When he held up his palm to the lantern, he saw that several of them were japanned: black mourning pins in token of Mrs. Leach's bereavement.

Though a confirmed bachelor, Chase nonetheless had no difficulty in understanding the significance of these pins. Ladies used them, endlessly and religiously. They carried them in their reticules. They pinned their veils with them and secured their flounces and fichus. They kept them on their dressing tables and regularly purchased papers of them. When Chase, as a boy, had embraced his mother and sisters, he recalled laughing with them when one of their pins had jabbed him. Bristles, he'd called one sister who had peppered her person with the things.

"Sure as sure, you'd best come out," said Deeds, sounding uneasy. "What's there to see?"

Chase hardly heard him. He was staring fixedly at his hand, and now he perceived it was faintly sticky with a jelly-like substance that had adhered to his fingertips while he was picking up the pins. And when he put his lantern down next to the trough, he saw a shiny patch half the size of a saucer and knew it to be blood. He put his hand in the water trough to cleanse his fingers and fished up a sopping bonnet with veil still attached. He plunged his hand in the water again and groped until he found another object, which he managed to grasp between his fingertips. Shaking the water from his hand, Chase held the object next to the lantern. It was a button covered in dark broadcloth, from a coat or a cloak.

He looked up. "Spring your rattle, Deeds." Then the loud vibrations mingled with the watchman's hoarse shouts, spilling into the night. In response, the cows began to bellow.

Chase found Mary Leach immediately. He had not seen her before, abandoned as she was on some sacking in a corner that had shunned the beam of his light. He knelt at her side, putting his ear to her mouth, seeking a pulse at her throat, and pressing his hand against her chest to find a heartbeat. She was dead.

Deeds was standing over them, wordless for once, and in the increased illumination, Chase saw Mary. She was lying on her back in a pool of blood draining from her broken skull. All too clearly the light revealed her ruined face. All too clearly he saw that one lock of her dark hair curled delicately around her split cheek, as if molded there by an artist's hand. When he ran his hands over her, he discovered that her entire upper body was sodden, not just with blood, and his gaze went back to the water trough in sudden, grim understanding. Gently, he closed her staring eyes and straightened her limbs, wishing he could shut out the din of the animals, thoroughly disturbed and crying in distress. Perhaps they had some glimmer of understanding of what had happened here tonight. These cows lived out their lives in the dark, never feeling a fresh breeze or seeing the sky. Tonight they had been witnesses to a murder.

Chase heard footsteps and raised voices. Men clustered in the doorway with their bobbing lanterns, which seemed too bright, almost indecent in their ability to expose this hideousness. "Stay back," he called. "Do not disturb the area."

One man ignored this command, rushing straight toward them—Mary's father Horatio Rex. Dropping to his knees, he extended a hand and turned his daughter's face toward the light. "Mariam?" he said.

PART TWO

Say, where am I? Can you tell?
Is my heart within my breast?
Am I bound in magic spell,
Or by fiends of hell possest?

Say, what horror sways this brain?
Do I sleep, or do I wake?
If I sleep—oh, dream of pain!
From my lids thy fetters take.
—Charlotte Dacre, "The Musing Maniac"

Chapter XIV

"May I join you?" said Chase. Horatio Rex stood on the terrace that overlooked the river, his coattails stirring in the breeze, his head lifted toward a sky in which dawn's rosy streaks had faded. Now that the light had increased, a banquet of beauty lay revealed before them on this unusually clear morning. Immediately to their left stretched the expanse of Somerset House and the incomplete arches of the new Strand Bridge. Beyond, the dome of St. Paul's floated amid the spires of City churches. To their right, Westminster Bridge sparkled like a fairy road in the sunshine, while the Abbey seemed as if it would last forever.

Turning from his study of the horizon, Rex sent Chase a veiled look, the old hostility still lurking. The man looked years older than he had in his drawing room just four days before, his urbane polish dulled, his eyes furtive and haunted.

Chase leaned his elbows on the parapet. "I need you to answer some questions."

"Ask them." Rex looked back at the river, where skiffs and lighters and coal brigs had already begun to crowd the waterway as London went calmly about its business.

Chase watched them too. They all had somewhere to go, but when he thought of the ugly futility of Mary Leach's death, he couldn't see why they bothered. *What the devil was the point?* There was no answer to this question. What he mostly felt now was guilt—guilt that he had not been quick enough and smart enough to save her. He would much preferred to have arrested her and let her take her chances in court defending herself against the charge of stabbing her husband. She might have pled insanity perhaps. Then he decided there *was* an answer to his unanswerable question. There was a point, and he would find it. He would find out who had murdered Mary Leach and why. Completing this task would not assuage the guilt, but it would allow him to lay it aside, one more loss, one more disappointment, an old letter hidden away in a drawer.

Chase spoke into the silence. "We've brought Mrs. Leach home, sir. The surgeon has examined her, and the housekeeper sits with her."

"Good. She should not be alone. They must keep candles burning by her side."

"If it can be any comfort to you, she was not violated."

Rex let his eyelids drop and opened them slowly, as if even so small a movement was an effort. He kept his face turned resolutely forward. "Thank God for that small mercy."

"I've inspected the stable, sir, and the Coroner has been summoned." Chase paused. "There's more. A pistol Leach kept in a desk drawer in the library has gone missing. Mrs. Leach must have taken it to defend herself, but there was no sign of it where she was found. We must assume she never had a chance to fire and her murderer removed the weapon."

When there was no response, Chase took the button from his waistcoat pocket and laid it on the parapet. "I found this along with Mrs. Leach's bonnet in a water trough. Do you recognize it?" As he spoke, he was running his eye down the other man's coat; Rex's buttons were of metal, not cloth, yet he'd had ample time to change his garments, Chase thought.

"A common enough thing," said Rex indifferently, barely glancing at it.

"Why would Mrs. Leach refer to herself as a 'wretch' and pen a note to arrange the care of her children? She was getting her affairs in order because she knew she was in danger." Chase allowed Rex to read the note but kept the memorandum book in his own hands.

"This means nothing." Rex pushed the book away. "My daughter believed we are all sinners. She understood the fragility of life; after all, she lost a child of her own body less than a year ago. She merely took precautions."

But Chase had glimpsed a flash of fear behind the raw pain in the other man's eyes. At any rate, the explanation failed to satisfy. "Your daughter's fate is terrible enough, but we must consider her husband's death. You've been helping Mrs. Leach hide the truth."

"I have no idea what you're talking about, Chase. Of course I dealt with the surgeon and promised to handle the parish authorities for Mary. She needed me. Any father would do the same."

"Mrs. Leach told Fladgate a cock and bull story about a masked assailant. Did you open your purse wide, hoping to ensure his silence? Maybe you even bribed the porter at the *Daily Intelligencer* to disappear."

"That's a lie."

"Who then?"

Rex shrugged. "I don't know. Someone must have wanted the porter's information. I've seen the watchers in Fitzroy Square, and they followed us from Greek Street last night too. I'm sure they are agents employed by the Home Office. Last night Mary said…she was afraid, Chase."

"We are speaking of Leach. The porter Peter Malone was a witness to what happened at the newspaper office. Did he see—a woman?"

"What does it signify if he did? Who would believe a mere woman capable of such a crime? Any man could defend himself. In any case, if Malone saw a woman, it could just as easily have been Mrs. Wolfe. I'm told she had called on Leach at the *Daily Intelligencer*."

Fury swept over Chase. "You dare to imply Mrs. Wolfe had something to do with the attack? You know perfectly well your own daughter was there that night."

"I insinuate nothing. I only hint at the construction the world may put on these events. What good can it do to destroy my

Mary's reputation? The only thing that matters is to find out who did this to her and why."

"I don't know yet, but I suspect the villain was after information." Chase had decided it would do no good to mention that Mary Leach had been tortured by having her head thrust into a trough of dirty water, though this information must come out in the inquest. Besides, he wanted to see if Rex would betray any knowledge of the scene.

Rex lowered his face to his arms. "My God, how frightened she must have been. Why did no one come to her aid?"

"The beggars in the Arches are unlikely to intervene."

"It's bad enough that Mary's children must suffer the loss of their mother, but think of the scandal."

"You're right. The journalists are bound to seize on the story. She must have told you something, Rex. Mrs. Leach left the house to meet someone, and you said she was afraid. Who was it?"

"I tell you, I don't know! She didn't take me into her confidence. She didn't trust me, her own father. I'll live with my failure for the rest of my life."

"You must have a theory."

His bent head shifted, and his voice was slightly muffled when he answered. "She needed to escape an intolerable situation. She was trapped. She mentioned you, Chase. When I told her Mrs. Wolfe was your friend, she asked me whether I thought you a decent man. What could I say? Should I have advised her to consult a Bow Street Runner?"

"A pity you didn't, isn't it?" said Chase wearily. "Why did she want to see Mrs. Wolfe?"

"To put her on her guard? I had tried that myself when I told Mrs. Wolfe's fribble of a husband about the masked man. I wanted to see how he would react, and I thought he was sure to repeat the story to her. A miscalculation, as it happened."

"Yes, because after you rushed to your daughter's side, you learned *she* was the one involved, not Mrs. Wolfe."

"I did think Mrs. Wolfe might be Collatinus."

"Why should you suspect her?"

"She might have tried to resurrect the past or hoped to profit from old secrets. Her father was suspected of murdering a woman when he was last in London."

"You mean Nell Durant?"

In his astonishment, Rex jerked upright. "You know about her?"

"One of the fashionable impure, once the Regent's mistress. Your daughter owned a pocketknife bearing the device of the Prince of Wales. Did Nell give it to her?"

"Probably. They were friends. That was before Mary married Leach and turned Tory. My wife promoted the match because she thought Mary was wasting her life, dwelling in the past. Nell's death along with the accusation against Sandford ruined my daughter. She was never the same." He looked around vaguely. "Where is Mrs. Wolfe? If I am to explain, Chase, we must go back nearly twenty years to my friendship with her father."

"Wolfe thought it best to escort her back to Greek Street. She was terribly distressed by the news of Mrs. Leach's death. You say your daughter did not trust you enough to confide in you. Well, you have been guilty of the same fault with Mrs. Wolfe. We have been stumbling around in the dark. I do know Sandford was the original Collatinus."

"True enough."

"And Nell?"

"She was a woman who felt her power. Her smallest smile drew men like bees to a blossom. She used to hold court in her opera box like a queen. She'd already had several protectors by the time she came to the Prince's notice."

"Nell was also a wronged mother, according to the letters."

Rex nodded. "She had a son a few months before she died. There were rumors."

"What kind of rumors? Who fathered the child?"

"I heard reports it was the Prince of Wales. Nell once told me His Royal Highness had treated her shabbily. He cast her off as he casts off every woman after he's had his fill. And promised her a settlement that was not forthcoming. Which explains why—"

"She resorted to blackmail?"

"She'd written her memoirs, you see. She meant to demand hush money from her former lovers and acquaintances in exchange for having their names expunged from the manuscript, and, of course, she wanted to embarrass the Prince. Then she came to one of my routs and met Sandford. He was one of a group of young men of good family and advanced opinions I'd been cultivating."

"Whose idea was it to write the Collatinus letters?"

"Sandford's. Nell had been made a plaything for rich and titled men, according to him. He convinced her to sell him information for his letters, which I agreed to publish. Her knowledge could thus do good for the world."

"She agreed?"

"When an injury is done to a man, he may seek retribution at law or on the dueling ground. A woman has no such remedies, or so Nell claimed."

"She sold the pair of you the secrets of her fashionable friends at an immense profit. Pay up or see your soiled linen exposed to the world. What were these secrets?"

"Oh, the usual," Rex replied, a ghost smile flickering at his lips. "We took aim at the Prince's debts, of course, and I recall there was a colonel who forced his mistress to sell her favors and thereby satisfy his creditors. A duchess, mistress to a government minister, who gained lucrative places for all her relations. The cuckolded aristocrat whose children all had different fathers. But would you believe that profit was not our primary motive, at least not my motive or Sandford's? We intended nothing less than to discredit the aristocracy's right to rule. If our targets refused to pay up, we would publish the information as paragraphs in the next Collatinus letter. Or, if they met our demands, as they usually did, we funneled some of the money toward the defense of the republicans or toward the families of the men who had been arrested. We couldn't lose. One way or the other, our enemies paid."

"Nell Durant paid a far higher price. What happened to her?"

"She was found murdered at her home in Marylebone. Her sister implicated Sandford."

"What possible motive?"

"I don't know. Someone offered to pay more for her memoirs, or Sandford discovered she had betrayed him."

"You were in difficulties with the authorities. Maybe you decided that Nell had grown too troublesome and killed her yourself?"

"No, it must have been Sandford. There was no one else."

"You are convinced of his guilt?"

Rex's expression shifted uneasily. "He ran away, didn't he? Yet I've always regretted our falling out right before he left. He said he was innocent, but I'm afraid I didn't quite believe him. A friendship destroyed."

"Perhaps he told you the truth. Sandford certainly *didn't* kill your daughter. Two women are dead. If the same person murdered both of them, he was innocent. And what of you? I hear your political allegiances underwent a change. Did your daughter suspect you of having something to do with Nell's death? Was that why she didn't trust you?"

"Damn you, Chase. What can you know of my life? Nell was dead, Sandford gone for good. Nothing to be done for either of them. The authorities would show a man of my race no mercy, assume the worst, and put the blame for Nell's murder at my door. I acted to save my family and myself. Do you judge me for it?"

"You made a bargain?"

"I betrayed no one," he said proudly. "I told the scoundrels only what they already knew, but they made sure I was humbled. I was to renounce my belief in the rights of man at a public assembly and defend the English constitution in print. Ralph Hewitt, a connection of my wife's, conducted the negotiations for me."

"And you thought it was all over until the letters started again? You went back to your usury and found better ways to profit by fleecing young men with expensive tastes who were stupid enough to put themselves in your power."

"You judge me by the world's prejudice." Rex looked into Chase's face and sighed. "My father was a street hawker. What professions do you imagine were open to me? Do you know how often the wellborn have failed to honor my contracts? You wonder why I am forced to charge such high rates of interest? They are all liars and cheats, from the Prince of Wales down to the merest sprigs of nobility out to indulge their pleasures without paying for them."

"His Royal Highness borrowed money off you?"

"He did—when I was fool enough to enter into financial engagements with him and his cronies. He has never repaid a shilling."

"Will you bury your daughter in accordance with your faith, sir?" inquired Chase, suddenly curious. He knew next to nothing about Judaism, he realized. He had encountered few Jews in his life, and he had never before spoken at length to one.

"We do not observe the ceremonies of the modern Israelite. Mary was wed to a Christian. She had turned her back on her upbringing as I advised her to do and as I did myself, though I've never renounced my religion and never would. But I should have kept her safe with our people, who, I have always believed, are favored by Divine Providence. One more regret. I can't help thinking that if I'd kept to my first wife—a good Jewish woman—none of this would have happened. And, even if it did, maybe Mary's life would have been happier."

Rex had returned to gazing over the river, but Chase decided it was time to stop dancing around. "What happened to the child Nell bore?"

"He died soon after his mother. A pity, but what future would he have had?"

"And the recent Collatinus letters? Blackmail again?"

"Perhaps. They seem intended to vindicate Nell Durant."

"If Nell sold her memoirs to someone, where do you think this new Collatinus obtained the manuscript? The letters seem to contain extracts."

"I cannot tell you."

"You are an obvious suspect to have revived these letters. You knew Nell. You published the originals. You have reason to seek revenge on your own account."

"I am not Collatinus. Do you think I would take such a chance a second time? My wife is not in robust health. As it is, she has been distressed by this business and looks on Mrs. Wolfe with disapproval, unfairly perhaps. Now I must tell the Countess about my poor Mary."

"Did your daughter mention the letter she received yesterday?"

"She never said a word, but then there wasn't an opportunity for much conversation. Her husband was dying, Chase."

"What time did you leave her last night?"

"Around ten o'clock. Leach wasn't going to last more than another hour or two, and Mary wanted to be alone to pray for his soul. I was to bring Mrs. Wolfe to her in the morning."

"Why didn't you wait?"

"Mary seemed so desperate. I thought it might comfort her to talk to Mrs. Wolfe, relieve her mind of a burden. I couldn't bear the idea of leaving her on her own, to tell you the truth."

"You went home after you left the Adelphi the first time? Your coachman or your wife can vouch for your movements?"

"Damn you to hell! Do you think I would beat my own child to death? No, I didn't go home until later. I took a long walk, then made my way back to Fitzroy Square to rouse my coachman. You know the rest."

Chase stared at him, eyes narrowed. Was Rex so depraved as to take his daughter's life? It was possible, especially if Mary had become a threat to him, as it seemed Nell had before her. Horatio Rex had sacrificed his heritage to claw his way to respectability, and if Mary had endangered his business interests or his position in society, he might have struck out in self-preservation. Her killer had felt strong feelings for her, must have hated her, in fact, to hurt her so viciously. Mary's father might have considered it his right to control his child and chastise her for her rebelliousness, and he could have staged the scene with Penelope as an elaborate charade to give himself a sort of alibi. On the other hand, Chase supposed that one of the other men in Nell Durant's life could have killed Mary.

"I need names, Rex, names of the men you and Sandford blackmailed along with the names of Nell's protectors."

"It's been nearly twenty years! Some of them are dead. Others have risen high in their careers. You'll never touch them."

When Chase didn't respond, Rex finally gave the information, his reluctance obvious. Chase was careful to keep the reaction from his face. These were men of enormous power and influence: a government minister, a fashionable gentleman, a wealthy aristocrat who owned vast property in London, and a rakehell who had recently wed a young heiress. Chase would be lucky to gain access to their secretaries, let alone the men themselves.

"This George Kester. He was in attendance at your rout party the other night?"

"He's an old friend. Part of the Carlton House set, a crony of the Regent."

An old friend Horatio Rex had blackmailed, but Chase let this inconvenient fact pass. "Mrs. Wolfe also mentioned meeting Mr. Hewitt. It was he who helped you evade arrest back in the '90s?"

Rex laughed shortly. "He's a sort of cousin to my wife, but, make no mistake, Hewitt didn't offer his aid out of any regard for me. He owed me a great deal of money. I was forced to forgive the debt in exchange for services rendered."

"Tell me," Chase said, keeping his tone even, "did your daughter use Nell's pocketknife to stab her husband? Did she do it to forestall Leach's next revelation in the paper? She was shielding someone, or she wrote those letters herself."

"You say that to *me*? You lower yourself to spread such filthy slander? A masked man murdered Leach, and there's an end to it. Very likely it was this new Collatinus. You cannot deny he had reason enough to hate Dryden Leach. You find him and leave Mary out of it."

"I won't lie for you," said Chase.

He spent the rest of the morning, trying to find anyone who might have seen Mary Leach or her murderer, but had no luck. Next he knocked at the door and questioned the Leach servants, including the footman Albert. Albert repeated his story about the letter Mrs. Leach had received, adding only that it had been addressed in a neat hand. No trace could be found of this correspondence—or indeed of any letters or papers except Mary's memorandum book and some innocuous household documents in Leach's study. Chase questioned the lady's maid (rude and contentious) and the chambermaid (flighty and evasive). The former acted as if he were accusing her of negligence when he inquired about the button and stated positively that it hadn't come from anything Mrs. Leach owned. The latter was the girl called Susan who had gossiped to Packet about finding her mistress' wet cloak and boots on the night of Leach's attack. When challenged, Susan burst into tears and denied the story.

"Don't be afraid. Just tell the truth." Chase kept his voice gentle.

"I am telling you, sir. I never said so."

"Has someone instructed you to keep quiet?"

"Who would do that? I never said a word about my poor mistress. I'd never tell a lie about her."

No matter how hard he pressed, the chit only cried all the harder, and he couldn't get a word of sense out of her. He had no doubt Horatio Rex had made sure she wouldn't talk. Similarly, he thought it would do little good at this point to interview the prostitute who'd told Packet she saw a veiled woman running down the street—for what did this prove, after all? The prostitute had caught only a glimpse of a fleeing form, and she hadn't seen where the woman went. No, Packet had gleaned whatever information was to be had from that source, but Chase would ask him to keep looking for other witnesses.

He managed to get a few words with Miss Elliot, the governess, by requesting that she step out of the nursery into the corridor. Pale and distracted, she barely concentrated on his questions and repeated several times that the children would wonder what had become of her.

"Did you speak to Mrs. Leach yesterday?"

She was gazing over his shoulder, but at this she turned her terrified eyes to his face. "No…I mean…yes, she visited Thomas and Emily."

"How did she seem?"

"I will never forget the way she kissed them." She shuddered and fell silent, tears welling up and trickling down her cheeks.

"What did she say, ma'am?"

"Why, nothing. I…I am not myself today. I beg you to excuse me."

Instinct told him she knew something. He felt the knowledge in the tension crackling between them—the governess was a remarkably poor liar, he thought. He persisted in his questioning. "Mrs. Leach did not confide in you, ma'am? If I am to discover who committed this deed, I need your help."

"Mr. Chase!" Isherwood, the butler, bustled up to challenge him, the footmen in his wake. "You are in a house of mourning. I must request that you leave at once, sir. This is not the time for such inquiries."

"This is precisely the time before the trail goes cold."

"Mr. Rex gave me instructions to deny you. Indeed, as he departed this morning, he warned me you might become a nuisance. You have no authority here."

Unfortunately, this was true. Chase stared down the sanctimonious butler for a moment, then decided to give in before the stalwart footmen did him some violence. "I'll come back later."

Isherwood bristled "Don't bother. You will not be admitted, sir."

Though Chase's knee ached fiercely and he longed for his bed as a repentant sinner yearns for salvation, he turned his steps toward Bow Street, where word of the murder had been received. There he waited for two hours in a small, uncomfortable anteroom until the Chief Magistrate was ready for him. This time Read did not offer a chair but kept Chase standing in front of the desk.

"I take it you're tired of your employment at Bow Street?" the magistrate said without preamble. "Otherwise, there's no accounting for your blatant disregard of my instructions."

"I'm sorry, sir. I did tell you I would pursue the inquiry."

"Now we have two corpses on our hands instead of one. Dear God, what were you doing at the Adelphi last night? How were you the one to find the body?"

"Mrs. Wolfe summoned me to search for Mrs. Leach."

"Mrs. Wolfe again. I won't have it. How dare you, Chase? I told you to stay out of this mess. If you think I will stand for your bringing this office into disrepute, you've chosen the wrong man to cross."

"Disrepute?"

"I've had a word dropped in my ear. It seems your Mrs. Wolfe's father was a traitor, a blackmailer, and likely a murderer. And I don't doubt she is cut from the same cloth. Damned disreputable, I say, sir. Damned disreputable. A connection of mine at the Home Office says this woman and her husband are being looked into as possible conspirators in the Collatinus matter. It wouldn't surprise me in the slightest if Mrs. Wolfe's husband turns out to be the one putting on fancy dress and sticking knives in people."

"They are innocent, Mr. Read. At all events, I don't believe in the masked man."

"How can you be so sure? Mrs. Wolfe could be a pretty face playing you like the fool you are and ruining your prospects into the bargain. If Graham didn't speak so well of you, you'd be on the street by now. As it is, you'll do just as I say. You'll have to testify at the coroner's inquest tomorrow, but when that's done you'll stay quietly at home for a week or two and hope this thing dies down or the authorities make an arrest. Don't show your face here for a while."

"I must seek Mrs. Leach's murderer and find Collatinus."

"One and the same, Chase. Everyone says so. You stay home. God knows, you look like you need a rest, and the Home Office has the matter well in hand without any more interference from you. Disobey me this time, and you're out."

Bracing himself, Chase said, "I'm sorry to disoblige you, sir, but I won't abandon a friend."

Read held out a peremptory hand. "I am sorry too, but it seems you've made your choice. Give me your tipstaff."

Chase slipped a hand in the pocket of his greatcoat, bringing out his ensign of office, the baton with the brass crown that represented the authority vested in him by the British Crown. For a moment he let it rest in his palm, remembering the dissatisfaction that had acted like a slow poison in his system for the last year. At the Brown Bear when this investigation began, he had reflected upon the emptiness of his life, and now he would have to find a new way to fill it. This was a daunting prospect. For a decade he'd been an officer of Bow Street. For two decades before that, he had served in the Royal Navy, and before that he'd been a poor clergyman's son, a boy who hated his father, wishing him dead for inflicting a cold religion and a crop of dead babies on his mother. A daunting prospect, indeed, to find out what real emptiness might feel like. Chase laid the tipstaff on the desk and thanked Mr. Read for his time.

Chapter XV

If Chase had been able to see below the Adelphi Terrace while talking to Horatio Rex, he might have observed the sign of a shabby public house. The Fox-under-the-Hill could only be approached through a closed-in, narrow passage called Ivy Bridge Lane that led to a landing on the Thames, where passengers embarked on boats bound for London Bridge. On the next afternoon, the pub's back room was the site of the coroner's inquest into the deaths of Dryden and Mary Leach. With the cooperation of the parish authorities, Rex had offered an enormous reward for information leading to the capture of his daughter's murderer, and in the various police offices around the city, suspects had already been questioned, though whether any of the men who happened to possess black cloaks and domino masks had the slightest connection to the crime was doubtful, at least to John Chase.

As he had foreseen, a storm of reaction had erupted. Two corpses: a staunch government loyalist killed defending his country from a traitor and a helpless woman caught in a wicked conspiracy. All London was talking about the masked assailant known as Collatinus, who must be apprehended if people were to sleep peacefully in their beds. Crowds roamed the surrounding streets, hoping to catch a glimpse of the jury on their return from seeing the bodies laid out in the Leach residence, and at the Fox-under-the-Hill, journalists plied the Leach servants with pints of porter to elicit fresh details.

This story had almost but not quite trumped the latest news in the Princess of Wales scandal. Reformist MP Samuel Whitbread had gone on the attack in her defense, challenging Lord Castlereagh, leader of the House of Commons, and lambasting the Tory press for its slanderous statements against the Princess. Whitbread referred scornfully to Carlton House editors given license to sit in judgment on the innocent, even as they raked in honors for publishing perjured depositions. As Chase waited his turn to testify, he found his thoughts returning again to Dryden Leach and his connection to the Prince. Leach had stood to profit from the Collatinus affair, but his wife had put a stop to that—and to him. *What a vile world we inhabit, and then we dwell with the worms.*

In their testimony, the surgeon Thomas Fladgate and Horatio Rex repeated the tale of the masked man. Sidestepping ticklish questions about why he had kept Leach's true condition a secret, Fladgate asserted that Mrs. Leach had begged him to be silent because her family was in danger. Predictably, Rex corroborated this evidence and spoke of escorting Penelope Wolfe to visit Mary and discovering his daughter's absence. Fladgate also described the injuries of both victims in graphic detail, with those of Mrs. Leach evoking grimaces and head shakings from the crowd.

Soon it was Chase's turn in the witness box. Aware of Penelope and Buckler watching him from the back of the packed room, he also felt the mocking, baleful regard of Fred Gander, sent his way from the specially designated area for journalists near the front.

"According to the footman, Mrs. Leach could not have gone out by the front entrance," Chase told the jury. "The butler found the kitchen door unlocked about midnight and secured the bolt. I assume Mrs. Leach stole out of the house unseen, intending to return the same way. It appears she carried her husband's pistol on her person, probably to defend herself."

The Coroner showed his disapproval. "Why on earth would she go out of doors alone so late?"

"Her husband had just died under tragic and mysterious

circumstances," Chase replied carefully. "A note was delivered to her earlier in the evening. I take it she had urgent business."

"What of this Mrs. Wolfe we've heard about? Mrs. Leach stepped out to meet her perhaps?"

Chase did not look in Penelope's direction. "No, sir. She believed her father would bring Mrs. Wolfe to her the next morning."

"Mrs. Leach would hardly go voluntarily to the Dark Arches, Mr. Chase. Which makes me question whether the villain somehow broke into the house and abducted her!"

"No sign of forced entry. The house was full of servants. It seems logical that she went out to meet someone and this person is responsible for her murder."

"Well, sir? What do you think happened?"

"Whether or not she went on her own to the Dark Arches, her life ended there in a hidden place where the crime could be perpetrated."

"Indeed, the poor soul stood no chance. This Collatinus likely held a knife to her throat. It wasn't enough to silence her husband, but the villain must also slay an innocent woman."

Sitting up straighter, Chase delivered his next response in a ringing tone. "We have no evidence that Collatinus murdered either victim. Neither is there evidence that the same person killed both Dryden and Mary Leach."

"Of course it was Collatinus. Do you suppose we have two masked assassins roaming the streets of London at one time? I believe we've not yet come to that in a civilized country." The Coroner laughed at his little joke, then turned a sneering look on Chase. "You are singularly uninformed, sir, for a Runner."

He lost his grip on the fraying ends of his patience. "You asked me what I think happened. I believe the murderer sought information from Mrs. Leach. Her clothing was soaked. He pushed her head down in a water trough to make her speak. Possibly, she refused to comply, so he beat her to death. Is that enough information for you?"

"What *lady's* knowledge is of interest to an outright devil?"

"She knew a murder victim called Nell Durant. Perhaps Mrs. Leach could identify Mrs. Durant's murderer—or she had found out who Collatinus was."

"You cast aspersions on a poor murdered lady? You saw what that monster did to her with your own eyes!"

"A vagrant boy came upon a gentleman in the Arches sometime after midnight. We must find this man."

"No gentleman in this case. 'Tis plain enough. Mr. Leach had enraged Collatinus with his courageous replies to these infamous letters"—here the Coroner rustled the pages of newsprint in front of him and slapped his hand on the table—"and the wicked brute attacked Mr. Leach in his own office. When he feared Mr. Leach had named his attacker, Collatinus went after Mrs. Leach too."

"The porter Peter Malone was a witness to the attack on Leach. He has disappeared. If you are right, sir, where is Malone? Why hasn't he come forward? Moreover, Mrs. Leach wrote a note in her memorandum book, which suggests she knew her danger. The note designates a relation to care for her children—the tone is desponding, that of a woman who meant to put herself in harm's way or take her own life."

"By asking a murderer to pummel her to death? You dishonor her memory."

It was no good. The Coroner maintained his obtuse hostility, and the panel merely stared at Chase, horrified by the possibilities his testimony raised. The jurors wanted the simpler explanation, the one with the most dramatic appeal. They did not want to imagine that people of wealth and influence had done anything to deserve this tragedy. Far easier and more entertaining to believe in a masked villain.

After the inquest ended with the expected verdict of "willful murder against person or persons unknown," Chase caught Buckler's eye, nodding toward the door. They should escort Penelope home without delay in case the journalists, especially Gander, had observed her presence. She allowed her friends to take an arm on each side as they walked briskly up the steep passage leading toward the Strand. But they had not gone more than a few yards when a voice called, "A word with you, Chase. My, you're in a hurry. I'll take but a minute of your time."

They halted, and Buckler directed a worried glance at Chase. Slowly, Chase turned to face Fred Gander who hovered a few feet away, his face wearing a gleeful expression. "Not now, Gander. I'll speak to you later at the Brown Bear."

"That won't do. Besides, I see you've got your friend Mrs. Wolfe with you. As it turns out, I've a few questions for her."

"I said not now, Gander. We are late for an appointment."

"No, no. You won't fob me off. The public has a right to know. You've done me a scurvy turn, Chase. You took my money and left me high and dry."

Releasing Penelope's arm, Chase opened his pocketbook to extract several notes. He strode over to Gander and shoved the wad in the journalist's coat pocket. "There's your money and a bit more for your trouble. Come to the Brown Bear tonight. I'll see you satisfied."

Gander pantomimed moral outrage. "Hush-money? It won't work. The public won't like to hear of a principal officer of Bow Street stooping so low. Consorting with a suspect in a murder inquiry too."

"You don't know what you're talking about. Stop making mischief."

"I don't, eh? I might have tumbled to your game sooner but for the uproar over the Princess of Wales. But this masked man story will round out my pamphlet delightfully. I see just how to do it. I'll make a heroine of the Princess—a woman, like poor Mrs. Leach, beset by an unscrupulous man. Not content to hound his poor wife almost to madness, the Prince Regent gets himself involved with a woman who turns up dead. Twenty years later, her friend is killed too! I've been reading the Collatinus letters, old and new, and having a few interesting conversations with my sources. It's been suggested I cast the Prince as victim of this piece, but I'm not having that version."

"You may rip His Highness' character to shreds for all I care," said Chase. "Leave Mrs. Wolfe out of it."

"You see, I had to ask myself, why did Mrs. Wolfe visit Dryden Leach on the very day he caught a knife to the chest? And I had no answer until it was whispered to me that her father was the original Collatinus and this N.D. was a celebrated courtesan in league with the Jacobins! And the Prince's lover. Too, too delicious, my friend. All too opportune for those of us taking up Princess Caroline's cause."

Buckler said to Penelope, "Stay here." Approaching the journalist, he seemed to loom over him. Though the barrister was not a tall man, he could give a good five inches to Gander, and the shadows playing over Buckler's face in the dim passageway made him look markedly dangerous. "Watch yourself," he said. "You don't want a libel suit. You have plenty of meat to offer your readers without dragging Mrs. Wolfe's name through the muck."

"Mr. Edward Buckler? I've seen you plead in the Old Bailey. Here's another deliciously interesting question: Are you Mrs. Wolfe's knight *sans peur et sans reproche*? I should think a married lady would stand in no need of such defense."

"Buckler." Chase laid a hand on his friend's arm.

But Buckler shook him off, eyes alight with a cold fire that made him look like an altogether different person. He leaned forward to grasp Gander by the lapels of his coat.

"I grow tired of being manhandled by you and your friends, Chase," the journalist observed in a plaintive tone. "It ain't polite. Tell Mr. Edward Buckler to release me."

By this time Penelope had joined them. "Let him go, Mr. Buckler. If I agree to speak to him, he may at least report the truth."

"No," said Chase, "you do not know this man. He will twist your words out of recognition."

"A sensible lady," approved Gander. "Would you care to tell me why you went to Mrs. Leach's house on the night she was killed? Strange, isn't it? You always seem to be on the spot for a bit of villainy."

Penelope addressed him like a teacher scolding a rather dim-witted student. "She was an old friend of my family. You don't understand, Mr. Gander."

He smirked at her. "I understand one thing, madam. If we are looking for the new Collatinus, we must consider you a prime candidate. But in that case, who is the masked man?" His gaze scanned insultingly over Buckler, who stared back into the gloating face with its avid eyes and twitchy mouth.

Before the journalist could say more, Buckler's fist had struck him in the nose. Blood spurted out and dripped down Gander's chin to land on the hand still holding the journalist's coat. With an exclamation of disgust, Buckler let go and, reaching in his pocket, took out his handkerchief. Deliberately, he wiped his fingers clean and turned away in disgust.

"We're leaving," said Chase.

Gander smiled through the blood staining his teeth red. "Mr. Edward Buckler," he said thickly, "you may be sure your blow will be repaid with interest."

◇◇◇

Two spots of color rode high in Penelope's cheeks. She twisted her gloved hands in her lap and tapped her foot on the floor of the coach. "It was foolish and wrong of you to strike the journalist."

"Yes," Buckler admitted ruefully. He avoided Chase's sardonic eye, instead meeting her severe one. To give him a chance to make his excuses, he had insisted on escorting Penelope home. He noticed that Chase had shunned the first hackney stand they came to, but now they were settled in an appropriately shabby coach bound for Greek Street.

"Mr. Gander will only shout his lies all the louder. He'll sling his filth in your direction too."

"Let him try, Mrs. Wolfe."

"I have enough to worry about. I don't wish to have you on my conscience as well." She folded her lips tightly together and turned her head away to gaze out the window.

"I can only say how sorry I am," said Buckler, his spirits sinking low. Almost of its own volition, his hand stretched out toward hers; then he retracted it quickly. He was amazed at his own folly. What had possessed him? He had risen to Gander's bait with a vengeance. In his profession, he had learned to exert a rigid control even in the face of extreme provocation from opposing counsel, such control being necessary if he intended to triumph in a cause. But today he had acted like a green boy or a lovesick swain.

His back to the horses, Chase sat listening to this exchange and looking amused. "It doesn't matter, Buckler. If you hadn't given Gander material for his paragraphs, he would have simply invented it. I believe you gained a measure of satisfaction in return."

"Oh, I did." They exchanged a glance of perfect understanding.

"This is absurd," Penelope burst out, frowning at both of them. "How did Mr. Gander discover that my father was Collatinus?"

"Apparently from one of his unnamed sources."

"Someone in the ministry, do you think, Chase?" asked Buckler. "I can see it would be convenient to blame the radicals for these deaths, but surely the ministers don't want the Regent's connection to Nell Durant known?"

"Unless they hope the Prince's role in the scandal might be swallowed up in a general condemnation of traitors everywhere."

Penelope pulled at one of her gloves, tore it off, crumpled it into a ball, and shoved it in her reticule. The other one quickly followed the first. She studied her fingers, as she seemed to consider her next words. Finally, she said, "The Coroner and jury had already made up their minds about Mary. A blessing for her family that she is not suspected of causing her husband's death."

"You won't call it a blessing when you read Gander's witticisms at the breakfast table tomorrow," Chase told her.

"Will it be very bad?"

"Yes. Talk to your husband about leaving town for a week or two. That is my advice."

"He has commissions to finish. I won't be driven away by a sneaking worm when I've done nothing wrong."

"Mrs. Wolfe," said Buckler, "you have no idea how awkward it will be. Your husband can finish his portraits in the country. There will be fewer distractions."

"The world will say I've run away out of guilt."

"Leave it, Buckler. You won't convince her. Let us determine our next step." Chase related his conversation with Horatio Rex, then said, "For one thing, I intend to learn more about Nell Durant, starting with the men who knew her: George Kester, for one. Rex claims he was one of her protectors and a blackmail target."

Buckler nodded. "I was up at Cambridge with his son. Kester is attached to the ministry, joint Secretary to the Treasury or something like that. An important man who won't care to have his past resurrected. Why was he blackmailed?"

After a measuring glance at Penelope, Chase told him.

Her angry color faded, replaced by dismay. "My father was right to attack such corruption. How many disgusting secrets must we uncover before we are through?" She turned to Chase. "How do you intend to investigate Mary Leach's death?"

Though Buckler found it difficult to read Chase, he had learned to discern certain signs. In this case, the aggression of his jaw and his withdrawal into terseness revealed that he was both unwilling to speak and stubbornly determined on his own course. Buckler kept his eyes on the other man's face. "The magistrates have told you to steer clear, haven't they? Is the Home Office taking the lead?"

"Is this true, Mr. Chase? You must do as they bid you."

"Must I, Mrs. Wolfe? We'll see, won't we? I am convinced Nell Durant is the key to Mrs. Leach's murder. The deaths are connected."

"*Have* you been asked to step aside?" demanded Penelope.

Subtle indications of a struggle were visible, but Chase's innate honesty won out. "I've been dismissed."

"Dismissed?" She stared at him in horror.

"I'll thank you to remember I am well able to take care of myself. Leave off, ma'am. There is much to discuss."

Though Buckler was equally concerned by Chase's news, he stepped manfully into the breach. "I assume you plan to ask Hewitt about the bargain Horatio Rex struck with the government? If Nell Durant stood in the way of his political regeneration, Rex might have killed her to save himself or stop her from revealing his treachery to the other Jacobins."

"Possible," said Chase. "What of the serjeant-at-law you told me of? He too was acquainted with Nell Durant. The more we dig, the more men we find lining up to be suspects."

Buckler was startled. "Quiller? He's a dull dog, I assure you. Far too cold-blooded to involve himself with a courtesan or allow himself to get blackmailed." He paused. "What about the printer of the *Free Albion*? Every journalist in London will be on his trail and the authorities too."

Chase opened his mouth to reply, but Penelope forestalled him. "We've not discussed your fee. I have been remiss, but indeed I never thought of it. Since I am the one to employ you, I can just as easily dismiss you. Surely if you tell the magistrate you have bowed out of this affair, he will restore you to your position."

He grinned at her. "You can't dismiss me, Mrs. Wolfe. I answer to nobody now."

Chapter XVI

When Penelope stepped into the hall, Lydia informed her that Mr. Wolfe had given orders he was not to be disturbed. Several visitors had called wishing to tour the showroom, but he had told the servant to ask them to return another day.

"They were a bit vexed, ma'am," said Lydia.

"It can't be helped, I suppose," replied Penelope absently. "Is my daughter upstairs with the other children?"

"Yes, ma'am."

Sarah and Frank were sitting on the hearthrug, playing with dolls, while little Jamie tried to insert himself into the proceedings. Maggie sat with her omnipresent mending in her lap, her feet stretched toward the fire. There was a dreamy expression on her pointed, freckled face.

Penelope smiled at them. "You look cozy."

Sarah ran to greet her mother, throwing her arms around her legs. "Come and play, Mama. Look, we've made a fine house for the dollies." She pointed to the spools, handkerchiefs, and buttons they had used to fashion a miniature dwelling.

The hour Penelope spent with the children did her good, though the innocent game did not allow her to forget Mary Leach. It was impossible to banish the thought of what Mary had endured in the Dark Arches. Penelope could only too easily imagine the stygian darkness—the beasts in the stable bringing a stench to Mary's nostrils—the blood and the pain and the fear.

She wished she could have spoken to Mary before her death, for she was convinced Mary had wanted to tell her something vitally important, a truth that might now remain unknown. When the children went off to beg Cook for a treat, Penelope began to tell Maggie about the inquest, warning her about the looming scandal. Maggie looked worried but said comfortably that people would soon forget all about it once a fresh story came along. Unconvinced, Penelope continued to think of Fred Gander's malice, Chase's news from Bow Street, and the flurry of bills raining down on her every night in her dreams.

Jeremy did not emerge until bedtime. Tea had been sent in, but the tray came out again, untouched. It was always this way. Once the desire to create had been kindled, Jeremy became lost to the world; then he would go for weeks without picking up a brush before the fever of creation returned. Of course, this was no way to make a living. At least some of this inconstancy could be attributed to his parents, respectable innkeepers who had not known what to make of their volatile son. Their incomprehension and constant belittlement had scarred him deeply so that even now at nearly thirty years of age, he continued to meet their low expectations.

"I have finished the *Psyche* portrait," he announced when he entered her sitting room. "This one I shall submit to the Annual Exhibition. If I can get the hangman to place my portrait in a favorable spot, our fortune will be made."

Penelope handed him a cup of tea, smoothed the hair back from his brow, and kissed his cheek. "I am glad, Jeremy." She sat down again at her desk.

"Come away from there and sit next to me. What are you doing?"

"Oh, just trying to make sense of these bills."

He surprised her by saying shortly, "Bring them here. Let me see them."

Sweeping up the pile, Penelope obeyed, pulling a low table next to the sofa and spreading the accounts in front of him. There was a long silence as he picked them up, one after the other, and a scowl settled over his brow. "So much as this?"

"A London establishment is expensive. But if you complete some of the commissions, the portrait of Mrs. Hewitt, for instance, we'll soon come about. I should think she might be willing to pay a hundred guineas, don't you agree? And you must exhibit *Psyche* and hope to gain further business."

For a moment the stricken look remained in his eyes; then, true to form, he smiled and set aside the problem. "You're right, my love. I shall do precisely as you advise. I am ready to show your portrait. Will you come?"

Looking at him, Penelope felt a profound sadness. She did not love her husband as she should; she did not accept him for who and what he was. In his way, he did care for her, and she wished suddenly that she had the power to alter the stubborn essence of their relationship. "Yes, I'll come."

They went upstairs, Jeremy pulling her impatiently by the hand. In his studio he bade her wait while he arranged the lighting, and she watched as he set two branches of candles on stands next to his easel. When he was satisfied, he beckoned.

Leaning against his shoulder, Penelope stood drinking in the portrait. She recalled that his rendering of Constance Tyrone had impressed her—this was the philanthropist who had been murdered soon after sitting for Jeremy. But this portrait…Jeremy had captured her heart. Her eyes looked out of the canvas, speaking love and longing; her skin glowed with earnest hope; her mouth smiled a little secretively, as if she must keep her feelings contained, or they would overflow, rush past any boundaries and sweep aside all inhibition. As Penelope examined his work, she was amazed that Jeremy saw her like this. She had always thought he took her for granted, saw her as the nagging, practical wife who had lost her youth and spirit of adventure. For a full minute she couldn't say a word.

"Don't you like it?" he asked anxiously. He turned her toward him, eager to read the truth in her upturned face.

"It's beautiful, Jeremy." She blinked rapidly to keep her tears from falling.

His eyes searched hers; then he smiled again, satisfied. "Lord, I'm tired. Let's go to sleep, love, shall we?"

The next morning Penelope awoke to find herself notorious. She had sent Maggie out to purchase the newspapers and tried to keep calm by supervising the children's breakfast. While Penelope coaxed Jamie into finishing his bread and milk, Sarah and Frank made slurping sounds at each other, managing to blow bread-crumbs all over the carpet. Penelope smiled at their pranks but reminded them to keep their food on their plates. As they rose from the table, Maggie burst in, a bundle of newspapers in her arms, words trembling on her lips.

Penelope quelled her with a glance. "Let's go to my sitting room. Lydia will soon be here to clear up. She can stay with the children for an hour."

The maidservant came in, and Penelope said, "I have need of Maggie this morning, Lydia. Please take these dishes to the kitchen and return to the nursery. I'll have a word with Mrs. Porlock to let her know I've asked you to mind the children."

Lydia grudgingly agreed. Ten minutes later as Penelope and Maggie descended to the first floor, Maggie whispered, "Come with me, mum, before we read those papers. I have to show you something."

Maggie drew her into the front room, where the curtains had been opened to admit the cheerful morning sun. This was Jeremy's showroom, a place to display his paintings to the visitors who came out of curiosity to tour an artist's premises. But there would be no callers admitted today, for he was already busy next door in his painting room, putting some finishing touches on the *Psyche* portrait.

Maggie sidled up to the window, keeping to one side, and beckoned to Penelope. "They're still there."

"Who?"

"Come see, mum. Who are they?"

Joining her, Penelope peered into the street. Standing on her doorstep was a cluster of three men, talking and laughing amongst themselves. She heard their voices clearly through the glass. One had a spotted Belcher handkerchief knotted about his skinny throat; another wore a garish waistcoat, an ugly pair of mustard-yellow trousers, and tasseled Hessian boots. The third, in need of a haircut and a shave, had a shabbier, more disreputable appearance. This man had a pencil stuck behind his ear and a notebook in his hand.

"Journalists. I'll tell them to go away."

She took a step toward the door, but Maggie laid a hand on her arm. "No, mum. Fetch Mr. Wolfe or send Robert out to get rid of them. You'd best not go yourself until you understand what's what."

Penelope was very aware of the newspapers under Maggie's arm. "I don't want to disturb Jeremy yet. Maybe they won't stay long."

In the sitting room Penelope spread out the newspapers, drawing a breath of relief when she found no reference to her or her father in the reports about the murders, which covered two full columns in the first two papers she consulted. But she was appalled to find the following paragraph in the *London Daily Intelligencer*:

"We note the attendance of Mrs. W___e of Greek Street at the Coroner's Inquest into the tragic deaths of Mr. and Mrs. Dryden Leach—but where was the lady's *charming and accommodating* husband, the portrait painter, on this occasion? Perhaps his absence will cause little remark, for it is well known that Mr. W___e finds solace in other company and indeed has often left his forlorn wife to her lonely crust of bread. It is fortunate then that Mrs. W___e had not one but two *Gallants* on this occasion: J.C., Principal Officer of Bow Street, and E.B., barrister of the Inner Temple, a gentleman entirely *dedicated* to his lady fair in her plight. Mrs. W___e, it may interest readers to know, is the daughter of an eminent author of liberal opinion, who departed the Metropolis some years ago—how shall we say?—rather suddenly. It seems the letters that have so outraged the Publick are not the first to be published under the infamous name of

Collatinus. We will have more to say on this subject anon when we hope to communicate our knowledge of a certain lady of the *frail sisterhood*—once beloved of a most *Illustrious Personage*—a lady who died under mysterious and horrid circumstances, not unconnected with Mrs. W. ___'s father, as it chances. In the meantime, dear readers, we leave you with the wise words of the poet, who reminds us: *'Be it the Task of every British Dame / To guard with nicest care her Sacred Fame!'"*

As Penelope read this gem of execrable style and absurd innuendo aloud, Maggie's eyes got rounder, and anger for her mistress flushed her cheeks. "Oh, what will Mr. Wolfe say, mum?"

How would Jeremy respond? Despite their frequent separations, no breath of scandal had ever touched Penelope; he had always been the one to raise eyebrows and cause comment. But to call Chase and Buckler her "gallants" was to imply impropriety in her relationships with them, and, as for the ending quotation, she felt the humiliation of this insult, as Mr. Gander intended she should. She didn't recognize it, but no doubt it came from some diatribe attacking adultery among the upper classes. Tossing the paper aside to page through the rest of the stack, she was relieved to find that this paragraph was the only one—so far. And yet he must have whispered the story among his journalistic cohorts, or they wouldn't have located her so quickly. The paragraph would soon have company.

"Jeremy won't like it, Maggie. But it's all nonsense, and I won't let it trouble me overmuch. I only hope it won't damage his prospects. He needs to establish himself for all our sakes."

Maggie nodded her understanding. It was unnecessary to explain how precarious was their position. Penelope and Jeremy would need to close the studio and find cheaper lodgings, and they would have to dismiss the servants, except for Maggie. But how was Penelope to ensure they would have a roof over their heads and enough to eat? After receiving the inheritance from her cousin, she had written to her father to decline her allowance. Though she had loved being able to make this gesture, she knew it now for the utter folly it was. She picked up Gander's paragraph and read it a second time, her fingers itching to put it on the fire.

Robert, the manservant, entered the room. "A Mr. Blackbourne has called, ma'am. He begs the favor of a few minutes of your time."

"She'll see no one today." Maggie glared at Robert, not her favorite person even in happier times.

Penelope frowned at her and turned to Robert. "Did Mr. Blackbourne state his business?"

Robert looked abashed. He was a lazy, sometimes unpleasant young man whom Jeremy had hired because he insisted that a passel of female servants did not give him sufficient credit before the world. But Robert would not relish the disgrace of his employers, as it would only reflect on him too. He paused, then blurted, "He's the chandler, you know, ma'am, and he says he'll have his account paid up or take drastic measures. He's out there talking to three men on the doorstep. Who might they be?"

"Why didn't you rout them?" Maggie scolded. "I suppose I'll have to go myself."

"No, Maggie," said Penelope. "I'll take care of it. Mr. Blackbourne has every right to his money."

Chapter XVII

After twice trying to see the Earl of Wendlebury, one of Nell's former protectors, and twice being told his lordship was "not at home," Chase admitted defeat. Rex alleged that his lordship had once been suspected of having secret ties to a faction in France, but even when Chase sent up a note with not-so-veiled allusions to this charge, no reply was forthcoming. Short of lying in wait for the man and catching him as he left his house, there was little Chase could do.

He also tried his luck in Berkeley Square, attempting to beard Sir Oliver Cox, another one of Nell's blackmail victims, in his stately den. Thinking to catch Cox at his breakfast, he presented himself at an early hour, only to be routed by a supercilious butler. He was retreating down the steps when he saw a gentleman approaching. Swaying on his feet, his clothing stained and disheveled, Cox was just returning from a night of dissipation. A known rakehell at least fifty years old, he had recently wed the seventeen-year-old heiress to a vast fortune, but apparently even her charms were not enough to keep him at home.

Chase bowed. "Sir Oliver Cox?"

"What do you want?" Cox slurred his words, peering at him owlishly out of bloodshot eyes.

"A word, sir, about Nell Durant."

For an instant, the baronet looked blank; then his face cleared, and he gave a high-pitched giggle. "A name I've not heard in years. What of her?"

"Nell was your mistress at one time?"

"We shared some laughs for a few months. It didn't last long."

"You parted friends?"

"Why wouldn't we? I paid her well enough. I gave her a sparkler for her pretty neck."

"Was this before or after she'd had a relationship with His Royal Highness, the Prince of Wales?"

"After. Look, Nell's been dead these twenty years."

"She was in league with the blackmailer Collatinus who wrote letters to the papers. Did they blackmail you?

"Probably."

"Did you pay Collatinus' demand, sir?"

Cox put a hand against a streetlamp to steady himself, his face a greenish color in the merciless morning light. "I've never yielded to a blackmail demand in my life. I sent a message telling the rogue to do his worst."

Chase believed him. This was not a man who cared what the world thought of him. According to Rex, Cox was fond of rough sexual games with the Covent Garden ladies and had suffered repeated bouts of the pox during his decidedly disreputable career. He probably hadn't changed much, thought Chase, as he studied the baronet's slack face and loose, wet mouth.

"Have you heard about the murder of Mary Leach, sir? She's the journalist's wife found in the Dark Arches."

"Who?" said Cox.

◇◇◇

A frugal man with modest tastes, John Chase had put by a sum that would maintain him in reasonable comfort for a year or two. When this investigation was over, he planned to visit his mother's grave, or if this ill-advised war with Britain's former colonies ever ended, he might take a trip to America to meet his son. It seemed there would be plenty of time for whatever he chose to do.

The loss of his Bow Street emblem had left a surprisingly large hole in his pocket and his life. He hadn't realized how much he'd come to depend upon his position as a Runner for countenance.

Can a man with no particular role to play in the world be called a man at all? This thought he shook off impatiently and just got on with his inquiries. After another fruitless attempt to locate Samuel Gibbs, printer of the *Free Albion*, Chase spent an hour at the Adelphi Terrace, avoiding the curious spectators and knocking on the neighbors' doors but discovering nothing to the purpose. He lingered in the vicinity, hoping Miss Elliot would emerge to take the children for an airing, but the windows draped in black crepe stared back at him with blank hostility. If the governess had any secrets to divulge, they would have to keep for another day.

Chase damned the expense and saved his knee some discomfort by taking a hack to Albermarle Street, where he was surprised to be immediately conducted into Ralph Hewitt's pleasant bookroom. A heavy-featured man in his late forties, Hewitt rose from behind his writing table, coming forward to offer a seat in one of the comfortable armchairs. He was, he confided, the son of a gentleman-farmer from an old Lincolnshire family. His ancestors had fought and fallen at Bosworth and Marston Moor, but his family had since, he added with a loud laugh, exchanged their swords for the ploughshare.

"We have a manor full of ancient portraits and rotting wood. As well as damp air and agues, I'm afraid. One day my brother hopes to drain our land to make it more productive, but I won't live to see it. I haven't been back in years. Now, Chase, what may I do for you?"

"Thank you for seeing a stranger."

"You see, I know who you are. You're the Bow Street Runner Rex tossed out of his house."

"The same, sir." He saw no point in admitting he was no longer attached to Bow Street.

"Rex lacked finesse, wouldn't you agree? I am curious, I suppose, as to why you pushed in where you were not welcome and why you wanted to see me today."

Chase explained that he was assisting a friend, an acquaintance of the Rex family.

"You mean Mrs. Wolfe? I saw the paragraph in this morning's *Daily Intelligencer*. Nasty business. I assumed you were the principal officer referred to, but who the deuce is E.B., barrister of the Inner Temple?"

Inwardly, Chase groaned. "I haven't seen this paragraph. Do you have a copy?"

With a gleam of curiosity in his gray eyes, Hewitt handed him a folded newspaper and watched him scan the column. Seething, Chase quickly read the paragraph, which was just as bad as he'd feared it would be. Fred Gander had better play least in sight for the foreseeable future, he thought. Keeping his expression impassive, he handed the paper back.

A smile tugged at Hewitt's lips. "It won't do to concern yourself with such malice. But I understand why you wish to defend the lady as well as preserve your own reputation."

"You've been acquainted with Mr. Rex and the Countess for some years?"

"The Countess of Cloondara is a distant cousin of mine, yes."

"I'm told you aided Horatio Rex at the time of the treason trials. You extricated him from his difficulties with the authorities?"

He looked gratified. "A neat piece of work, I must confess. I did not do it for Rex, however, but for the Countess. You might say I saved him from arrest and disgrace, and the Countess was grateful. To be honest, I've never understood—"

"Why she stays with him?"

Hewitt shook his head wryly, acknowledging the point. "They met years ago when she broke with the Earl of Cloondara and came to London. She got herself in debt to Rex. I shouldn't be at all surprised if he took advantage."

"By extorting certain favors in return for loans?"

"So I believe. Very attractive woman in her day. She has been an enormous asset to him socially, but now there's this scandal with Leach and Rex's daughter. Well, I can only imagine the Countess may have regrets. Far too late, of course."

"You blame Mr. Rex?"

"I don't imply that he is *personally* responsible. But at the time when Rex got himself entangled with the radicals, Mrs. Leach was a foolish and headstrong girl. The Countess was worried about her, especially after that courtesan was murdered. Later Mrs. Leach seemed to have put her past behind her with marriage to a dependable man. Still, one wonders."

"You don't think her an innocent victim?"

"Oh, tragic; that goes without a saying. But it's a strange business nonetheless. What brought her out in the night?"

Chase showed Hewitt the button he had fished up from the water trough. "I found this near her body. Do you recognize it?"

He took it between his fingers. "This? Should I? I'm afraid not."

"It's a button, possibly from the killer's cloak. I've determined it didn't come from Mrs. Leach's clothing." Chase retrieved it and slipped it back in his waistcoat pocket. "You imply she was involved with the Jacobins in her youth and again before her death, sir?"

"Nothing of the kind. You quite mistake me. But the Countess once told me that Rex had allowed his daughter to become too friendly with Mrs. Durant. And the Countess feared for Mrs. Leach's reason when she was murdered and Eustace Sandford fled the country."

"You too were acquainted with Mrs. Durant, sir?"

As though in the grip of a pleasant memory, Hewitt leaned back, allowing his eyelids to droop. "The most beautiful woman I've ever seen. She had a number of titled and wealthy protectors in her time. A pretty little barque of frailty."

"If you don't mind my asking, were you one of her protectors?"

"Too much of a high-flyer for me, I'm afraid. It was Kester who introduced the girl to the *ton*. He found her in a shop, I believe. She became all the rage."

"She had given birth to a son soon before her death?"

He opened his eyes to grin at Chase. "I recall some talk about that, yes."

"Nell Durant claimed the Prince of Wales himself was the father. You knew of their liaison, sir?"

"Of course, common knowledge. She would say the babe was his, wouldn't she? She must have hoped for a fat settlement. I suppose the father could have been anyone."

Chase kept his tone casual and impersonal. "Did any of her former protectors have a reason to kill her?"

"Perhaps, if she'd been playing off her tricks."

"Tricks?"

"If she'd made one of them jealous or got greedy. I can only speculate. There was the business with Rex too. I wondered whether her death had anything to do with that."

"She had written her memoirs." He watched the other man carefully.

Hewitt gave a contemptuous snort. "Memoirs? Just another whore out to titillate the public and line her pockets."

"Was Eustace Sandford guilty of her murder, do you think?"

"He could have been. Or it was one of the other radicals or even, as you say, one of her protectors, though that seems unlikely as most of them were gentlemen."

"And Mrs. Leach?"

He folded his plump hands on the table, regarding Chase seriously. "Ah, that was a dreadful thing. But I heard an encouraging report recently. It seems the authorities are on the verge of arresting this Collatinus. They believe the villain is Mrs. Durant's son, out to milk a profit and avenge his mother's death. You've not come across such a person in your investigation?"

Chase leaned forward. "No, sir, I haven't. Mr. Rex told me Nell Durant's son died in infancy. Where did you hear this report?"

"From my wife, actually. The story was making the rounds at a party we attended last night."

The pieces in Chase's mind assembled in a new pattern. If Mary Leach had found an ally in her feud against her husband, that could explain how she managed the delivery of the letters and also why she had chosen to help her friend's son in the first place. What if Nell's son was present when Leach was stabbed? For that matter, he could have done the deed himself with his mother's knife. And perhaps this alliance went sour after the attack on the journalist if one of the conspirators had threatened to turn on the other. According to her father, Mary had been afraid of someone, and this someone could have been Nell Durant's son.

Hewitt rose to tug the bell pull, signaling the interview was over. He spoke over his shoulder. "It seems we are about to find out the truth, Chase. These letters have stirred up a hornets' nest, and Mrs. Leach was badly stung. Let us hope we may soon be quit of the whole affair."

◇◇◇

When the porter of the Cocoa Tree Club whispered that a visitor awaited him, George Kester had been dozing over his newspaper in the coffee room. He put aside his paper and got to his feet, smoothing his perfectly tailored coat with a well-tended hand from which several rings glinted. Strolling toward the doorway where Chase waited, Kester motioned him into a luxuriously furnished visitors' room across the corridor.

The Treasury Secretary wore assurance like a second skin, displaying a well-bred politeness coupled with haughty indifference. George Kester's face was marked by years of rich living, but Chase had done his research, and he knew that Kester was also an astute, successful politician who had worked in various ministry posts.

"How may I help you?" He reached in his coat pocket to extract his gold and enamel snuffbox. Surreptitiously studying Chase from under his brows, he placed a pinch to his nostril and inhaled. Kester's stare seemed to take in his plain garb and dismiss him.

In response, Chase withdrew a leather case from his own pocket. He opened the case, removed Nell Durant's pocketknife from its silk compartment, and passed it to Kester, haft first. Then he took out the button and held it up.

Startled, Kester looked as if he wanted to drop the knife. He gazed down at it in his hands and drew back in his chair. "What is the meaning of this?"

"The knife once belonged to a murdered woman. It was lately found in the possession of the journalist's wife killed in the Dark Arches. You knew Mrs. Leach, sir?"

Kester had recovered his composure. With obvious distaste, he laid the knife on a small table between them, pointing the blade at Chase. "What have you to do with so unsavory an affair?"

"Have you lost a button from one of your coats recently, Mr. Kester?"

"What the devil are you talking about? Who are you?"

"I am here on behalf of a friend, purely in a confidential capacity. I need to ask you some questions about Nell Durant and Mary Leach."

"Give me one good reason why I should speak to you. In the pay of the newspapers, hmm? You'll get nothing from me." Kester rose to his feet.

"A reason? Charles Lavenham. Your personal secretary back in '88. He hanged himself after you started a campaign of rumors about his 'unnatural desires' in liking little boys. It might have been true for all I know. At all events, I know why you did it."

The Treasury Secretary went white with rage. "I'll make you sorry you spoke to me like that. Wait, I've seen you before— you're the Runner from Rex's rout. You'll be out of a job by morning."

"Too late, Mr. Kester. Is this how you react when someone crosses you? Lavenham found out that you cheated at cards. He saw you marking them and threatened to tell. You had ruined some young fool, who promptly blew his brains out, and I suppose Lavenham pitied him. I doubt you needed the money. Did you do it for fun, or for a challenge?"

"What are you after? A bribe?"

"Information. Tell me about Nell Durant."

Kester resumed his chair, crossing his booted feet. He pulled out his watch, frowning as he saw the time, and glanced toward the door. "What is there to tell?" he said. "She was a courtesan under my protection for a short time before we parted ways.

Amicably, I might add. My parting gifts were generous. She went on to gull far richer prospects."

"You found her in a shop?"

"I? You mistake the matter. My memory may be at fault, but I recall she was the mistress of a fellow named Fowke when I met her. A silly ass who hadn't a hope of breaking her to bridle. Nell was the daughter of a watchmaker and a stocking repairer, you know. I've no notion where she got her impudence."

Chase stared at him. Finally, he said, "You won't have forgotten blackmail surely? Collatinus blackmailed you, using information provided by Nell Durant. He gave you a choice. Pay up or see your baseness exposed in a letter to the newspaper."

"*Nell* gave Collatinus the information? I see I underestimated her."

"You didn't know she was involved with the radicals? How did she discover the secrets she sold?"

Kester gave a wintry smile. "Bedchamber talk, I should think. I was by no means the only string to her bow. The Prince of Wales had even shown some brief interest. It makes perfect sense now that I think of it. She knew everyone in society during her reign—the gentlemen, at any rate. She was there when they dined or gambled or drank themselves to a stupor. A clever girl, too clever for her own good."

"Because she made someone hate her enough to kill her?"

"Exactly."

"Who?"

He shrugged. "That's the question, isn't it? Why the devil should I know or care? I haven't thought of her in years."

"You paid the demand?"

"It would have been inconvenient to have that lying slander in the papers. My wife was expecting a child. I didn't want her upset."

"How did you deliver the money?"

"I left it at a tavern for Collatinus."

"Was your relationship with Nell over by then?"

"Long over. She'd been under the protection of another fellow, Tallis I think his name was. He's been dead for years before you think to go bothering him! He'd set her up in a neat little place in Marylebone, she and her sister. Tallis used to complain that Nell had saddled him with another mouth to feed, but Nell said she needed her sister to play propriety."

"The sister's name?"

He reflected a moment. "Amelia. She married a man called Ecclestone. She was a harpy. Always poking around and creeping in corners and scolding Nell when she thought no one would hear. I swear she'd peep through the keyhole at us when we were in bed together."

Chase jotted the information in his memorandum book. "How can I find her?"

"Ecclestone used to keep a tobacconist's shop in the Haymarket. It may still be there. I wandered into the shop some years back."

"When was the last time you saw Nell?"

"Nell? I looked in on a masquerade ball given by Jew Rex, and she was there in high spirits, queening it over the other women. Someone broke into her house later the same night and stabbed her. I suppose it might have been a robbery. She had plenty of trinkets to her name. Look, I've been very patient even though you've been damned insolent."

"I have two more questions. Was Mary Leach at the ball?"

"How do you expect me to remember? I was never on more than nodding acquaintance with Mrs. Leach, and what any of this has to do with Nell Durant is more than I can tell you." Kester got to his feet again. "Your last question? Make it quick."

Chase stood too, restoring the knife and button to his pocket. "Were you aware that Nell had given birth to a son shortly before her death?"

"It was a joke making the rounds of the clubs. She'd managed to hide her condition from poor Tallis, and he had to pension her off in a hurry. You can imagine he came in for some ridicule."

"Who was the child's father?"

"No idea, I'm afraid. She was a courtesan. What can it matter?"

"I heard it was the Regent's."

This seemed to strike him as exquisitely funny. He gave a shout of laughter. "You be careful. You don't want to repeat such malicious slander. I suppose I should be grateful Nell never claimed the brat was mine." Kester was still smiling, though the smile never reached his eyes.

"Have you heard any recent gossip about this boy? He'd be, what, about nineteen?"

"If I had, do you think I'd repeat it to you?"

"According to Mr. Hewitt, Nell's son is about to be arrested. He's the one who's been writing the seditious letters for profit and revenge. What say you, sir? Could Nell's son be the new Collatinus?"

"This boy, if he exists, could be the man in the moon, as far as I'm concerned."

Chase took a step closer to look down his nose at Kester. "What if Collatinus knows secrets someone wants to keep hidden? A reasonable motive for murder, don't you agree? The revelations in the paper would be…embarrassing. We may have further surprises from Nell's memoirs in store for us."

"Get out before I summon the porter to eject you."

Sketching a quick, ironic bow, Chase complied.

Chapter XVIII

Since that cursed paragraph's appearance, Edward Buckler had read it at least twenty times, and every time he discerned new shades of meaning, possibly even beyond the author's sly intention. Finally, on the second morning after Gander's public blast, Buckler decided that honor demanded he explain his conduct to Jeremy Wolfe, so after picking at his breakfast and dressing himself with unusual care, he took himself off to Greek Street. Buckler gave his name to the manservant and asked to speak to Wolfe, but as the servant opened his mouth to reply, the artist himself appeared, carrying several draping cloths over one arm.

"Mr. Edward Buckler to see you," said the servant.

The two men measured each other in the gloom. Outside, the day was blustery and cold, and very little light had penetrated the paneled entrance passage lit by a single wall sconce. After an awkward pause, Wolfe smiled and extended his hand. "Are you here to see my wife? She's gone out to do some shopping."

"Can you spare a few minutes, sir? I would like to see Mrs. Wolfe but had hoped to speak to you first."

The artist bowed. "Certainly. Step upstairs, and I'll show you my gallery. I am arranging a private showing. A friend comes later today to see one of my portraits." He glanced at the manservant. "Bring Madeira."

Wolfe led the way up the stairs to a large chamber at the front of the house that had once been a drawing room. Plaster busts of Greeks and Romans on pedestals overlooked the riot of color that was Wolfe's collection of portraits, placed high and low on the walls with some propped on easels. Other canvases leaned in a corner along with some stretching frames. But Buckler's attention was pulled irresistibly toward the painting hung over the chimney. He went to stand before it.

"You show good taste, Mr. Buckler. My *Psyche*, my most recent effort, my masterpiece. What do you think of it?"

"A work of genius." Buckler did not trust himself to say more, for he was gazing at Penelope with all his eyes and was afraid to think what he might reveal. Even if he did not find this man's wife impossibly beautiful, he would have admired the work. This surprised him. He was accustomed to deeming Jeremy Wolfe an utter failure of a man, an irresponsible, buffle-headed fop.

The artist looked complacent. "I agree with you, of course. I wish I had the means to tear out this hideous yellow wallpaper. It clashes. But that is not to be. Perhaps my *Psyche* will soon gain a setting more worthy of it."

"You won't sell it?" Buckler had spoken too quickly.

"Not exactly. As you are an old friend of my wife's, I don't mind owning that our affairs are in a bit of a tangle. But I have a friend willing to make me a substantial loan with *Psyche* as collateral. A decent sort, my friend. He will keep the portrait for me until I can redeem it."

Buckler was saved from having to reply by the servant entering with the wine decanter and two glasses on a tray, which he set down on the three-legged table under the window after removing some gallipots of color. After the man had poured out, Wolfe dismissed him. Seating themselves in two hard chairs, they sipped in silence a minute or two. Buckler had met Jeremy Wolfe once before in Newgate Prison, but, oddly enough, Penelope's husband had displayed a good deal more lighthearted flippancy on that occasion. This time he seemed rather subdued.

"I wanted to speak to you about the paragraph in the newspaper," said Buckler. "I was afraid you might have the wrong idea."

Wolfe grinned. "Do you intend to satisfy my honor, sir?"

"If you mean we should meet each other with pistols at dawn, no, I hadn't thought of it."

"I've no intention of calling you out even though Penelope is terribly cut up about the matter."

"I'm not surprised. I only wish there was something I could do. But perhaps Fred Gander has expended his malice and will leave her alone in future. I'd see the man myself if I didn't think I'd only make matters worse."

"There *is* something you can do for me, Buckler. You can stand my wife's friend whenever she might need you. Even if just to advise her. We both know—" Wolfe broke off to take a long pull of his wine, still gazing at *Psyche*, as if the portrait could give him the answers to his problems. Then he put down the glass and picked up a hog's-hair brush lying on the table. He inspected it, keeping his face averted. "Never mind. Will you do it?"

"I'm not sure I understand you." Buckler felt acutely uncomfortable.

"I'll ask you to keep this conversation to yourself. You know Penelope's written to the Great Man to ask about Collatinus? The thing is, she can't depend on him. He's just as likely to take *her* to task for getting herself in trouble."

"You don't get on with your father-in-law?"

"I wasn't good enough for his daughter. Well, that's the only thing he ever said I agree with. I took her away from him, and he never forgave me. You see, he had made her childhood a misery. He forced her to spend every waking moment in study and improving activities—never a bit of understanding, never any praise for her efforts, never any…love. It's no wonder she wanted to get away. And he worried her mother into an early grave."

"He was unkind to his wife?"

"Not openly from what Penelope has told me, but he let her know in a thousand small ways that he held her in contempt. She was a simple woman, daughter of a Sicilian shopkeeper. She'd been educated, but, of course, she couldn't hold her own with Sandford."

"A sad story."

"Quite. Now he's got Penelope involved in this Collatinus business."

"Do you think Sandford capable of murder?"

Jeremy Wolfe frowned. "It's possible. In a fit of passion or temper, not otherwise. I suppose any man is capable of murder under the right circumstances." He tossed the brush aside and looked Buckler full in the face. "Are you going to answer my question?"

"I will always stand her friend, Wolfe. You can rely on me."

The sound of church bells drifted on the wind, louder and softer and louder again. Rain fell from the sky, soaking the black silk mantilla that covered Penelope's head and shoulders. No one paid her any attention—the veil rendered her invisible. Years before, in Sicily, her mother had worn it to church in token of her submission to God, and on the day of her funeral, the nurse had wrapped it around Penelope and led her to the same church to say good-bye. Later she always associated that day with the odor of incense and antiquity and with a terrible fear she could not assuage.

Today she had worn the mantilla as a gesture of respect for the dead and for another reason too. From her window this morning, she'd seen the watchers lurking outside, two of them, ordinary men in heavy overcoats and hats that shadowed their faces. They weren't the journalists strutting around as if the city belonged to them; these were men who moved furtively and slouched in doorways. But she had fooled them. Using her mother's mantilla to shield her face, she had gone up the area stairs and slipped past them without being identified. They had likely thought her a kitchen maid.

Now Penelope stood on the pavement, waiting. She could smell damp wool, horse excrement, and a hint of rosemary from the bunch the old woman next to her clutched in her hand. After a while the woman called out "It's coming!" and brandished the bunch of rosemary in her fist. Two mutes appeared, their countenances suitably somber; they wore black sashes and carried crepe-covered wands. Holding their own staffs, pages in black suits and gloves followed. The pages showed far less decorum, laughing and shouting vulgar remarks to the crowd, some of them obviously inebriated. Penelope saw one of them take a long swig from a flask stored in his coat pocket and stumble on after his fellows. But the old woman didn't seem to have noticed. She looked at Penelope, wrinkled her face in glee, and pointed at the hearse, driven by six perfectly matched blacked horses, all with ostrich feather headdresses gleaming with moisture and drooping in the damp air. Bearers accompanied it, pacing slowly as they lifted the corners of the black velvet silk pall draped over the two coffins. Dryden and Mary Leach, bound together in death and soon to rest in a burial vault.

The people around Penelope were all intent on the procession, and one or two were crying, their tears mingling with the rain. The papers had reported that the outpouring of grief for Mary continued, with crowds gathering in Adelphi Terrace where the bodies had lain in a room lit by innumerable wax candles burning night and day. Mary was the gentle wife, the angel, ripped from her home and children by unimaginable evil. No one knew she had likely stabbed her own husband.

Who had killed Mary? Penelope's own father had admitted to being the long-ago Collatinus. He might have murdered Nell Durant, but he certainly hadn't killed Dryden Leach or his wife. Though Penelope had no evidence to support her theory, she felt instinctively that the same person had murdered both women. He could be a part of this crowd, watching this funeral procession. He could even be one of the mourners riding in the line of coaches. The blinds of these vehicles were drawn.

She watched as the last of the coaches rumbled through Temple Bar, the narrow, blackened gateway serving as the boundary between Westminster and the City. The cortege would proceed down Fleet Street to its destination at St. Bride's, where the funeral service and burial would take place. But Penelope would not be there to see. She waited until the crowd had thinned, then melted into the current of pedestrians, walking with her head down, the cold seeping through her half-boots, probably spoiled by this excursion.

She was almost home when she came upon an urchin hawking copies of a newspaper. He wore a tattered livery with trousers short enough to display ankles like ghostly twigs. He looked cold and miserable, but he blew his postman's horn with vigor. "Collatinus is back!" he was shouting at the top of his high, clear voice. "See for yourself. He's written another letter!"

With chilled fingers, Penelope groped to find a coin in her reticule, and a moment later she had the paper in her hand. She rushed away, eager to gain the privacy of her sitting room. She quite forgot about the watchers, only remembering them when she was taking out her key for the front door. Now she saw an agent on the opposite side of the street strolling by. He flicked a glance at her but kept going. In her anxiety Penelope fumbled at the lock but finally got the door open and stepped into the hall to find her husband with Edward Buckler. The door closed behind her with a soft click, and she shot the bolt home. Removing her veil, she smoothed her hands over the wet silk, not looking at either man.

Jeremy came forward to help her with her pelisse. "How was your shopping, my dear? Rather a dismal day, isn't it?"

Buckler stared at the newspaper tucked under her arm and said nothing.

Chapter XIX

"What do you think?" asked Edward Buckler.

Chase set aside the newspaper and leaned forward to replenish the wine in his friend's glass. He had cracked his best bottle in honor of the barrister's visit. "Collatinus grows desperate. He knows London is out for his blood and denies responsibility for the deaths of the Leaches."

"Since we have a fourth letter, we've established one fact. Mary Leach could not have been Collatinus unless someone has taken over her alias."

"A partnership? Yes, I thought of that."

Buckler studied the newspaper again. "I am intrigued by this reference to the Regent: *Let us enquire who were the confidential associates of the P_____e of W_____s at the time of N.D.'s death. They were the very dregs of society: creatures whom a person of morality could not endure; creatures capable even of murder to serve their own base interests.*"

"Men like Sir Oliver Cox, Ralph Hewitt, and George Kester?" asked Chase. "I must discover their movements on the night of Mary Leach's death."

"I had my clerk nose around in the taverns. Kester's a placeman; he's been in government service for years, the type who always manages to land on his feet. As for Hewitt, he earns a handsome salary as Paymaster of Widows' Pensions, profiting at the expense of poor widows and orphans. And I'm told he's got hold of another sinecure recently."

Chase snorted in derision. "Faithful servants of the Crown. Cox, on the other hand, is simply a rake. And Horatio Rex is unquestionably a scoundrel, though at least he makes his own way in this world. His Highness saddled him with an enormous debt years ago, so there's another royal connection for you."

"But whether Collatinus levels a specific accusation or merely a general indictment is anyone's guess," said Buckler. "What do you make of his declaration of innocence?"

"Why should I believe it? If Mary Leach was his confederate, Collatinus could have killed her to safeguard his identity. At any rate, when they catch him, the authorities will make sure he rots in prison—or execute him for murder."

"I could throttle him myself when I think of Mrs. Wolfe's situation." Buckler rose to take his leave, settling his hat on his head, donning his greatcoat, and collecting his walking stick.

Chase sent him a sharp glance. "You've seen her?"

"I've just come from Greek Street. She went to view the Leaches' funeral cortege."

"She's fortunate she didn't get her pocket picked or worse. Ruffians have been known to attack the coaches in these processions."

"Go to her, Chase. She won't sit still for long."

That was true enough, he reflected, recalling certain dealings he'd had with Penelope Wolfe in the past. He must persuade her to listen to reason this time and see how much safer it was to allow him to act for her. Thinking aloud, he said, "I need to find Nell Durant's son before the government does. If we are lucky, her sister Amelia Ecclestone will have word of him."

"Can you imagine the scandal if the Regent is, in fact, the boy's father? I lay you odds the Home Office is eager to silence him."

"Perhaps Nell gave the memoirs to her friend Mary, and Mary gave them to Nell's son."

Buckler nodded. "These memoirs may not be kind to Eustace Sandford either. There may be more scandal in store for Mrs. Wolfe."

"For God's sake, don't even hint such a thing to her."

"Do you think I would?"

"No, you'd probably try to protect her, not that she would thank you for it." Chase paused, debating whether a warning would serve in this instance. Then he decided he didn't care. Had matters been otherwise, he supposed the barrister would have made a good match for Penelope, though the knowledge gave him no particular pleasure. Casually, he said, "It cannot be, Buckler, as I'm sure you realize."

He halted in the doorway and swung round, his eyes kindling. "What the devil do you mean by that?"

"Mrs. Wolfe is a married lady and a virtuous one. Don't add to her troubles."

Watching the hand that clenched and unclenched around the walking stick, Chase thought a jab in the nose might be coming his way too, but Buckler merely responded, "I thank you for that entirely unsolicited and unnecessary advice."

Chase said no more but made a motion for Buckler to precede him into the corridor, then accompanied him down the stairs. He ignored Leo Beeks, who had contrived to be on hand.

At the door Buckler shook hands with something less than his usual cordiality. "You'll let me know what else I can do?"

"As soon as I know myself," said Chase.

Chase had scarcely settled down to parse each one of the Collatinus letters for the third time when Leo knocked at the door and put in his head. "Mr. Farley has called, sir," he said, his voice vibrating with excitement. After closely questioning Chase about his Bow Street colleagues, Leo had learned all their names. And if Farley's purple-veined cheeks and unkempt side-whiskers now proved a disappointment, the boy gave no sign of it as he ceremoniously ushered him into the room.

"Shall I ask my mother to make coffee?"

Chase knew his friend too well for that. "We'll have brandy." He went to the sideboard to pour two glasses. Observing that Leo still hesitated in the doorway, Chase straightened his spectacles and directed a quelling look in his direction. Reluctantly, he withdrew.

Farley relaxed in his chair with a sigh of relief. "Got news you'll want to hear, though I can hardly square it with my conscience to tell you. We ain't supposed to be on speaking terms, you and me. I know you, Chase. You'll be after him before I can say Jack Robinson." He gave his brandy an appreciative sniff. "How do you like being a gentleman of leisure?"

"Cut line, Farley. What news?"

"You remember Kirby? The green Runner getting above himself because the Home Office tapped him for some secret business? He was in his cups at the Brown Bear and boasting to Vickery, as was kind enough to drop a word in my ear. Bow Street's been called in to help nab Collatinus. Now what are you going to do?"

"Get there first."

Farley smiled. "I heard you was interested."

Chase sat up straighter, setting aside his glass. "Go on."

"The printer of the *Free Albion*, man called Gibbs, has turned crown witness to escape an information laid against him for seditious libel. He'll put Collatinus under hatches, you mark my words. The authorities have got Gibbs in their eye and won't thank you for spoiling their game."

"How do I find the printer?"

"Can't say. They're hiding him until it's time for the show. They're using him to bait the trap, and he'll cooperate to save his skin. When Collatinus comes to deliver his next letter, they'll clap the Jacobin in irons before he knows what's what." Farley held out his own heavy wrists in demonstration, the buttons on his waistcoat bulging.

Chase stared into the fire. "This Collatinus, what can you tell me about him?"

Farley appeared to debate his next words. "Here's an interesting thing," he said finally. "He's an educated fellow. Gibbs says Collatinus looks and talks quite the gentleman, though his clothes are well darned. And young, not more than twenty."

"What else?"

"He's the bastard son of a courtesan."

So the rumor Ralph Hewitt's wife had heard was true, thought Chase. "When and where will they take him?"

"Damn it. I'm not sure I should tell you. Bound to do something stupid." The Runner gulped the rest of his brandy, tapped his thick fingers on the table, and sighed. "Well, you've been decent to me in your way, Chase, and I ain't a man to forget that. All right then. Just don't say it come from me. Tomorrow night. The Crown and Anchor tavern. The radicals are holding a banquet. We'll get Collatinus there."

Chase was already at his writing desk, dipping his pen in the ink to write a hurried message for Packet. When he had sealed this document, he strode to the door and bellowed for Leo. "Deliver this into the hands of the barkeeper at the Brown Bear," he said when the boy had dashed up the stairs to meet him on the landing.

"Yes, sir!"

◇◇◇

The message had instructed Noah Packet to keep watch on the office of the *Free Albion* in the Dials. Chase didn't think the Home Office would suspect a common pickpocket of any interference in its plans, and Packet could be extricated should he find himself in difficulties. In the meantime, Chase had other urgent business. Nell Durant had lived in Marylebone, so he would first go there in search of her and then seek an interview with her sister Amelia Ecclestone.

When Chase entered St. Marylebone parish church, a brick edifice that struck him as unusually cramped and primitive, he found a chaotic scene presided over by a beleaguered young curate, flitting from one ceremony to the next. Two mildly odiferous corpses requiring burial were laid out in the pews near several new mothers, who waited in another pew to be churched or blessed for having survived childbirth. There was no font. Huddled around a basin on the communion table were a half-dozen baptismal sponsors, rocking wailing infants in their arms. No one, not even the curate, paid the slightest attention to the sponsors' responses to the traditional questions of the service.

Moving methodically, Chase examined the tablets and monumental inscriptions, though he didn't really expect to find evidence of Nell or her child. Churches always reminded him of his own family. In his childhood he had spent many uncomfortable hours listening to his father preach in the drafty village church. He was reminded, too, of the churchyard, where he used to stand over the graves of his tiny brothers and sisters and rail against his father for putting his mother through another ordeal of bearing and losing a child. His father hadn't approved of him either, then or later when Chase had lowered himself to join the police.

But he did locate Nell's tablet on the south wall, and as he read the inscription, the din in the church seemed to fade from his ears: *In Memory of Eleanor Durant. Her afflicted Sister Judith Ecclestone has placed this marble as a pledge of her affection. Born March 27, 1765. Died June 6, 1794. Open me the Gates of Righteousness that I may go into them and Give Thanks unto the Lord.*

A gentle voice spoke. "Good day, sir. I have come to Mr. Stapleforth's assistance. We are quite busy today, as you see. I am Augustus Lively, parish clerk. May I assist you?"

A prim, old gentleman stood smiling at him. After greeting him, Chase pointed at the memorial. "Did you know this woman, Mr. Lively?"

The clerk lifted a frail hand to finger the lettering. "Sad, she died young. I'm afraid I do not recall her, sir. Is she a member of your family?"

"No, but I am very anxious to discover word of her or her son. Will you check the parish books for me?"

A gleam of interest stole into the clerk's faded eyes. "An inheritance in dispute, perhaps?"

"On the contrary. A murder—or rather murders."

"Indeed?" Lively elevated his white brows. "You surprise me. What is your name and your interest in the matter, if I may inquire?"

Chase started to reach for his gilt-crowned tipstaff; then he remembered that, of course, it wasn't there. "My name is John

Chase. I am investigating three deaths, Nell Durant's among them. She was one of the murder victims I mentioned. My interest is purely personal, Mr. Lively. I wish to uncover the malefactor."

The clerk studied him as if attempting to read his character and motives in his face. After a pause, he said, "Come with me, sir, and we will see whether our christening record can offer any illumination."

Lively led Chase toward the back of the church and through an oak door into the small vestry. This was a damp, low-ceilinged room ringed with aged wooden presses. The clerk went to one of these cupboards and opened it with a rusted key he took from a ring at his waist. "What month and year would you like me to check?"

"The spring of 1794." Penelope had told Chase that Eustace Sandford had departed England in June of that year to elude arrest for the courtesan's murder. Nell's son would have been a few months old, he assumed.

Lively retrieved one of the registers, a heavy volume bound in dark leather, and placed it on the long deal table that ran across the room. "You wish me to look for a child born of Nell Durant?"

"If you would, yes."

Silence fell as the clerk painstakingly perused every entry in the ledger until Chase was ready to tear it out of his hands. The only sounds in the room were the old man's breathing and the rustling as he turned each page. "Nothing in March, April, or May."

Chase felt a tired disappointment. This inquiry seemed like the hydra to him: a monster with heads of wriggling snakes that grew new heads to baffle and taunt him every time he thought he might have chopped one off for good. "Check June," he suggested, not really expecting any result since Nell had died early in that month.

"Ah, here we are." Lively flipped the ledger around, pushing it across the table. "You didn't tell me the child was illegitimate," he added with a note of condemnation.

Chase reached for the book and hunched over to read the spidery hand. About halfway down the page, he found the following entry dated the 9th of June: *Lewis, son of Eleanor Durant and putative father Eustace Sandford, by the report of the child's mother base begotten. Born 27th April.*

"According to the memorial, Mrs. Durant was dead by then," said Chase hoarsely. If he had thought this situation was bad for Penelope before, it had just got much, much worse. Nell Durant and Eustace Sandford. Why should he be surprised? It seemed the woman had pursued affairs with most of the gentlemen in London. Penelope had been worried about her father's role in the courtesan's death, and unfortunately they had found no evidence to prove him innocent of this crime. But now she must face that Sandford had abandoned his own child, escaping to live a comfortable life abroad. And he had left behind his only son, Penelope's younger brother.

Lively interrupted these reflections. "It matters not that the mother had died, sir. Sponsors may bring a child to be baptized. Christians who have a babe's best interests at heart." The old gentleman peered at the record. "See here. There's an annotation in the margin. The sponsors were Edith Cantrell and Mary Rex. Does that help you, Mr. Chase?"

When Chase stepped into the crowded tobacconist's shop, he was obliged to wait his turn. Several patrons stood at the long glass counters, either sampling snuff mixtures or chatting animatedly with the proprietress. The proprietor, a hulking fellow with arms that strained at his coat, hovered nearby. He rarely addressed the customers himself but instead fetched and carried at his wife's smiling command. Often the tobacconist seemed to anticipate her needs and pop up with just the right variety as she made a recommendation to a customer.

For some minutes Chase pretended to study a pamphlet explaining the relative merits of snuff that had been rasped to a texture of "fin, demigros, or gros" and informing him that papier-mâché was the best receptacle to keep the snuff moist, though one was never to cram too much of the mixture in any container. Keeping his eyes planted on the pamphlet, he listened to Amelia Ecclestone (for he was sure this was Nell Durant's sister) converse earnestly with a dandy sporting impossibly high shirt points about the virtues of such sorts as the Prince's Mixture, Martinique, and Bolongaro. This gentleman, who took his snuff with nary a sneeze in prospect, sampled these and many more before finally making his purchases. Probably the most important decision the man would make all day, thought Chase. When the other patrons had completed their business, Mrs. Ecclestone approached him.

"Good day, sir." Her smile seemed to stretch her thin lips in a polite grimace. "I apologize for the delay. May I help you?"

"Not at all. You have a pleasant establishment here."

She curtsied. "Thank you, sir. I am Mrs. Ecclestone, wife of the proprietor."

"Is there a Mr. Hanson too? I saw his name on the sign outside."

"Passed on, I'm afraid. It's just the two of us and a shopboy."

Standing closer to her, Chase saw that she had never been a beauty even in her youth, which was long past. Her chin was too weak, her brow too heavy over smallish blue eyes, her nose too pronounced. And yet he thought her face compelling in its mercurial movement, its constantly shifting emotions. "I'll ask you to show me some of your snuff. The gentleman who just left seemed highly knowledgeable, but you'll need to offer me more advice."

A faint contempt communicated itself in the downward sweep of her eyelashes, but it was gone so fast Chase might have imagined it. "If you are a beginner, sir, you will want something rather mild. I can also show you some snuffboxes."

As the proprietor moved away in quest of the snuff, Chase said, "A gentleman recommended your shop to me, ma'am. A Mr. George Kester."

She looked surprised. "Oh, indeed? I've not seen Mr. Kester in years. He is well?"

"Quite well. He mentioned that he was once acquainted with you and your sister."

Ecclestone's bustling hands stilled, and he shot a warning look at his wife. After a pause, she answered in a high-pitched voice. "Yes, Nell had many friends among the *ton*."

"Your sister's death was a tragedy, ma'am."

Passing a hand across her forehead, she stepped back from the counter, putting distance between them. "Why do you ask about Nell?"

"Because I mean to know who killed her. I'm sure you've heard that another woman, Mrs. Dryden Leach, has recently been murdered. The two crimes are connected."

The proprietor stumped forward to place several jars of snuff on the counter, pouring out a small amount of each variety on a cloth and pushing a handkerchief at Chase. "You wish to try the snuff or not? Use the wipe to protect your neck-cloth." His accent was considerably less refined than his wife's.

"Certainly." As Chase had seen the dandy do, he took a pinch from one of the piles, brought it to his nose, and inhaled—an entirely disagreeable sensation in his opinion. He dusted his upper lip with the handkerchief. "I need to talk to you about Nell Durant," he told Mrs. Ecclestone.

"You a journalist?" demanded Ecclestone.

"No. I have a friend concerned in the matter. Her father is Eustace Sandford." He watched them both carefully to see if they recognized the name and was rewarded when he observed Mrs. Ecclestone's slight stiffening.

"All that is long buried. There's no call to resurrect it."

"I'm afraid there is, ma'am." He removed the knife from his pocket and showed it to her. "This was found in Mary Leach's bedroom. It belonged to Nell, didn't it?"

They stared at the knife but made no move to touch it. "It was Nell's," admitted Mrs. Ecclestone. "She must have given it to Mary after—"

"After the Prince abandoned her?"

"He never met his obligations to her, and she had debts. Perhaps she sold it to Mary. Lord knows, they always had their heads together, those two."

An angry flush mottled the proprietor's cheeks. Before he could interrupt, Amelia Ecclestone said quickly, "A day doesn't go by that I don't grieve for my sister, but we don't want any trouble. It's bad enough that monster never paid for what he did to her."

"Who, ma'am?"

"Your friend's father, Eustace Sandford. He was the one. That I always said and will go to my grave saying. I would have been a witness against him in court, but he turned tail and ran."

Chase felt his pulse accelerate. Could this woman be telling the truth? "What evidence do you have?"

"Why, I was in the house the night she died. I heard Mr. Sandford's knock and saw him in the hall. I went to bed, but I heard them shouting at each other. I found Nell the next morning, stabbed to the heart…the blood, you can't imagine what it did to me to see that sight."

"You lived with your sister?"

"I was Nell's housekeeper. Oh, she lived a fine life while it lasted, but she'd have been better off without her fancy liveried servants and her silly opera box hung in pink satin. Nell thought she could turn everyone up sweet. She thought no one could resist her." Mrs. Ecclestone was practically spitting her words, her voice rising higher. "Better to dine on a single joint of mutton at home and live in peace, I always said. Money ran through her fingers like sand. She was always in debt, always worried about being put out in her shift one day. She was spared that much at least."

Jealousy and rancor and rage had passed in quick succession over her mobile features rather like a summer squall at sea, but now her mouth drooped in sadness. Glancing at Ecclestone, Chase saw that he stood with fists clenched, not looking at either of them. Did the tobacconist resent his wife's preoccupation with Nell Durant? It seemed that Nell was a third person in their marriage.

Amelia Ecclestone added more quietly, "She used to say she'd never be wholly at any man's disposal. But they owned her, body and soul, every one of them."

"What happened on the night of the murder?"

"She'd gone to a masquerade ball dressed as a shepherdess, and I knew the gentlemen would be after her in droves. Still, she came home early just before midnight. She went into her sitting room, told me to go away. All she would say was she'd had a quarrel."

"She didn't tell you what it was about?"

She regarded Chase coldly. "She kept her own counsel. It was no good my asking her to confide in me."

Ecclestone reached out to slam his hand on the counter, and the two little piles of snuff went flying. "That's enough. Have you made your selection, sir?"

Chase remembered Kester's remark about Amelia Ecclestone prying and listening at doors. He ignored her husband. "You must have some notion of what Eustace Sandford wanted that night. Midnight seems a strange time to visit a lady."

An odd smile lit her face. "Not for them two."

"They were lovers?"

Her eyes glinted in triumph, and when she spoke again, her voice dripped venom. "They were lovers, all right. I'm sure he killed her because he got jealous of the other men sniffing around. I never saw a man more enamored. Or maybe he finally realized that she cared only for herself. She would betray him and his Jacobin friends as fast as she'd change her silk stockings."

It was Chase's turn to draw back, disconcerted by her savagery. "Did you hear Sandford leave the house, ma'am?"

"I told you. I went to bed. He was the last person to see her alive."

"Did you know your sister had written her memoirs? What happened to the manuscript after her death?"

"It wasn't among her effects. She must have given it away or sold it to someone."

"And Nell's child? She had recently given birth to a son, I understand. Where is he?"

"Dead. Nell had sent him to be cared for by a widow, who took the babe into her family for a few extra coins to feed her own children. He was a puling little creature. He died the month after the murder. It was a relief to me. I wanted no reminders."

"Did the Prince of Wales father this child?"

She shrugged. "Nell said so, but it doesn't matter, does it?"

"Do you recall the widow's name?"

Her eyes shifted away, and she moistened her lips with her tongue. "It's a long time ago, sir. I've forgotten."

Chase said softly, "You're a liar, ma'am. Your nephew Lewis Durant is alive and well. Suppose you tell me the truth."

Goggling at him like a sheep about to get its throat cut, she swallowed and gulped. "Alive? Why, what can you mean?"

"When was the last time you saw Durant? I need to find him."

Ecclestone wrapped an arm about his wife's shaking shoulders. "Get out of my shop before I land you a facer."

"In a moment." Chase turned back to Mrs. Ecclestone. "Tell me what I need to know, and I'll leave you alone. Why did you lie?"

"I…I…men came round asking questions the other day."

"What men? And what did you tell them?"

Her husband spoke for her. "They were from the police. We didn't tell them nothing for the simple reason that we don't know where the boy is. Amelia's not seen him since he was a babe."

Mrs. Ecclestone nodded. "It's all Mary's fault. It was her idea to lie. We told everyone the child had died. She said he'd be safer that way."

"Who was the father?" Chase held her gaze to be sure she told the truth this time.

She was crying hard, her face flushed and distorted. "Who do you think it was? It was that villain Eustace Sandford, that's who."

Chapter XX

As the light faded from the sky, Chase waited on the street outside Penelope's house. He had come here for the first time nearly a fortnight ago, and he could not then have imagined that he would be steeling his nerve to tell Penelope she had a brother—a brother about to be arrested and tried for seditious libel and murder. John Chase had always believed in plain dealing. Telling someone an unpalatable truth had never bothered him. If he were honest, he would admit he often relished such telling. But this was Penelope Wolfe. She had been hurt by this business, and he must add to her burdens. Standing there, Chase was aware of the watchers that lurked in the shadows. He couldn't see them, didn't know where they were, but he knew they were there. Let them look, he thought. What could they see? A man hesitating before he knocked at a door, no more than that. He reached up and banged the knocker defiantly.

When Maggie Foss opened the door, her face split into a smile. "Mr. Chase! Come in, and I'll let Mrs. Wolfe know you're here."

"Are the other servants occupied, Maggie? I'd expect you to be with the children."

"We got no servants anymore, sir. Mrs. Pen turned them all off and with full wages for the quarter too. We come into some funds from Mr. Jeremy's painting, but what must she do but throw good money away?"

Chase absorbed this news, understanding its significance. "Is Mr. Wolfe at home?" He had decided it might be wise to have Jeremy Wolfe on hand to support and comfort his wife if he could be counted on for that much.

"He's out, sir. If you'll come with me, I'll light you to the sitting room." She lit a candle from a lamp on the hall table and conducted him down the passage to the room where he had sat with Penelope before. Once inside, Maggie built up the fire and excused herself. "I'll fetch Mrs. Wolfe and make some tea, sir."

Moving to the hearth to warm his hands, Chase thanked her, feeling strangely nervous—which was utterly unlike him. To relieve his feelings, he seized the poker and drove it into the pile of coals, sending flames roaring up the chimney.

Penelope came in. "I told Mr. Buckler I was anxious to speak to you, but I had hardly dared hope you would come so soon."

He took her hands. "Of course, I came, Mrs. Wolfe. Maggie is bringing us some tea. Shall we wait until it arrives before we have our talk?"

She released him, stepping back to study him. "What is it? I can see you have something to tell me. Don't keep me in suspense."

Chase was busy mocking his own stupidity. What had made him think he could be two minutes in the same room with this woman without her detecting there was news? She had always been perceptive and annoyingly forthright, and she was looking at him now with more than a hint of impatience in her brown eyes. Stubbornly, he waited until Maggie had come in with the tea-tray and some cakes. Realizing how hungry he was, he ate a few cakes and used the delay to marshal his forces.

Too polite a hostess to challenge him while he refreshed himself, Penelope waited but seemed incapable of small talk. She left the plate of cakes untouched, sipping her tea and observing his every move.

Finally, Chase swallowed a tasteless bite and launched into a rather disjointed description of his interview with Amelia Ecclestone, emphasizing that he found her an untrustworthy witness and he himself did not credit her accusations against Sandford. Penelope did not react, and he forced himself to come to the heart of the matter. "I've also been this afternoon to the church of St. Marylebone. I was seeking Nell Durant in the parish records. You recall that she lived there prior to her death?"

"Mr. Rex told you that?"

"Yes."

"And what did you discover?"

"I found a memorial erected by her sister Mrs. Ecclestone and an entry in the parish's christening record. It says Nell's child was illegitimate, as we knew already. According to this record, the babe was called Lewis. He was baptized in the church in June of '94, a few days after her death and around the time you and your father left London. I checked for a death record, but there wasn't one. Nell's son is still alive."

He held up one finger to forestall the eager words trembling on her lips. "There's more, Mrs. Wolfe. Today a colleague from Bow Street brought me word that the Home Office has identified Collatinus as Nell Durant's son. The authorities are preparing to lure him into a trap. He will likely be in custody by tomorrow night."

"Why do you look like that? You seem afraid to speak. It's not like you, Mr. Chase." She was getting nervous, and he heard a hint of accusation in her tone.

He took a breath and plunged on. "When a child is baseborn, often the father's name is not indicated in the record, but in this case the clergyman recorded it. Though it's possible this information is not accurate, I've had confirmation from another source."

"Nell claimed the Prince of Wales was the father of her child."

"She was in debt. I believe she invented the story to seek her own advantage and obtain financial compensation."

"If it wasn't the Prince, then who?"

Chase reached across the table to grasp her hand. It was a small hand, sturdy and elegantly formed, a hand that would be deft about its daily tasks and gentle to a child in illness. He held it firmly. "The record states that your father sired this babe, Mrs.

Wolfe. As I said before, this information may not be accurate, but if it is, then Lewis Durant is your brother—or rather your half-brother."

Her face went white. "My brother? I have a brother, and he is Collatinus? Are you telling me he is guilty of killing Mary Leach? At least we know he couldn't have killed his mother. No, it seems that honor belongs to my father."

"Drink your tea."

For once, she obeyed him. She dropped his hand and sat in silence while she drank the tea, holding the fragile cup so tightly he was afraid she might shatter it. Finally, she said, "Did my father know about this child?"

"I don't know."

"What are we to do?"

Ah, the question she was bound to ask. He only wished he had a better answer. Chase told her that he hoped to obtain more information before the rendezvous at the Crown and Anchor and would try to locate Lewis Durant before the Home Office did. She listened, a faraway look in her eyes. Some color had returned to her cheeks, but he could see a rapid pulse beating at her throat.

She interrupted him as he was laying out a plan to prevent the arrest or arrange for Lewis' defense if they were unsuccessful. "I am certain my father knew about this child," she said. "One night when he was drunk—the time he told me about Collatinus—he made a remark I didn't understand. He said the worst thing he'd ever done was to abandon an innocent. At the time I thought he meant *her*, his mistress, the woman he had injured."

"I will do what I can for the boy. I promise you."

"He's not even twenty," she murmured in wonder. She sat up straighter in her chair and seemed to banish the mists from her brain. "Yes, we must help him, Mr. Chase."

After Chase departed, Penelope sat at a table in front of the fire, spooning up soup from a bowl. Maggie asked no questions but simply bustled about, delivering a low-voiced monologue about the naughtiness of the children, the chill of the evening, and any other commonplace topic that rose to her lips. She didn't seem to expect any response, so Penelope allowed her thoughts to wander.

For years she had banished her memories of the days when she was five years old and always afraid. Her father had gone out a great deal, leaving her with a young maid called Laura, whom Penelope detested with every fiber of her small being. She cried for her mother and stormed at her father. She tormented herself with jealousy of the people who took him away from her, whose company he seemed to prefer. In retrospect, this conduct astonished her, for in later years she would never have dared flout his authority. She had dared then because she somehow understood he was absorbed in some private drama all his own. With a child's simple logic she decided that her father had broken his promise to be everything to her in her mother's absence. Memory suddenly assailed her, and she saw him standing in front of the glass in their dreary lodgings, as he adjusted his domino and secured a mask to cover his face. He had gone to the masquerade ball to see Nell Durant, she realized. And afterward, said Amelia Ecclestone, he'd followed Nell to her house in Marylebone…

Penelope set down her spoon. She would not believe he had lain with a woman, put a child in her belly, then raped and murdered her—just as she would not believe Lewis, a boy not quite nineteen, capable of beating Mary Leach to death with his fists. The world would say the father had killed the one woman and the son, cut from the same infidel cloth, the other. Penelope had been upset when Fred Gander published his nasty insinuations about her in the newspaper, but how small a matter that seemed as she sat brooding over her father and Lewis Durant.

When Jeremy came in about an hour later, she got to her feet, pasting a pleasant smile on her face. "Have you dined? There's not much, but I can give you some bread and cheese."

He went to lean against the mantelshelf, his posture elaborately casual. "I've eaten. Is Sarah asleep?"

She looked at him curiously. "Hours ago. She was asking for you, but I told her you'd be out late. You can see her in the morning." Her instincts prickled. "Is something wrong, Jeremy?"

"No, nothing. What should be wrong?"

"I don't know." Watching him closely, she sat down again in her chair. "You seem worried. Did you have a good day?"

In an instant he had lurched across the room to throw himself to his knees and bury his face in her lap. As her hand went out automatically to caress his hair, he began to shake with sobs.

"I'm sorry," he said when he could command his voice. He lifted his head, and she was appalled by his expression of agony. For one wild moment, she thought he had come to tell her that Lewis Durant had been arrested or even killed. But then she perceived how foolish this was and felt an angry impatience. He was about to treat her to more of his dramatics—on this night of all nights. Any impulse she had to tell him her own news evaporated immediately.

"What is it?" When she reached out to touch his shoulder, he turned his head away.

"I cannot stay here, Penelope. One of my creditors has taken out a writ, and I will have the bailiffs at my heels tomorrow. There are debts I cannot pay."

"We'll pawn your watch or my pearls and settle them that way."

He forced a weak laugh. "A mere drop in the ocean. I am bankrupt, my dear. They'll take it all, everything we possess, and arrest me into the bargain. I can do nothing to prevent them."

"How much?"

"I don't know for sure. The creditors can claim nine hundred or a thousand pounds of me. Maybe more."

Penelope's hand dropped back to her lap. "How can you owe so much?" she said blankly. She could have told him to a penny the total of the household bills she'd struggled with for weeks, but Jeremy's response made clear how foolish she had been to think she could salvage the wreckage. Roughly, she took his chin in her hand to stare into his eyes. "What about your friend Mr. Rex? He will help you. You must go to him."

"I tried. He won't even see me. I'm finished." His voice broke. "The only thing I can do for you and Sarah is get away and save you the disgrace."

Pushing him aside, Penelope got to her feet and took a few steps across the hearthrug. "You will leave me to face the bailiffs by myself?"

"You know you can't be held responsible for my obligations. If I could do any good here, I would stay, but I will only end up rotting in prison. There will be other creditors—too many of them. I'll never find a way to satisfy them all. What's worse, I have debts of honor. I am ruined, Penelope. I'll never hold up my head again."

"Gaming debts? How could you? What about me and Sarah?"

Seeming to realize that he cut an absurd figure on his knees, he stumbled back to his feet. Shame seemed to rise in his throat and choke him with harsh, ugly sobs. After he had himself under control, he said, "I can't ask you to come with me. But I swear I'll send for you and the child as soon as I can put a roof over your heads."

"Where will you go?" She heard her own voice from a distance. Her anger had died; she felt nothing. Later she would cry for Sarah's inevitable confusion and grief. Now she merely wanted to get out of the room.

"I don't know. I suppose I could go to Calais and let the French arrest me instead—or maybe I'll returnt o Ireland. Somewhere I won't be known."

He raised his arms to embrace her, but she stepped out of his grasp and went to the door. "Go and kiss your daughter good-bye, Jeremy."

Chapter XXI

Late in the afternoon of a blustery day, Chase and Buckler had the porch of St. Clement Dane to themselves. As they conversed in low tones, both men huddled in their greatcoats, and when Buckler stepped out of the building to envisage the lay of the land, the shrill March wind bent back the brim of his beaver hat, threatening to rip it from his head. Hastily, he withdrew to give his attention to Chase's terse instructions.

Across the Strand lay the enormous Crown and Anchor tavern, stretching over an entire block behind the houses and shop-fronts on the southern side of the street. The guests had already begun to pour into the tavern's dining room to attend a reform dinner, where countless glasses would be raised to the Princess of Wales and the cause of English liberty. Lewis Durant, attempting to deliver the final Collatinus letter, would be somewhere in the crowd. Chase wished he had succeeded in preventing this meeting, but at least Packet had obtained a description of Durant from a printer's devil, an apprentice he had managed to question at the office of the *Free Albion*.

Chase studied the barrister, thinking that Buckler looked a trifle overexcited, too likely to respond without calculation. It was always like this with civilians who were useful but possibly risky allies—not that there was any choice this time. "Noah Packet will be somewhere nearby. He will try to warn Durant. You must stand on Arundel Street in case Durant comes that way."

"How will I recognize him?"

"Longish, curly dark hair and brown eyes. Tall. Slender. He has an aquiline nose and a pleasant voice. Looks the gentleman but purse-pinched."

"What should I do if I see him first? I don't want to scare him off."

"Tell him he's walking into a trap. Tell him he has a sister who wants to help him escape the city. That should get his attention."

"Right," said Buckler. "What time does the dinner start?"

"Five. The constables and patrol officers will position themselves as soon as the crowd provides some cover. They'll wait until Durant approaches Gibbs with the letter; then they'll make the arrest."

"Where will you be?"

"Initially in the vestibule outside the dining room. I'll station myself behind one of the columns. Thorogood will be inside the dining room, standing ready to give the signal if Durant slips past us somehow. Thorogood's presence won't raise any eyebrows?"

Buckler smiled. "Thieves' attorney, they call him. He's known to be reform minded. Chase—"

"Yes?"

"You'll take care Thorogood doesn't put himself in harm's way? I promised Hope I'd see to his safety."

"Pluck to the backbone, eh? Never fear. I'll watch him." Chase extended his hand. "Good luck, Buckler. Let's get this right for Mrs. Wolfe's sake."

Chase crossed the Strand, traversing a narrow passageway cut between two shops to reach the front of the tavern, an immense structure of four stories. His eyes measured the arched windows on the ground before scanning the iron balconies on the first floor. After he had walked up and down the street a few times to impress the geography of the area on his memory, he entered the stone-paved lobby, which was illumined by a huge overhead lantern and ringed by a gallery. Men were going up and down the staircase to the upper floors. Other men, laughing and talking, paced the lobby. Chase strolled over to position himself in the shadow of one of the enormous Doric columns near the entrance to the dining room. He watched the room filling up, no one paying him the least attention. Every time a publicly recognized guest made his entrance, cheers erupted.

As a mass of humanity streamed into the building, Chase was surprised by the obvious respectability of many of the radicals; there were well-dressed swells along with other men who had the look of tailors, butchers, or carpenters. And mingling among the guests were men Chase recognized: nearly a dozen Bow Street patrolmen and a clutch of men from Great Marlborough Street, as well as Bow Street Runner Victor Kirby, who came in alone, his arms resting nonchalantly over the pockets that held his pistols. Reading Kirby's intent look and confident gait, Chase felt his isolation keenly. If any of the officers spotted him and realized he was trying to throw a rub in their way, they would call him a Judas. And yet Dugger Farley had taken a sizable risk to tell him about this trap. Chase would not forget his loyalty.

Damn. This would not go well if Packet and Buckler failed to catch Lewis Durant outside, and it would be easy to miss him in this crowd. Chase's worry grew. He made sure his queue was well tucked up out of sight under his hat and averted his face, trying to slouch like a bored porter or some other menial employed by the tavern.

After a while, Ezekiel Thorogood walked by, arm-in-arm with another man. Smiling broadly, Thorogood chatted with his friend in robust tones. The two men promenaded a short way across the lobby and disappeared into the main room, but Thorogood's slight nod at Chase told him the lawyer had noted his presence there next to the column. For a long time nothing else broke the monotony of the wait. The anxious minutes stretched to an hour, then two, and Chase started to think perhaps Lewis Durant would not come at all. In which case they would just have to find him and convince him to flee London as his father had before him.

The after-dinner toasts had commenced. After each speaker, voices roared with approval or bellowed, "Kick the rogues out."

Chase, growing more and more restless, mused that if he were Durant, this would be the moment he'd choose to make his move, when the guests' tongues had been loosened by wine and everyone's focus was on the toasts and the speeches to follow. Chase slipped inside the dining room.

A confused impression of blazing light, clinking glasses, and clamorous voices overwhelmed him, but he quickly absorbed the contours of the room, which was dominated by fireplaces at either end. A door, through which waiters moved to and fro bearing laden trays, gave access to the kitchen. His eyes picked out a few of the patrolmen and officers ranged around the expansive chamber, sitting among the hundreds of diners or lounging against the walls, and he knew there must be more agents he would not recognize. Victor Kirby stood quite near Ezekiel Thorogood, who was up to stretch his legs again, plying his walking stick energetically and engaging anyone who came in his way. Thorogood tossed a remark to a small, gray-haired man in a drab coat, sitting at a table near one of the fireplaces. This, Chase thought, must be Samuel Gibbs, editor of the *Free Albion*. Chase had seen the man jump like a rabbit and stare glassy-eyed into Thorogood's beaming countenance as the lawyer passed with his measured pace. The journalist looked ready to jump out of his skin.

The current speaker, winding to the climax of his toast, suddenly shouted, "To the people, the only source of legitimate power, not to be subdued by the forces of tyranny!"

Applause and cheers broke out, and five hundred glasses lifted into the air. Gibbs rose with the others, stepping behind a cluster of guests. When Chase shifted to get a better view of the journalist, he was startled by a voice in his ear. "You part of this business?"

He turned to confront a member of the Bow Street patrol, a man named Ellis. "Just an observer," he said coolly. "None of my bread and butter this time."

"I ain't seen you around lately. Where've you been?"

Chase held the man's gaze, addressing the patroller in his lordliest tone. "I've been busy. Don't make a stir, Ellis."

Giving him a skeptical look, the patroller sidled away, but unfortunately this brief distraction had been enough for Chase to miss the approach of a dark-haired young man, now tapping Samuel Gibbs on the shoulder. Hemmed in by the table at his back, Gibbs had nowhere to retreat, and he cowered in fear. Lewis Durant, however, seemed unaware of his danger. He continued to speak earnestly to the journalist while his hand fumbled at the pocket of his coat. Ezekiel Thorogood finished his stroll in one direction and turned back. An anxious expression on his face, he glanced toward the door.

Suddenly, from behind Chase, someone called, "Watch yourself, Kirby. He's got a weapon." He had no time to try to place this teasingly familiar voice from the crowd because he was already running.

One of the other constables shouted, "We are peace officers. Lay down your arms."

Chase sprinted toward Durant, knowing he wouldn't get there in time. Chairs scraped across floorboards, and panicked voices cried out. Lewis Durant froze, his hand still inside his coat. Metal glinted in the candlelight as Victor Kirby, standing not five feet away, raised his pistol. Durant took one step away from Gibbs—a single step that gave the Runner a clear shot. But Thorogood was there. He leaned forward, sweeping up his cane in a fluid motion to strike the barrel of the pistol. It exploded, and the bullet lodged in the carved flowers on the ceiling.

Kirby was reaching for his second pistol when Chase pushed him aside. Wrapping his arms around Durant to form a shield, he forced him face down over the table, holding his own body against the boy's to keep him still; next he yanked his wrists behind him and rapidly searched his narrow frame, thrusting his hands in Durant's coat pockets. When his fingers encountered a sheet of paper, Chase grabbed it and shoved it down the waistband of his own trousers, praying no one had seen. Finally, he put on the handcuffs.

"No weapons found," he announced in a loud voice. Turning the boy over, he stared into Durant's frightened, defiant eyes. "You are my prisoner."

Only then did Chase turn to face the men gathered around them. Victor Kirby was glaring at him murderously, and Ezekiel Thorogood had stationed himself, arms akimbo, at Lewis Durant's side. The cane that had spoiled Kirby's shot was now tucked under the lawyer's arm.

Before anyone could speak, Thorogood laid a hand on the boy's shoulder and pressed down hard to silence him. Then he said, "I am watching you, Mr. Chase. Be more gentle with my client."

Eyelids lowered, Psyche reclined on her gold brocade couch, framed by scarlet drapery. Incongruously, this couch had been placed in a garden so that Psyche's delicate sandaled feet were cushioned on a bed of verdant green. Her golden butterfly dangled from a chain wrapped around her waist, and the artist had added a second charm: a tiny dagger hinting at Jacobins and French assassins. Words streamed from her lips: *"My Cupid has abandoned me. Oh, how shall I achieve my quest and save Collatinus?"* Above her head, Princess Caroline in the guise of Aphrodite floated on a cloud, her pendulous breasts spilling from a low-cut gown. She exclaimed, *"Drat that girl. I'm far, far more beautiful than she. 'Twill be all her doing if Collatinus is hanged. I can't allow my fat guts husband to triumph over me!"*

At Psyche's feet, an army of black-gowned ants toiled across the grass, carting off a horde of golden coins. The red-haired ant leading this procession remarked: *"I'll sort your grains for you, Psyche. Let me serve you, lovely one."* And to the right of Psyche's dark head, an eagle (or was it a vulture?) bore in its beak a flask of water from the River Styx. *"I will go to hell and back for you, my dear!"* it croaked as its queue of graying hair, tied up in crimson ribbon, wafted in the breeze. And, last, a masked man in a swirling black cloak could be seen in one corner, tiptoeing away. Clutching a letter in one hand and a dagger in the other, he hissed, *"I am innocent, but I'll be hanged yet."*

This was "Psyche's Quest," a satirical print making its appearance on the day after Lewis Durant had been examined at Bow Street and committed to stand trial for the murders of the Leaches. Edward Buckler was walking down St. Jame's Street when he came upon a huddle of mechanics and artisans clustered around a print-shop window. Excusing himself politely, Buckler edged into the middle of the group and gazed at "Psyche," displayed in a position of honor among an array of other prints. Around him the men exchanged wild speculation about Collatinus and his shadowy allies, said to have hatched a radical conspiracy to discredit the government and murder supporters like Dryden Leach. As for Leach's wife, one of the mechanics repeated a rumor that the villain Collatinus had played on her sympathies and lured her into a clandestine relationship, the better to strike at her husband. Opinions varied as to the strength of the evidence against Durant in the matter of Mary Leach's murder. Not that it mattered. After all, they mused, a man could only be hanged once. Everyone agreed that, one way or the other, Lewis Durant was doomed. The masked man in the print was deemed a particularly clever touch.

It was not hard for Buckler to detect Fred Gander's malicious hand somewhere behind "Psyche's Quest," its release timed to coincide with the shocking news that Durant was Eustace Sandford's son—and Penelope Wolfe's brother. Buckler was amazed at how well informed Gander and his colleagues seemed to be. Who was Gander's source? And Buckler wondered too how John Chase would feel about his role in this satire. For his own part, he supposed he'd rather be portrayed as a greedy lawyer-ant than as something even more ridiculous.

But how the devil had the caricaturists gained access to the *Psyche* portrait? Perhaps the so-obliging friend who had made Jeremy Wolfe a loan had allowed a print artist to copy the portrait in order to recoup his capital. No doubt the artist had recognized the profit potential in a story with all the elements of melodrama, especially now that Lewis Durant could be counted on to entertain Londoners for days to come. After a while, the men drifted away, and Buckler went inside the shop. He laid a half-crown on the counter, slipped his copy of "Pysche's Quest" in his leather case, and went on his way.

As she waited for Buckler in Greek Street, Penelope was wishing for her father's presence so that someone else could make the necessary decisions. But her letter would not have reached Sicily yet. Her father could not help her. She was alone. Jeremy was gone—again—and she had found a brother, perhaps only to lose him to ignominious death. She could not allow Lewis Durant to die without doing her best to save him, let the newspapers make of her actions what they would. After all, she reflected, what had prudence ever done for her? She had made one impulsive mistake in choosing a husband, and it seemed that her whole life ever since had been about atoning for this error. She would not shrink from Lewis for fear of making another mistake.

At the conclusion of the magistrates' examination, she had been given no chance to speak to him. The constables hustled him off from the unruly crowd to transport him to Newgate Prison, where he would be held until his trial. Thorogood and Buckler accompanied Lewis to make arrangements for his accommodation while Chase escorted Penelope home.

Treating her with a patience that surprised and touched her, he had stayed with her for several hours, conversing rationally with her about the case. Together they would fight for Lewis. He would uncover the truth of these murders, Buckler and Thorogood would mount the criminal defense, and none of them would rest until her brother was free. Believing him, Penelope had been comforted. When they were finished making their plans, they put the letter Chase had snatched from Lewis' pocket on the fire, standing side by side to watch it burn. Collatinus' farewell. Ironically, it contained no new revelations, as if Lewis had run out of inspiration, but it ended thus: *I break my charms and take my leave. Here my vengeance dies. I still the mutinous winds to peace and calm dread rattling thunder.* Collatinus, it seemed, was a literary man. He had appropriated Prospero's forgiveness of his enemies and abandonment of his magical powers. Collatinus had checked his thunderbolt of scandal.

Penelope heard a knock at the front door and lifted a hand, straightening her hair and smoothing the cuffs of her morning gown. Then she looked up in some surprise as Maggie rushed in to seize the fireplace poker.

"Where is Mr. Buckler?" said Penelope.

"It ain't him, mum. The bailiffs are here." She quit the room abruptly.

Penelope hurried after her. When she caught up, Maggie was screaming through the door for the bailiffs to go away before she had the law on them.

"No, Maggie." Putting her aside, Penelope unbolted the lock and motioned the two men into the hall.

"You are here to see my husband?" She tried to speak calmly.

"Yes, ma'am," said one of the bailiffs, a fresh-faced, anxious young man. "We are here to execute a writ on the person of Jeremy Wolfe. Is he at home?" He proffered his writ, as if afraid it might scald her fingers.

Penelope took it. "He has gone out of town, and I can't say when he'll return. Is it the matter of a debt?"

The other bailiff showed a hard, watchful expression. "That's just about it, ma'am. You'll understand why we need to see for ourselves." He glanced at his companion meaningfully. "Stay with them, Tom."

Nervously, Tom eyed the poker in Maggie's white-knuckled grip. When Penelope saw how the Irishwoman's baleful stare unnerved him, she intervened. "Go upstairs, Maggie, and stay with the children."

"You want me to leave you alone with *him*?" She pointed with the poker.

"Yes," Penelope snapped. "Do as you're told for once."

Maggie withdrew, hurt and worry evident in every line of her stiff form. Penelope, left with the younger bailiff, heard her stamping up the stairs and calling to the children, who were upstairs in the nursery. "Your partner won't find my husband, sir. He really is gone, and I don't think he'll be back for some months. What will you do then?"

Tom kept his eyes fixed on the wall over her shoulder. "We have a writ to execute for your goods and chattel, ma'am. We'll take an inventory. The goods are to be sold at auction."

"All our possessions must be sold to satisfy the debts?"

"Yes, ma'am."

"Not our personal belongings? My clothing? My daughter's toys?"

"Everything. You understand, ma'am? We must do our duty."

"I have one or two pieces of jewelry I inherited from my mother. You won't take those?"

At this, the man called Tom lowered his eyes to hers. "Go upstairs and pack a valise. Don't be greedy now. Just a few of your dresses, toilet articles, and the child's things. And the jewelry you mentioned, one or two pieces, mind. You set aside the valise before we take our inventory, and tell your maid to gather her traps too."

"Yes, thank you." She offered him a small bow and fled up the stairs.

She came down again half an hour later to find Buckler in Jeremy's gallery with the bailiffs. Holding the writ in his hand, he was discussing the appropriate valuation of the paintings in this room as well as the ones stored next door in the painting room. As she entered, Penelope overheard him giving the bailiffs the name of an art dealer to give to the auctioneer's clerk, and the stern bailiff was noting this information in his memorandum book. When Buckler became aware of her presence, he broke off to address her.

"Good day, Mrs. Wolfe. I've explained to these men that I am your legal counsel. Unfortunately, their writs are quite in order, ma'am, so we must ensure a fair valuation of your household effects. That is the best way to assist your husband under these distressing circumstances."

Penelope felt ready to sink with shame, but she answered him with composure. "Thank you, sir. Your advice is most appreciated."

"Come, I think we can rely on these men to carry on with their duty. We will discuss your position and determine an appropriate course of action." He nodded at the stern bailiff. "You've finished in the rear of the house?"

"Yes, sir."

Buckler and Penelope went together to the sitting room. He closed the door behind them and stood near the mantel. "I'm afraid we won't stop this seizure, Mrs. Wolfe. You must secure your private papers and prepare yourself for an auction. This will be no place for Sarah with strangers tramping through to prod and pry and gape. You will find new lodgings?"

"Do I have a choice? We cannot pay anymore. In truth, this house oppresses me."

"Your father will help you?"

"If I care to ask him, he will."

"He's too far away to offer immediate assistance. Don't you have some cousins residing in Brook Street? Could you pay them a visit for a few weeks?" He stood watching her, his gaze never leaving her face. "Whatever you decide, you must know that I will not see you or Sarah in want."

The effort to smile was painful. "My cousins did not approve of my father before the extent of his radical activities was generally known, so they can hardly wish to acknowledge me now. They are eminently respectable. At all events, I am too accustomed to my independence to relish hanging on anyone's sleeve." Stepping briskly to her desk, she threw open one of the drawers. Not looking at him, she pulled out the stacks of papers, the pens, the ink jars, and the glove with the hole in it that she'd been meaning to mend. And the bills, those endless, ever mounting bills that had so tormented her. "They'll need an inventory of these," she said, wafting them in her hand.

Buckler took one step toward her. "Where is your husband?"

Penelope put down the bills. Slowly, she approached him, and his arms came out to enfold her. They looked somberly into one another's eyes for a moment; then Buckler lowered his head to kiss her. When he broke the embrace a long time later, there were tears on Penelope's cheeks.

She answered his question. "He's gone. Jeremy is gone, and I'm glad. I don't ever want to see him again." Buckler had retrieved his handkerchief and was drying her tears, pressing on her cheeks with a quick, light pressure that managed to feel both uncertain and urgent. His other arm still rested at her waist. Reluctantly, she drew away. "His absence cannot matter to us, Edward."

"I know, my love."

"What can we do?"

"Nothing for now. Will you go to the Thorogoods?"

"I suppose I will. I had a note from them this morning. They asked me to stay with them at least until this trial is concluded. Is there a chance for Lewis, do you think?"

"Can you doubt it? Between us, Thorogood and I will present a defense to go down in the history books and bring us fame and fortune. I shall be buried in briefs after defending the great Collatinus. Mark my words, we'll secure your brother's freedom."

"I want to meet him, Edward."

"Why do you think I'm here? As soon as the bailiffs have done their worst with their inkhorn and ledgers, you shall put on your bonnet. And I hope you understand how fortunate you are, ma'am? A barrister does not generally show himself among the riffraff of Newgate."

Chapter XXII

The turnkey unlocked another gate and secured it again after Penelope and Buckler had passed through. As they followed him down the stone passage, the locks of the gates and gratings yielded, one after the other, with monotonous clanks like thunder. Voices, the restless murmur of prisoners in captivity, drifted from behind the iron bars of the wards that led off the passage, and through these bars Penelope glimpsed forms moving back and forth. Soon they came to the felons' quadrangle, where they found Lewis Durant pacing the yard under a gray sky. Other prisoners conversed and laughed with a potman selling beer through the grating, but Lewis, staring at the paving stones under his feet, did not at first notice the turnkey, who jerked a thumb in his direction. Thus, it happened that Penelope got a good look at her brother before he observed her presence.

She saw at once that the christening register at St. Marylebone church had not lied. The resemblance to her father was too marked: the same curly, black hair; pronounced brow; long nose; and lean cheeks. Lewis Durant was tall and slender, thin really, as if he hadn't eaten a good meal in weeks. When the turnkey called his name, he started, turned, and looked straight past Buckler at Penelope. Then his spirit leapt to hers in sudden recognition, a light springing up in the dark eyes that seemed to mirror her own.

"Permit us to speak privately to this prisoner." Buckler put a generous tip in the turnkey's palm.

"You his lawyer? I reckon so." The turnkey's curious gaze lingered over Penelope, but he withdrew to the other end of the cage-like barrier that gave visitors access to the prisoners, though the gap between the double rows of bars prevented actual contact.

Buckler addressed Lewis Durant. "You passed a comfortable night? They are treating you well?"

"Yes, sir." Lewis' attention was still on Penelope.

She said, "Lewis—do you know who I am?"

"I imagine you are Mrs. Wolfe."

"You already knew of me?"

"Yes, from Mary. Mrs. Leach." He broke off, embarrassed. "I am sorry to see you in this filthy place, ma'am."

Listening to the deep but youthful voice, Penelope felt her throat tighten. Buckler had told her that Lewis' foster mother, the brewer's widow from Marylebone, had apprenticed him to a schoolmaster at the institution, where he'd been educated and working as a junior teacher before his arrest. *What of his child-hood? Was the widow kind to him? Had he wished for a real family? Was he docile or rebellious? Did he prefer books or rough and tumble games? Did he grow up to have a sense of duty and decency—or had his upbringing ruined him?* There were so many questions she wanted to ask. She could ask none of them.

"I'm not sorry to be here. I wanted to meet you. I want to do what I can to help you."

Lewis grinned engagingly. "You have already, ma'am. Without you, I would be a dashed sight more uncomfortable." When she looked surprised, he explained. "I have little money and no connections. With your kind assistance, I was able to pay for easement to have my irons removed and could forgo the plea-sures of the commons side. Here I have only three men to bear me company in my cell and only one man with whom I must share my bed. Princely accommodations."

Silently, Penelope vowed to ask Buckler and Thorogood for an accounting. She would make certain this money was repaid.

"Will you tell us what you can about these murders? How did you meet Mary Leach and her husband?"

His long fingers tightened on the bars. "Her husband? I never set eyes on him in my life. He was never at home when I visited Mary."

"You went to the Adelphi Terrace?"

"A few times, but she was worried about the servants gossiping, so we would meet on the Strand. We'd walk together and look in the shop windows."

"Why, Lewis?"

"To make our plans, of course," he said impatiently, as if the answer were obvious.

"You planned the Collatinus letters. Nothing else?"

The disturbingly familiar eyes flared with anger. "You think me capable of murder, ma'am?"

She corrected him. "No, I don't believe you dressed up as a masked man to stab Mr. Leach, but it won't be easy to prove your innocence. We think it was Mary who killed him. But even if a jury can be brought to accept her guilt, which I doubt, they will only say *you* murdered Mr. Leach at her behest. You must tell us everything—every detail—and give us a chance to save you."

Oddly, it seemed her lecturing, elderly sister tone had reassured him, for a smile began to play about his lips. "Just how do you know I am innocent, Mrs. Wolfe?"

"First of all, you must call me Penelope. Formality is ridiculous under the circumstances, don't you think? Second, I know you are innocent because—" She drew a deep breath and said, "Because you are my brother."

The smile vanished. "You are remarkably trusting."

Strange. Mr. Chase had said these exact words to her after the inquest, warning her that he could not control where the investigation might take him. They knew nothing of Lewis Durant, and what there was to learn might not be pleasant to discover. Chase advised her to hold herself aloof—in case she had to retreat altogether if Lewis were incriminated further—and he cautioned against this visit to Newgate. Though Penelope had acknowledged the value of this commonsense, she knew it could make no difference to her.

She held Lewis' gaze. "Then you must not betray my trust. Answer Mr. Buckler's questions."

Buckler glanced toward the turnkey, who was engaged in a bantering exchange with some prisoners clustered near the barrier. "Tell us about your dealings with Mary Leach, but keep your voice low. How did you meet her?"

"After Mrs. Cantrell died, I found a letter from Mary among her effects. She had sent money to finance my education. I called on her to ask why."

"Why did she?"

"She was my mother's friend."

"And Mrs. Cantrell was your foster-mother?"

"Yes, sir. She always refused to speak of my parents, but I knew there was something wrong about my mother's death. I was determined to learn the truth."

"You did not seek out your mother's sister, Mrs. Ecclestone?"

"I've never met her, though Mary told me about her. Mary didn't trust her."

"So it was Mrs. Leach who told you Nell Durant's story?" Buckler said evenly.

"And my father's." Lewis' eyes assessed Penelope again, and she met his look of inquiry. She wanted to read his character if she could—in his words, his intonations, his willingness or unwillingness to answer the questions. Watching him fascinated her. She found herself catching phantom reminders of her father: the tilt of his head when he spoke or the arrogance in the dark eyes when he imagined himself under scrutiny. But added to these was a hesitation, a painful reserve, in his manner that wrung her heart.

After a pause, Buckler continued. "Whose idea was it to write the Collatinus letters?"

"It was Mary's, sir. Except for the last two, she wrote them, and I delivered them to the editor of the *Free Albion*. Only one of mine was published."

Penelope laid a hand on Buckler's arm. "Edward, a jury might believe him. Mary had written poems and puffs for her husband's newspaper. She would know far more about the business than a boy of nineteen." She said to Lewis, "What purpose did these letters serve?"

"Revenge."

Her grip tightened on Buckler's sleeve, and his hand covered hers. "Whose revenge—Mary's or yours?"

"Why, revenge for the both of us, ma'am," he responded, the chill in his tone making her shiver. "Mary said the letters would likely give some nasty people a few turns, but that was merely to add a bit of relish to the game. She was after only one person, my mother's killer. She wanted to make him suffer."

"Mrs. Leach knew who murdered Nell? Who was it?"

"She wouldn't tell me, Mrs. Wolfe. She said he was a dangerous man, and she had no proof to bring the crime home to him. Hence the letters."

"To provoke him?" asked Buckler.

Lewis nodded. "I think she wanted him to panic and expose himself. He wouldn't have suspected her right away because of Mr. Leach, you see. She thought she was safe as long as we were careful and the killer didn't realize she had my mother's memoirs."

"Where is this manuscript?"

"I don't know, sir. It should have been among Mary's things, but the authorities have sent constables to Newgate to question me about it. They wouldn't believe me when I said I never had it in the first place."

Buckler said sternly, "Say nothing to them, Lewis. Will they find anything to incriminate you in your lodgings? Tell me now."

"Nothing, sir. The Runner took the last Collatinus letter off me when I was arrested. He is my friend?"

"A better one than you deserve. The letter has been destroyed. But if Mary Leach knew the identity of Nell's killer, why didn't she tell anyone?"

"No proof. And for another reason." He paused, giving himself time to consider his next words. Abruptly, he dropped his head over his outstretched arms. "If I speak, I will only malign a dead woman. What good can it do? She suffered enough. I'll take my chances in court."

Buckler bent forward to whisper in his ear. "And you will end on the gallows. Don't be a fool! Why did Mrs. Leach stab her husband? Were you an accessory to the crime?"

Lewis Durant drew himself up. "No! I didn't even know until afterward. She did it to protect me and to…atone."

"Atone for what?" cried Penelope. "Lewis, you must tell us."

She saw his fear for the first time, but he answered her composedly enough. "Mary had encouraged her husband to bandy words with Collatinus. It amused her to duel with Mr. Leach in the press without him knowing his enemy. She hated him, you see. But he found out—the servants told him about my visits. She suspected that her butler had been paid to spy on her; then Leach had me followed. When he confronted her with his knowledge, she told him who I was and begged for mercy. He wouldn't listen."

Buckler said, "So he came after you?"

"He intended to sell my identity to his ministry contact and unmask me as Eustace Sandford's son in his next column. By having me brought up on charges of seditious libel, he'd shield his own reputation. He and his paper would score a great triumph over the radical menace, making a pile of money in the bargain. If Mary didn't cooperate, he'd send her away and she'd never see her children again."

Penelope thought that Edward would be worried—and with reason—about his ability to convince a jury of so improbable a tale. Yet hadn't she discussed this very aspect of the case with Mr. Chase? The masked man, the mysterious watchers, Mary's dread vigil over her dying husband. And later the murder in the Dark Arches and the discovery of Nell's knife, used to commit another crime. *A Gothic tale indeed. But who would believe it?*

All of this flashed through her mind in an instant. She rushed into speech. "You mean, don't you, Lewis: Mrs. Leach killed her husband to save you?"

"For that reason and for Nell. Mary felt she'd betrayed her friend."

"Betrayed how?"

"I…I'm not sure. By not denouncing her killer? I asked Mary how she got my mother's memoirs as well as her pocketknife set." His dark hair fell across his cheek as he turned his head away.

"She showed you the knife?"

"Yes, Mrs. Wolfe. My mother had given her the knife and the manuscript to keep safe. After Nell died, Mary kept silent for her father's sake. But she wanted to strike back at my mother's killer with her pen. To stab him with her words."

"She used the real knife against Dryden Leach," said Buckler. "A war of words turned deadly. Did she admit to stabbing him?"

"Not outright, but I knew."

Penelope lifted a hand to cover her eyes. "Poor Mary. What she did was evil, but she was crazed with fear and hatred. Lewis, did she ever speak to you of our father?"

"She said that for years she'd wanted to believe him guilty of Nell's murder but had always known his innocence." He added, his tone gruff, "You've been anxious about Mr. Sandford? Don't worry, Mrs. Wolfe. He made a convenient scapegoat."

Buckler brought them back to the purpose of this visit. "Where were you when Leach was attacked?"

"I dined with a friend and went back to my lodgings to mark some papers."

"Can anyone vouch for your movements?"

"My landlady saw me, sir, but I could have gone out again. She retired for the night, and she's a heavy sleeper."

"Describe your last encounter with Mary Leach. When and where was it?"

"The day before she died at our usual place in front of the stationers. We had an arrangement to meet in the late afternoon around four o'clock if she could get away. I waited, walking up and down in front of the shop, and she arrived when I was about to give up and go home. I knew at once something was wrong. I could see she hadn't slept. Her eyes were…wild like a cornered creature. She drew me down one of the passages off the Strand and told me we'd been found out. She was calm, as if she were already dead and nothing could harm her further."

Observing his anguish, Penelope felt helpless. "Why didn't you run away?"

"Where would I go? I thought Mary might need me. At first she argued with me, but then she said maybe it didn't matter. I would be safe if she could make me so." His voice had got softer and softer until she had to strain to hear him.

"What did she mean?"

"I was too stupid to understand, Mrs. Wolfe, but she meant she would make the villain pay, at long last, for Nell's death. She knew I would try to stop her. But she failed—he murdered her instead."

Buckler didn't look at Penelope, but his arm went around her shoulder, and she rested in his embrace briefly. After she had pulled away, he said, "Where were you on the night Mrs. Leach was murdered, Lewis?"

"I went to meet Mary the next afternoon; only this time she didn't come. I waited for hours, even after it grew dark. When I was sure it was hopeless, I went to the Adelphi Terrace. I thought about knocking to inquire for Mr. Leach, but I didn't want to make trouble for her. I went home."

"What time?"

"I don't know, about nine o'clock?"

"Did your landlady or any of the other tenants see you?"

"I used my key, Mr. Buckler. She'd retired for the night."

"After you found out Mary was dead? What then?"

Lewis shrugged. "I wrote another Collatinus letter. I couldn't think what else to do."

Buckler stroked Ruff's head as he bent over Peake's *A Compendium of the Law of Evidence*. On the table at his side, a stack of books seemed about to topple to the imminent danger of a half-empty, chipped coffee cup and a candelabrum in which candles guttered in their sockets. Out of long habit, he had turned the chipped side of the cup away to keep it from catching his lips, but the coffee had long since grown cold.

Ensconced in his usual armchair, Thorogood puffed at his pipe, the vapor mingling with the black smoke thrown forth by the candles. Accustomed to Buckler's abstraction before a trial, he hadn't bothered to speak in at least an hour, yet Buckler could sense in his friend an unusual disquiet. Ruff, on the other hand, was merely bored. He snorted and sprawled across the scattered pages of notes spilled across the hearthrug.

After the dog had shifted restlessly for the third time and scrabbled at the sheets trapped under his heavy paws, Buckler called to his clerk, who was slumped over his desk, his forehead resting on his arms. "Bob, have you taken Ruff out?"

Hair on end, cravat askew, Bob lifted his head to glare at his master. "How the devil was I to do that? You haven't given me a moment's peace in days. Take him out yourself."

Thorogood's sardonic smile dawned. "Now, Bob. You don't want the dog to have an accident. Who do you think will clean up the mess?"

"Oh, very well." Bob got to his feet, stretching his arms high in the air and wriggling the muscles of his shoulders. All he had to do was cock his head in Ruff's direction, and the animal leapt to his feet, eager for his evening constitutional. As Ruff raced across the room, his paws churned up the papers on the rug, and Buckler was forced to rescue one that drifted too near the fire. Ruff was at the door before Bob had managed to collect his coat and muffler. Grumbling to himself, the clerk went out, dog in tow.

"The man's a treasure, Buckler. Increase his wages before some other lawyer steals him from you."

"Who? Bob?"

"Yes, you dolt. Put aside your book. I want to talk to you about Richard Grouse."

Buckler had not been pleased to learn that Grouse had been engaged as solicitor to mount the prosecution against Lewis Durant, or, for that matter, that the formidable Latham Quiller had been employed as lead counsel. Grouse was known to be methodical and unstinting of effort in preparing his briefs, and he would relish any opportunity to see Buckler defeated in court as payback for the personal humiliation he'd suffered in the crim. con. matter.

"What of Grouse? A man who seeks to profit by dragging his wife's name through the muck, not once but twice, is a scoundrel beneath my notice."

Thorogood rolled his eyes. "His marital antics are beside the point. An acquaintance of mine encountered him at the Grecian last night. Grouse was in high spirits and seemed to think the outcome of the trial could not be in doubt."

"Delightful."

Buckler gazed for a while at the trio of flickering candle flames engaged in their futile battle to stand upright. He could not allow this boy to go to the gallows. The shame and sorrow would linger, tainting his relationship with Penelope and branding him a failure in her eyes, not to mention that Buckler had grown to like the boy for his own sake. Still, when he considered the might of the forces arrayed against Lewis, he doubted his ability to bring him off safely. Buckler had seen neither the indictments nor the depositions of the witnesses. He knew little of the prosecution's case beyond what he'd been able to glean from the preliminary hearing. He would not be able to address the jury on his client's behalf and could only strive to sow doubt about the prosecution's case and present a few character witnesses. Lewis' employer, the schoolmaster, had refused to speak on his behalf, but the boy's landlady, as well as the friend he had dined with on the night of Leach's attack, had agreed to testify. This would not be enough, Buckler reflected. And with this thought, melancholy—black and deep—stirred, like a beast waking from an uneasy slumber, or an unwelcome memory clouding a happy day. He pushed it down. He had no time for his old foe today.

Irritably, he kicked at the papers with the toe of his slipper. His strategy and legal precedents were already committed to memory, so he didn't really need the notes anymore. Most of the sheets consisted of scribbles, incomprehensible to anyone but him, as he had mapped out the different avenues his cross-examination might take. His usual method was to do as much planning as he had time for, then let his instincts take over. Often, he had received a brief but a few minutes before a cause came on, forcing him to rely on his wits and any knowledge of the law he had managed to pick up along the way. This time he would be ready to fight.

Buckler took a sip of cold coffee and grimaced. "Quiller will cast Lewis Durant as a masked devil, Zeke."

"Without a doubt."

He could feel Thorogood watching him, tapping his fingers on the arm of his chair, his brow furrowed, his expression gloomy. Buckler hadn't seen him this way since the time they'd visited the family of a wet nurse accused of smothering an infant in her charge. They'd lost that case—the wet nurse had been hanged.

"Out with it, old man." He was aware of what ailed his friend and knew Thorogood wouldn't rest until he said it, as if saying the words aloud could somehow protect them.

"She would forgive you, Edward."

Before he could respond, Bob and Ruff ushered in Grouse himself. The solicitor was a tall, well-formed gentleman with a shock of black hair and an air of clever industriousness. Grouse came forward to meet them, stepping nimbly over the clothing, newspapers, papers, and books.

"I beg your pardon for this interruption. Can you spare a moment?"

"Certainly, Mr. Grouse," said Buckler, struggling to hide his surprise. He motioned toward his own vacated chair. "Won't you sit down?"

"No, no. My business is soon discharged." Grouse bowed a curt acknowledgement in Thorogood's direction but kept his focus on Buckler.

As the two friends exchanged a glance, Ruff fled to Buckler's side, and he put a reassuring hand on the dog's neck. "How may we assist you, Mr. Grouse?"

"In the matter of Lewis Durant: I would like an assurance you will not bring dishonor upon those to whom we are bound by the most sacred ties of obligation."

Buckler narrowed his eyes. "And who would that be?"

Thorogood affected shock. "Do you really think I would insult my own mother, sir?"

Grouse ignored them both. "You can hardly wish to revive the past, Mr. Buckler. The defendant is, after all, less than twenty years old. He can know nothing to the purpose about his mother's disreputable life."

Running a hand through his unruly hair, Buckler tightened the belt of his dressing gown and studied Grouse's uncomfortably red face. "Oh, indeed? You refer to Nell Durant? I'm sorry to disoblige you, but she is central to my defense."

"Illustrious persons, to whom you would not wish to give offense, will take it very much amiss if you publish malicious tattle with no bearing on this case. You are yet a young man, Mr. Buckler, with a long career ahead of you."

"Do you seek to frighten me?" asked Buckler gently. "Well, sir, you quite mistake the matter if you think you or anyone else can have the slightest influence on how I choose to defend my client."

Thorogood stalked to the door. Throwing it open, he spoke over his shoulder. "Take yourself off at once before I tear your ties of obligation to shreds and make you eat them! We'll see you in court, Grouse."

Chapter XXIII

Sarah soon adjusted to a new home offering delightful playmates and a large garden, especially since the bailiffs had not seized her small treasures and familiar belongings. With scarcely a pang, Penelope had relinquished the costly gowns Jeremy had purchased for her to play her role as the wife of a successful artist. She kept her mother's pearls, her plainer dresses, and her books, finding herself oddly satisfied with the bargain. As the fashionable sofas and carved gilt picture frames were carried away, it seemed to her she watched the dismantling of a life that had never been right for her. Well, let it go.

This complete change distracted the child from the reality of Jeremy's desertion, though in the following days Penelope would often see a look on her daughter's face, a sudden realization of loss so perplexing that Sarah threw herself with all the more determination into her games. At these times her play took on a frenzied quality as she darted around the Thorogoods' garden, one moment laughing and boisterously calling to the other children, the next creeping back to hide behind Penelope's skirt. But after the first morning when she had awakened to find her father gone, she did not again mention his name. And every time Penelope noted the child's bewilderment, she felt the guilt rush back to weigh her down like a stone.

"The children frisk like new lambs today," observed Hope one April morning when the tender leaves sparkled with raindrops from early showers, and a watery sun struggled to spread its warmth.

Penelope watched her daughter tagging at David's heels as he launched his kite in the breeze. David, Sarah's new idol, was remarkably tolerant, generously allowing her to share in his pursuits and only teasing her when irresistible opportunity presented itself. It had been amusing to watch Maggie's Frank vie with Hope's son for Sarah's attention, for Frank was not sure what to make of this big, open-hearted boy who had welcomed them into his world. Penelope had just been explaining to Hope that David made the wait for Lewis' trial at the next Old Bailey sessions much more bearable.

"He's a dear boy," Hope replied with pardonable pride, then moved hastily out of the way as her son charged toward them, his face turned up to the sky. "Come, my dear. Let's retreat to the shrubbery before these children knock us down with their rumpus."

As they paced together down a neat, wide path surrounded by tall greenery, Hope said, "Have you prepared yourself for this trial, Penelope?"

"Better to have it over, and I know Lewis thinks so too. When I visited him the other day, he'd been arguing with one of the other prisoners before we arrived. Some of the men torment him, while others seem inclined to glorify him for daring to attack the nobs, as they put it. And the Ordinary has been after him to confess his crimes and repent of his sins. No doubt the chaplain hopes to profit in selling Lewis' story to the public."

"Lewis must keep silent. Newgate is rotten with jail informers."

"Mr. Thorogood and Mr. Buckler remind him of that repeatedly." As she steered Hope around a puddle, she said with diffidence, "I know you worry about Mr. Thorogood contracting a fever when he goes to that vile place. I…I thank you, Hope, for all you have done for me."

"Nonsense. Do you think I could stop him? He is never so happy as when big schemes are afoot. He brags continually about the magnificence of the brief he has presented to Edward to use

in your brother's defense. And Mr. Chase's services in interviewing the witnesses have been most helpful. If this business can be
accomplished, together they will do it."

Keeping her eyes on the gravel walk, Penelope drew Hope's
arm closer to her side. She understood her friend's meaning.
Hope wanted her to remain optimistic about the outcome but
to preserve in some dark corner of her mind the awareness that
their utmost efforts might not be enough. The only trouble,
thought Penelope, was that the darkness in this corner had a
tendency to thicken and expand until it choked out the light.

"We need to find Peter Malone, Hope. I'm certain he saw
Mary Leach at the *Daily Intelligencer*. Why else should he run
away unless in fear of his life from someone who didn't want
him to tell his story? Mr. Buckler must make the jury question
the government's version of events."

"I pray all will be well."

"Mr. Gander continues to evade a confrontation with John
Chase. So far, I have obeyed Mr. Chase's instructions to remain
quietly at home, but despite what he says, I intend to call on
Nell Durant's sister, Mrs. Ecclestone."

"You must be patient, Penelope."

How was that possible? In his daily paragraphs and his popular pamphlet, Gander trumpeted arch speculation about Lewis
Durant and the entirely fabricated history of his relationships
with his sister and his celebrated father. Men like Gander knew
how to twist public perception like a lump of dough under
their hands.

But if Penelope had to rise each morning dreading what her
morning paper would reveal, at least Princess Caroline had won
the publicity battle handily. The *Times* had declared her complete innocence and advised her to take no more notice of any
"vague aspersions" cast on her character. The ministry was on the
defensive as Caroline's supporters vociferously championed her
in the press. Soon after Lewis' arrest, the work simply entitled
The Book, Spencer Perceval's original inquiry into the Princess'
conduct, had begun to appear in various editions. Despite its

scandalous nature, the public had made a heroine of Caroline and a villain of her selfish, blundering husband. It was said that the Lord Mayor himself would present a proclamation to the Princess to express the undying loyalty of the City of London, and Penelope had even overheard Buckler and Thorogood discussing whether the Regent's increasing unpopularity might sway the jury in Lewis' favor. A faint hope, she feared. Popular or unpopular, the Regent was too powerful.

"Can patience serve anyone when the liars and bullies of this world would destroy us all?" she said wearily.

Before Hope could reply, David ran up the path toward them, Sarah and Frank following. "There's someone to see you, Mrs. Wolfe," David announced.

"He's at the garden gate, Mama," added Sarah.

Penelope and Hope looked at each other. "That's odd. Why didn't the visitor go to the front entrance?" murmured Hope.

Accompanying the children, they set off down a stone path across the garden. At the gate into a lane bordered by fields and dotted with other homes, a neatly dressed man in a tall beaver hat awaited them. Yellen, the Thorogoods' aged gardener, hovered nearby, calling out as they approached, "A gentleman to see Mrs. Wolfe, ma'am."

"Thank you, Yellen," said Hope and nodded pleasantly to the stranger. "What can we do for you, sir? You have come to the rear of our home. Have you lost your way?"

Rudely, the man ignored her friendly smile. Keeping his eyes fixed on Penelope, he stepped closer and put a sealed document into her hand. "Mrs. Jeremy Wolfe? You are summoned to appear at the trial of Lewis Durant."

◇◇◇

"I read about you in the newspaper," said Amelia Ecclestone after Penelope had identified herself. The tobacconist's wife was alone, sweeping up the droppings on the floor. There was no sign of the husband Chase had described. Setting the broom to one side, Mrs. Ecclestone ran her hands down her apron and stepped behind her counter. She had greeted Penelope's entrance with a welcoming smile that soon withered to cold suspicion.

"You're Mr. Sandford's daughter and Lewis Durant's sister."

"Yes."

"The man who came here before—Mr. Chase. He pursues his inquires on Durant's behalf?"

"He works to free your nephew."

She glanced nervously around the empty shop, as if worried they would be overheard. "I've had no contact with the boy since his early infancy. It's nothing to do with me."

"Lewis Durant is your kin," Penelope reminded her.

"What do you want? I have many tasks awaiting me this morning, and a customer may come in at any moment. State your business."

"I want you to tell me anything you can remember about your sister's last days. Lewis Durant is innocent. His life is in danger. If you know something, it is your duty to speak out, ma'am."

"If people find out we are connected to Collatinus, our business will be ruined, the labor of a lifetime spoiled. Leave us alone, Mrs. Wolfe. What harm have we ever done to you?" Amelia Ecclestone leaned across the glass, extending her arms in appeal, but Penelope, seeing the calculation in the gesture, was disgusted.

"You can't hide your relationship to Lewis forever. George Kester knows of your connection to Mrs. Durant, and Mr. Chase said that constables have visited you." As she spoke, Penelope was taking in the prosperous shop with its gleaming glass and rows of jars. She was remembering what Lewis had told her of his boyhood in the charity school: days of hunger, loneliness, and submission to stern authority. His recounting had been terse, bare of detail, but she had filled in the gaps only too easily. His foster-mother had meant well by him, but she'd had her own family, after all.

Mrs. Ecclestone broke the silence. "As soon as the letters started in the papers, we knew Mary Leach was making trouble. I'd always thought Nell a fool to take up with her."

"Why did you tell Mr. Chase my father killed your sister? And you lied when you said Lewis died as a baby."

"I'd never seen your friend before in my life. He was prying into our private family affairs! Besides, for all I know, Mr. Sandford *was* guilty."

"Because he visited Nell on the night she died?"

"Exactly," she said triumphantly.

"Did you hear something of Mrs. Durant's conversation that night? You must see it's important, ma'am."

"How dare you. I've read about you in the papers. You're a woman who can't even keep her own husband at her side! I have nothing to say to such as you."

Penelope grew cold with anger. "Either you tell me what you know, or I will stand in front of your shop and shout to the world that your nephew is to stand his trial for murder."

Mrs. Ecclestone turned away to tidy her jars, lifting them one by one and placing them on a shelf behind the counter, her hands visibly trembling. "You don't understand. I was frightened. Mr. Sandford was shouting at her and accusing her of playing him false. I didn't know what he might do—that's why I listened at the drawing room door."

"She'd been with another man?"

She paused and faced Penelope again. Doubt, fear, and cunning chased each other across her face. "No," she said at last. "He was angry at Nell for saying Lewis was the Prince's bastard. I don't know exactly what it was about, some arrangement. Mr. Sandford warned Nell to stay clear, but she wouldn't listen. She told him she could handle herself."

"What kind of arrangement?"

"Business. She was negotiating with the other gentleman, the one who ruined her in the first place. I always knew that man had an eye to the main chance. He saw Nell when she was still a respectable girl, and he thought he'd make a handsome profit on her. I suppose his pockets were to let, and my sister could fill 'em up for him. And she did, for a while, until she got above herself. Your father came along and spoiled the party."

"What gentleman was this, ma'am?"

Mrs. Ecclestone sent her a scornful look. "Nell needed money to pay her debts. She kept insisting it was owed to her, but Mr. Sandford said she was lying about their child and risking their lives and the lives of his Jacobin friends. I heard his footsteps coming toward the door, so I dashed up the stairs. By the time I came down again, there was nothing more to hear. I went to bed."

"She was in the drawing room with my father, but you said she was found upstairs in her bed the next morning."

"I never spoke to her again." Now she was rubbing her hands across the glass counter and smudging it with finger marks.

"You accused my father. Why? You had no evidence other than his presence in the house."

"It was my duty, Mrs. Wolfe. As for Lewis Durant, Mary told me to lie when Nell's gentleman came round asking questions. We said the baby died."

"*What* gentleman, ma'am?" Penelope asked for the second time.

Mrs. Ecclestone shook her head. "Get out of my shop. Do you think I'm going to have you making more mischief for us? I acted to protect that boy and give him a chance to grow up free of the past. What a pity he's been led astray and will likely hang for his folly."

A fresh burst of fury stopped Penelope in her tracks, and she paused at the door to confront Nell Durant's sister once more. "Since you never bothered to find out what became of your sister's child, you can hardly be sorry."

She left Amelia Ecclestone to her memories.

Chapter XXIV

Chase nodded politely as he passed Bow Street's chief clerk and rapped on the door of the magistrate's office. When a voice bade him enter, he stepped over the threshold.

Read looked up from his papers. "You received my message, eh? It struck me we might have been a trifle hasty when last we spoke. I thought another conversation would not come amiss." He shot Chase a sharp glance. "You won't like to hear that Farley and the others have taken up the slack in your absence. Not that you don't deserve it."

"Am I to resume my duties, sir?"

"I've had a fresh complaint, Chase. This grows more than tiresome. I can't have a man in my employ who goes off half-cocked at every opportunity."

"You'll permit me to answer to these charges?"

"Certainly. You thrust yourself into the middle of Victor Kirby's arrest and damn near scuttled it. Apparently, you also stole Collatinus' last letter and did who knows what with it. Kirby claims you did all this for the glory and the reward money."

"That young jackanapes can take his reward money and—"

"The jackanapes, as you call him, has a point. You were told to stay out of this affair. However," Read added tartly, "I don't say you stuck in your oar for money, if I know you as well as I think I do."

"Kirby failed to deliver a warning. If a bystander hadn't spoiled his aim, Lewis Durant would be dead. A boy of nineteen, sir."

"And an accused murderer." The magistrate frowned in the direction of the wall where a web of grimy cracks had marred the plaster. He looked pensive, a little distracted, like a man with his eye on a sky filled with thick-bellied clouds, bracing for rain. Abruptly, he nodded toward a chair.

Chase took a seat. "Kirby's bullet could easily have gone awry. He was a fool to fire in so crowded a place. Besides, the boy is innocent."

"You may be one of the only people in this city convinced of that. You and his sister, I suppose?"

"Yes, sir. She's been served a subpoena to testify at Durant's trial. They will try to implicate her in the conspiracy."

"Funny I should listen to you when the Home Office tells such a good story. Collatinus got his blood up when he was attacked in the press. He stabbed the newspaper editor, then killed the man's poor wife. Perhaps murder wasn't in the original plan, which was to avenge his mother's death and line his pockets through blackmail—but there can be no excuse. At all events, your friend Mrs. Wolfe is said to have abetted him in this foolish quest."

"Mrs. Wolfe had nothing to do with the Collatinus letters, though she wishes to help her brother. Natural, of course."

"Most admirable."

"So why *are* you listening to me, sir?"

Read looked up, a spark brightening his eyes. "The case interests me. Just when the Prince Regent has undergone a thorough drubbing in the press over his cruelty to his wife, this Collatinus gets himself arrested. An awkward business all around, considering the Prince was once involved with Durant's mother. So the Regent has a few stories planted in the papers about Princess Caroline's Jacobin supporters and casts himself as the innocent victim of a treasonous prostitute and her equally unscrupulous son. He'll get the traitor safely hanged: a much needed coup for our Prince—and for my colleague Mr. Conant."

"You see it too? Since Collatinus' arrest, I seem to have picked up a few of the Home Office agents who've been dogging Mrs. Wolfe. It makes a man curious."

"Yes, well, it was curiosity that got you in trouble to begin with, Chase." Read slid open a drawer of his desk to retrieve an ebony baton topped by a gilt crown. He laid it on the desk and met Chase's gaze, his eyes challenging. "If you choose to pick this up again, I'll thank you to remember the loyalty due to this office. And to mind your tongue in future. Too much to ask?"

Chase looked down at the Bow Street tipstaff, and his hand went out to grasp it. The wood felt solid and cool in his hand as he restored the baton to his pocket. "I suppose not, sir. I'll do my best to remember your advice."

Read snorted. "I won't hold my breath."

A loud rap at the door made them both start, and Read called a curt "Come in."

Victor Kirby appeared in the doorway. "My apologies, Mr. Read, but I was sure you'd want to hear the news. We've got him. By God, we've got him!"

"Who's that, Kirby?"

"Collatinus." Pointedly, the Runner ignored Chase. "May I speak to you in private, sir?"

Studying Kirby's set face, the magistrate motioned Chase out of the room. "Get out of here and make yourself useful for a change."

Instead Chase waited in the anteroom for Kirby to emerge, passing the time in gossip with the chief clerk James Winkle, who set aside the depositions he was copying into an occurrence book. A spare, dry man who masked a kind heart under a choleric manner, he confided frankly that it wouldn't be easy for Chase to regain his professional standing. "They say your judgment has been grossly at fault in this Collatinus business. Don't expect Mr. Read to stick out his neck any further. He has his own concerns." Blinking rapidly, Winkle managed to convey both regret and censure.

Chase leaned down to whisper in the clerk's ear, "As long as you stand my friend, Winkle, I don't despair."

He gave a bark of laughter. "You know me, sir. I don't forget my friends just because the wind changes direction. I take it you don't share in the general rejoicing about our deliverance from Collatinus?"

"Kirby say anything to you?"

"Big with news, even I could see as much."

"You know where he was today?"

"Maybe I do. But what I don't know is why I should tell *you*."

Chase retorted, "Maybe you should because Mr. Read is not the one pulling the strings. I don't think he relishes all this poking and prying into the Princess' private affairs."

The clerk sniffed. Fanatically loyal, he was often vigorous—and sometimes hasty—in his defense of Read's interests. According to office lore, he had once smacked an insolent servant so hard he broke his nose. Now he said, "Maybe Mr. Read prefers that his men occupy themselves with nabbing downright villains, bless him. I'll tell you one thing. It goes both ways, doesn't it? His Royal Highness can't afford any more bad reports. They'll put this Collatinus to bed, fast."

"You mean the reports about the Regent's relationship with the boy's mother?"

"Just so. He should've kept his breeches buttoned when it came to that bit of muslin. A few of the radical sheets have even picked up a rumor that Collatinus isn't the radical's son. Surely the Prince wouldn't hang his own flesh and blood?" The eyes behind Winkle's spectacles glinted with curiosity.

The door to the magistrate's office opened, and Kirby emerged. He would have swept by had Chase not seized his arm. "Stop a minute, Kirby."

"I have nothing to say to you." He attempted to pull away.

"You'll talk to me." Chase's patience with this arrogant idiot was at an end. A boy, a mere few years older than his own son Jonathan, languished in Newgate with the full might and power of the English Crown arrayed against him, and Chase could not but recall the toll exacted on Penelope. Today when she'd told him about her encounter with Amelia Ecclestone, he had noticed her pallor and her heavy, haunted eyes. Chase's grip tightened, and Kirby, looking up into his face, shrank back.

"Mr. Chase," said Winkle sternly, "let's have no brawling, if you please." He picked up his pen and returned to his work. "Not in my presence, at any rate."

Ten minutes later Victor Kirby slipped inside the stairwell at the rear of the building. As the door closed on him, Chase stepped out from an alcove across the corridor and followed him. In the narrow space, he paused to get his bearings. The smell of dust and stale air. Darting shadows cast by candles in wall sconces; a pool of darkness below. Voices drifting up from below and the tramp of Kirby's heavy boots as his form receded in the gloom.

Chase set off in pursuit, catching the other Runner about halfway down the flight of steps. He grabbed Kirby from behind and slammed his head against the wall, holding it there. Looming over the younger Runner, he took full advantage of his superior height and the leverage provided by his position.

"Get your hands off me, you bastard." Kirby struggled to pull out of his grasp. He kicked back with a booted foot, catching Chase in the calf and just missing his vulnerable knee. Kirby swayed, nearly losing his balance, but Chase held him up. Drawing his fist back, he gave Kirby one sharp blow to the jaw.

"What'd you find?"

When he didn't respond, Chase hit him again. "What did you find?"

Kirby fingered his jaw. "Peace," he mumbled. "My head is ringing. Damn you, you've probably cracked my skull."

"I doubt it. It's hard enough. Don't you understand you're being used?"

"You don't fight fair, Chase. Creeping up on a man, you coward." He sounded confused yet belligerent.

"Fight fair, you die. Best learn that lesson now, bantling." Chase swung Kirby around and thrust his face so close he could smell the ale on the other man's breath and observe his pupils, wide and black with fear. A dribble of snot trailed from one nostril.

"Milling me down won't save Durant," Kirby said, twisting

his face away. "We found his cloak and mask. He killed Leach, all right."

"Where?"

"We emptied the privy at his lodgings."

Chase absorbed this information. Until now, he'd had no reason to question Victor Kirby's integrity, but the masked man tale had been invented. For Kirby to find this new piece of "evidence" on the eve of Durant's trial, well, that was more than suspicious. "There was no masked man," he said. "Are you telling me you agreed to plant false evidence?"

Kirby brought up both hands to shove back. Chase fell and this time his knee cracked hard against the wall. Pain exploded. Blindly, he reached out, his hand groping for the banister, but as he hauled himself to his feet, Kirby's fist caught him in the belly, and he fell again. Kirby sprinted down the stairs.

Ignoring the agony in his knee, Chase went after him and caught him on the landing. The voices were louder here. On the other side of the wall, the magistrate would be conducting hearings: prisoners, witnesses, officers, and a motley crew, all jumbled together in the courtroom. In the din, they would be unlikely to hear a scuffle. Chase stationed himself at the door leading to the corridor and held up his arms in a defensive posture. The candle in the wall sconce burned brightly, shadows flirting down the walls to dance over Kirby.

"Why did you fire your pistol at the Crown and Anchor?"

"What do you take me for?" Kirby whispered.

"An ambitious man who should have asked more questions. Were you told to shoot Durant?"

"No…of course I wasn't." But doubt, hostility, and guile flickered over his face, each battling for supremacy. "A suggestion merely that the country might be better spared a trial. I was to act only if he resisted arrest."

"Who called out, telling you to fire? Durant had no weapon. Was it one of the officers? Whoever it was knew your name."

"I…I don't know."

"Did you find anything else at Durant's lodgings?"

"Nothing much."

Kirby had been looking for Nell's memoirs, Chase thought. The authorities would be desperate to stop them from becoming evidence in the trial.

"Who told you to examine the privy? I guarantee it wasn't your notion, Kirby."

The Runner's eyes went wide, and he looked a little sick. "Chase," he said urgently, "I thought I did right. I believed him when he said I would earn His Royal Highness' gratitude."

Chase was staring at the shadows on the walls. Yes, he thought, and the idea he'd been turning over in his mind for the past week suddenly crystalized. How easy to manipulate Kirby, just as someone acting for the Prince had influenced the journalist Dryden Leach on his royal master's behalf. What was it Gander had said? *Leach is well paid for his loyal support, which, I can tell you, is needed now that Prinny has turned his back on his Whig friends. I've seen the Prince's man around lately—there's bound to be something in the wind.* The "something in the wind" was the investigation of the Collatinus letters.

According to Amelia Ecclestone, inquiries had been made about Nell's infant son after her death. The Prince would have wanted to know the fate of the child he was rumored to have fathered, and who better to send than his own man, his faithful servant? The Prince's Man had sponsored the courtesan's debut in aristocratic circles and probably brought her to his master's notice. When she later resorted to blackmail, her perfidy must have enraged him.

Nell would have confided her plans to Mary Leach, who sat by watching the destruction of a friend she loved. But Mary had stayed silent to protect her father, whose life had been in the hands of Nell's killer, the preserver of his freedom. The killer had made doubly sure of Mary by seeing her wed to Dryden Leach, his press contact. So, yes, she had kept quiet until she met Lewis Durant. And that meeting led her inexorably to the night when she wielded Nell's knife to attack her husband, a proxy for the true villain of this piece—the Prince's Man.

Nell's knife bore the triple plume device with the inscription: *Ich Dien. 'I serve.'* What a shame that this particular offshoot of the royal line had so little interest in serving anyone but himself! Fortunate for him, he had a minion only too willing to do anything to remain in his favor, a minion who simultaneously advanced his own vicious interests. Chase did not believe the Regent could have known what kind of man he honored with his patronage, but then again he was unlikely to have inquired too closely. The Prince's Man must think himself secure. He had lied about his connection to Nell Durant—he must have been the gentleman who had discovered her in the shop. He had even attended the dinner at the Crown and Anchor to oversee the success of his plan. His was the voice Chase had heard calling out to incite murder.

Still awaiting an answer, Victor Kirby seemed frozen as Chase lifted his gaze from the wall and said casually, "It was Ralph Hewitt, wasn't it?"

Three weeks earlier
A sunless place, forbidding and strange. Tunnels, an intricate weaving of stone, a warren of passages in which they could have wandered for hours. As they passed down a corridor, hemmed in by the curving brick walls, a ragged form in its foul nest of straw flung out a bare foot. When Mary started in fear, Ralph Hewitt laughed softly.

"Surely we've gone far enough," he said, his voice amused, and they hesitated at a fork where the passage branched in two directions. When she turned to look at him, he was still smiling, relaxed, his broad face wearing an interested expression, as if he wanted to be friendly. They might have been strolling in the park, exchanging pleasantries.

"Not quite." She pointed to the left, shielding her candle from a sudden draft. In truth, Mary wasn't sure which way to go. Leach had sometimes met his more disreputable contacts down here in the Arches, but she didn't know where. The warehouses and wine cellars would be locked at this hour, but what choice did she have? When Hewitt's letter had come earlier that day, she had known she couldn't confront him in the open street, or get in a coach with him, so she had chosen the Arches for their meeting. To reassure herself of the wisdom of this decision, she felt for the pistol in her pocket.

They descended some steps to find more vaultings, stretching as far as she could see. She had not realized the size, the extent, of this place. Ahead, through a hole at the end of what seemed a long cavern, she glimpsed a heavier darkness—the river. Suddenly, she could hear a faint lowing and smell the pitiful cows housed underground here, living out their lives in squalid misery. Her hands shaking, she tried a few doors until one, aged and frail, yielded to her touch.

"In here?" Hewitt's nose wrinkled.

"We can speak privately."

Once inside, she crossed the space to set the candle atop an overturned crate, wanting to have her hands free. Lifting the veil of her bonnet, she faced him. The pistol was in her hand, and she prayed she could hold it steady.

"Oh, like that, is it? Put that away. I need to talk to you, Mary. Why don't you tell me what's happened to your husband? He had some important information for me."

"He's dead."

"Leach found out who Collatinus is, didn't he? Who is it, Mary? You've been helping the villain, is that it?"

"You killed Nell."

"Nell?" He sounded genuinely surprised. "She's twenty years dead. What can she matter to you? If you know so much about her, why didn't you denounce me?"

"How could I when you held my father's fate in your hands? Later you convinced the Countess I should marry Leach, a safe man, your puppet. What choice did I ever have?"

"My poor darling. Who is Collatinus?" Hewitt took a step closer, smiling into her eyes in a grotesque parody of intimacy.

"Do you really think I would tell you? You are going to die, Ralph Hewitt."

"Why? Because I rid the world of a troublesome whore? I suppose you gave Nell's memoirs to Collatinus. Clever little girl, aren't you?"

She raised the pistol. "You crept into her room and raped her. You stabbed her to the heart and left her to bleed to death."

"I had made Nell what she was, but she turned on me to take up with Jacobin rubbish. Never mind that. I need that information. You may as well tell me. You can't save Collatinus, so you may as well save yourself. It suits me to find him before my friends in the Home Office do. Put the gun down, Mary. You don't want to hurt anyone."

"*I* am Collatinus." Mary raised her arm to fire her pistol, but Hewitt grabbed her wrist, wrenching it. The pistol clattered to the ground. His arm dragged her closer, and, staring into his eyes, she could see twin pools of candlelight pulsing in their depths. He ground his face closer, thrust his tongue in her mouth, and a river of hatred poured out to drown her, choking her with its vileness. He pulled back to shake her.

"You didn't work alone. You must tell me who he was."

Mary was thinking furiously. Better he should think her a doll, a silly toy to dangle at his whim. "Just a boy. He knows nothing about you. I used him to deliver the letters, but I never told him your name."

The other hand drew back. "I don't believe you. Who is Collatinus?"

She could only shake her head.

A fist smashed into her cheek, and the pain was so intense she went momentarily blind. She raised her arms in a futile gesture of protection and shrank away as another blow struck her nose. Blood began to pour down her cheeks. Another blow, and a hand was ripping at the front of her gown. Then Hewitt tore the bonnet from her head, and Mary tumbled to the ground. Her hair, coming loose, swept down in the dust in a black tide as she wrapped her arms over her head. The cows were quiet.

Stealing a glance up at Hewitt's countenance, set like stone in the flickering light, she felt a surge of terror.

Hewitt pulled a water trough to the center of the floor. Roughly, systematically, he thrust her into the foul water, down and then up and then down again. Each time he pulled her up, he asked the same questions, again and again. When she was down, she could do nothing but reach back and clutch at his coat, trying to get free and lift her head to take a breath. One of his buttons came loose in her hand, and she dropped it. Mary's awareness began to fade.

It seemed to her that Nell was with her. Nell, not as Mary had last seen her, a frightened woman begging protection for her child; instead, Mary saw her revolving in a man's arms on the dance floor, her head thrown back as she laughed: a little moth turning round and round a candle, never stopping until its wings were ablaze. Mary's heart twisted with love and longing and grief. In the instant before unconsciousness overtook her, she acknowledged that she had been a fool to come here, a fool to think she could stop this evil. The Prince's Man had won. *I'm sorry, Nell*, she thought, and was gone.

Chapter XXV

"You are restless tonight, sir," said Sybil Fakenham, as he went to the window and looked out for the third time.

It was after eleven o'clock, and the seamstress was sitting in one of his easy chairs by the fire as she put her tiny stitches in the bodice of a silk gown. Tonight, her flyaway hair was scraped back in a tight knot that made the bones of her thin face poke out.

"I am expecting someone," Chase told her.

"We'll hear his knock below." She glanced at the open door. They were always careful to leave this door ajar during their late-night encounters in case Mrs. Beeks should come upon them unexpectedly. They both knew the landlady would have Miss Fakenham packing her boxes on the spot if she were to suspect any immorality under her roof.

"My friend is not one to knock. Besides, I don't want to rouse the household."

Miss Fakenham absorbed this without comment, merely snipping off a thread and lifting the dress to examine it in the light of the candles arranged for her convenience. Chase had never met someone (other than himself perhaps) who worked with such joyless determination, such utter disregard of her own comfort. Several times, when sleep eluded him, he had sat, watching her droop with fatigue over a task so that she had to rise and bathe her eyes or take several rapid turns around the room in order to continue. But the next morning there she'd be, garbed in the same ugly gown, ready to deliver another commission.

"I'll go as soon as your visitor arrives," she said, still not looking at him, careful to mask her curiosity.

Perversely, this made Chase more expansive. "What would you do if you discovered the existence of a brother whose existence you had never suspected?"

"That would depend on the brother. If he were an honorable man, I might be glad of him. If not…" She shrugged.

"Yet they say blood is thicker than water."

"Not to everyone. You have a son, don't you? What would you do if he were called a rogue?"

"Stop the mouth of any man who said so." Chase heard the weariness in his voice. To have a son he had never met who lived on the other side of the world. To have loved only one woman, this boy's mother, so that after she refused him, he had been forced to satisfy his needs in occasional fumbling encounters Sybil Fakenham couldn't begin to imagine. But the fault had been in Chase; he could have tried to make a real life for himself.

She was watching him closely. "You've known about your son all along, but you never thought of making a push to meet him?"

"At least I don't spurn all human sympathy."

Glaring at him, she did not at first respond, and Chase realized how little he knew of Miss Fakenham, just that her father had died and she was destitute. He wondered why she seemed to have no one to care what became of her, no friends, no family, no connections. One day he would ask her.

She returned to her task. "I'll answer your question. Whether I would come to a brother's aid must depend on circumstances. Whether I believed in him and had the power to act on that belief."

"No, you're wrong. In the end, you'd stand by him if he were in need."

Sybil gave her enigmatic smile, hardly a smile at all, merely a quirk of the lips that managed to express both self-mockery and acknowledgment of his point.

Chase got to his feet to wander the room. "Tomorrow a foolish boy goes on trial for his life while the real villain, a murderer who has killed two women, watches and laughs and feels secure in his triumph. But I know him, this man with the cruel heart. He will not escape me."

"This friend you wait for—he can help?"

"Let us hope he can, Miss Fakenham."

She lifted her eyes from her lap, and he was astonished to glimpse the sheen of tears. "Cut down the heartless man, Mr. Chase. I quite rely on you to do so."

He was about to address her further when he heard the rattle of pebbles at the window and, peering out, saw a diminutive form separate itself from the surrounding blackness. Chase checked the street, up and down, but could see nothing to worry him.

Miss Fakenham had already gathered her belongings in preparation for departure. "Your visitor has arrived? Take the light with you, sir."

"I'll see you to your room first."

Opening the door to her own chamber, she said softly, "Good luck, Mr. Chase." Before he could reply, the door had closed.

Downstairs, Chase turned the bolt and put out his head to beckon Packet inside. Packet stared and seemed worried. "You want I should come into your ken?"

"Be quiet. Follow me."

They went upstairs together, Packet stepping lightly to keep the old floorboards from creaking and Chase leading the way. When the thief had taken the easy chair vacated by Miss Fakenham and been fortified with brandy, he leaned back with a sigh of satisfaction, his eyes darting around the room. "Nice crib you got here."

"What word of Malone?"

"There's a costermonger called Angel, a man what's married to Malone's sister. This Angel was a greengrocer but took to a barrow and goes his rounds, selling fish. He's the one hiding your quarry."

"How do I find them?"

"Won't be easy—folk like that. Aye, Malone's a downy one. Fooled us, didn't he, when all the time he's been under our noses? That's why we got no word of him on the roads."

Chase blew out a breath of irritation. "Damn it, Packet."

"Done my best, eh?" he said philosophically.

"What's this fish-seller look like?'

"Plump fellow about thirty years old. Round face. Pale hair and skin. You try Billingsgate, Chase. You find him there, and if you're lucky he'll give you word of Malone. I got a score to settle with him. Here's a touch for luck." He reached over to poke one grimy finger at Chase's wrist.

"I'm sure that'll accomplish the business." But Packet was right. Given that he didn't know Angel's usual route, his only hope was that the costermonger would show up tomorrow at Billingsgate Market, where the fishmongers congregated to purchase their stock for the day. Packet sat back in his chair, daintily sipping his brandy and drying his muddy boots at the fire, while Chase, lost in thought, frowned at the dirt his guest had tracked onto the hearthrug.

Packet's gaze continued to flit. He seemed fascinated by the thick curtains that kept out the draft, the stack of books that beckoned invitingly on the nightstand, the polished furniture, and the shaving gear lined up on the bureau. Finally, he said, "Ain't you going to ask my advice?"

"What?" Chase was startled out of a daze. It had been a long day, his knee hurt, and he would be rising at five to depart for the market.

Packet displayed his rotting teeth in a grin. "Mark me, Malone won't be easy to turn to account. He'll run again, Chase."

In the hour before dawn, John Chase emerged into darkness, the empty pavement stretching before him. Near at hand, the coaches rumbled by on their way to Covent Garden; a few early birds chirped; the black sky awaited sunlight; the windows of the houses gazed down, empty, no stirrings yet. Alert to the possibility of watchers, Chase set off through the streets, his breath visible in the cold, hands thrust in the pockets of his overcoat. Once or twice he caught the echo of footsteps at his back, but when he cut off down an alley to peer back through the tenebrous air, he saw nothing. To be certain, he took several quick turns and detours along the way, moving by gradual degrees toward his goal.

It was still dark when he arrived at Billingsgate to find a tumultuous crowd swelling the market square. Along with a seaweedy odor wafting from the Thames, the smell of the fish that had been delivered overnight to the nearby wharf was overpowering. Large, flickering oil lamps gave the scene an unearthly glow, though the babble was purely human: raucous, unceasing, and salted with loud calls of "What price?" Chase headed toward a man in a jaunty cloth cap who was perched on a salmon box, conducting auctions to sell his lots of fish. A mass of fishmongers and costermongers with their barrows, carts, and baskets surrounded the auctioneer as they bid for the lots in quick transactions, punctuated by his hands clapping to conclude each sale.

Chase stepped around a little girl selling baskets and moved through the mass of people, his eyes darting from face to face, trying to find a man who fit Packet's description. As he went, he bellowed the question at each clump of market-goers: "Know a fish-seller called Angel?" Most of them ignored him, their attention fixed on the sales that would determine their livelihood for the day. A few glanced at him, shaking their heads. One man swore, elbowing him aside rudely. Chase stiffened but forced himself to swallow his spleen and keep going.

The hour grew later as he circled the square, and the fishmongers had begun to take down their stalls when a young woman turned in response to his query. Dressed in a brown stuff gown tucked up at her waist so that her muscular calves were visible, she tilted her head, flashed her crackling blue eyes at him, and unleashed an unintelligible stream of words.

"I beg your pardon?"

Grinning, the woman abandoned the lingo of her trade to answer him somewhat more comprehensibly. "What yer want with Angel?"

"Something to his advantage. He here today?"

"'E's 'ere right enough, guv. I saw 'im." Lowering the basket she carried on her head, she raised her other hand to plump the purple ostrich plume on her bonnet.

Chase slipped a coin in her hand. "Where?"

In response, she jerked a thumb over her shoulder and, with one more flirtatious grin, hoisted her heavy basket again to disappear into the crowd.

When he looked in the direction she'd indicated, he saw a man wheeling his barrow along the edge of the square, apparently having completed his transactions. He had a sweet, round face and closely cropped fair hair under a dirty cap. He smiled frequently as he deftly maneuvered his barrow around the people in his path.

"A word with you, Angel," said Chase when he was close enough to be heard.

The street-seller set down the barrow, regarding him courteously. "Sir? How do yer know me name?"

"I need to speak to you about Peter Malone."

Angel's face closed, his friendly smile fading. "Yer a constable, guv?"

"I'm here on a private matter. My name is John Chase. It will be to Malone's advantage if I speak to him."

"Malone, yer say? Sorry, don't know 'im."

"A friend of mine says you do." Observing the man, Chase saw that Angel was tugging at the red kerchief around his neck and shuffling his boots, clearly anxious to get away.

"Don't know yer friend neither," said Angel after a short silence.

"You don't have a brother-in-law staying with you and your family? In a spot of trouble perhaps? Tell me, and you'll be glad you obliged me."

"I don't know nuffink. Good day ter yer, sir." Touching his cap, Angel lifted the handles of his barrow.

Chase sighed. He would have to follow the costermonger to a less congested spot and give him a little encouragement to tell his story. He debated whether he should simply step in his path, grab him by his kerchief, and hope the other costermongers would not immediately rally around their own.

"Wait, Angel," he called in carrying tones that made one or two of the nearby patrons glance at him curiously. Angel stopped and turned, gazing back with a sullen look that seemed ill-suited to his frank countenance.

Chase approached him to lay a hand on the sleeve of the costermonger's old brown surtout. Caked with the slime and scales of fish, it was stiff and slippery under his fingers. "I met Malone when he was employed at the *London Daily Intelligencer*. I must find him—to warn him. You would do me and him a great service."

"Say yer gives me word for this fellow. If 'appen 'e come me way, I can tell 'im about yer. 'Ow 'bout that?" So saying, Angel pulled free.

"No time. A man is on trial for his life today, and Malone has information that could help him."

"Don't rightly know where 'e is, now do I? See, nuffink to do."

"Don't lie to me."

The costermonger drew back. "Begging yer pardon, sir, but 'e ain't never mentioned yer ter me." Suddenly his attention shifted, and he went rigid, plump cheeks puffing out in distress as he directed his eyes somewhere over Chase's shoulder.

Chase spun around to see Peter Malone. Malone was pushing his barrow of fish, smiling and relaxed among the barrow-men. The same long face and awkward air, the same hunger Chase remembered, but Malone had exchanged his suit for a pair of dun trousers and a shapeless coat left open to reveal his knobby frame. A neckerchief of a sickly yellow hue dangled loosely over a corduroy waistcoat fastened to the throat with pearly buttons. Malone didn't seem to have observed Chase standing there, or possibly didn't recognize him. A touch of Packet's luck was with him, after all.

But as soon as this thought crossed his mind, Chase's luck fled. Two men converged on Malone, each seizing one of his arms and beginning to drag him away. Chase took in the brown felt hat that one of the men wore, which he had last seen on the street outside the *Daily Intelligencer*, bobbing along behind him and Penelope as they walked down the Strand. "Damn and blast," he swore and pushed into the crowd after them.

Angel huffed at his side. "Who are they?"

"Officers. Don't do anything stupid. They'll be armed."

Chase and Angel caught up with the men at the edge of the square as they were attempting to thrust Malone into a hackney coach. While several bystanders gaped, one man was pushing on the porter's torso while the other leaned down from above to yank on his shoulders. Malone was kicking his long legs and shouting at the top of his voice. The jarvey looked on, bemused.

With a quick apology to a passing fishwife, Chase lifted the basket from her gray-haired head.

"Fancy a bath, gentlemen?" He upended the basket, and fish rained down in a silvery shower.

Chapter XXVI

The prisoners to be tried on that April day walked down the enclosed, brick-walled passage that connected Newgate Prison to the Old Bailey. There, behind a semicircular wall cut off from the curious public, they waited their turn in the bail dock, Lewis Durant among them. Inside the courtroom, Edward Buckler took his place at the table provided for counsel under the bench of high court judges, City officials, and aldermen, but Penelope would not enter the court until the clerk summoned her as a witness. Thorogood sat at Buckler's side, and Hope Thorogood observed from the gallery above the jury's box. They were ready for what the day would bring, though Buckler had never imagined he would have to watch the woman he loved testify in court.

"Did you instruct her?" he asked Thorogood.

"I told her to tell the exact truth. She didn't know of Lewis' existence until Mr. Chase uncovered the christening register. She did know her father was the original Collatinus—and that's why she went to see Dryden Leach and later Mrs. Leach."

"Quiller won't be gentle."

"There's no help for it, Edward."

Buckler looked away, catching sight of George Kester, a man he had met years ago when he was acquainted with Kester's son. And why was Kester here? Perhaps because a scandal, even one several decades old, would hardly enhance his political career. He must hope it would remain buried. A solicitous usher pointed out Mary Leach's father, Horatio Rex, and Buckler studied him covertly: a man with a flashing eye and a brittle hardness that spoke of bitter experience. Resolutely, Buckler quelled a twinge of remorse, for if all went well today, these proceedings would not be kind to the memory of Rex's daughter.

The usher was also able to indicate Ralph Hewitt. He looked a prosperous gentleman, well dressed, certain of his place in the world, his thick shoulders hinting at his Lincolnshire farmer origins. For a moment Buckler was amazed that Hewitt had dared to enter the Old Bailey and watch Lewis Durant be tried for murder. Then he realized Hewitt must be here in his capacity as the Regent's confidential agent.

After Chase's letter had arrived last night, Buckler and Thorogood had remained thunderstruck for some time. Chase had asked them to extend the proceedings as long as possible to give him more time to find proof of Durant's innocence. They could not accuse the Prince's Man without something more solid than a web of supposition, however logical and persuasive. *Will the prosecution call him as a witness?* Chase had written.

"Doubtful," Thorogood had said when he'd stopped exclaiming. "They won't wish to reveal details of Carlton House's relationship with the newspapers. Hewitt can only be effective from the shadows." Another thought struck him. "You don't suppose His Royal Highness—"

"No. I imagine Hewitt acted alone. Still, if our Prince weren't such a reprobate in his own right, the villain might not have been emboldened."

Now Buckler cleared his mind and tried to settle his nerves as Lewis Durant went to stand at the bar. Assessing him, Buckler was surprised when the young man returned his look with composure. He wore the new suit his sister had purchased for him; his posture was erect, giving him a confident air. Black eyes alert, cheeks faintly flushed, black hair tamed, he made a gallant figure that would surely appeal to the jury. But Buckler's spark of hope died when he looked away from Durant toward Latham Quiller, flanked by the junior counsel for the Crown. Quiller nodded indulgently in his direction and resumed his conversation with his colleagues. The solicitor Richard Grouse sat at his side.

Buckler had been surprised to learn that the Lord Chief Justice would not preside over so notorious a trial, but rumor had it that the Chief Justice was sulking after having erupted in anger during a debate in the House of Lords. Having been a member of the original commission investigating the Princess of Wales, the Justice had reportedly been outraged by attempts to suggest improprieties in this inquiry. Instead, conducting the trial today was Mr. Justice Worthing, a reasonably fair-minded, though occasionally sarcastic, judge whom Buckler had faced before.

The clerk read the indictments for two felony counts of murder, making no mention of the additional misdemeanor count of seditious libel, which would be tried in a separate cause should Lewis Durant somehow escape the noose. There was no need to mention this charge—the newspapers had already laid the groundwork for the prosecution, openly accusing Lewis of depicting "the Prince Regent as sanguinary, despotic, and cruel."

As Buckler listened attentively to the opening statement, Quiller clarified the prosecution's strategy: "If your Lordship pleases, we will address the indictment for the murder of Dryden Leach, and if the jury shall find the prisoner guilty of that crime, we need not give the court any further trouble. Though the fate of the second victim is not our primary object, the story of Mr. Leach's murder cannot be told without also disclosing particulars of the horrid murder of his wife and the defendant's seditious activities."

"Proceed by your own method," said Worthing.

Quiller laid out a case that sounded damning enough. Lewis Durant, the son of an acknowledged Jacobin, had conceived a conspiracy to extort money from men of high degree and sow discontent in the people through seditious letters in the press. When Dryden Leach had threatened to expose him, Durant, like the Frenchified assassin he was, crept into Mr. Leach's office and stole his life. Later he terrorized an innocent woman and feloniously beat her to death with his fists. "If this man appears innocent," Quiller concluded, "God forbid you should find him guilty. But if the facts are proved beyond any doubt, you must do your duty. You must deliver us from this heartless rogue."

Theodore Blagley, the acting editor of the *London Daily Intelligencer*, was called to the stand. A nervous, exhausted man, he described Dryden Leach's eagerness to counter the treasonous letters and the growing enmity between Leach and Collatinus. Then Quiller skillfully elicited information about Penelope's visit to the newspaper office on the day of the stabbing.

"Mr. Leach declined the honor of seeing Mrs. Wolfe? He thought her not respectable?"

Buckler rose to his feet. "My learned friend poses a leading question."

Quiller smiled seraphically. "I did not mean to lead the witness. If you knew me, you would not suspect it of me."

"Brother Quiller, Lewis Durant is on trial for his life here," reproved Mr. Justice Worthing. "That is an improper question."

Bowing his acquiescence, Quiller continued. "Do you recollect what Mr. Leach said on the occasion of Mrs. Wolfe's call?"

"That she was the daughter of a Jacobin and her husband a spendthrift who would come to a bad end. Though Mr. Leach's Jew father-in-law had taken up the Wolfes' acquaintance, he was not inclined likewise."

The laughter swelling from the gallery was Quiller's reward, and Buckler, glancing in Horatio Rex's direction, saw that the banker had grown even more coldly remote. He seemed to overlook the squirming machinations of his fellow man, all the while knowing his superiority.

"…Mr. Leach had planned a big revelation, is that correct, sir?" Quiller was saying.

"Indeed. He meant to unmask Collatinus and put a stop to his villainy."

Quiller led Blagley through the events on the night of Leach's attack. Blagley's story was much the same as the one Fred Gander had told Chase about Leach taking "ill" in the street outside the office and calling the porter Peter Malone to assist him to a coach.

"Where is this Peter Malone?" inquired Quiller, injecting the right note of puzzlement into his voice. "Surely his testimony must be invaluable in this case."

"Gone. Two days after the attack he failed to report for duty. He has not been seen since."

"You can't tell us where he went?"

"I heard that Collatinus bribed him to make himself scarce."

Mr. Justice Worthing intervened. "Mr. Blagley, you must tell us only what you know at firsthand."

"Yes, my lord."

Buckler rose to cross-examine. "Did Mr. Leach make any specific allegations against Mrs. Wolfe?"

"He said he didn't care to see her."

"He did not accuse her of associating with Collatinus?"

"He didn't tell me so."

"Did Mr. Leach accuse the defendant Lewis Durant in connection with the Collatinus letters?"

"No, I never heard Durant's name until his arrest."

"You've testified that Mr. Leach did not call for help when the intruder broke in. Could that be because he knew his attacker and did not, at first, perceive a threat?"

"I suppose but—"

"Nor did Mr. Leach give the alarm after following his attacker to the street? Why?"

"I don't know! Perhaps he didn't realize the extent of his injuries."

"Did Mr. Leach name Lewis Durant as his assailant?"

"No, as I've explained already, I saw Leach getting in the carriage, but Malone was the only person to speak to him. Leach waved us all off."

"So it's possible he had his own reasons for keeping silent?"

"I'm sure I don't know what you mean." With trembling fingers, the editor retrieved his handkerchief from his waistcoat pocket and used it to dab at his perspiring forehead.

"I mean," said Buckler deliberately, "that we don't know why Mr. Leach concealed his plight. And two of the witnesses who might be able to reveal his motives, his wife and Peter Malone, are either dead or missing."

"He cannot speak to your question," said Mr. Justice Worthing.

"I apologize, my lord." Buckler turned back to Blagley. "Did you see the masked man?"

"No."

"Did anyone at the *London Daily Intelligencer* report seeing such a man?"

"Not to my knowledge, sir."

"Whence, then, originated this tale?"

"I cannot tell. It became a matter of common report after Mrs. Leach had also been slain."

"Hearsay, in fact."

Buckler allowed the silence to draw out before saying, "Thank you, Mr. Blagley." He was pleased to see Quiller and his cohorts exchanging uneasy looks.

Quiller and his juniors questioned the surgeon Fladgate, the watchman Abraham Deeds, and the Leach servants, who testified to Lewis Durant's visits to the household and to Mrs. Leach's devoted nursing of her husband after the attack. The footman Albert spoke of the letter Mrs. Leach had received on the day of her death, though he could offer no further information about its sender or contents. The maid who had found Mary Leach's wet cloak and muddy boots was not in court.

Next in the witness box, the butler Isherwood dropped the first bit of damaging evidence. "I saw Durant through the window that night. Lurking in the street."

"You're certain you saw the defendant?" said Quiller.

"Quite certain."

"At what hour was this?"

"About eight o'clock in the evening. I was watching for the surgeon Mr. Fladgate, and I saw Durant clearly. When I went back a few minutes later, he was gone."

"Did you tell anyone?"

"We were at sixes and sevens that night, what with Mr. Leach breathing his last and the mistress going missing. It slipped my memory. I did mention the matter to Mr. Rex, and he told me the boy had likely come to inquire about the master. We didn't know then that Lewis Durant was the masked man."

Quiller moved past this response quickly, going on to question Isherwood exhaustively about his recognition of Lewis. Yes, there'd been enough light to see him, for he'd stepped under an illuminated window and raised his face. He'd seemed to be looking up at the second floor windows, Isherwood had thought. The butler also described Mary Leach's self-imposed isolation, her father's regular attendance on her during the crisis, and her request that Mr. Rex fetch Penelope Wolfe.

"Do you know why Mrs. Leach wanted to see Mrs. Wolfe?"

"I assumed she was an old friend of the family and could offer comfort in Mrs. Leach's affliction."

"And after Mrs. Wolfe arrived, what happened?"

"Why, when the mistress didn't answer us, we broke down the door to the bedchamber and discovered her gone and the poor master a-lying a corpse in his bed. Mr. Rex, Mr. Wolfe, and some of the servants left the house to begin a search. Mrs. Wolfe insisted that Mr. Chase of Bow Street be summoned. After the searchers left, Mrs. Wolfe asked to see Mrs. Leach's room in case she had left a clue to her whereabouts."

"Mrs. Wolfe suggested that Bow Street be summoned?"

"Not Bow Street—she and Mr. Rex were quite explicit on the score. Just Mr. Chase in his private capacity. I understood him to be a friend of hers."

"You remained with Mrs. Wolfe until this Runner arrived?"

"I left her there in Mrs. Leach's bedroom. Mrs. Wolfe instructed me to go below to await Mr. Rex's return, and when I came back, I saw her—" Here he broke off in mingled embarrassment and distaste.

"What did you see, Mr. Isherwood?"

"She was holding Mrs. Leach's knife in her hand. I was relieved when the Runner took it off her. She looked that strange and desperate."

A murmuring erupted in the gallery, and one of the judges sent the spectators a quelling glance. Buckler stood to cross-examine. He tried and failed to shake the butler's identification of Lewis, though he did get Isherwood to admit that Mary Leach had left the house with her husband's pistol, which was now missing. Once that was established, Buckler said, "Let us be clear, Mr. Isherwood. Mrs. Wolfe was merely holding the knife in her hand when you entered the room?" Scorn laced his tone.

Flushing, the butler agreed. Buckler placed a small memorandum book in Isherwood's hand. "Do you recognize this book?"

"It belonged to the mistress. Her pocketbook where she kept her accounts and memoranda."

"Open it, please. Do you recognize the handwriting?"

"It is Mrs. Leach's hand."

"Thank you." Taking the pocketbook back in his hand, Buckler bowed and retreated.

Then Penelope entered the courtroom. Dressed in a black silk gown, she glided forward at a deliberate pace, her head held high and her countenance serene. After she was sworn in, she delivered her responses in a clear voice that carried to the corners of the courtroom, turning her gaze frequently toward Lewis Durant to emphasize her belief in his innocence. Knowing her, Buckler saw what it cost her to be the focus of hostile attention, but he also saw her courage. He could never doubt his love for Penelope Wolfe, but on that day he learned how much he admired her.

When he was finished establishing her parentage and domicile, Quiller said, "Your husband is not in court with you, madam?"

"He has left London."

"Isn't it true that a warrant of commitment and detainer has been issued against him? If he shows himself, he will be arrested for debt."

"Yes, that is true." She spoke firmly, with dignity, but her voice sank a little, and her eyes inadvertently sought Buckler's. He tried to smile, but his lips felt stiff.

"Unfortunate—and yet it seems you are more fortunate in your friends? We've heard of the Runner John Chase, who, I believe, was recently dismissed from Bow Street for disobedience of the magistrate's orders. And I'm told you also call my learned colleague Mr. Buckler your friend? I'm sure you will correct me if I'm wrong, madam, but I believe I read something of the sort in the papers." With a lift of his brows, Quiller indicated Buckler, who felt the jury's eyes on him. At his side, Thorogood gave him a nudge of his elbow, and Buckler busied himself writing notes he didn't need.

"Indeed, sir," Penelope said, "I am very fortunate. My friends work to free my brother, who is innocent of these terrible crimes."

Moving on to inquire about Eustace Sandford's activities at the time of the treason trials, Quiller easily drew forth that Penelope's father had owned to being the original Collatinus. And, when asked outright, she did not deny her father's participation in a scheme to blackmail influential men.

"Political motives, you say?"

"Yes, on his part. He thought society had grown corrupt and selfishly indulgent, uncaring of the common man. He believed that Mrs. Durant had been wronged by the men using her for their pleasure."

"Wronged? A courtesan? A prostitute? A strange way to speak of a female in such a position. Few would agree with you."

"Perhaps they should reconsider, sir."

"What did your father tell you of Nell Durant's murder?"

"That he had led her into danger."

"He was responsible for her death?"

"I think he meant he should have tried harder to protect her. And after Mrs. Durant died, my father was blamed. Which is why I went to the *Daily Intelligencer* to see Mr. Leach. I wanted to discover the identity of the new Collatinus."

"But you have no proof of your father's innocence?"

"My brother told me so. Mrs. Leach believed it."

"Your brother. You refer to the defendant? When did you learn of this relationship?"

"When Mr. Chase told me about Lewis, and I visited him in Newgate Prison."

"You had no contact with Lewis Durant before his arrest?" His tone, almost nonchalant now, conveyed clear disbelief. "And yet you were in the Adelphi Terrace on the very night Mr. Leach died of his injuries and his wife was brutally slain. We've heard testimony that Durant was seen in the vicinity too. Why were you there?"

"Because Mr. Rex had asked me to visit his daughter."

"For what possible reason? I'm told you'd not seen her since you were a small child. It seems, if you don't mind my saying so, rather odd of Mrs. Leach to summon you, a woman practically a stranger, to a house newly cast into mourning."

"We cannot ask her, can we?" Penelope shot back. "I am sure she wanted to tell me about Lewis and share her secrets before it was too late. I only wish I had been in time to stop her from leaving the house."

"Secrets, madam? A respectable woman can have no secrets of this nature. For shame, you imply ill of a woman who died tragically."

She looked away, struggling to retain control. After a tense silence, she said softly, "Whatever Mary Leach did, I bear her no malice."

Quiller snapped his fingers, and an underling brought forth a volume bound in dark leather, which was placed before Mr. Justice Worthing. "The christening register from St. Marylebone parish church, my lord," said the serjeant smoothly. "It records the birth of a baseborn son to Nell Durant and Eustace Sandford. Mrs. Wolfe's father."

He turned back to Penelope. "You've heard the wicked rumors Mrs. Durant circulated about the parentage of her babe?"

"I've heard the speculation that the Prince of Wales was the father."

Now Quiller pointed at Lewis, who stared back at him haughtily. "And yet you call this man brother—Nell Durant's child grown to manhood and accused of sedition and murder. It seems you are right, Mrs. Wolfe. The christening record is proof these rumors were foul lies. You own this bond of blood freely?"

"I do, sir."

Quiller withdrew, satisfied.

Buckler kept Penelope's cross-examination short, wanting to get her off the stand as quickly as possible. He emphasized Eustace Sandford's status as a respectable scholar and pointed out that, after all, Sandford had not returned to his native shores in years. He could hardly be guilty of any nefarious plots from so far away, nor had scandal ever before tainted his daughter. Through further questioning, Buckler also introduced Penelope's theory that Mary had summoned her to reveal the existence of her brother Lewis Durant.

Next on the stand, Samuel Gibbs, printer of the *Free Albion*, produced several closely written pages. "Here they are, my lords. The Collatinus letters."

Quiller half turned his body toward the jury and spoke in a deliberately restrained tone, somehow managing to convey a sweeping accusation. "Whose hand brought them to you?"

"Lewis Durant's, sir."

"The same letters you published in your newspaper under the Collatinus pseudonym?"

"The same." Gibbs, a fine representative of the gutter press, was said to have made a fortune out of his chapbooks and ballad sheets, many of them capitalizing on the theme of Princess Caroline as wronged mother. He was an imp-like creature with hair, gray and matted with dirt, and nose, red and veined from drink. As he answered the questions, he glanced around the court like a child, eager to please.

"Did Durant admit to authoring these letters?"

"'Course, he did. He quoted 'em at me."

"You knew who he was? The son of the radical Eustace Sandford and Nell Durant?"

"I'd not be publishing his letters else," said Gibbs earnestly. "We meant to introduce him to the world as Collatinus, son of

Collatinus. We'd have made some gingerbread with that one, I can tell you. Only he got nabbed."

"Did Durant tell you where he got the information for the letters?"

"Why, from his mother's book. The one she used to record her doings when she spread her legs for fine gentlemen."

Buckler heard several gasps of horror punctuated with shouts of laughter, and Worthing snapped, "Mr. Gibbs, you will curb your tongue."

"Sorry, my lord. It's just, that *is* what he said."

"About his own mother?" Quiller injected the right note of dismay into his tone. "Did you see this book, Mr. Gibbs?"

"He kept it close. He told me his foster mother had given it to him when he was a boy. He knew its value."

"Value? You mean that Durant hoped to profit. Blackmail, in short."

"Why, of course, he did. Old secrets, mind you, but still worth a bit to keep *sub rosa*. He'd send a begging letter or two; maybe he did it already for all I know. I told him I'd have naught to do with such wickedness."

"That, then, was the purpose of the letters?"

"And to take a poke at the nobs what never gave him nothing. He hated His Royal Highness like poison, he did. He'd say anything about him; he called him a pig and spit out the side o' his mouth when he said his name. Blamed him for his mother's death, in truth."

Quiller picked up one of the letters to quote, "*This PRINCE— this monster of rapacity, this enemy of mankind…*" He paused for effect. "Who is the author of this sentiment, sir?"

"Lewis Durant. Without a doubt."

Buckler rose to his feet. "I object to this, my lords. Mr. Gibbs is an interested party, bent on evading punishment. We must ask what reward he was promised for this testimony."

"The defendant's counsel grows impatient, I see. No matter. I am finished. You may ask this witness any questions you like." Quiller gave his polished bow.

Buckler approached the witness box, and for the second time that day, presented Mary Leach's pocket memorandum book, open to a page in the middle. "Do you recognize this hand?"

Gibbs gaped at him, perplexed. "How should I?"

"Do me the honor of comparing the hand in that book to the first Collatinus letter." As he made this request, his palms were sweating. If Gibbs were to pick up the *last* published letter—the one Lewis had actually written—Buckler's maneuver would fail. Thanks to John Chase, there was only the one.

Suddenly Quiller was at Buckler's side. "My lords, my honored friend outdoes himself with this feint. What does he mean by it?" He plucked the book from Gibbs' nerveless fingers, holding it aloft to decipher the neat script. "*This day I trimmed my white chip hat with some old gauze.*" Quiller smiled at the jury. "We must admit that Mrs. Leach sounds a right villainess in these pages."

Laughter erupted again, and Buckler felt his face flush. "The hand is the same. Allow Gibbs to make the comparison, if you please. You've heard Mrs. Wolfe's testimony about Mrs. Leach's note to arrange the guardianship of her children. Something had gone seriously wrong in her life."

Quiller swept an expansive arm to invite the judges, the jury, and the spectators to share his outrage. "Is it not enough the poor woman should be murdered? No, you seek to rob her of character and virtue. You deprive her of reputation, the jewel of her soul."

Buckler's gaze went out over the gallery to find Horatio Rex, and their eyes locked. "You are right, Mr. Serjeant Quiller. But I cannot see an innocent man hanged to protect her. Mrs. Leach was caught in an evil not of her own devising and swept along by events. If she did evil in her turn, we must temper our condemnation with mercy."

Fish everywhere. They perched on shoulders and decorated the officers' hats. They slid into pockets and plunked on the pavement. The old woman, whose precious stock lay around her like corpses on a battlefield, began to wail. "My fish! You 'ad no call ter do that. Who's goin' ter pay?" Tears pouring down her withered cheeks, she began to retrieve the casualties, dusting each one on her filthy apron before replacing it in her basket.

"You will be compensated," said Chase as he went to Malone's assistance.

Taking advantage of the distraction, Malone had kicked back with his heavy boot to catch one of his captors in the stomach. Off balance, the man slipped on some scales and fell. Above, the agent in the brown felt hat held grimly to the prisoner's lapels, but Malone, with another kick and a mighty wrench, broke free. He too would have fallen to the ground had Chase not stepped forward to steady him. Chase drew Malone away from the coach, a firm arm encircling his neck.

"Angel?"

"Here, sir," said the costermonger. Glancing over his shoulder, Chase was surprised to see that the sweet-faced fish-seller bore a distinctly menacing aspect. He stood, fists raised, ready to charge into the fray should fraternal obligation require.

The jarvey had descended from his box to join them. "What do you think you're doing? You interfere in police business."

"I am the police," said Chase.

The jarvey looked confused.

The agent in the brown felt hat jumped down to confront them. "He's lying. Help us get this man back into the coach."

In reply, Chase retrieved his Bow Street tipstaff from his pocket and addressed the jarvey pleasantly. "John Chase, Bow Street. These officers are acting illegally. Ask them to produce their warrant."

"I ain't done nothing wrong," said Malone, appealing to the jarvey, man to man.

Chase looked at Malone. "You'll come with me voluntarily? You are needed to answer some questions. A summons has been issued for you to tell your story in court. You are likely the only man in London to have seen the masked man who killed Dryden Leach."

"Are you mad?" said the agent in the brown felt hat. "I'll see you locked up for this, Chase."

"For helping you locate a witness who is wanted by the Crown to testify today? I should think you would thank me. I assumed you had the same intentions as I in regard to this man. By what authority do you detain him?"

"Mr. Conant must interview him."

"And so he shall. I'll escort Malone to Great Marlborough Street myself after the trial. You may follow us to the Old Bailey if you wish, gentlemen."

Malone, chalk-white and sweating, took a step back. "I'll go nowhere with none of you."

In the end, Conant's officers, uneasily eyeing the vociferous crowd gathered around the coach, agreed to terms. One of them would follow Chase and Malone to the Old Bailey, while the other would proceed to Great Marlborough Street to learn Mr. Conant's instructions. As for Malone, Chase overheard Angel saying to him, "You'd best go along, Peter. What's ter do? Go and tell yer story. Then yer'll be safe belike." That seemed to decide the matter, and when Chase had recompensed the old fishwife for her stock, they were ready to depart.

Once inside the coach, Malone retreated to the corner and rested his head against the squabs, eyes determinedly closed, a sullen look on his face.

"Why did you run away?"

"I'm a poor man, Mr. Chase."

"Not so poor as when this business began, eh? Were you bribed to make yourself scarce?"

"I thought maybe I'd be in bad loaf if I stayed. When all's said and done, I'd already made a bit on what I could tell."

"Tell it again now. What did you see that night?"

Malone opened his eyes. "What about me? I don't want no more trouble."

"You'll stand up in court like an honest man and tell the truth, what else? What did you see?"

"They got the villain what done for Mr. Leach. I read it in the papers."

"Oh, for God's sake, Malone," said Chase, restraining himself with some difficulty. "Did you—or did you not—see Mary Leach enter the building that night?"

"I never saw her go in. But I saw her run out right enough."

"What else?"

He blinked rapidly. "Sir?"

"What happened next?"

Malone had stared after Mrs. Leach. Though she hadn't stopped to speak to him, she'd noticed him sitting there, and never before had he seen a look like that on a human face. *What in the name of Old Scratch is this? Where'd she come from?* "Mrs. Leach," he called after her; then she was gone, a lady alone in the night. He had a dim sense it might be his duty to go after her, to make sure she was all right. But the next thing Malone knew, footsteps were pounding down the stairs, and Malone saw his employer Mr. Leach stumbling after his wife. He ran to open the front door for him. Leach's progress was erratic, and at first Malone thought he was drunk, very drunk. But he wore a look of stunned amazement—this cold man who had always seemed untouched by his fellow man. He had never had a kind word or a smile of greeting for his porter. He had walked right by Malone every day for three years with a growl of complaint if Malone didn't get the door open fast enough.

"Help you, sir?"

Leach did not reply.

"Sir, are you ill?"

By this time, they were outside, and he was holding Leach up as they watched the woman escaping down the street. She looked back once to see them standing there, her face a white blur in the dark.

"Get me a coach," bit out Leach, speaking with difficulty. When some of the other journalists came out of the building to see what had happened, he waved them away.

Malone obeyed, motioning frantically at a passing hackney coach. "Can I summon Mr. Blagley to you? Or a doctor?"

"I'll go home."

"What shall I say has happened, sir?" He wrapped his arm tightly about his employer's shoulder and guided him down the pavement.

"Keep quiet if you value your position. I'll speak to you in a day or two when I return."

Malone helped him into the coach, giving the driver Leach's address, and it was only then that he discovered the blood on his hands. As his heart began to pound, he wiped the blood off on his trousers and returned, slowly, to his post.

"Only Mr. Leach never came back. Three days later, I heard he was dead."

"What of this masked man tale?" Leach had discovered the identity of Lewis Durant, Chase thought. Even in his agony he might have believed that he and Hewitt could pin the stabbing on Durant, and perhaps Leach had also decided he could rid himself of his rebellious wife without too much fuss. He certainly wouldn't have wanted the humiliation of being known as the man whose own wife had dared to joust with him in the public press and then pinked him with a knife. With Mary out of the way, he could have published the story of his career and taken credit for bringing down Collatinus.

"She was his wife, wasn't she?" said Malone. "Stands to reason. Better a masked man than a murdering she-devil."

"But you told someone about Mrs. Leach, didn't you?"

"That's right. The Prince's Man came around asking questions. He was supposed to have a meeting with Mr. Leach. He were generous, but all the same…"

"Why'd you run away, Malone? You could have sold your information a second or a third time, to me for one."

"Mr. Hewitt told me Bow Street might be nosing around. He said there was treachery afoot against the realm and our Regent. I would play into the scoundrels' hands if I opened my mouth. Even the police weren't to be trusted. There was something about him. I wasn't going to chance it."

Chapter XXVII

Penelope took a seat in the gallery. Marveling at Hewitt's tranquility, she kept thinking of Mary, Nell, her father, and Lewis, and her anger threatened to leap its banks like a swollen river. As she waited for John Chase and watched the parade of prosecution witnesses, she repeated to herself, over and over, that she wanted Hewitt to pay. But Buckler's attempt to force a penmanship comparison hadn't worked, and now Victor Kirby's testimony seemed to strike the jury with renewed belief in Lewis' guilt. Here, finally, was a piece of concrete evidence—the mask and cloak. Listening to Quiller's measured questions and Kirby's replies, she felt a queer trembling in her limbs. Then, to her enormous relief, it was Buckler's turn to cross-examine, and the momentum shifted.

"Who instructed you to examine the privy at Durant's lodgings?"

Hesitantly, Kirby said, "It wasn't a directive. A suggestion we thought might bear fruit."

"Who is 'we,' sir?"

"Mr. Hewitt broached the matter to me."

"And he is?"

"A gentleman often engaged in the Prince Regent's affairs."

"This gentleman told you to look in the privy? It was kind of him to tell you your business. Did Mr. Hewitt give you any other…suggestions in regard to Lewis Durant, specifically at the time of the arrest?"

"He said Durant was a desperate a villain and might even fire into the crowd if cornered."

"A desperate villain?" Buckler stood gazing with a puzzled expression at the defendant who waited, still and composed. Point taken: he did not look the part.

Buckler went on. "Which is why you fired on Durant without warning, though he was quickly apprehended with no weapon in his possession?"

"Yes."

"Was anything in particular found in Lewis Durant's pockets when he was arrested? For example, was he carrying the promised Collatinus letter?"

"No, nothing, but I'm sure that was because—"

"Did you not find Mr. Hewitt's conduct strange? A gentleman involving himself in police affairs?"

Kirby bristled. "I did not. Everyone was eager to catch Collatinus."

"Should not such instructions have come from your superiors? You didn't consider that?" Before Kirby could respond, Buckler added mildly, "Well, after all, perhaps you were a trifle distracted by the rewards at stake."

He started to withdraw, then turned back, as if suddenly recalling a thought to mind. "One more thing, Mr. Kirby. Were there any witnesses to the finding of this mask and cloak?"

When the Runner just glared in impotent rage, Buckler offered him a polite smile. "Thank you. You may step down, sir."

Penelope had seen the jurors exchanging worried glances, for they knew that the Runners had at times been suspected of entrapping criminals in order to obtain reward money for the convictions. Remembering that the jury was composed of freeborn Englishmen, she began to feel more hopeful.

And then John Chase entered the Old Bailey.

To the end of her life, Penelope was to remember this moment. There in that dark place that had seen so much suffering, so many desolate souls condemned to the gallows, her heart lifted to watch him stride toward the judges' bench, shepherding the porter under an authoritative hand. Chase had an air of easy confidence and a look of grim satisfaction that spoke of a job well done. Ducking his head, Peter Malone seemed anxious to avoid the crowd's eager scrutiny, but Chase hurried him forward.

Buckler came forward to meet them, and his hand went out to grasp his friend's in welcome. Jubilantly, he said, "Mr. Serjeant Quiller, it appears the missing witness has been found." As he spoke, he looked up, seeking Penelope in the gallery, and smiled, a small, private smile closing out the rest of the world.

Caught up in this drama, Penelope forgot to keep her eye on Hewitt, but Hope Thorogood, sitting at her side, squeezed her arm in warning. Head down, the Prince's Man edged along the gallery. "Mr. Chase," Penelope shouted. "Stop him! He's trying to get away."

At the sound of her voice, Chase dropped the porter's arm and set off in pursuit.

He caught Ralph Hewitt at the door. Hearing Thorogood's heavy footfall behind him, Chase told the lawyer to stay back, but it was quickly apparent Hewitt had no intention to fight. He put up no resistance when Chase clapped a hand to his shoulder and wrestled his arms behind his back.

Thorogood spoke into the murderer's ashen face. "You'll go nowhere, sir. You are wanted to testify."

Every person in the Old Bailey had observed this confrontation, and Hewitt seemed to shrink, as if trying to avoid the sea of eyes. He allowed himself to be conducted to the front, where Chase sat him down and stood guard over him. As Peter Malone spoke, Hewitt remained silent. The judges studied Chase curiously but seemed to have decided to permit matters to unfold without interference. The prosecution lawyers conducted low-voiced conversations with the exception of Latham Quiller, who waited like a statue in his red robe, fur-trimmed cloak, and white lawn coif. Quiller's look said he was prepared for anything.

With one part of his mind, Chase listened to the porter's testimony, but he was conscious of a restlessness, a feeling that something still eluded him. It was a nagging irritant, a thorn in his thoughts, until he noticed the cloak and mask, discarded on the lawyers' table after Kirby's testimony.

Chase bent to whisper in Thorogood's ear. "What's that?"

"The cloak and mask Kirby claimed he found in the privy. A shame that Buckler didn't get him to confess he put them there or Hewitt did. They don't matter now. They can't be used against Lewis if there never was a masked man."

"You're wrong. They matter more than ever."

No one, except Thorogood and perhaps Latham Quiller, paid Chase any heed as he walked over to spread out the folds of the black cloak. Made of broadcloth, lined with satin, and sporting several capes, the cloak had three buttonholes but only two flat buttons at the neck. Its material was slightly stiff in places, caked with unmentionable substances and probably also with dried blood. From his pocket, Chase withdrew a plain button covered in thick black cloth—a perfect match. He held it up to the cloak, smiling to himself. Watching him, Thorogood grinned too.

In the witness box Malone had finished his testimony. Buckler stepped forward to address the panel of judges, accompanied by a buzz of excited anticipation. "My lords, we have a fatal variance between the indictment and the proof. The prosecutors have undertaken to prove that Lewis Durant, in the guise of a masked man, stabbed Dryden Leach." He paused. "But according to the testimony of Peter Malone, no such masked man was seen in the vicinity. On the contrary, the evidence suggests that the person most likely to have committed this crime is Mary Leach herself."

Worthing nodded. "I am inclined to agree. Here is no evidence against the prisoner in the first felony count."

Buckler gestured at Ralph Hewitt. "My lords, we have not yet got to the bottom of this matter. Peter Malone related the particulars of Mr. Leach's attack to Mr. Hewitt on the day after the stabbing. And yet Mr. Hewitt, who has connections in the Home Office and friends of the highest degree, appears to have shared this information with no one. Instead, he allowed the prosecution of Lewis Durant to go forward and, as we've heard, even intimated that Durant's life could well be dispensed with. We must hear from Mr. Hewitt."

"My brother Quiller?" said Worthing.

Quiller raised an ironic eyebrow at Buckler. *Your move now.* "I have no objection," he said. "Let Mr. Hewitt be sworn, and my learned friend may pose his questions."

The tension in the court was palpable as Ralph Hewitt rose to his feet. His effort to maintain calm was a failure, Chase thought. He was not used to the glare of the public gaze—he had always worked in shadows. Sweat glistened on his broad forehead, and he raised his hand, a fleshy dead thing, to his forehead to dash away the moisture. There was a stiff, mechanical quality to his movement, as if he were propelled, unwillingly, by some inner voice instructing him to face all, dare all, and somehow come off the victor. As he walked haltingly by the journalists' table, Fred Gander waved his quill in greeting and gave him a cheeky grin. Hewitt closed his eyes briefly before mounting the witness box.

Chase took out Nell Durant's knife and handed it to Edward Buckler. When Buckler extended his palm to Hewitt, the spectators drew an audible breath. "Tell me about this knife, sir."

Hewitt tried to look away, but the knife drew him inexorably. "It appears to be a pocketknife. What significance it holds for you, I cannot say."

"The device on the knife—the three feathers atop a gold coronet. Would you identify it, please?"

"That is the badge of the Prince of Wales."

"And the motto?"

"*Ich Dien.* I serve. It refers to the ruler's duty to serve his people."

"In turn, you have loyally served the Prince of Wales these many years?"

"His Royal Highness has been good enough to favor me with his patronage, yes." This he said with more confidence.

"Surely, His Royal Highness did not command you to bribe the porter Peter Malone?"

"No," Hewitt answered in a low, strangled voice.

"Why did you so?"

"I thought the matter warranted discretion."

"Because you feared what Mrs. Leach might reveal if she were accused of writing the Collatinus letters and attacking her husband? Because you feared she might denounce *you* as the murderer of her friend Nell Durant?"

Hewitt did not reply, and Buckler pressed on. "You do not recognize the knife? It was a present from the Prince to his inamorata, the mother of the prisoner, a woman murdered nearly twenty years ago. Do you remember her?"

"You know I do. Why bother to ask?"

"Your pardon, sir," said Buckler conversationally. "Possibly you aren't aware that after Dryden Leach was stabbed, this knife was found in Mary Leach's possession? The lining of its case was stained with blood. I assume Mrs. Leach didn't have time to clean it properly before she restored it to its sleeve. I have a witness to testify to this fact."

"That's nothing to do with me."

"Mrs. Leach had kept this knife as a memento of her dead friend, a reminder that justice was denied. And I believe she used it to prevent her husband from selling Lewis Durant's identity to you, sir. The man responsible for negotiating with the news-papers on the Regent's behalf. Three days later she was dead."

Here Mr. Justice Worthing intervened. "Mr. Buckler. You may impeach this witness to defend your client, and I confess I am strangely eager to hear this line of questioning. But I cannot permit you to cast aspersions on royalty."

Buckler bowed. "I have no such intention, my lord." Chase was at his side, whispering in his ear and slipping something in his hand—and a gleam of wonder dawned in the barrister's eyes. He faced the bench again. "Your pardon, my lords. If you will indulge me, I have a few more questions for this witness. We've heard about the mask and cloak supposedly tying Lewis Durant to these crimes. The person who put them in the privy would have assumed there was no reason for anyone to trace the garment to its real source."

Here Buckler brandished the button for all to see. "Do you see this button torn from a gentleman's cloak, from a murderer's cloak, in fact?" He turned back to Hewitt. "What if we were to seek intelligence of your valet to help us identify the cloak, sir? After all, it falls to every respectable gentleman's gentleman to know his master's belongings. You may be sure we will seek such an affidavit."

He picked up the cloak to hold the button in place. "Perhaps you had what must have seemed a clever notion, a way to kill two birds with one stone. We already know you had concealed Peter Malone's story. Did you then cause this cloak to be found where it would incriminate my client Lewis Durant? Did you thus rid yourself of incriminating evidence that pointed only to you? But where did you obtain the mask to go with your cloak?"

The Prince's Man was gripping the front of the box as if afraid of drowning. His shoulders were slumped; his perfectly styled hair had wilted over his collar; his eyes blazed with terror as he tried to hold himself straight. He started to choke out an answer to this question, but his voice caught in his throat and died.

Still Buckler's implacable voice went on. "Indeed, it must have seemed a clever scheme, though no doubt you see it now for the colossally stupid mistake it was. But perhaps we shouldn't judge, sir. After all, why should we link the cloak and mask to anyone but Lewis Durant? We believed in the masked man; we believed he was Collatinus; we were sure Durant was the culprit. And who would presume to question *you*? But if there was no masked man"—he prodded the cloak with one finger—"this garment belongs to someone else."

He dropped his words into the hushed court, pointing toward John Chase. "Mr. Chase found this button at the bottom of a water trough in the underground cow-pen where Mary Leach was killed. Whoever owns this cloak is almost certainly her killer."

Now Buckler's voice thickened with revulsion. "I have nothing further to ask you at present, Mr. Hewitt."

The next day the newspapers reported that Ralph Hewitt was dead by his own hand. He went into his study, locked the door, and shot himself with Leach's missing pistol. Though he left no confession to his crimes, his valet confirmed Hewitt's ownership of the cloak. The news reports also informed the public that the murderer had returned home late on the night of Mary Leach's death, having told his man not to wait up for him. The article speculated that somehow he must have washed himself and disposed of the bloody water, but the next day the valet had noticed the missing cloak as well as a missing shirt. To silence him, Hewitt had told a tale of a nocturnal adventure with a prostitute who had stolen his clothing along with a favorite ring when he had unwisely fallen asleep in her bed.

After Hewitt's examination at the Old Bailey, Lewis Durant had been discharged. At Thorogood's urging, he retreated to the house in Camden Town to escape the journalists, and Penelope wrote another letter to her father to convey the news of his son's deliverance. It was a hard letter to write. Lewis hadn't said much since his release; he studied the Thorogoods and their happy, noisy family as if they were creatures from another world. But the ordeal was over—an official gentleman had quietly given Buckler the word that the pending charges for seditious libel would also be dropped.

At breakfast, Penelope sat at her brother's side, making sure his plate was filled and trying not to be too obvious in her solicitude. She saw that he was tired to the bone and wary of everyone. She tried to explain this to Sarah, who had developed an instant fascination for her new uncle, but the child couldn't seem to stop staring. Lewis seemed most comfortable with Buckler, whom he had thanked after the trial with a few brief but obviously sincere words. Now he responded as Buckler addressed the occasional remark to him about books they had both read, neither participating in the general discussion about the trial and its outcome.

They were lingering over their coffee cups as Thorogood read aloud from the papers when the maid announced Mr. Chase. "Bring him in," said Thorogood, waving a genial hand, "and set a place for him."

"He is with a lady, sir," said the maid.

Thorogood went to meet his guests and returned leading Mary Leach's governess, Miss Elliot, and John Chase into the room. Taking in the many pairs of eyes fixed on her, the governess seemed ready to sink, but Thorogood escorted her to Hope, who welcomed her kindly.

Chase said, "Miss Elliot has come to bring you something, Mrs. Wolfe."

Blushing, the governess added, "I am sorry I didn't give it to you before, ma'am. My late mistress entrusted it to me. Only I wasn't sure—" She broke off in confusion.

Chase came to her rescue. "Miss Elliot saw the reports about Mr. Sandford and Collatinus. She feared Mrs. Leach had been taken in by a nest of vipers."

"I...I didn't know what to do," stammered the governess.

"I'm sure you did what you thought was right," said Hope, handing her a cup of tea.

"Now that Mr. Durant has been freed, there can be no reason, and I don't want it in my possession, I assure you. Oh, I didn't read it. It is wrapped up just as poor Mrs. Leach left it."

"Nell's memoirs," said Buckler.

Chase nodded gravely. "That's right. Mrs. Leach burned every scrap of paper in her desk before she went to face Hewitt, but she couldn't destroy the manuscript. It didn't belong to her really, and she didn't know whether it might be needed as evidence."

"The memoirs belong to Lewis." Without looking at him, Penelope groped for his arm under the tablecloth and gave it a small pressure. It felt like iron under her fingers.

Hesitantly, Miss Elliot passed the wrapped package to Sophia Thorogood, who set it in front of Lewis' plate. He didn't touch it.

"You can decide later what you wish done with your mother's memoirs," said Buckler, watching Lewis' face. "No need to make a hasty decision. I've no doubt there will be plenty of interest in the manuscript from the Prince Regent's people and others."

"The Regent? Ha!" cried Thorogood. "*A most notable coward, an infinite and endless liar, an hourly promise-breaker, the owner of no one good quality...*"

Miss Elliot turned a shocked face to him, but Buckler grinned at his friend. "If you're going to spout Shakespeare at breakfast, Zeke, how about *'there's no more faith in thee than in a stewed prune'*?"

Amid general laughter, Lewis said to Buckler eagerly, "Sir, what if I were to make a fair copy of my mother's memoirs and send it to the newspapers?" When Penelope stiffened in alarm, he added, "These men deserve nothing less, Mrs. Wolfe."

"I quite agree with you, Lewis," replied Buckler, lifting his coffee cup to his lips. "However, when all's said and done, you may prefer to honor your mother's memory in another way."

After the gathering broke up, Lewis retired to his room with Nell's manuscript, and John Chase left to escort Miss Elliot back to the Adelphi, where she was still caring for Mary's orphaned children. Penelope and Hope promised to visit the children, who in future would make their home with Leach's cousin. Removing her husband, who seemed inclined to engage Buckler in boastful reminiscing over the glories of the case, Hope went off to attend to her housekeeping. So, as once before, Penelope and Buckler found themselves alone in the Thorogoods' entrance hall.

She slipped her hand in his. "I spoke to Mr. Chase and Mr. Thorogood yesterday but never had a chance to thank you."

"We did it together."

"That's true, but you were truly magnificent in court. You and Mr. Chase have restored my brother to me. I can learn to know him—because of you."

His fingers tightened on hers. "I've already told you I would do anything for you. Repeating myself will grow tedious for us both. What will you do now?"

"I must wait for word from my father, and I want to establish a home for Sarah and Lewis. I will return to my writing and help Lewis to some profession; perhaps he may teach again if he wishes. My father will assist us until we can manage better on our own."

The words came out of their own accord. "What about us, Penelope?" Then Buckler looked more closely at her pale face.

He saw that it would take time for her to come to terms with her altered circumstances—and he could have bitten out his unruly tongue.

But she gave him the direct response he would always expect from her. "We must be the dearest of friends, you and I and Mr. Chase, all three together. There is no other way. Jeremy is still my husband."

He nodded. Undoubtedly, he was a fool. In a more romantic day, he could have worshipped her from afar and written verses to her beauty. Upon her rejection, he could have renewed his oath of fealty, reveled in his lovesickness, and dedicated himself to deeds of valor for her sake. *Alas, we live in unimaginative times,* he thought, mocking himself and feeling better in the process. He leaned forward to kiss her briefly on the lips. "You do know that Wolfe asked me to look after you and Sarah, and I shall do just that. Don't try to stop me, ma'am."

Penelope smiled in exasperation. "How very like Jeremy." Suddenly she kissed him back, her lips lingering on his as his heart thumped an instant response. "I wouldn't dream of trying to stop you, Mr. Buckler," she said.

Author's Note

This novel began with a story I read in *Seven Editors* by Harold Herd. In the chapter "The Strange Case of the Murdered Editor," Herd writes, "Imagine that one night the editor of a London morning newspaper is murdered in his office by a masked man and that the next day neither his own journal nor any other paper makes any reference to the crime." Well, I started to imagine how such a crime *could* have unfolded. I emphasize the "could" because to create this story I tampered with the historical timeline by creating a fictional version of the mysterious attack on the journalist and moving this event back in time twenty years. I thought this alteration justified for two reasons: the event is obscure—I doubt you will find it mentioned in many sources—and it may even have been apocryphal, in which case I felt free to re-imagine the tale.

Citing Wilfrid Hindle's *The Morning Post: 1772-1937*, Herd repeats a story from late 1832 or early 1833 when the *Post*'s outspoken Tory editor Nicholas Byrne was assassinated in response to a reactionary article (something to do with the editor's opposition to the new Reform Act). Hindle had discovered a report of November 2, 1872—forty years after the supposed murder—in which Byrne's encounter with the masked man is described. As in my version, Byrne followed the assailant into the street, but he, or in my case *she*, fled. Herd concludes that Byrne did not die in the initial attack, the death not being reported until June 27, 1833, when the journalist expired after "an illness of many months." Or so says a curiously uninformative *Morning Post* announcement, which contained no mention of an inquest or funeral.

In *Gossip of the Century*, Julia C. Byrne, Nicholas Byrne's daughter-in-law, describes an 1820 incident during Queen Caroline's divorce trial in the House of Lords when public feeling ran high in her favor. The mob attacked the pro-George *Morning Post*, breaking windows and smashing everything in sight, causing the editor Byrne to fear for his life—he brushed through this incident only to later lose his life to the masked man (perhaps). Harold Herd trots out other oddities of the case of the murdered journalist, such as that Julia C. Byrne recounts this mob violence against the *Post* but doesn't mention a word about her father-in-law being stabbed!

According to Herd, the early nineteenth-century *Morning Post* (in my version, the fictional *London Daily Intelligencer*) expressed a "slavish" admiration for the Prince Regent, later George IV. Indeed, a sycophantic poem, written under the pseudonym "Rosa Matilda"—in which the author apostrophized the Prince of Wales as an "Adonis"—was responsible for provoking Leigh Hunt's famously scathing riposte that opens this novel. For Hunt's temerity, he and his brother were found guilty of seditious libel, paid stiff fines, and spent several years in prison.

Once I started my own digging, I learned so many improbable and startling facts about the slain editor's family circle that I was for a long time puzzled as to how to accommodate them, though, of course, these details are merely the basis for a murder plot of pure invention. First, Nicholas Byrne's wife was Charlotte Dacre, whose poetry I quote at the beginning of each section. Byrne and Dacre conducted a liaison for some years, and Dacre bore him three children before their eventual marriage in 1815. Dacre was also a Gothic novelist, author of, among other works, *Zofloya or The Moor*, a reviewer opining of this particular novel that the author had been *"afflicted with the dismal malady of maggots in the brain."* In addition to her literary pursuits, Dacre was Leigh Hunt's journalistic foe "Rosa Matilda," proving to me at

least that a female Collatinus does not stretch the bounds of possibility. As a side note, the practice of adopting the pseudonym
of a Roman patriot for political letters was common in both
England and colonial America. Often these names are repeated,
so it's difficult to tell who's who. I believe there may have been
a Collatinus or two, but my Collatinus is fictional.

There's more to this complex web of interrelationship. It turns
out that Charlotte Dacre's father was a man called John King,
a Jewish moneylender or "cent-per-cent," a cultured man and
gentleman upstart. My character Horatio Rex is based on the
colorful figure of John King: he was falsely accused of assaulting
two women; he was a printer, who renounced his radicalism to
escape prosecution; he may have betrayed his fellow Jacobins as
a government spy; he lived high and engaged in shady financial
dealings; he was "married" for forty years to an Anglo-Irish
aristocrat, the Countess of Lanesborough. In my portrayal of
Rex, I am particularly indebted to Todd M. Endelman's essay
"The Checkered History of 'Jew' King: A Study in Anglo-Jewish
History" and to a fascinating pamphlet written by King himself
entitled "Mr. King's Apology; or a Reply to his Calumniators."

I must add that, remarkably, John King and the Prince Regent
shared a mistress, Mary "Perdita" Robinson, the celebrated actress
and author with whom the Prince fell in love after seeing her
perform in Shakespeare's *The Winter's Tale*. The Prince of Wales
became her "Florizel," a nickname that rather inspires derision.
According to Paula Byrne (no relation to Nicholas Byrne) in
Perdita: The Literary, Theatrical, Scandalous Life of Mary Robinson,
King and Mary Robinson enjoyed a passionate correspondence,
which he later published in 1781—hardly very chivalrous of
him, but it seems she owed him money. In her turn, Robinson
blackmailed her lover's father George III to obtain a financial
settlement after the Prince of Wales tired of her charms. The king
paid this demand to ensure the return of compromising letters
his son had written to his inamorata! And, by the way, Robinson also wrote poems, which were published in the newspapers
under various pseudonyms, penned her memoirs, and produced

a feminist work called "A Letter to the Women of England, on the Injustice of Mental Subordination."

Now for the Prince Regent and his hated wife Caroline. Leaving for the Continent in 1814, she shocked all Europe by frolicking with her Italian servant Bartolomeo Pergami and only returned to England after her husband had ascended the throne. I had known that George IV tried and failed to divorce his wife, and I remembered the story about her banging on the door of Westminster Abbey while he was being crowned—she died a broken woman soon after. However, I didn't know that George and Caroline had engaged in a preliminary skirmish in the spring of 1813, airing their dirty laundry in the press. But the whole business is there to read in the newspapers of the day. In one incident, an effigy of the "perjurer" Lady Douglas, who had testified against Caroline in the Delicate Investigation, was carried through the streets and burned before an enthusiastic crowd. At this time Caroline had a useful friend in the lawyer Henry Brougham, who had also defended Leigh Hunt and later defended Caroline herself during her divorce proceedings. Brougham was responsible for drafting the Princess' letter to the Regent that initiated the 1813 press war.

I don't think I have been *too* unjust in my portrayal of the Prince Regent. He really did send an underling (his secretary Colonel McMahon) to bribe and browbeat the press into submission, and he was terribly unpopular—deservedly so, in my view. One more delicious tidbit: he reportedly had a habit of getting on his knees to blubber over women who had rejected his advances. There's also a story that he dramatically stabbed himself to get the Catholic Maria Fitzherbert to agree to an illegal marriage with him. But in the end, he abandoned her to marry Caroline so that his obscene debts would be settled.

The magistrate Nathaniel Conant participated in the 1806 Delicate Investigation and then headed a similar investigation in 1813. According to Lady Anne Hamilton, Caroline's lady-in-waiting, "Conant, the poor Marlborough-street magistrate, who procured the attested evidence for impeachment, was created Sir

Nathaniel, with an increase of a *thousand pounds* a year, as chief of all the police offices." Admittedly, Lady Anne was a Caroline partisan, but it's true enough that Conant was invested as a knight in 1813 and became Chief Magistrate of Bow Street this same year. His 1822 obituary in *The Gentleman's Magazine* has the following somewhat suggestive statement: "He possessed a very clear understanding and promptness in decision, which, added to a great mildness of disposition and manner, peculiarly fitted him for the situation he held, and were evinced on many trying occasions, when he was intrusted with the particular confidence of the government."

Finally, I found references to a solicitor and confidential agent of the Prince, whose name kept cropping up in the Caroline inquiries. This man—and I won't name him because, as far as I know, he is perfectly blameless—helped interview witnesses, including the laundress who deposed that the Princess' linen showed signs she had miscarried a bastard child. From this historical footnote, I developed my concept of the "Prince's Man."

March 7, 2014

To receive a free catalog of Poisoned Pen Press titles, please contact us in one of the following ways:

Phone: 1-800-421-3976
Facsimile: 1-480-949-1707
Email: info@poisonedpenpress.com
Website: www.poisonedpenpress.com

Poisoned Pen Press
6962 E. First Ave. Ste 103
Scottsdale, AZ 85251